GHOSTLY
EMBRACE

GHOSTLY EMBRACE

BRENDA HURLEY

Matador
9 Priory Business Park,
Wistow Road, Kibworth Beauchamp,
Leicestershire. LE8 0RX
Tel: (+44) 116 279 2299
Email: books@troubador.co.uk
Web: www.troubador.co.uk/matador

ISBN 978 1789017 120

British Library Cataloguing in Publication Data.
A catalogue record for this book is available from the British Library.

Printed on FSC accredited paper
Printed and bound in Great Britain by 4edge Limited

Typeset in 12pt Adobe Jenson Pro by Troubador Publishing Ltd, Leicester, UK

Matador is an imprint of Troubador Publishing Ltd

For Natalie, Sue and Bethany

Thanks for the encouragement you gave me

THE BEGINNING

In that small bedroom, the cold grey corpse lay surrounded by his art that was testimony to his extraordinary skills. If the bed could speak it would have told a story. A love story that would seal his fate and cause his death.

Louis didn't feel the knife as it plunged into his heart. He would never wake from his deep slumber. Never again would his mortal eyes see the light of day.

There was not much blood to be seen but the little there was seeped through the thin mattress that he had laid on and into the wooden slats that supported it.

Louis's lifeblood and his spirit were absorbed into the wood, just as his sweat had been when he carved and tooled the bed he was to die on.

The carved love token that told the story of the creation of life.

Every chip and every mark he made under his hands became a real place in his imagination. He could feel that world growing under his hands as he worked, he could see beyond the wooden surface into a pleasing and beautiful countryside.

From the first mark he made, he was realising a dream. It was a labour of love fashioned from oak, a desired world that was made for and by Louis.

Louis had carefully planned the headboard's design, its shape and size. It was his blank canvas of wood on which he could shape his fantasy.

Using the high central curve to depict the crown of the tree, the trunk stood solidly rooted in the centre of the headboard. Louis carved the tree heavy in leaf. Its spreading branches stretched out, reaching and disappearing into the upright edges of the board that connected to the posts of the bed. Grapes, apples, figs and oranges hanging heavily from the branches were immortalised there in the carved oak, a rich variety of fruit, part hidden under the leaves of the trees. There would be no hunger in his kingdom.

On a low horizon behind the tree, the sun stretched out its rays of light to touch the edges of this world; warmth, too, would be his gift.

Sheltered by the leafy branches of the tree on either side of the trunk, two figures stand. The couple, a man and woman, face each other in profile, their eyes locked, their steady stare shutting out all that is about them, everything save themselves. Their arms reach out, their hands clasp together, sharing the simple touch of love.

That gesture of love put them in the centre of Louis's world.

1

THE END OF THE
18TH CENTURY

LOUIS

Was it his good nature that attracted people to him? Or perhaps it was his smile that appeared so readily on his face when he was talking to someone.

You couldn't deny he had charm; whatever the cause, it made him friends.

Most would have said he was handsome. At five feet ten inches he was regarded as quite tall standing against the rest of the men in his village. His eyes were dark under his hooded brows; as to whether they were brown or black one couldn't say at first glance, but they twinkled under his lashes when he was engaged in conversation, especially with a female. His nose was straight but not too long and his lips were soft and full. He had long unruly dark hair that habitually fell over his eyes when he was working at his bench. He would constantly be pushing it back from his eyes until in frustration he would tie it back in a leather thong in a tail at the nape of his neck.

He didn't go unnoticed by the young females of his village whose hearts beat a little faster when he was near. A few dreamt of capturing him for themselves and imagined their wedding day, but none of the ladies captured his heart, though he enjoyed flirting well enough. He was never short of a lady companion if he wanted one, though love had never visited him.

The attractive thirty-year-old was already a master carpenter but he also had a gift for carving. He had an insight when he touched the wood in his hands. The knives and chisels became one with his sensitive fingers as he cut away through the bark and the outer layers of the wood until he found the birds, animals, fish or fowl hidden deep within, allowing the precious forms to be liberated from the prison that had locked them within the wood, or so it seemed to him.

He drew his inspiration from folklore and local legends that heightened his imagination when planning a new piece of work in wood. He loved the idea of spirits living in the trees and forest. Pixies, fairies, trolls, water sprites and the like intrigued him. How many trees had faces on their gnarled old bark with eyes that looked back at him as he walked through the wooded paths. They reminded him of the myths from long ago like that of the Green Man, a deity of pagan England that became an instrument of harmony between the pagans and the Christian church.

The pub in the village was called The Royal Oak; it too had the iconic face of the Green Man painted on its sign. Carving the strange mask-like face with hair and beard made of oak leaves and acorns stirred Louis's imagination, as it had for many men for the last thousand years. The green man was a god of wilderness, nature and agriculture, wine, ecstasy and sexual abandonment that had been used as a decoration in stone on many churches since the New Christian Order.

Louis's mind was flooded by the inspiration that came from the source of nature, feeding his imagination; his skill grew along with a reputation for his fine work.

He was his own boss and after a day's work with no one to please but himself, you would find him in the local public house in the evening.

The Royal Oak served hot meals and with a tankard of beer in his hand to wash the meal down, it seemed a much better idea than cooking for one in his kitchen.

It became his regular habit, week in, week out. It was a way of unwinding the tensions of the day and relaxing his stiffened muscles. The other benefits of his habit meant that he met up with other workmen from the village; they made good company for each other, enjoying men's talk and having a laugh over a pint.

When love came it turned his life upside down.

Sophia was a goddess in his eyes, socially in a sphere that was far too lofty for a man like himself.

He dreamt of her becoming his one true love, knowing it was only a dream because there was no hope of courting such a fine lady.

But fate had other ideas and when he did meet her she became the inspiration of his creation, the carved headboard that told the story of the Garden of Eden and the tree of life.

She was his Eve and he was her Adam, if she would have him.

2

⁓

THE VILLAGE

Everyone knew Louis in the village of Ravensend. It nestled in a valley sandwiched between moorland on one side and fertile fields of crops that rolled on, reaching the tree-lined hills in the distance.

The village of Ravensend was made up of ninety homes, several shops, one public house and a small chapel. There was a factory just beyond the boundaries of the village that employed many of Louis's neighbours, sorting wool, dyeing it and weaving the spun threads into fabric.

Louis's workshop was in a small stone house. It comprised of a bedroom and a living room-cum-kitchen that led off into a decent-sized workshop, well lit by a large window and the only access door that opened onto the main road that ran through the village. It was a cobbled road that led from the factory to Broadwater Town that was some eight miles away. Pavements of dark grey stone slabs lined the main road, standing inches above the cobbles of the road.

The carts that rattled over them with their metal wheels spinning slowly and noisily were drawn by tired-looking horses pulling heavy loads as they carried the finished woollen product from the factory to the town.

Ravensend was a large prosperous village. The factory had brought money to the pockets of the villagers. Many earned more now than they could have done working on the land. For the folks that lived there, the shops were well stocked with all manner of goods and supplies. The monies that came from the businesses were spread and spent on making the homes of the businessmen as elegant as the owners could afford. Orders of fine furniture, elaborate doors, banisters and wall panels to dress the studies and offices of the middle-class merchants came from Louis's workshop.

It had taken many years of dedicated work to create the elegant furniture he was producing now; since becoming a carpenter he had steadily built up a business from nothing, and thanks to his father he had fulfilled both their dreams.

Working alone in the workshop he often remembered the sacrifices his late father Massie had made for him so that he could live the good life he had now. His father Massie had been a farmhand since he was a lad; he met his wife on the same farm he worked on. He came from agricultural labourers just as his father had and his father before him. He had worked on the land since he was twelve years old and life was hard. Labouring in all weathers, dealing with torrential rain, standing in mud up to his thighs with only sacking to use as protection. The summer was no better, toiling under the baking sun in fields with no shade. The seasons came and went. But winter was probably the worst season, dealing with ice and snow in the short dark days. The land gave much but it took much too. Living from hand to mouth was normal when you worked on the land. Despair was never far away for the families who scraped a living on it. That sort of living was not what Massie wanted for his son. If he could spare his child from that, he would.

Any spare time he had, he took on odd jobs and he saved the money he earned for his boy's future. Begging, borrowing, but stopping short of stealing, Massie raised the necessary amount of money to pay for Louis to have an apprenticeship. Cash, which would pave the way to give his son a different kind of life.

From being a humble apprentice with a good local carpenter, just a village away from the farm where his father worked, Louis learnt his skills quickly and eventually became even more skilled than his teacher.

More than that, his appetite for learning was insatiable. From the mere mechanics of his craft, he soon moved on to the more ambitious and creative items, which required fine tools and clever hands.

The gift that poured out from him came from his artistic soul. He was soon producing decorative carvings on chair backs, table legs and any other blank area of wood he could tool. After a few years, he was earning enough to repay the debts his father had taken on for him.

After his mother died, Massie, then an old man, came to live with Louis and for a few years he worked with his son in the workshop. How proud he was of Louis. His son was independent, his own boss, making his own way in the world. All his efforts to help Louis had been worth it and because of it, Massie was able to escape the hard physical work in the fields in his final years and to be with his son. Massie polished and varnished the finished articles Louis had made before they went to their new owners. He was incredibly proud of his son and marvelled at his extraordinary gift until the day he died.

Now Louis was on his own again, still grateful for his father's gift to him.

Louis was at his happiest when he was releasing the forms, whether it was animal or vegetable that he found trapped within the wood under his sensitive hands. But his mainstay was making quality furniture. His reputation grew and he lived well.

He was well known for his skills, carved doors, ornate tables, chairs with carved backs of vines, fruits, leaves and occasionally figures. His trademark was a tiny butterfly stamped and hidden on his work. Life was good and commissions came in regularly.

It was through one of those commissions that he met Sophia.

THE FIRST MEETING

He was busy in his workshop when he heard the knocking at his door. He cleaned his hands before opening it to a servant who had come down from the large house that was situated two miles from the village. It was early morning; the weak sun was trying hard to light his workshop and warm the day. It crept through his doorway, silhouetting the poor man in front of him. He looked as though he had had a brisk walk and was perspiring.

"Will you come in?" asked Louis.

"No, thanks, got to get back, I been sent to give you this," he said, holding out a letter.

"What is it about?" asked Louis, looking at the white envelope now laying in his hand.

"Yur better read it," advised the servant. "But I can tell you Mr Pennock wants to see you about a commission."

It was quickly read and needed an immediate response. Louis wrote a message to send back with the man; he would call on Mr Pennock the next day about noon.

The servant touched his forehead in a gesture of farewell, turned away and was gone.

Louis became restless and spent the rest of the day wondering what sort of commission he would be offered. He knew of Mr Pennock but had never done any work for him and he had never had the occasion to go up to the house. He was rich, that much he knew; it could be a sizable commission, and dwelling on that thought he could feel his excitement rising.

But work was work and he needed to finish off the chair that had taken more than a few days to make. The order of six would be finally ready to deliver that afternoon. He would get the carter to do that later in the day and then clear up the workshop ready to start his next order.

By the evening the carter had been and gone, delivering the chairs and his invoice at the same time. He cleaned and tidied his workshop and at last he could get ready for the meeting with his new client tomorrow.

He worked until mid-morning before setting off at a gentle pace. The house lay just two miles away from his workshop; it was a mere forty-minute walk away.

It was spring, his favourite time of the year, and the day was especially warm with the sky the colour of cornflowers. He enjoyed a walk in the country on a day like today.

The large country house that stabled horses and had many outhouses stood at the top of a narrow lane lined with trees. The branches of the trees splayed out over the track he walked on, making a canopy of green that was shady and cool. The track was broken by dappled light coming from the sun that shone through the branches and leaves on to the dirt floor. The patterns they made moved with the branches as they swayed gently in the breeze.

It is like a giant umbrella, thought Louis, *shade from the sun and giving some protection from the rain on wet days.* Louis's mind wandered as he walked along the dusty lane, enjoying the sounds of the different birds as they whistled and cawed from their nests. It was nesting time. Soon young birds would be learning to fly.

He was nervous at the thought of meeting this rich man. What would he be like? Arrogant? Lofty? He would have to wait and see, but not for long as each step brought him nearer to the house and the meeting.

He concentrated his mind and watched the rabbits playing around the holes that served as front doors to their warrens. *The tunnels must certainly run the length and breadth of the surrounding meadows*, he thought. The grey cottontails seemed unaware of the lone man invading their space; they jumped and hopped openly on the grass borders that protected the narrow lane.

Seeing nature along the way lifted Louis's spirit, calming his nerves as he walked along the lane to the meeting with a man that could change his life.

It was a private lane used by the farmers and their labourers who worked on the estate. They used it regularly, passing through on their way to the home farm and cottages where they lived, but none were about that day.

With no company but his own, Louis enjoyed the warmth of the spring day as he strode forward to his destiny, the house growing larger as each minute passed.

The mansion house could be seen through black wrought iron gates as he neared his destination. They were supported on each side by large stone blocks with two sandstone eagles carved on top; they appeared to be there to protect the property.

He walked on, passing that entrance. That way in was not for him. Through the bars of the gate he could see an arch leading to a centre courtyard. He needed to find the entrance used by the tradesmen. He continued walking along at a pace around the outer wall, searching until he found a wooden gate.

Pushing the old wooden gate open he stepped into an unfamiliar world, one so out of reach for a man like himself that it filled him with awe. The residence was surrounded on all sides by a large garden, lawns and flower borders, manicured to perfection by the gardeners.

That day the yards and gardens were bustling with gardeners and servants going about their business tending the grounds. They hardly raised their heads as the stranger moved among them looking for the way to the entrance. He had not gone many yards when one man, who seemed to be an overseer, stopped Louis.

"What does tha want here?" said the man, addressing Louis.

"I have an appointment with the master here, but I'm not sure of the way to the back door," responded Louis.

"Are you that carpenter chap from Ravensend?"

Louis nodded.

"We've been expecting you." The man nodded and pointed. "Tha goes through the gate between the stable and the laundry. It'll lead you to the front door."

Front door. He had said *front door*. Louis hadn't expected that.

Louis turned and quickly followed directions that led through the house gardens. Neat rows of vegetables and salads had been planted, looking fresh and green. The kitchen garden was edged with borders of rosemary and lavender. The air was filled with a delicate scent. Louis could hear the bees busily collecting pollen to take back to the hives to feed their young and supply honey to the house.

Following the sweet-scented rosemary bushes that bordered the garden by the kitchen, he could see a figure of a woman in the formal garden beyond, tending the flowers in a raised bed.

She was lovely.

This was the first time he laid his eyes on Sophia. For a moment the sight of her took his breath away. They were yet to meet and may not meet at all, but he had heard that Mr Pennock's daughter was beautiful and this woman must be her.

This was the place Louis first saw Sophia. This was her home where she lived with her widowed father and this was where Louis had come to discuss an offer that could change his life.

Remembering quickly why he was there, he took a deep breath and moved on to the oak door that appeared to his right, set back in a wall covered with ivy. He reached up to the brass knocker. Taking it firmly, he rapped the door soundly, stood back and waited. A smartly dressed young man opened the door. *Yes, he was expected,* was the reply when Louis stated his reason for calling. And Louis was escorted by the man through the house to a large room on the other side of the building.

The sunlight streamed into the pleasant room from its two long south-facing windows.

Louis was impressed; a fashionable fireplace was decorated with candles and china dogs on its high mantelshelf. A huge mirror also reflected the light back into the room enhancing the elegant chairs and the three fabric sofas that were arranged in front of the fireplace.

A stout man with a grey frock coat, a high standing collar and fancy waistcoat stood up from the sofa on his right and walked across to Louis with a smile on his face and a hand outstretched in welcome.

The welcome was unexpected but here was a gentleman who valued artistry and skill, both to be found in Louis. Why else would he have sent for him? Louis immediately felt a liking for this unassuming man.

Mr Pennock moved Louis towards the windows, describing as they walked into the light an idea that had come to his daughter Sophia.

And there she was, still standing in the flower garden cutting tulips. Mr Pennock tapped heavily on the window. Hearing the knock, Sophia straightened up and turned to face them.

Louis's heart missed a beat. She was very beautiful.

Smiling, she waved. Gathering up her flowers, she added them to the blooms already in the basket at her feet and made her way indoors.

The door was pushed open into the room where the men waited with a force of energy that almost had it slamming into the wall. Sophia, armed with her flowers, bustled in, full of life and beaming as she approached the men.

Sophia was in her early twenties. She was petite, a little over five foot tall, with hair as dark as the darkest ebony and large blue eyes that seemed to smoulder under her long dark eyelashes when she looked at him. Her hair was piled on top of her head with small curls fashionably framing her lovely unblemished face; a face of such perfect proportions that the artist in him desired nothing more than to make an image of her loveliness. Her slim frame was silhouetted against the light. A goddess indeed, and now here she was standing right there in front of him.

It was so disarming; she was unlike any other women he knew.

Louis was already besotted and understood the saying 'love at first sight'.

Louis looked at the father and daughter; there was not much of a family resemblance apart from the colour of their eyes. The overweight middle-aged man in a fancy waistcoat was going to fat round his middle and his chin bulged over his rather tight collar. It was obvious he enjoyed a healthy appetite. He was pleasant and his eyes were full of good humour In fact, Louis felt they both had a huge enthusiasm for life and felt oddly relaxed in their company.

As in all small villages, the gossip about the gentleman up at the big house was rife; that he wasn't quite a gentleman in the old sense, he was 'new money' and not gentry by their standards, but was a good sort of man who looked after his workers and so he deserved some deference.

Mr Pennock was a widower; he and his young daughter had lived some seventeen years at the Avondale Hall. She was an infant when they came. Tragically, her mother had been lost giving her life.

A series of nannies and governesses had come and gone over the years, according to the gossip in the village. Sophia was loved so much by her father that she was indulged and spoilt and in consequence she had become quite headstrong.

Louis would not pass judgement based on tittle-tattle from the village, he would make up his own mind on the subject but how could this lovely woman be like that and he decided that it was often jealousy that started rumours.

There was no doubt that Mr Pennock loved her. Sophia was uncommonly like her departed mother. A very fine painting of her was hung on the back wall of the room, it was so like Sophia but obviously not her. Sophia's mother had such fine features that it was easy to see why her father had fallen in love with her and by the way Mr Pennock looked at his daughter Louis could see that he loved her very much too.

It was reported that Mr Robert Pennock had made his money importing goods from the all over the world. Tea, sugar, rum and tobacco, was his main import. But he also traded in raw cotton, silks and spices; in fact, anything that turned a tidy profit. He exported to the British Empire around the globe, textiles of cotton and wool. His supplies of woollen cloth were made into uniforms for the army.

It was thought he had started from humble beginnings but that part of the story was also very vague. The gossips had no idea where Mr Pennock originally came from, but for the last seventeen years he had lived in the mansion house and raised his daughter.

When Louis received the note from Mr Pennock requiring him to call and give him an estimate for some work he wanted doing, Louis was curious and excited. He had lived here all his life but had never met indeed, he had never laid eyes on the Pennocks, but of course he knew of them.

Now he was in deep conversation with a rich and powerful man who was explaining the plans he and Sophia had put together. They wanted him to make new shutters for that reception room.

The windows were high and wide. His task to measure the windows of the main reception room could not be achieved without the aid of a stepladder.

With tape in hand he started to measure the vast frame. The heat of the sun that reflected through the glass soon caused his body to perspire. When at last the stepladder came and was stood in place, he glanced at Sophia. She didn't divert her eyes and she smiled back at him; there was no haughtiness on her part and she seemed, at least to him, to like what she saw.

Without any airs or graces and seeing how hot Louis had become, she offered a cool glass of water to him. How gracious she seemed, how thoughtful. If his estimation of her could have reached new heights at that moment, it would have.

Louis was already designing the shutters in his head. His skill as a carver was well known and Mr Pennock had made it clear that Louis was free to design and make them as he saw fit. Mr Pennock wanted a price for the commission but until Louis could sort out the measurements and put together some sketches, they could not move forward on it.

The price would be expensive for this type of work and it would take some considerable time to complete. And it could leave no room for any other work to be done from other sources, which was a worry. Louis hated turning work away. But if he was successful this commission, it would certainly make his name and his future would be secure.

Quickly, he measured and re-measured, for there was no room for failure in the calculations. He could not get it wrong; it was all so important. What type of wood, where to get it from? All these thoughts ran through his mind as he went through the motions of business.

The shutters would be twelve-feet high from floor to ceiling and fold into a recess on both sides of the window, which measured one and a half yards wide, and there were two windows to fit. They would be situated in the best room of the great house, facing south and looking out on to the flower garden.

The cleverly designed gardens with winding gravel paths that separating the flowerbeds, met up at a stone built circle in the centre of the garden. The circular raised bed was filled with a variety of brightly coloured flowers and at its centre stood an ornate sundial.

Louis could see that the shutters would frame the gardens from the window. A flash of memory came to Louis's mind of Sophia. There she was, looking like an angel, her slim silhouette outlined against the sun as she stooped to cut fresh flowers to bring indoors. He hurriedly brought himself back to his business and tried not to stare at her, though he couldn't help glancing once or twice as he measured up the window. She stood close to her father, talking and smiling before stretching up to kiss her father on the cheek. Then she was gone, rushing out of the room as suddenly as she had entered.

Louis resumed the task in hand; this was going to be a big job and probably the biggest he would ever work on in his lifetime. He could not afford to offend Mr Pennock or his beautiful daughter with his silly daydreams.

Basic shutters were easy to construct but these were to be anything but basic; these were to be unique. English oak was the material of choice. They would have a façade that faced into the room, a façade carved and polished with an intricate hunting scene, one that reflected the land of northern shires and the life that the Pennocks lived. Hunters with gundogs. Foliage of every kind, beetles hiding under leaves, frogs, fish and fowl, rabbits, hares and deer. All these animals would be included. The commission was the best he had ever been offered; he was keen to have the job even though it would take months of work to complete it.

After a lengthy discussion an estimated price was agreed between the two men. They shook hands on the deal and subject to contract it was done. A contract would be drawn up within the week once the design was confirmed. It would be signed by both of them and then Louis could concentrate on making this unique piece of art.

It would be the work of a lifetime. Louis was exhilarated; with a piece like this, his name would become famous and the piece could last for centuries.

His business completed, Louis set to take his leave when the door flew open and Sophia entered the room with as much liveliness as when she had left it. She carried a large vase filled with highly scented flowers cut from the garden; gently, she settled it down on a small table by the windows where the sunlight enhanced the glorious colours of each delicate head. Smiling, she walked across to her father, putting her arm through the crook of his elbow, and took his hand. Her father, enjoying her affection, patted her hand and returned her smile. Then Mr Pennock turned towards Louis and formally introduced Sophia to him.

"Sophia, my dear, let me introduce you to Louis properly, the man we spoke of. He's agreed to take on our little commission." There was a slight chuckle in his voice as if a private joke was being enjoyed between the both of them. Looking directly at Louis, he continued. "You will be interested to know that the shutters with a decorative façade were my daughter's idea," explained Mr Pennock proudly. "She had gone up to the Great Hall, you know, Sir Oliver's Place."

Louis nodded but he didn't know, he had never set foot in the great hall. Louis didn't move in such grand social circles.

"Well!" continued Mr Pennock. "Lets see a couple of years ago. Sir Oliver brought some rather splendid panels back from a visit he had had to Italy. The panels are carved with an assortment of plants and he had them fixed to the window shutters, and that started my little girl thinking that we could do with some shutters ourselves. You wouldn't believe the trouble we have with this room. Too hot in the summer, too cold in the winter and when we have a storm, the gale we have in this room." He raised his eyes to heaven. "The windows rattle and moan, I tell you, they would scare the ghosts if we had any." Winking his eye at his daughter, he turned back to Louis.

Louis had seen diagrams and prints of such work from Rome when he was an apprentice and was aware of the talent and beauty that came out of Italy. He was brought back into the conversation as Mr Pennock continued.

"She pleaded with me until I agreed," said Mr Pennock in a triumphant tone, pride showing on his indulgent face. "I can never say no to her for long," he added.

"I am delighted that you thought of me," Louis said, suddenly filled with a new kind of confidence. "I'm sure I can match and even do better than the Italians for you," offering his hand to Sophia, which she took. Louis bowed slightly, lifted her hand to his lips and kissed it lightly in an automatic gesture before realising what he had done.

3

One month later Louis started the commission as spring was steadily progressing towards summer and the length of the days grew longer, and it seemed to Louis that nature itself was lifted with a sense of optimism. By mid-May, Louis was hard at work on his project knowing that this commission would be life-changing for him. He had spent weeks already sourcing the wood that he would use.

He carefully drew the images he wanted to use on the shutters, tracing out the objects in detail before transferring them to the timber. Slowly but surely the project started to grow, and with it, a kind of adventure grew with the story he was telling through his work. The whole development took on a new life, the story growing under the knife and chisel as his hands nursed the images from the wood.

An added bonus for Louis was that Mr Pennock visited Louis's workshop weekly and always brought Sophia with him.

His daydreams about her grew with each meeting. As the weeks went on his desires and his fantasies got so bad that he thought he might go mad with frustration. He needed her love so badly. Would there ever be a time when a workingman such as himself would be able to court such a perfect creature?

Each new meeting was a challenge for Louis. Her eyes, as clear and bright as water with sunlight dancing on it, smouldered under her long lashes when he was near but looked away coyly when their eyes met. Her apparent shyness when they met only added to her allure and she knew it.

His heart raced when he was in her company. He longed to touch her skin, so fair and smooth. When she stood beside him her perfume encroached his space, filling his nostrils with the heady scent of fresh flowers. She always smelt so good.

The weeks passed into months; spring was long gone and summer was starting to slip away. The long days were shortening but it was still warm with pleasant, comfortable evenings. It was sometime in August when the madness of love overtook his common sense and he decided to risk letting her know how he felt towards her. Somehow over the weeks she had managed to confer that she was not indifferent to him. Her face and body language convinced him that his feelings were reciprocated and each visit convinced him more, until he became certain that she had strong feelings for him too.

As the visits rolled on from weeks into months, she had become bolder with her body language. She managed to press up against him as he showed her some particular image of design he was working on. Her father always stood in the background, he watched their interaction and presumed that they were only involved in a discussion about the project. The shutters were proceeding at a good pace; each weekly meeting saw new shapes, new animals and a story evolving before Mr Pennock's eyes. He didn't suspect the growing bond between the two young people; he assumed their excitement was the same excitement he felt for his growing commission. He could not see his daughter looking at Louis under lowered lashes, coy yet forward all at the same time, a little pout on her perfect lips adding an unsaid invitation to Louis.

Louis was intoxicated. Throwing caution to the wind, he decided to risk everything and on her very next visit to his workshop he managed to slip her a note. But fear gripped his heart almost as soon has he had done it. His love for her was now out in the open.

Oh my god, what have I done? Thought Louis soon after she had left with her father. The commission was so important to his future. What if he had put it in jeopardy? Would he lose everything in his moment of rashness?

What if I have mistaken her attitude towards me? What if she is offended by my boldness? Her father could crush me and I'll never work again. Panic flooded his thoughts.

The note had been simple, he earnestly pledging his love for her and begging her to meet him. He must wait before he would know his fate; she had not attempted to read the note, nor did she seem annoyed or surprised by receiving it.

In that, he dared hope.

He had to wait yet another week before he saw her again. There was no pretence this time. Her father was not with her; instead she came with a chaperone. She said her father was away on business and a girl companion who Louis did not know had accompanied her to the workshop. Under the pretence of scrutinising his latest carving, she passed a note to him; it was done silently and out of sight of the girl, a secret note for a secret love.

Louis was reassured by Sophia's response. She had not betrayed him, he was safe and his commission was still intact.

Sophia returned a note with a time and date for their secret rendezvous. She suggested that they met that evening a little way from her home in the copse of hazel trees by the river. It was a beauty spot that was well known to all the locals and where many courting couples met. The thought of meeting her in the hazel grove that warm summer night under a pale August moon excited him.

The day passed slowly, much slower than he would have liked. As the sun went down and dusk crept in he was relieved to down his tools and prepare himself for the assignation. He made himself a light meal that he could hardly eat because of the anticipation of the night ahead. Instead he played with the food on his plate until he finally discarded it and walked out into the quiet of the evening. The village was settling down for the night and with most of his neighbours at their evening meal, he wasn't seen as he silently left his home and strolled out of the village towards the rendezvous in the hazel grove.

The warmth of the night air surrounded him in such a pleasant way that it seemed to hold his anticipation of an evening of romance.

He was walking quickly now, his eyes adjusting to the dark as he followed the well-worn path that led to the copse and their secret meeting. The moon cast a pale light on the rough path as it snaked through the trees. It led him to a half-concealed figure sitting on a bank of grasses.

She looked so small and fragile sitting under the heavily leafed tree, a great well of emotion stirred his heart and he felt a pressing need to protect her. As he drew nearer he could see how lovely she looked sitting there in the moonlight. Her dark hair softly draped around her face and her full lips welcomed him with an inviting smile. Raising her hands up to him she indicated her need for his help to get her to her feet. As he did, he pulled her to him, feeling for the first time her young soft body next to his.

His strong arms held her to his chest while his lips searched for hers. Finding them as eager as his, he pressed hard against her lips, feeling them opening slightly, inviting passion rather than greeting. All the pent-up emotion released as they slipped slowly down to the warm grassed earth beneath their feet until they lay together, drinking in the scents of the night, the wild flowers under and around them. Their hands eagerly explored each other, their frustrations at last set free; inhibitions gone, it was not surprising that they tasted love together for the first time.

As the many kisses passed between them, he held her face. His fingers laced through her hair as he kissed her eyelids, nose, mouth and chin, finally reaching her long neck that was soft, white and scented with lavender. She tasted and smelt sweet, and was ready and willing for his eager lips. She responded with her hands clutching his dark curls, guiding his lips down her neck and towards her pert breasts.

Louis's sensitive hands glided over her bodice, down onto her hips, feeling his way on a voyage of discovery and passion. Peeling the layers of clothing away slowly, delicately, discovering more and more white flesh that responded with full consent as he went. She in turn helped him free of his shirt, going on to undo the fastenings on his trousers, touching him through the cloth, arousing him in anticipation of things to come. Her bodice was fully open. He sat astride her, drinking in the beauty of this woman that lay before him under the August moon, looking every bit like a goddess in the pale ghostly light.

Her arms splayed out openly, inviting and tantalising, waiting for him to make love to her. Her breasts were soft under his searching hands, her nipples hardening has he held them gently between his fingers. Taking the weight of his body on his knees, he bent forward, kissing her neck, teasing her, making her wait until she arched her back and took his head, pressing it towards her breasts, releasing a sob of relief when at last he found the delicate target, her desire increasing until the time for sensibility was quite gone.

Louis would not allow his passion to overcome the moment. He made love to her slowly until he felt her to be ready to go further. His hand slipped down, feeling for her knee, lifting the heavy skirt that hid and protected the most intimate part of her, pulling at her skirts until finally he raised his body and the skirts were lifted to one side. When he settled over her once again, only a thin layer of cloth divided them from each other. This moment was almost too much for him. He had held back his passion for so long; now, suddenly, he was released. Freed of clothes he entered her, rejoicing in the final act to become as one. Their bodies moved together as one in rhythm that went from passionate to a crescendo, and for the next few minutes neither one of them was aware of anything in their world but each other.

When at last they finally separated in an exhausted state they lay together in each other's arms, hot, sweaty and deeply satisfied, sharing the moment and wanting the night to last forever in their newfound love.

The owl in full flight, looking to find a small rodent for his supper, didn't disturb them as it flew overhead, nor did the yelp of a fox on the prowl not far away in the undergrowth reach them.

High above their heads, the moon's soft light reached out through the gaps made by the branches and caressed their bodies with its glow. They were still entwined and lying on a carpet of fallen leaves and soft grasses. The moon had moved a good pace across the dark heavens in which it voyaged every night.

In the warm night air the couple resisted the call of sense inside their heads that told them they had better be heading home. The night was too good to end. They wanted that moment to last forever.

His arms were wrapped around her body while she contently rested her head on his bare chest. She could hear his steady heartbeat and her outstretched arm that was draped across his body made her aware of the strength of his muscular torso.

She felt protected and safe. His arms tightened around her as he kissed her hair tenderly. Soon they would have to go back to their very different lives. Just now they lived for the moment but they were certain in the knowledge that they were at the start of a journey, a journey filled with love.

Whenever they could, the couple would steal away to meet each other, neither wanting to be separated from each other for long. The meetings would become a regular occurrence over the next few weeks with Louis falling even more madly in love with Sophia, if that were possible. He desired her desperately each day and thought of her every waking moment. Not that any of his thoughts relieved his deepest fear that this love affair would not survive.

He recognised that although he was more than able to support himself and a wife, he was still only a craftsman, while she, though not gentry, was still the daughter of a rich and powerful merchant who could use his influence and destroy him and any hopes the couple might have of marriage.

He was not happy with the situation, his moral compass did not really approve of the clandestine meetings. But what other avenue could they use? He wanted to marry Sophia, his passionate lover that he loved with a need he couldn't describe.

Somehow he had to find the courage to ask her father for her hand and convince him that he loved her more than life itself and was seeking nothing more from her father but his daughter.

Finding the right time and place was essential. Months had passed and the commission was almost completed. The work had gone well and the story in wood was almost told. Mr Pennock's weekly visits only reinforced Louis's feelings of true worth; the gentleman showered prolific praise on him. The extraordinary skill in Louis's hands and fingers was there before him in wood, soon the commission would grace his living room and become a talking point for every dinner party he held.

Soon Louis would not have a legitimate reason to see Mr Pennock. Time was getting short, and he must ask him soon.

Louis was due to fit the decorative panels within the month. November was almost out and the festive season was about to start. It had taken almost a year from start to finish but every mark he had tooled had been worth it. He was filled with pride looking at his work and was looking forward to fitting the shutters, just as eager as Mr Pennock was to see them in their final location.

Louis finally decided to ask his patron for Sophia's hand in marriage after he had fitted the commission, but first he must ask Sophia. Hardly daring to hope that that was what she wanted too, it was a huge step for both of them. She would become a craftsman's wife if she accepted him, gone the lifestyle she enjoyed now. Parties, balls and the social life would be replaced by a much simpler lifestyle governed by his business and how successful he became.

At their next meeting, before they made love, he went down on bended knee and asked her to marry him. She accepted without hesitation, falling into his arms and vowing to love him forever.

Asking Mr Pennock for her hand in marriage was Louis's next goal and getting his permission could be difficult because, regardless of the fact Sophia had agreed to marry him, there was no guarantee that her father would give his blessing. Although Mr Pennock was not nobility, he was rich and powerful and might be horrified by the thought of a craftsman being a son-in-law, however skilled and clever he might be. Louis was well aware of the change of status he was asking Sophia to accept and so was she. Would Mr Pennock be willing to allow her to follow her heart? Sophia and her father moved in a social circle that Louis could only dream about. If Sophia married Louis she would lose all of that and her father may not allow it.

There was an expectation and a buzz of excitement in the air on the day when the shutters were to be fitted. It was also the time that Louis had chosen to ask Sophia's father for her hand.

No one could help but admire these pieces of art he had made. Louis had used all his talent, imagination and skill in their execution.

From Louis's workshop they were wrapped in thick blankets as they were carried by the local deliverymen to the cart and gently placed there for transfer up to the large house, tied firmly for the journey. The local carter sat up front ready with the reins in his hands, and once the cargo was safely lodged he urged his horses forward over the rough road onwards up to Avondale House.

For the actual fitting, Louis would have help from a number of Mr Pennock's labourers from his estate. A lot of brute strength was needed for the lifting and fitting of these beautiful pieces. Apart from the weight that needed strong arms and hands to support it, they must be held in place until they were fixed within the inserts by the windows. It took manpower and many hours but finally the men with Louis were able to step back and view the fruit of their labours.

By the end of the day they were in place. The shutters were magnificent.

Mr Pennock and Sophia stood in front of their new acquisition, drinking in the stories carved in wood. Louis was looking at their faces, searching for the right reaction. After all the months working on these pieces, the carpenter in him knew they were good work, but the artist in him feared that they might not be liked, even though they had been overseen all the way through the months.

The silence in the living room was deafening. Louis had knots of tension biting his stomach as he waited for someone to break the silence and speak.

A shrill laugh of excitement from Sophia broke it. Clapping her hands in a childlike way, she turned, smiling, to her father, who by now was smiling too.

Looking as pleased as Punch, he hugged her and then marched over to Louis and shook his hand with real feeling.

The pleasure on Mr Pennock's face was unmistakeable. He moved forward to the nearest panel, reaching out to touch the warm rich wood. He traced his fingers over the fruit and animals that were raised up in full lifelike detail. His eyes were filled with moisture and for a moment he was overcome.

Mr Pennock, thrilled with his new purchase, was suddenly gushing with praise, giving Louis a semi-hug while slapping the young man firmly on his back. Tears of joy ran down the face of the older man while his daughter looked lovingly at Louis, her eyes filled with pride.

Louis could see that he had reached the heart of the older man and he knew that this was the right time for him to ask that all-important question. He could not afford to miss this opportunity. Feeling a new confidence in himself, he took the plunge and faced the older man and asked him for his consent to marry Sophia.

Mr Pennock liked Louis, he admired his gift and he himself had started from a humble background. One did not choose where and to whom one was born; Mr Pennock preferred to judge the man, not his background.

Mr Pennock had noticed a change in his daughter over the months and now he realised that the change was due to Louis. She came to Louis's side and waited for the answer that could map out her future.

Mr Pennock could see the love in the faces of this young couple and remembered the love he had felt for Sophia's mother. He considered the new life Sophia would share with Louis, so different from the one he provided for her. He could see how badly she wanted Louis and so, with some reservations, he gave his blessing, crossed his fingers and hoped he had made the right decision for the both of them.

Louis the modest journeyman was so happy, it seemed that heaven had blessed him.

The date for the ceremony was decided. Both Louis and Sophia wanted a spring wedding. The first week in May was penned in on the calendar.

Both of them loved the spring, so fresh and new after the winter, they looked forward to the long days and mild weather. But for now, a long winter stretched out before them. Time enough for the planning of their wedding day, and gathering together furniture and such for the home they would be making together.

It was during one such meeting that Louis was taken by the thought of making the marital bed, one that they would share for the rest of their lives.

He conceived the idea of carving the headboard, featuring the tree of life, and cast himself and Sophia in the roles of Adam and Eve. The sun would always shine on the two of them in his Garden of Eden; he saw it as a little piece of heaven on Earth. His bed would be so special, so unique, with their love story depicted in wood. A gift made with love to a soul mate who would make his life complete.

Her father had been surprisingly encouraging of the union between them. And was more than happy to pay for a lavish wedding. Even more surprisingly, he had given Louis a substantial amount of money to 'get them settled', as Mr Pennock put it. Louis could only suppose that her father wanted to make sure that Sophia would be comfortable and have some luxuries about her that she was used to once she was married. Luxuries that Louis could ill afford. Louis was grateful for his father-in-law's generosity.

Mr Pennock had worries about their forthcoming union. He knew his daughter very well and in the past Sophia had been wild and sometimes uncontrollable. Mr Pennock had great hopes that Louis was the man who would help to settle his daughter down. Her father loved her but she had been troublesome since she realised that men found her attractive and from her mid-teens had actively sought out male attention. She had been a mischievous flirt who loved to be courted and enjoyed being the centre of attention.

Men could not help but be attracted to her and she had had a number of suitors. But sweet little Sophia could quickly become a viper, her incendiary temper would explode if she didn't get her way. Not surprisingly, her conquests retreated quickly when faced with the experience of one of her rants.

Louis was unaware of Sophia's past and that Sophia was not as sweet as he thought. Love was blind.

Louis had only seen what Sophia had wanted him to see. She had been careful not to expose her temper in front of Louis. She genuinely loved him and had no intention of losing him through an angry moment of rage. Her perfect beauty hid a violent temper and a jealous nature. The men to whom she had attached herself in the past had had a lucky escape. Louis would not be so fortunate.

4

When the winter came, it was bleak and bitterly cold. There was not much movement in the village, the neighbours kept indoors as much as they could. It seemed to snow most days through December and January and the icicles that hung from Louis's guttering were growing longer daily.

Everyday he would be found in his workshop. Since making the shutters for Mr Pennock his customer base had grown along with his reputation. New commissions came from all over the shires, giving him work that would see him financially secure for the forthcoming year and beyond; his new clients all expounding praise about the elaborate hunting scene he had created for Mr Pennock. They, in turn, wanted to own something of beauty and excellence for themselves.

Louis spent all the hours that God sent fulfilling his new orders but although he was always busy, he somehow still found time in between jobs to work on his personal project, his wedding present to his Sophia.

Sophia and Louis met infrequently through the winter, and when they did meet they could not spend much time together. The weather being cold and damp excluded meeting in the open air and meeting in his home was out of the question. It would have surely set the tongues wagging in the village. So for the sake of decency and reputation, they only met in company and at her father's home. Their passion for each other for now would have to wait. Though they both felt frustration at the forced condition, spring was not too far ahead and warmer weather would soon break through the cold. Already a few green shoots had pushed their way through the snow. Soon the snowdrops would be raising their heads, announcing that spring would soon be here, and in May they would be wed.

The wedding day arrived on a warm and sunny day. The wedding party was smaller than they had planned. A few of the guests they had invited felt it inappropriate for a craftsman, however good, to marry a lady of money and position. But despite that, the day was a great success. They were very much in love and no one or anyone was going to interfere with their day. By late afternoon Sophia had become a carpenter's wife.

At first, love carried them along. Life was sweet. Sophia loved Louis's gift, his love token to her. His clever hands had depicted his and her likeness in the form of Adam and Eve in minute detail; she was thrilled that her image would be there well after her time on Earth was over.

Making love on the first night of their marriage in the bed he had made for her was ecstatic. Their bodies entwined were eager to touch and be touched. Her full breasts were firm and round under his searching hands, nipples hard in anticipation of the pleasure that was before them. Her hips rose up to meet him, moulding them together as he readied himself to make them one. The wonder of love bound them together. They were ecstatically happy for the first year of their marriage.

By June of the following year, small changes in her attitude had started to worry Louis; Sophia seemed restless, she could quickly become angry at the smallest thing. There were many needless arguments, which he did not understand. They had been married just over a year and now he wondered if he had made a huge mistake.

Sophia, who had married for love, was starting to miss her old life. Yes, she did love Louis but it was so dull being his wife. No one invited her to parties any more. She no longer had her garden to work in, where she had spent so much of her time, and she missed it dreadfully. Concerts were also out of her reach but the hurt she felt the most was because of her friends. She had thought they would stay friends with her after her marriage but they had distanced themselves from her. Her sin was that she had married for love and beneath her station, a sin that couldn't be forgiven, so she had become ostracised by the ladies.

Her insecure and jealous nature, which she had hidden so well, came to the surface every few weeks. Without any real provocation her temper surfaced, making Louis's life very difficult.

Louis! She reasoned he had a life, he was always busy, had friends and he didn't give her the attention she felt she deserved. He would sometimes go out after work for a drink and join his friends for a chat. It was just like he had done in the days before he was married. She didn't like that.

She wanted all his attention. He should be taking her out, not leaving her at home alone. After all she had given up for his love she surely deserved that much. Village life had some diversions – visiting musicians, the odd barn dance – but they were infrequent and the people that went to these venues she felt were beneath her.

She had not made any friends in the village, partly because the village women were afraid of her and partly because she was always rather lofty when she addressed them.

Her home help that came into her house to see to the chores was the only person she spoke to, but it was to order and never in friendship. Only when she visited her father did she feel normal and her charm returned for a limited time.

In her dark moods, she seemed unable to listen to reason from Louis or her father. She was intent to only have her say, no matter what. In effect she was always in the right or the victim.

She could be kind and loving but her episodes of being unreasonable were becoming more frequent and more embarrassing for Louis. As more years passed, her attitude became so bad that she seemed to go out of her way to pick fights and to humiliate him. At times, even his workshop offered no escape from her. Several times she had found him in the public house having a beer; he knew her temper would be ready to explode and so not to have a scene in front of his friends and neighbours, he would quickly take her home. Once they were back in their home she became his caring wife again but he was aware that his life's space was shrinking, he was never given time for himself anymore.

She seemed to want to control every aspect of his life, suffocating him in the process.

The heaven that Louis had dreamed of was turned into a living hell, her behaviour was so unpredictable. The occasional invites they got to evening supper with Louis's friends should have been fun but instead they became an ordeal. She would misinterpret Louis's natural charm and easy manner as flirting. She accused him of being disloyal to her when they returned home. It became clear that his friends would rather not be exposed to Sophia and the tension she brought with her.

Louis's patience was stretched to the limit. Unable to pacify her most of the time, he opted for a quiet life, keeping his thoughts to himself or finding work to do in his workshop to get out of her way.

She could not control her rage. It was not unusual for her to throw precious pieces of china in temper, smashing them into a thousand pieces. Gifts that Louis had bought for her with his love. With each piece that was smashed, a little piece of his heart was also crushed. These gifts of love that had meant so much to him meant so little to her. Even when she apologised for her behaviour she would still try to justify her actions and would ultimately convince herself that she was the victim.

The fifth wedding anniversary came and went. Five years of struggling with her temperament had exhausted Louis; it was having an effect on his creativity and livelihood. Love that was shared in the marriage bed was no longer sustaining their marriage.

After all she had done to win him, now she recognised the signs she had seen before in her younger days with other suitors. She no longer held his focus like she had and her tears did not move him anymore. She could no longer persuade him by a kiss or making love to have her own way.

She knew that Louis was losing interest in her and was becoming restless; even making love now was at her bidding. She sensed he was looking for a way to get away from her. Divorce was so scandalous that she wouldn't allow it to happen. Marriage was for life; divorce was such a public disgrace. In her society it just didn't happen.

She asked herself why he didn't understand her, hadn't she given up her privileged life to be with him? She reasoned it was his fault that they argued so much. He was a flirt and a magnet to women. She couldn't bear it. Maybe if they had a child...

5

The heat had been building all day and the evening was very sultry. The humidity was so high that even doing the slightest chore caused heavy perspiration and when Louis came in from the workshop he was hot and sweaty. He was surprised to find that Sophia had prepared him a warm bath and the tin tub sat waiting for him in the bedroom.

"God, Sophia, that's just what I need," he said, pecking her with a kiss on her cheek before stripping off and settling into the warm water. Lying back on the upright of the tub, Louis closed his eyes, enjoying feeling the warm fluid around his tired limbs. He was dozing in the warm water, when he felt her hands touching his chest and her lips kissing his neck. It brought him back to the moment.

Hell, can't she even let me have a bath in peace, he thought but instead he said, "Just give me a minute, love, and I'll be out of here."

"No need for that," said Sophia. She was already stripped naked and testing her toe in the water as she got in.

Pulling his legs up to his chest, he made a space for her. Not to do so would mean another row and one in the state of tiredness he was in, he could do without.

What had seemed such a lovely gesture on Sophia's part was fading now as he realised that she wanted something and this was all part of her conditional love; he got something, she got something! That was the deal. But not tonight!

As she got settled in the water he stood up and got out.

"Where are you going? We always loved to bathe together," her face looked rather peevish but she was able to keep her voice sweet.

"Hungry, really hungry," he lied and went off towards the kitchen. He could hear her movement in the water as she made use of the bath. She soaped herself all over, freshening herself in the warm water. For what she had in mind was an intimate night, a night when a child might be conceived. Louis would not escape, not tonight.

Salad was laid out on the kitchen table – radishes, tomatoes, onions and some lettuce with blanched cauliflower. There was fresh bread on a board and cheeses lay on a plate next to it, all ready for supper.

Drying himself on a linen towel, he walked to the table. The loaf smelt so fresh. It was long and twisted with crusted ends. He could not resist the end of crusty bread. It tantalised him sitting on the breadboard, just asking to be pulled off and eaten. It always irritated Sophia if he nibbled before the meal, but she wasn't there to see, so he enjoyed it all the more.

"Bring me a towel, love," came the cry from the bedroom. "Then help me to clear the tub away and we'll have supper."

The bath had made Louis feel fresh and strong. Despite himself he was feeling warmer towards Sophia than he had a few minutes ago.

"Coming, love," he called out and he went to help.

He could not help admiring his wife's lovely body. The small towel he had brought hardly covered her. She patted herself dry in front of him, and seeing the roundness of her breasts and the soft curves over her stomach stirred his blood and he felt himself becoming aroused.

But then, that was what she had hoped for.

Keeping herself as cool and comfortable as she could on that oppressively hot evening, she dressed in a loose-fitting cotton lawn shift and nothing else. It gave her comfort and she had an opportunity to flaunt herself in front of her husband.

She had felt his interest in her as she was drying herself and hoped that his interest would lead them to bed after supper. The front opening of the shift gaped every time she bent forward, showing her breast briefly in a tantalising, teasing way.

He had not planned to make love with her but somehow the light-hearted talk over the evening meal and the relaxed atmosphere that so reminded him of the earlier years lulled him into desiring her again. After supper he was willingly led by Sophia into their bedroom and into the bed that had been carved so lovingly by him.

She slid out of the shift and lay passively, looking like a goddess. Louis stripped quickly and took her in his arms. Kisses and foreplay led to passion. The tensions that had been between them for months were forgotten for a few precious minutes while they re-enacted a journey they had travelled so many times before in making love. His lips found her breasts, her body rising, helping him to find his way. They were joined together again for the first time in many months.

When the passion was finally over they rolled back, sweaty from their intimacy and the heat of the night. Louis was exhausted from the day's work and making love. He pulled on his nightshirt and after giving Sophia a light goodnight kiss, he turned his back on her and was asleep in seconds.

The anger she felt was palatable. He used to hold her for a long time and stroke her hair after they had finished making love. Why had he turned his back on her? It never crossed her mind that her husband was beyond the point of exhaustion, she only knew she felt slighted and used. Her plan had not gone exactly as she had planned. Her thoughts were in chaos. Was there someone else in his life? Was that the reason he had lost interest in her? Would she end up old and alone? Panic replaced her anger. God! Was she going to lose him?

Had Louis made love with her that evening only because she had tempted him? Had he fallen out of love with her? He had not been interested in her sexually for months; unhappily, she felt she was losing him. Once again anger filled her; she was so agitated that sleep was beyond her now. Her thoughts came rolling rapidly into her head, memories of their life together, all the love that they had shared. She had given up so much to be with him and there he was lying beside her but he didn't love her anymore. Lying there in the dark, resentment was building up as the time ticked away into the early hours.

She tossed and turned, restless, not able to sleep, but Louis had not stirred in his sleep beside her. His breathing was steady and deep but sleep evaded her. What could she do to keep him? Brooding anxiety built up through the long dark hours until the morning light started to creep into the bedroom. Lying in the half-light with tiredness affecting every part of her body, passion, jealousy and despair overcame her. If she couldn't have him, no one would.

Just as dawn was breaking, she slipped out of bed and picked up the pillow she had laid on. She thought it would be so easy to smother him. Walking around to his side of the bed, she looked down at his face, so peaceful in sleep. Yet the hate she was feeling was now stronger than love.

Standing over him with the pillow ready, she had a moment of panic. What if he woke as she was trying to smother him? He was much stronger than she was and he would stop her. Changing her mind, she flung the pillow to one side and ran out of the room, taking her hate with her.

Standing in the kitchen with her head spinning with thoughts of jealousy and hate, the mixed emotions fused together until a numb blackness took over her mind. Seeing nothing and moving by instinct she stood staring down at the table that still held the remains of their evening meal. The bread knife was still on the table by the bread. She picked it up and in a trance she retraced her steps back to the double bed.

He had not moved; he was still half-curled, laid on his side in deep slumber. The thought, like a chant, repeated itself in her head. The bed that had been their bed of passion would now become his deathbed. *His deathbed, his deathbed, his deathbed.* With tears running down her face, she lifted the knife in her two hands high above her head and plunged it into the sleeping figure.

Sense suddenly returned. Her hand jumped off the knife handle as though it was red hot. She stared down at her husband's still body, shocked at what she had done. Blood was seeping around the knife and down the white nightshirt he was wearing. She could see it covering the bed sheet where he lay and being absorbed into the mattress. Too late she realised what she had done. Sick to her stomach she mouthed a silent word, "Louis", as though trying to call him back to her before fleeing the house, leaving the knife still in her husband's back.

Sophia gave herself up to the local constable in the village and was sent to jail to await trial. Her father could hardly come to terms with the fact she was a murderess, his little girl the daughter he loved, who through jealousy had killed.

Money could not save her. It seemed the only person who still cared for her was him.

Her defence counsel tried to claim it was a crime of self-defence but with the evidence being what it was, that her husband was apparently asleep when she attacked him, the law naturally decided it was premeditated. Her rash and jealous actions had sealed her fate.

The punishment for murder was to hang until dead and justice in the Georgian courts was without mercy. Her father, who had loved her too much, was a shattered man. His daughter was a convicted killer and her body would never be allowed to be buried in consecrated ground, so when he claimed her corpse he took her back home to bury her in the grounds of Avondale House, close to the rose garden she loved so much.

6

A piercing pain in Louis's back invaded this strange dream he was having. A dazzling white light at the end of a tunnel had formed in front of him and it seemed to be drawing him into its incredible brightness, pulling him along like a rag doll towards it.

Suddenly he was aware of many memories flashing before his eyes, memories he had experienced during his life.

The pain in his back suddenly dissolved and he felt strangely peaceful and weightless for a moment. Then, shaking his head, he struggled to wake from this bizarre dream he was having. Shutting his eyes and with all the strength he could muster, he pulled himself back from the blinding light. The luminosity of it dimmed slowly before disappearing completely.

Damn this dream, I must wake up, he thought, shaking his head, trying to wake himself. He propped himself up before rolling over in the bed and was shocked to see a body beside him. Pushing up to sitting position, he was feeling light-headed with shock – the man laying face down next to him had a knife in his back!

He leapt off the bed, his stomach retching. God! What was he to do?

Not knowing how to react, he found a chair and sat down heavily. His head was spinning with questions.

What was happening here? What the hell was going on, who was the man and where was Sophia? What the devil had she been up to while he was asleep?

His hands nervously pushed his hair back from his face.

Who is he? Could he be alive? he questioned.

Louis got up and moved nearer the bed but there was no movement on the man's chest, he wasn't breathing. He was dead!

Louis leaned over to move the covers that were draped around the figure, he wanted to see this man's face, but to his horror his fingers could not grasp the fabric. Indeed, they seemed to slip through the cotton sheet that he had slept under that night.

He tried again, grabbing hard at the sheet, but it was all in vain. Try as he might he was unable to fulfil the task. He was frightened now, once again doubting that he was really awake.

What in God's name was happening? He was still dreaming, that was it, he was having a terrible nightmare. Why the hell couldn't he wake up?

He sat on the bed, drained and exhausted, his head in his hands. How long he sat there he didn't know. His downcast eyes watched the morning light move across the carpet. A rectangle of light spread over the bed cover and across the figure. It was then, and only then that in his distress, Louis had not realised the body he was looking at was his own earthly remains.

Unbelievable panic hit him. The pit of his stomach turned and lurched as he fought to steady himself. His eyes tightly shut, his hands balled into fists pressing hard against his temples. He rocked himself backwards and forwards on the edge of the bed. He was in a state of total disbelief. When the panic within him subsided a little, Louis took stock of his situation. He remembered stories, stories of people having near-death experiences, about tunnels of light, voices of angels and people being shown their past lives, even stories of loved ones coming to meet the newly departed and helping them to pass over into the afterlife.

Some people were turned back from the light, made to return to the living world to fulfil their destiny; they would never be afraid of death again. He had never believed the stories. They were just that, stories made up for the weak-minded. Those that couldn't face up to the fact that once you were dead, you were dead, and that was the end of it. No heaven, no afterlife, nothing but nothing. Everything ends.

The lightness of his disembodied spirit scared him. Having rejected the tunnel of light to the afterlife, he realised he was trapped in a netherworld. Would it be for eternity? God! How long was eternity? There was no one to ask.

THE BED

The bed, so precious to him in life, was bonded to Louis by his own blood. He was transported with it each time it was sold.

At first, being trapped in this dead but un-dead state left Louis anxious and angry. He could not believe that this was his fate to be left in limbo forever. Never to communicate with people he could see and hear. The realisation there was no way out for him but existing in this netherworld was not to be contemplated. The choice of heaven or even hell might be preferable to this state he now found himself in. Was despair the only feeling he would have as a companion for all eternity?

Even in this spirit state, in the narrow world he was confined to, he still felt emotion; he could see and hear even if it were on a different level. He would not give in, he must find a way back somehow.

This, he promised himself.

7

Louis's landlord John Ridley was shocked and rather put out; he was left with a house and workshop without a tenant and even worse, his tenant had been murdered. It was unlikely he would find a new tenant quickly in the circumstances. Who would want to move into a home where a murder had taken place?

In lieu of lost rent, he intended to sell whatever he could from Louis's effects and arranged for an auction to take place as soon as he possibly could.

He was unaware of any immediate family belonging to Louis; he had been an only child as far as he knew. There was only his father-in-law who would be classed as family but he need not worry about him. The old man had his own money and had withdrawn from society after the trial.

Mr Pennock had become a recluse and his health was in a poor state, according to the locals. The shutters in his living room that had been his pride and joy only held sad memories now. They reminded him of Louis and the madness of his daughter. He had become so troubled that he had given orders that the room should be locked and took to spending his time in his library, hoping that the old saying 'Out of sight, out of mind' would work for him.

Louis stood by the bed. The noise from the people in his small cottage invaded his mind. He was contemptuous of them – how could they be there to bid for his possessions?

But then he thought, *What good are belongings to a dead man?* He didn't feel hunger and was never thirsty since that awful day when he was killed. His shell that he had used in life had been taken away but here he was still in his home, not part of either the living or the dead.

"Bugger off, get out of it!" Louis found himself shouting at the fools who were in his house. He didn't get any response – how could he? How futile it was. He recognised that he could hear and see them but no one could see him or even feel his presence.

How on Earth am I to survive? He suddenly laughed out loud at the preposterous thought he had had. This new world of his was empty of normal acts and ghosts don't need to survive. Eternity was eternity; he could not escape from the sentence he had inadvertently given himself. He somehow would have to learn to live on this plane and not to think of all the tomorrows that were in front of him.

All Louis knew was that his home had become a kind of circus, with people passing through his rooms at regular intervals. They lifted and touched all the items he had bought or made over the five years he had been married to Sophia. He was helpless to stop them and anger built up within him on a daily basis. Strangers coming to view his possessions had little regard for the way he had died. They were, in the main, more concerned with getting a bargain, buying something on the cheap.

On the day of the auction a great deal of bartering went on. A few of his friends and neighbours had come in to his workshop, looking for mementos that would remind them of him and his incredible skill. That was something Louis appreciated and he listened to the praise they still bestowed on him; what a good fellow he had been and how they missed him. He was standing among them drinking in the words.

Flooded with mixed emotions and unable to make himself known to them, he knew the true meaning of isolation and despair.

A lot of money changed hands that day, with most of it going into his landlord's pocket. Only the amount that the undertaker was due to was deducted from the landlord's haul. Louis could only watch as his pieces were carted off in all directions. Only one item stayed in place: his bed.

He sat on the bed feeling tired and angry. He leaned heavily against the headboard looking for support for his back but found that the wood gave way under him, it reacted like a soft pillow. Puzzled, he pulled himself back into an upright position for a moment. He touched the wood with his hand, pressing it slightly. Again the wood moved under his palm. *How strange*, he thought, but curious, he leaned against it again. The wood was pliable, more like a curtain than wood. It opened up, allowing the spirit of Louis to enter.

The magic of the kingdom was all there, just as he had seen when he had carved it all those years ago, the tree, the meadow, the stream and sun. The curtain closed behind him, shielding him from the mortal world that he had died in. He had been allowed entry and was drawn into his kingdom.

Just as he had found the images within the wood when he lived, now the wood seemed to close around him to protect him from his strange situation. He was absorbed into his Garden of Eden. This was his new refuge, for when he needed to hide away and find some peace. Now was such a time.

It was a relief to get away from those awful people who had clamoured like thieves for his life's work. The quiet of his garden with the shade of the tree beckoned him to lie down and rest.

Mr John Ridley, the landlord, had plans for the bed. He was having a relationship with an attractive widow called Joan. Her late husband had been the local doctor and magistrate, and had left her rather well off financially. He had been a pillar of the community and she missed him dreadfully.

Five empty years had passed and Joan was very lonely. She had met John through the auctions that were held once a month in the neighbouring town. His many properties were partially furnished with items he had bought from them. She enjoyed buying the more interesting pieces, including fine china and crystal. Over the years a friendship had grown between her and John, and he was more than pleased to fill the role of intimate friend and lover.

John had described the bed in detail to her at one of their secret meetings. His description of the carved headboard with the tree heavy with many fruits and the sunrays that stretched from corner to corner fired her curiosity. She loved fine things and she had been intrigued about this piece of furniture. Knowing how much she appreciated beautiful things in her home, he guessed she would pay a sizeable sum for something as unique as Louis's bed.

John's principles were suspect. He never missed a trick when it came to making a few extra pounds and despite their relationship, he thought she could afford to pay the full asking price for the bed. John deliberately persuaded her to come to Louis's home before the auction to view it ahead of the other customers.

She was bowled over by its fabulous carving, stroking the wood gently feeling its warmth and silky feel. She recognised how precious it was and she could already see it gracing her bedroom. She bought it at once, paying extra than asking price, a price she knew could not be matched. John enjoyed making a little extra profit. Life was sweet.

Within a month from the date of his death, all Louis's effects had been auctioned and his small cottage stood cold and bare after the removal men had picked up Louis and his bed.

His landlord, happy with the sale, and Joan, pleased with her purchase, had no idea what she had bought and that they would be the first couple to experience Louis's anger. His anger at the injustice of his early death had turned him into a resentful spirit. In his aggrieved state he decided he would not allow his bed to be used. Louis could not choose who bought it, but he would have a say in who slept in it if he could.

She was completely unaware that her beautiful new bed was haunted.

Joan greeted the removal men like long lost friends when they delivered the bed to Rosewood Cottage in the next village along the road from where Louis had lived. The men carried the disassembled bed into the clean white painted bedroom, where they quickly assembled it.

"You've got yourself a bonny bed there, missus," the foreman could not help remarking as he made his way back out to the cart. "I've been moving beds for years but I haven't seen anything as fine as this."

"Yes, it is rather special, isn't it?" She was pleased at the compliment paid to her.

She paid them, giving them a generous tip before showing them out and watching them as they disappeared down the road back to where they came from.

In the quiet of her home, she busied herself making up the bed with soft cotton sheets and a bolster pillow. The quilted bedspread of circular patterns that she had made put the finishing touch to the bed in her bedroom.

She was proud and contented. It all looked rather grand in a homely sort of way but she thought it needed something else.

Making a decision, she thought, *I know, a few flowers on the bedside table will brighten up the room and make it look cosy.* She left the room, crossing the hall where her dog laid sprawled out on the clippie rag rug.

Why do dogs always lay out in places where you are likely to fall over them? she thought.

"Come on, mutt," she said cheerily, "lets go and cut some flowers from the garden." Her dog was by her side and out of the house before she could properly open the kitchen door. The air in the late afternoon was filled with the scents of the flowers she grew and it was still pleasantly warm for May. She made her way to her very favourite flowers, scissors in hand, ready to cut the heavy-headed pink peonies.

Her dog was fussing under her feet as she cut them.

"All right, all right, I'll take you for a quick walk in a minute." Flowers in hand, she quickly retraced her steps back to the kitchen and left them in water for her return. The dog was still fussing around her feet.

"I know," she said with a laugh in her voice. "Come on then, let's go."

With the lead in her hand, the two of them were out of the gate, walking at a fast pace and enjoying the last of the afternoon sun before returning for the evening meal.

The meal was soon over; cooking for one was a depressing affair. How she missed company at the table and the conversation. The need to make a proper meal was missing from her life now. But she must eat. Scrambled eggs were so quick to make and tonight her friend was coming later. She was so looking forward to it, and then she remembered the flowers. The dog had been fed and was laid out in his bed; he didn't raise his head as she entered the kitchen. She smiled – a good walk and food always tired him out. Over at the sink she retrieved the flowers and found a vase.

Putting the crystal vase down on the night table, she could not help thinking how splendid the peonies looked; they really did finish off the room. With a smile on her face she went back to the kitchen to clear up for the night.

Deep within the carved garden, Louis had found some respite and calm. He remembered vaguely being moved out of his bedroom and after some sort of journey, settled in another room. But it was all dream-like and in his delicate state he was happy to feel secure and out of harm's way within the headboard's protection.

It was the smell from the flowers that disturbed Louis. It reminded him of Sophia.

The heady perfume filtered through the wood into his garden. It came from the night table by the bed that held the vase of peonies. It brought Louis back into the living world. He stood there in the dazzling white bedroom, a room he did not recognise. The light of the early evening poured through the window behind the delicate pale pink curtains. The two bedside tables in French oak matched perfectly with the wood Louis had used for his carved headboard. A floral square carpet of creams and pink wool graced the floor. An old rocking chair sat in one corner covered with a throw, made from the same material as the bedspread that covered the bed.

Louis had no idea where he was. There was his bed that he knew so well only everything else had changed. He felt disorientated. Where was he? This was not his cottage, was it? And then there were the flowers by the bed; Sophia liked flowers in the bedroom, but this wasn't their bedroom. Then he remembered standing over the body, his body, and the knife sticking out of its back. He was dead, or rather he should be. He only knew that his memories were rekindling the anger deep inside of him.

Then she came into the room dressed in a nightdress and slippers. Who was she?

It was cold, very cold; Joan shivered as she got into bed. She couldn't understand it; the room had been so cosy when she had brought the flowers in earlier.

Even the hairs on her arms were standing on end. Well, thank goodness she had put a hot water bottle in the bed to air the mattress. *Where is it?* she thought. She stretched her arm down under the covers until she found the ceramic holder and pulled it up close.

Louis was standing next to the bed, looking down at her.

What sort of person is this woman? He thought, not that he really cared. She wasn't young or pretty but she had an air about her that echoed a similarity with Sophia, his oh-so-loving wife, who had killed him. Damn her. He wasn't pleased at his observation. That feeling of betrayal returned, raising his level of anger, and an involuntary oath left his mouth.

Joan felt an icy draught that came from nowhere and travelled around the room. *Damn. I must have left the window open, no wonder it's cold in here.*

But at that moment the front door creaked as the sneck was lifted. Louis heard the front door open and a dog, hidden from his view, growled deep in its throat. It was no greeting, rather a warning about this person who had just arrived.

"I'm in here," Joan called out from the bedroom to the newcomer.

"Just a minute," a man's voice replied. There was a sudden commotion coming from the kitchen. The dog yelped as though someone had hurt it.

A frown appeared on her forehead before Joan called out.

"What are you doing?" she said, turning the covers back as she made to get out of bed.

"Just putting the dog out, be there in a sec," a voice replied.

Joan sighed, settling back in bed. He really didn't like her dog; in fact, he didn't like dogs at all – memories of his childhood still clung to him. Ever since he had been knocked over by an Alsatian has a small boy, he had never forgotten the fear that he felt as the dog stood over him; he could still smell the dog's breath and see the sharp white canine teeth inches away from his face. However unreasonable it was now as an adult, he didn't want her dog in the house.

Louis stood stock-still looking over to the door where the voice had come from.

I know that voice, thought Louis. Seconds later, the man walked into the bedroom to the waiting woman. It was his landlord, John.

Louis was surprised. John Ridley was a man he had never trusted. He always seemed to look after his own interests rather than those of his tenants but perhaps all landlords were like that, Louis had thought. He also knew that he was married with several children but although he had distrusted him, he had never thought for a moment he could be an adulterer.

Oh my God, thought Louis, watching the man stripping down to his underwear before sliding into bed beside Joan. *I can't believe this is happening*. He shook his head in despair. Must he really have to watch this couple make love in his bed?

He couldn't bear it; uncontrollable rage became a thunderous roaring in his head that projected it's self by shouting and screaming at the couple. Needless to say, they heard no sound as they cuddled up together under the blankets.

Louis was beside himself. "Not in my bed!" He shouted over and over again, his voice rising each time he repeated the phrase.

Joan once again felt an icy draught sweep around the room, causing the curtains to flap together at the bedroom window.

"Hell's teeth, its bitter in here," grumbled John. "It's May! How can it be so cold?"

"I must have left the window open, sorry love," Joan said apologetically. She sat up, throwing the quilted cover to one side.

Just as she was about to get out of bed to close the window, her dog started barking to be let in.

"I'll see to it," she said, pushing her feet into her slippers. John reached out to pull her back into the bed.

"Let him wait, come back to bed," pleaded John, putting on a sad face as she pulled away.

"No love, it must be freezing outside if this room is anything to go by. I wish I'd banked up the fire," she said, almost to herself. She was across the room in two strides and out to the kitchen to let the dog in.

"Come on, you silly mutt, in you come," she said affectionately, stroking the dog as he pushed past her into the cottage, rubbing up around her feet, his soulful eyes pleading for a titbit.

John called her from the bed. "Shut the window on the way, will you?"

The dog followed her, trotting behind her until Joan got to the bedroom. She moved towards the window but the dog stopped short of the door. Again a growl sounded deep in his throat. It stopped Joan in her tracks. He had never acted like that, even though she knew John was not his favourite person.

"What's up with him?" grumbled John while pushing back the covers, motioning to Joan to get in beside him.

The hackles were rising on top of the dog's neck and he was backing away with his tail down between his legs, before turning with a whine and scuttling back to the kitchen.

"That's odd," said Joan. "He's been acting strange all afternoon, do you think he's ill or something? I better go to see to him."

"He's fine, he's just sulking 'cos I'm here. Never mind, love, come and keep me warm," persuaded John, his arms held out for her to come to him.

Joan giggled, completely forgetting about the dog and the window. She felt like a young girl again. It was always the same when she was with John. She climbed back into the bed, snuggling down under the covers, feeling the warmth of his body lying beside her. John enveloped her in his arms, raising her excitement at the anticipation of making love. John made her happy.

Louis had retreated back into the quiet and secure kingdom behind the carving. It was all too much to watch the lovemaking in his bed. The dog had sensed his presence, he was sure of that. Could it be that the animal could actually see him? He didn't know which, but when the dog turned tail as he went towards it, he felt it was the latter.

That was when Louis decided to turn tail himself and melt back into his retreat, back into the relative peace of his own kingdom though he was still able to hear the couple. Discontentment and frustration of not being able to stop the couple using his bed and hearing the couple in their lovemaking made him attempt another challenge. He would try again to put a stop to the couple usurping his bed.

The couple, though past the first flush of youth, were totally absorbed in each other. Their monthly rendezvous was intense; it was so exciting having a secret love and eating the forbidden fruit.

For the few hours that they spent together they were ecstatic, on cloud nine. It was a special time filled with kisses and the thrill of passion. That night was no exception. Both were naked now and they were enjoying the freedom of love making and knowing what gave each other pleasure.

The wood seemed to become transparent as Louis started to appear from the headboard. He was staring down into the face of the woman Joan, who had opened her eyes just as he was emerging. For a moment their eyes were locked together and Joan seemed to see him. He could see the terror on her face and heard the cry from the muffled scream. He pushed back again into his retreat. He was so pleased that for a few moments, he had succeeded in stopping them. More than that, he had shown himself to a living person, though he had no idea how he had achieved it. He hoped it might mean that he could find a way to pass from this netherworld and move on, to where he didn't know, but he hoped.

They were deep in an embrace in the half-light as night closed in, shadows playing on the walls of the bedroom as the sun went down. Joan lay against the pillow. John was kissing her neck, her body responding with each caress, her eyes were half closed and her head was raised and turned to one side. Excitement was rising through her body and she was eager for more, when out of the corner of her eye Joan thought she saw the shadow of a face.

God! It was the face of a man looking at her from the headboard. An involuntary sound came from her lips as she stifled a scream, her hand closing over her mouth as she froze in John's arms.

She threw herself to one side away from the headboard and started to shake.

"What's wrong?" asked John in an accusing voice, not understanding what was going on.

"I— I thought I saw—" She stopped mid-stream. It was so silly. She looked again at the carving and saw nothing but the beautiful Garden of Eden. "There was a shadow on the carving. It looked— well, it looked like a face staring at me."

She laughed nervously. A deep frown appeared on her forehead; she did not know how he would react. He was not known for his sensitivity and could be easily provoked.

He was indignant, as though she had somehow rejected him.

"Look! Are we making love or not? You're being stupid with your wild imaginings." But seeing the look on her face and her eyes filled with tears he softened his stance. "And it can't be anything more than a trick of the light. You're behaving like a silly goose. Stop worrying and come here."

His arms wrapped round her body, pulling her tightly against his chest, and he was kissing her with all the passion he had. He held her until her tears subsided.

Her fear dissolved lying in his arms and she allowed herself to be persuaded to give in to his sexual desires.

Louis was pleased with himself and after a couple of minutes emerged once again to make himself known to the woman, but the moment had passed. He could not be seen by the couple who were now totally engrossed in making love. He stood watching and waiting for the spectacle to stop, loathing and temper bubbling up in him all the while.

He screamed, unable to keep his emotions in check, but it was not heard. His temper gave him strength and he was able in that moment to shake the bed but the lovers didn't notice. For the third time that evening, the room's temperature tumbled to below freezing, followed by an icy draught from Louis's breath that touched the skin of the lovers. They didn't notice.

It was some time later that John realised how cold he was; even under the layers of blankets his back felt like an ice block. Joan was already dressing into her nightgown that she had abandoned earlier and she planned to refill her hot water bottle as soon as she was able.

"Someone just walked over my grave," said John, shivering, and he too reached out for his shirt and pulled it on with some haste. He was already thinking rather guiltily of the hot supper and warm bed that his dutiful wife would have waiting back at his own home. He would have to go soon. He loved his wife in his own way and loved Joan too. He could never leave his wife or his children for Joan, but he could not give Joan up either. He knew he couldn't be late back home without his wife being suspicious and that his time was almost over with Joan for another month. It was all so difficult.

The draught that spun around the bedroom was bitterly cold and lifted the curtains, billowing them out into the room, startling both of them.

"Lord! Let's get that window shut," said John, striding over to the window with purpose. Pulling the drapes aside, he was astonished to find the window wasn't open.

"What the h—" He stopped midway through the sentence. He was baffled to find a layer of ice on the inside of the window standing a full half-inch thick. Shaking his head and almost speaking to himself he muttered, "I don't understand it, how can we have a frost?" He motioned to Joan.

"Come and look at this," he said, making Joan hurry over to his side. "How very strange. How can we have a heavy frost in May? It's hardly dark yet and it's been a warm spring day. But look at that ice, no wonder we're so cold. Better make up a fire tonight and leave it banked up." He kissed her lightly on the cheek. "I must go, love. Sorry I can't stay longer but you know how it is," he said, pulling on his trousers, socks and shoes. "It was good tonight, wasn't it? I wish we could get together more often." She wished that too but knew it was impossible. He would never leave his wife.

Ten minutes later she lit the lamps and he was gone. She moved into the kitchen, putting on the kettle. She needed a hot drink and another bottle for the bed. She was cold; she had never experienced her bedroom as cold as it was now, even in deep winter.

She felt very unsettled. Usually after a visit from John she felt strengthened and invigorated but not tonight. Standing in the kitchen in her nightdress, she was conscious that she didn't feel as cold and that the room was warm. There was no icy chill in here. There was a small gap between the curtains at the window and she reached out, opening the curtains fully. The image was clear through the window, she could see the moon casting its light on her garden. The glass of the window was totally free of ice and there were no tell-tale signs of water on the sill. How very odd. She was puzzled; a few strange things had happened today, things she could not explain. The way the dog had reacted after the bed had been delivered – he wouldn't go into her bedroom, then the icy window and the bitter cold. Draughts swirling around the room as though the windows had been left open. What could it all mean?

The dog came for some attention and she was glad to give it. Her dog gave her unconditional love and companionship every day and, yes! security too. She patted his head as he pushed against her legs, those soulful eyes looking up at her as if trying to tell her something.

"Go on, back to your bed," she said, pointing at the rugs lying in the corner of the kitchen. "See you in the morning." And she went about the chores she had been doing before being distracted.

By the time she had made her tea, replaced the hot water in the bottle and returned to the bedroom, she was feeling a little better. But when she saw that her pretty pink curtains were stained and dripping with water, she was shocked. The water was pooling on the floor before being absorbed by the carpet.

"What on earth is going on?" she said out loud. She drew back the wet curtains to find that the ice that had been there fifteen minutes ago had completely melted.

She hurried back to the kitchen to get cloths to mop up the water. Only when she had finished clearing up the puddle did she realise that her bedroom was warm; in fact, very warm for a May night. Putting the damp cloths away in the kitchen, she shuddered. Now she was worried. It was as though someone or something was playing with her mind.

First the room had been so very cold, then her poor dog was disturbed, but the scariest thing that had happened was seeing that face, those eyes staring at her from the headboard. She shuddered again. Somehow she persuaded herself that she was being foolish. What would John say if he were here? Shaking her head, she smiled wistfully and got into the bed. She sat upright and for some time she was unwilling or unable to lie down, with anxious thoughts going round and round in her head. She knew that the owner of the bed, one of John's tenants, had been murdered and that he had carved the bed as a gift to his wife for their wedding day. Was there somehow a connection between his death and her buying this bed; were they linked to the strange episodes that had happened that evening? Surely not?

Back in his retreat, Louis was pleased. It had not all gone his way and he had not been able to stop them using his bed, but he was sure the woman had seen him and he had been able to disrupt their antics. He laughed out loud at the thought of doing it all again when he next got the chance. No one would rest in his bed if he had anything to do with it. That much he was sure of.

Just as Joan settled down to sleep, her head pressed deep into the feather pillow and feeling light as she drifted towards sleep, in the half-dreamlike state she thought she heard laughter coming from the bed itself. She sat up bolt upright and was wide awake instantly. That was all too much for Joan; now panic hit her, she was afraid. Pulling the blankets from the bed, she headed to the sitting room, calling to the dog as she went. She spent a very restless night on her settee, the dog at her side for protection.

But there were no further icy draughts and no more ghostly laughter and by the time dawn had broken she had promised herself that the bed would go back first thing that morning and John would have to repay her her money.

But would he believe it was haunted? She didn't care; right now all she wanted was to be rid of the bed!

By the afternoon of the next day, the bed was back in the possession of John and back in the cottage where it had started. It was sat back in its old position in Louis's old bedroom, but it wouldn't be staying there for long.

John, too, had his reservations about the bed. He had never believed in ghosts but he had experienced first-hand some odd events, like the real chill around the bed when the rest of the room was warm. He couldn't explain it even to himself.

Joan had been quite forceful in her demands once the bed was returned; not only did she want full payment for the bed but her costs for getting the bed to and from her cottage, and as she was now in need of a new bed, she expected John to find her one and deliver it to her that day.

Within a week, the carved bed was on the move to be sold in the Friday sales at the local Yorkshire auction.

8

The day before the auction Louis sat on his bed watching the people who had come to view the goods for sale. He wasn't angry anymore; he liked the people that passed through the saleroom. The bed was so admired, it was touched and stroked by the unsuspecting buyers and by the time the auction was over after a frenzy of bidding the bed, with Louis attached to it, had been sold again.

The new owners lay unsuspecting in the half-light of the candles that sat on the bedside tables. They were as pleased as Punch with their new purchase and snuggled up to each other. Just as they were settling down to sleep, they heard a whisper of ghostly laughter that got louder and vibrated somewhere beyond their pillows. The candles spluttered before going out with Louis's icy breath upon them. The noise of laugher quickly built up into an intimidating roaring laugh that echoed and bounced off the walls. It's sound was something like the devil might make when reaping souls. The new owners of the fine bed were terrified. The shaking couple were now hiding under the covers expecting the worst at any moment. Panic set in and for a time they were unable to move until in fear they leapt from the bed and fled to another room in the house, where they spent the night bolt upright on high back chairs, lamps lit around them, not daring to close their eyes.

The bed was sent back to the auction room.

The dealers in the auction houses soon noticed a regular pattern that developed around the bed, it was sold but repeatedly returned. Whispers and rumours about it spread, the stories of the haunting growing wilder each time it was returned. Finally, the bed was branded as possessed, if proof was needed it was thought that there was a history of the man who was murdered in it and that he was the ghost that possessed it.

The story of a haunted bed soon spread to other auction houses in neighbouring counties. No one wanted it, no matter how beautiful it was.

Years passed. It was eventually sold to a dealer who, being an educated man, did not believe in ghosts or the rumours. He lived in the Midlands and was charmed and impressed by the distinguished piece. He believed that the northern dealers were fools and that he would make a handsome profit selling it on. But Louis's spirit would not be sold.

All too quickly the dealer learned the rumours were true, that the bed was haunted. Each time he sold it, the bed was returned to him. He realised that history was repeating itself just had it had in the north and that the only way to get rid of the bed was to send it to a place where it's history was not known. With that in mind, it was sent with many other pieces of highly rated furniture to the south of England, to another dealer based near London.

When the dealer's men came to collect the bed, Louis once again found himself being moved; trapped as he was and bonded to the bed by his life's blood, the choice wasn't his.

A century had passed since Louis's death. He and his masterly carved bed were deposited in a small market town in the Home Counties at the start of the twentieth century.

It was just as Louis had promised himself. The bed was his, made by his hand and no one was going to use but himself. After all the love he had put into the making of it, how could he share it? He was determined to stop his bed being used by people who didn't deserve it. He hadn't deserved to die or be trapped like this, why couldn't these stupid people hear his cry for help?

The anger that had ruled him since his death was there in him; it burned away in his heart, growing like a cancer. Even his garden behind the curtain of carved wood was not enough at times.

In a small portion of his heart, when his anger was quiet, there was a yearning for someone to speak to, for someone, anyone, to be aware of his ghostly predicament. As the years passed, the yearning grew and grew but so did the frustration, and in the end his yearnings died along with his hope.

Little did he know that this move would be the start of a new chapter in his journey.

9

A NEW START

MARINA

A large middle-aged woman loomed into the small dark shop. Her voice was as large as she was; it dominated and demanded attention from all the people around her. She stood with her hands on her hips in the centre of the room. Her black curled hair, frizzed around her face and tied back into a bunch with a red velvet ribbon, gave her a common touch. Dressed entirely in black, she was obviously a force to be reckoned with. Her lace blouse stretched tightly across her ample bosom, stretching the fabric to its limit. She looked formidable. Her rouged full lips were just a scarlet slash across her face. Maybe once she had been a beauty but time and life seemed to have left their mark on her. Marina looked hard, a look that she cultivated. She wore her clothes as a prop, a screen to hide the soft heart that beat within her breast.

Across the room, Louis could see her making her way towards him. She had seen his bed. Had Louis been alive he would have avoided her like the plague; she was, on the surface, an image of all the things Louis hated – overweight, loud, and she appeared to be coarse and vulgar, a low life, best to be ignored.

But here she was as bold as brass, haggling with the shopkeeper for his bed, his masterpiece. *No, no,* thought Louis, *surely she won't buy it.* He wouldn't have it. This creature wouldn't own it if he could help it.

The shopkeeper wanted more for the bed than she was willing to pay but on the other hand, he wanted to sell it as quickly as he could, for not many folk in this area had the money to spend on or the refined taste for a bed like this. Or, if it came to that, the space for it; the small houses of this district would not accommodate a bed of its size within their bedrooms.

The haggling went on until at last, to Louis's dismay, the parties shook hands and a substantial amount of money was passed over to the man's eagerly waiting hands. The shop owner was delighted and he was keen to arrange delivery of the bed quickly to make space in his overcrowded shop. He had men on hand in the back of the shop waiting for instructions; they would wrap it to protect it before carting and delivering it to its new home.

The price agreed and paid in full, Marina was left only to instruct where the bed should be delivered to that afternoon. The address was written down in neat handwriting, with direction to her house on the edge of town, before she flounced out of the shop, only stopping in the doorway to remind the shopkeeper that it was to be delivered in perfect condition.

When the men came to move the bed, little did they know they were moving Louis as well!

The ride through the hot noisy town on the back of an old wooded cart, pulled by dray horses and being tossed around by every bump and pothole in the road, was difficult to say the least, especially having been warned to take special care of their cargo.

Louis had no idea where he was being taken. *Still, how many ghosts move house?* he wondered to himself. *What part of town will my new home be in? And more to the point, how quickly can I persuade them to return us to the shop?* He was surprised to find himself on a broad tree-lined road that led to the very edge of town. The noise and the bustling streets that were filled with people going about their business at the start of the journey were now far behind them. The quiet of the road, with only the steady tap of the horse's hooves pulling the cart, settled him. He could now hear the chirping of the birds calling to one another and relished the sight of bright flowers on either side of the grass verges that lined the road. It reminded him of home, his Yorkshire.

The men slowed up and turned off the road, pulling to the right into a small narrow lane. It led to a modest-sized house, partially hidden by large mature trees that must give shade and protection from the weather, thought Louis. They approached a large garden gate that was already open for them to pass through. He could see a garden filled with plants and flowers. His thoughts turned to the past and Sophia standing in her flower garden. He discarded the thought quickly. She had betrayed him. However, he couldn't lose a feeling of longing to be able to walk freely in the sun and enjoy the brightly coloured bloom and their wonderful fragrance. A pipe dream. He sighed, accepting that it was never going to be a possibility.

The trees acted as a screen, keeping the house private and concealing it from the road. Beyond the garden there was a backdrop of purple green hills and a vast sky. It could have been a painting on canvas.

It could belong to a local merchant, thought Louis, as the men pulled up to the front of the door. But almost immediately a voice rang out to the carriers to bring the bed in and up to the bedroom; it was the voice of the loud, coarse woman that Louis had heard in the shop. He was hit by the reality that she, that woman, had bought his bed.

But how long will she keep it? he wondered with a knowing smile on his lips. *Not long if I have anything to do with it.*

Marina stood in the darkened doorway, almost invisible in her dress of black, cursing the men as they struggled up the stairs with the bed parts.

"Be careful, you clumsy oafs, be careful. That bed's special, I don't want a scratch or a dent on it!" she shouted, as one of them stumbled halfway up the narrow stairs. "You ruin that bed and you'll not be paid," she threatened, but they had delivered to her before and knew only too well her bark was worse than her bite. She was always generous with a good tip at the end of each job; though it was true she was equally gruff and shouted a great deal until the task was complete.

Louis was completely unaware of this side to her and was horrified at the prospect of not only having to live with this woman, albeit for a short time, but she also would be sleeping in his bed. That thought was not to be contemplated.

Finally, the men, having brought up each section of the bed, assembled it and placed it against the wall of Marina's choice in her large bedroom.

They didn't know they had also transported an unhappy spirit, who resented being dumped in a room of gaudy taste. The room in which Louis now sat was decorated in a fashionable way but was too bright and feminine for his liking. Dark pink and beige striped wallpaper adorned the walls; vases of flowers were dotted around the room. A pink plush chaise longue scattered with red cushions was alongside a low round table that was placed in the centre of the room. A dressing table on another wall was cluttered with bottles and jars of creams that filled the air in the room with a light scent of lily of the valley. Laid out in the centre of the table was a silver-backed toilet set, tooled in finely worked filigree. Not what he expected to see at all.

"So this is to be my new home!" Louis said out loud. A ripple of cold air transported around the room and for a second Marina stood and shivered.

"I must be getting a cold," she remarked to herself and sniffed. She turned to dismiss the carters who stood by the bedroom door waiting to be paid. "Very nice, too," she said, looking at her assembled bed that was waiting to be made up. "A nice job, gentlemen."

Smiling, she indicated for the men to follow her downstairs and paid them the agreed fee. Once that was done she showed them to the door, slipping the gaffer a tip. "Have a drink on me," she said as they left. She knew all about hardship and because she understood it, she was always generous with the tradesmen who served her. Returning to her thoughts, she made her way back up the stairs to admire her new purchase that now graced her room.

Moving to the bed, her true self was for the first time displayed to the ghostly onlooker. Stroking and caressing the carving on the headboard, Louis heard her say in a soft voice, unrecognisable for the one he knew her for, "So beautiful, so very beautiful. I bet you would have a tale to tell, if you could talk."

Her eyes filled with tears; something in his carving had touched her memory. *Is it the lovers standing hand in hand before the tree of life?* Louis wondered. But true to the character that she showed to the world, she shrugged, shook herself and busied herself making up the bed with its new flock mattress, feather pillows and the finest cotton linen she could afford.

Louis deposited himself on a high-backed chair near the window and watched her while she worked. His opinion of her was changing but even as he questioned himself, he wondered why he should care. His thoughts were interrupted when suddenly a door opened into the room, revealing a small dressing room off the main bedroom where a young girl had been waiting. Bustling with energy, she ran as only youngsters do and she threw herself into the waiting arms of Marina.

"Oh, Mummy, Mummy, it's lovely, can we sleep in it tonight?"

"Tonight and forever, my sweet pea." She paused. "This bed is for only you and me Lucy, only you and me." She said it almost to herself; her gaze showed that her thoughts had moved elsewhere and whatever the memory was it was not pleasant.

Louis was suddenly intrigued, this was not the woman he had expected her to be and he was shocked to find she was a mother, and a loving one at that, judging by her expression and the intense hug she gave her child.

What had happened to her? What was in her past that so obviously hurt her and was still near the surface of her mind? Now in that room, a soft and gentle person emanated from her. Like an actress who had stepped out of her role the brash vulgar woman he thought she was had disappeared.

"Here, sweet pea, lend a hand," said Marina as she loosened her clothes. Taking off her outer layer, she exposed a layer of padded corset and a bustle that made her look two sizes larger than she was. Quickly, she removed them from her body and Lucy hung up the false paddings in the dressing room. After re-dressing in a pale lilac silk dress, she patted down her hair, removed the red ribbon and tied her hair back with a delicate comb; next, she wiped away the rouge from her lips.

Without the padded garments and the make-up she looked altogether different. Louis was astonished as the years vanished from her, revealing a lovely looking woman who was in her prime.

"Time to get ready, my angel," she said, and with that the two of them moved to the door. It was now late afternoon; food must be made and the girls awakened.

"Go wake up the girls, time to get ready for work!"

Lucy, who never walked, ran, whisking away down the passage and banging on the bedroom doors as she passed. Shouts and groans emanated forth from behind the closed doors.

"Go away!"

"Not already, let me sleep." But despite the protests, the rustling of bedclothes being pushed back and feet on floors could be plainly heard echoing around the first floor.

Louis could hear mother and daughter knocking on the doors and women's voices responding. Four voices. Four women. What sort of place had he come to?

Louis didn't know, but this was a sanctuary for the women he could hear moving about, making themselves ready for their evening trade.

The women of the house worked together in a strange sort of co-operative. Each woman lent their talent in supporting each other. The four girls, plus Marina and Lucy, lived together, each performing what they thought they were best able to do. It was that or living in the workhouse, where conditions were so bad that they would be half-starved and worked until they dropped, with no life and no prospects. What they did for a living was so much better than that, even with some risks attached.

Three of the girls worked as prostitutes, or 'ladies of the night', as they liked to call themselves; one worked as housekeeper and gardener. Marina ran the house like a business but she was also a mother hen, watching over them and protecting them the best she could.

And although Marina was her birth mother, Lucy was loved and cared for by the women. Each of them had become an adopted aunt to her, watching over her as she grew up. Over the years, Lucy had come to understand the comings and goings that went on in the house. She knew some people would sneer and be morally outraged at what was a normal life to her. It was just the way it was, and she knew these women and loved them. There was no choice in their lives; they worked to earn a living and keep a roof over their heads.

Marina had given the girls their own private bedrooms; their sanctuaries, hidden away from the rooms they used in their working life. Rooms for entertaining their clients were situated on the ground floor. There was the odd occasion when friends of the girls were invited up to their own rooms but the business was done downstairs where Marina felt she had some control of who came and went; she liked to keep any possible risks to a minimum.

Back in Marina's bedroom, Louis groaned to himself. Putting two and two together, he gathered from the wake-up calls and the females' replies that his new home was a brothel.

The sun was going down, he could see that from the window. Although the sky was still light, the sun was no longer high in the sky and the night was drawing in.

What else could it mean? *Get the girls up ready for work,* that's what she had said. He could only think that meant ladies of the night, working girls; not to put a fine point on it, prostitutes. He didn't know what to make of it all. It was an odd sort of set-up. The woman Marina was not what she seemed to be. Were these women he had heard just unfortunate women or were they sluts?

He was intrigued and curious about the situation he found himself in; he almost found himself wanting to stay. But that was never his plan. Anger and frustration welled up inside of him and he hit out at a vase, sending it crashing to the ground. Flowers and water scattered across the floor.

Hearing the crash, Marina came back into the room.

"Lord! How did that happen?" said Marina out loud.

"My thoughts exactly!" said Louis thoughtfully, his anger completely gone. Now he was amazed and excited at the same time. He had actually moved something. Instead of his hand passing though the vase as usual, he had smashed it. Maybe he could do other things given the right stimulus.

Mopping up the water and rescuing the flowers from the floor, Marina felt a chill pass through the room.

Nodding to herself, she said loudly, "Either that was a strong breeze from the window or I am getting a cold." But the window was not open, not even a crack, and from the look on her face she seemed none too sure where the breeze had come from. It was a mystery.

For the first time since his passing, Louis hoped that maybe he could do more than be idle in a futile existence. Scaring people half to death from time to time was no longer amusing and he was far away from his own county, lost to the living world yet not part of the dead world either. Perhaps God had a purpose for him after all. Maybe, putting his anger to one side, he could live side by side with this unusual household. One thing was certain: he may not be able to live life but he would see life here, that was assured. His yearning to be acknowledged came alive again. Was there a possibility that he could make himself known to the members of this household?

Who knows? he thought, *if they have a ghost amongst them they might even get a priest to exorcise me into the next life.*

He had refused the gateway of light but now he would welcome it gratefully.

Late afternoon turned to evening and darkness overtook the day.

After a late meal together, the women prepared for their evening work and clients as usual.

Marina dressed once again for her role as the madam; red lips, black shaded eyes, frizzed hair and padding to make her overweight. Smiling at herself in the mirror of her bedroom, she looked common and hard. *Nobody will mess with me or mine,* she thought. Satisfied with her look, she took herself off down to the parlour, and sat with the other women and waited.

Tapping was soon heard on the side door to the house, which couldn't be seen from either the driveway or the road. Their clients were mainly married men who were bored, over-sexed or just needed company without the ties of marriage.

In the small town in which the clients lived, they knew they were known by sight if not by name. These men needed to be discreet, lest their wives or others found out where the men's late-night walks had taken them.

The day had turned cold earlier and now a fine drizzle fell over the house and garden. A wind was rising; it promised to be a miserable night.

It's going to be a slow night tonight. Not too many would brave this weather! thought Marina, smiling to herself; she was rather glad of a wet night. It meant Lucy and herself could retire to the bedroom for a good night's sleep and they could enjoy the comfort of their newly installed bed.

Lucy helped to clean up the kitchen after they had finished supper and lay places for a late breakfast the next day. The house was still quiet. She could hear the murmur of the women's voices coming from the parlour. Soon the clients would be arriving, as they always did once it was dusk.

Men who needed love and company, her mother had said when she asked her why the men came. She sometimes wondered who her father was and why he didn't live with them. Her mother was the most loving and caring person she knew, but she avoided answering when she had once asked her why she didn't have a father. Marina had promised that one day she would tell her all about him. But the grief and pain that showed on her mother's face hurt her so much that she had not asked again.

Lucy was still regarded as a child by Marina. She was in fact fifteen years old and had finished school over a year ago. In a few weeks she would have her sixteenth birthday. She was already having teenage dreams of romance. She didn't see boys of her own age often now she had finished school but her dreams were her dreams.

She thought she knew what went on in the house, but when she fell in love it would be so different. She, like all young girls, dreamed of a perfect love and happiness with a man who would love and protect her. She hoped that in her future she would find that one man to love and be loved for the rest of her life by him.

The other women who lived in the house were, to Lucy, all surrogate mothers. They looked after her and cared for her and she loved them for that, but Marina was her birth mother and no one would ever be able to breach the love between mother and daughter.

Lucy knew her mother and the ladies had pasts that were filled with pain. She knew they had escaped from desperate situations where their lives were threatened. Marina had brought them under her roof and given them hope. Now they worked together, supporting each other as a family, for they had no one else.

Lucy had settled down to sleep by 10pm, well out of the way of the gentlemen who were still downstairs. By10.30pm the drizzle had turned to heavy rain and Marina heard the door bang closed as the last client left to make his way back home.

The regulars had come and gone. Marina decided to lock up for the night. From experience she knew that the bad weather would keep anyone else away. Local men would be at home indoors, with no excuse to take in the night air. Not even the dogs would want to walk tonight.

Louis was watching Lucy sleeping. He was sitting by the bed when Marina entered the bedroom quietly so as not to disturb Lucy. It was strange, but he hadn't had the impulse to stop Lucy when she had got into his bed. When she had come out of the dressing room dressed in her night shift, looking young and vulnerable he could not help feeling protective towards her and when she lay down to sleep he was happy to let her rest. Marina walked over to her sleeping child, moving a wisp of hair that straddled her face. Bending over her, she kissed her cheek lightly so as not to wake her.

Stretching her body in an effort to ease the aches she had accumulated from the day's work, she yawned. Tiredness had finally caught up with her. The lamp in the dressing room was turned down low and Louis could only see her shadow as she proceeded to undress. She removed the layers of her garments until she revealed a much slimmer and youthful-looking woman underneath. Dressed in her night attire, he watched as she brushed and braided her hair before getting into bed beside her young daughter. Louis approved of the attractive mid-thirty-year-old that played a game of charades with everyone except her household. He would let her rest too.

10

By 11.00pm Marina was washed, all make-up removed, her hair brushed and smoothed down. She sat in her nightdress, loosely braiding her hair, ready for the night's sleep.

Lucy had been asleep for over an hour when Marina finally climbed into bed, stopping only to run her fingers over the carving, smiling as she shuffled down under the sheets, sighing as she sank into the mattress. Stretching over, she moved another stray strand of hair from Lucy's young face and couldn't help leaning over to kiss her on her forehead.

"I love you, little lamb," she whispered, before reaching to the oil lamp on the side table. She killed the flame and the light in the room, and within seconds she was asleep.

Louis had been laying on the chaise longue, contemplating his new position in this house while listening to the rain being blown onto the windows.

The trees surrounding the house were moaning as the branches were stretched and pulled by the great gusts that buffeted them. Leaves and weak branches were torn away and scattered onto the garden below.

It was a wild night outside but inside it was warm and peaceful; he became aware of Marina's breath becoming deeper and regular as she fell into a deep sleep. It was strange but he felt rested too and for the first time for many years he felt relaxed and at peace. It was certainly not what he expected when he arrived in the house. If a ghost could put down roots, he felt he might be able to do that here.

When morning came, both Marina and Lucy woke refreshed and ready for the day ahead. Sun was streaming through the window and it promised to be a pleasant day.

"What a good night's sleep I've had, the best I've had for ages," said Marina in a sleepy voice, stretching out and touching Lucy as she did. "When I saw that bed, I just knew it was right for us."

Lucy turned on her side to face her mother, her hand reaching up to touch the figures carved in the wood.

"They look very happy," said Lucy. "Look at the way they are touching each other. Is that what love is like? Is that how you felt with my father?"

The words were out before she had thought what she was saying. There was a look of distress on Marina's face for a moment, then she smiled. "Yes, sweet pea, I suppose it was."

A smell of fresh bread came wafting up from the kitchen and a voice sang clearly from the garden below.

"Rosa's in good voice today," remarked Marina. "Come, love, time to get up," said a smiling Marina, tickling the young girl that lay at her side.

"Give up, Mum," gasped Lucy, struggling to speak through the giggles. Turning on her side, she slid from the bed to escape Marina's hands.

From behind the curtain of carved wood Louis was smiling. He had been right to allow this loving family to use his masterpiece. He suddenly realised that, at least for now, he was content there and had no reason to haunt that family.

After the rain and wind from the night before, the garden looked battered. Rosa was already out in the garden viewing what needed to be done. The flowers would need to be tied up to stakes to support them as they had been almost flattened with the force of the rain. But thankfully the vegetable plot was intact and the rain would have given the crops a good soaking. Apart from the debris from the fallen leaves, no harm was done, and they would be cleared up directly. The sun was already warm, the night forgotten and it promised to be a hot day.

Marina ran her household like a well-oiled machine. Chores needed to be done both inside and out, as always. Each day had a regular routine that started with a good meal. Breakfast was a noisy affair as the women gathered around the kitchen table, chattering while tucking in to a cooked breakfast of eggs, bacon and hot buttered toast topped with a generous layer of homemade marmalade.

The smell of newly baked bread and cooked bacon wafted up through the house into the room where Louis was stationed. The laughter and the smell of breakfast was just too much for him. He missed company and while he was never hungry, the thought of bacon filled him with fond memories. He wanted badly to join the happy group of women; if not to be part of them, at least he could observe them.

He wanted to see the faces that belonged to the voices he now knew. Agitated, he moved to the door, swinging his fist against the wood in frustration. It went through the door like a knife through butter.

He could hardly believe it; that had never happened before. Following his instinct and filled with hope, he stepped through the door and found himself on the landing.

Oh my God, a way out, he thought, his excitement rising as he took the steps down to the ground floor, following the voices until he found the kitchen.

The large room that he found himself in was truly a working kitchen. Herbs hung from a ceiling rack that also served as a line to dry and air clothes. A large black range stood practically covering one wall, incorporating fire, oven and water boiler. Over the fire, a kettle was set on an iron, steam rising from its spout as it reached boiling point. Pots and pans were arranged on shelves, with large pans hanging from hooks near the oven. A dresser stood behind him; lines of plates differing in size sat on the open shelves, with gaily painted cups hung from hooks below them. In the centre of the room, a large rectangular table made of oak was littered with the remnants of breakfast. The women sat, still in their night attire: Rosa, Nora, Emma and Roni. The women that Louis would soon come to know had no idea he was there, or so he thought. Double doors opened out onto the garden that was now bathed in golden sunlight. The emeralds of the grasses and the highly coloured flowers could be seen through the open doors. Louis was delighted; he hoped that with a little luck he might be able to move within that space too.

Rosa saw Louis come into the kitchen. She had felt a movement in the spiritual balance of the house yesterday afternoon and she had wondered what it had meant. It was neither unpleasant nor threatening. She had tried to analyse what it was all about and now here standing in front of her, was the reason.

A rather handsome ghost stood in her kitchen, wearing old-fashioned clothing, with strikingly dark eyes and dark curly hair tied back in a tail. There was a restless and rather lost feeling coming from him. What was he doing there? In all the time she had lived in the house she had never detected a ghost and even now, what she was feeling coming from him was not one hundred percent spirit.

There was no eye contact between them; she was sure he wouldn't even know that she'd seen him. When the time was right and there was an opportune moment, she would speak to him and find out what he was doing here. She smiled to herself; he looked as though he was enjoying being in the kitchen surrounded by the aromas that lingered in the room. He lifted his head and sniffed the warm smell of leftovers from the cooking with a smile on his handsome face.

To talk to him now would be quite out of the question with the other women still sitting finishing breakfast and engaged in talking. No, it wouldn't be fair to him, or her if it came to that. Better to wait.

She had a sixth sense, a psychic power that she had had from when she was very young. She had been able to see and hear spirits, a gift she preferred to hide from people. Only Marina knew her full story, and she had no intention whatsoever of drawing attention to herself or this spirit.

11

Rosa had chosen to become the housekeeper in Marina's home and spent much of her time cooking and gardening. She was often alone preparing meals for the family in the kitchen and that morning was no exception. She had got up at six to finish off the process of making fresh bread. Kneading and proving had all been done the night before. The bread had sat in loaf tins covered with buttered muslin cloths in the warm hearth for the bread to rise. Now the first of the loaves were cooking in the oven. She could rest awhile before preparing the late breakfast when the rest of the household came down to eat. It was going to be another fine day, with warmth already coming through the windows from the early sun. She was filled with an inner peace and without thinking her joy came through in song straight from her heart.

Throughout her childhood she had regularly attended church with her parents; she loved being able to sing and the words and music still stuck fast in her head. She had lost count of the number of hymns she had learnt in those years. The household loved her singing, old folk songs were also favourites with her adopted sisters and sometimes they would all get together around the kitchen table for a singsong.

She was in good voice that morning, singing at the top of her voice, filling the house with a rousing hymn.

The smell of baking filtered up the stairs and into the bedroom where Louis was resting half asleep under the tree of life behind the wooden curtain. It was Louis's second day in the household.

Rock of Ages wafted up to him along with the aroma of fresh bread. The tune was loud. It was a melody that he knew well and it brought back memories of his life back in his village.

The tune was running around in his head and the aroma of the baking filled his nostrils, both beckoning him to join the songstress down in the kitchen. He slipped through the door just as he had done the day before and drifted down into the warm kitchen. Perching himself on one of the stools by the table, he watched Rosa take the baked loaves out of the oven and turn them out onto the clean tea cloths on the table.

Rosa was not surprised to see him. She knew that spirits often enjoyed the aromas that they knew from their past life. The smell of the bread had obviously drawn him down into her kitchen and, being the only one up that morning, this was the perfect time to get to know this handsome soul.

"Well! Hello, have you come to join me?" asked Rosa, her eyes looking down at the bread in her hands, tapping it, making sure it was cooked through.

Louis looked over his shoulder. Someone must have come into the room very quietly and he hadn't heard them. There was no one there. Rosa looked up and she was staring directly at him, her hands on her hips, now waiting for an answer.

He was surprised. In all the years he had spent in his twilight zone, no one had been able to see him properly and now this youngish woman was looking directly at him and waiting for an answer.

"Well, are you going to speak to me?" Rosa inquired.

"You can see me." It was a statement more than a question.

"Yes! Yes, I see you. I saw you join us at breakfast yesterday," she replied softly. "What's your name?"

"Louis."

"I've not felt you here before, Louis. Where have you come from?"

For the first time since he'd died he was able to talk to someone. It was like opening a floodgate; he poured his heart out to her, telling her his whole story, missing nothing out.

He explained how he had stood over his own corpse, not realising it was his own shell that he was looking at, how he had been pulled towards a light. He now realised it would have helped him pass into the next world but he had resisted it, trapping him in a netherworld in which he had existed for more years than he could count.

His life's blood had soaked into the wood of his bed; it had trapped him in this void. He was neither dead nor alive and he could not pass on to rest or return to the mortal sphere.

He told her of how he had loved Sophia and had carved the bed that sat upstairs as a marriage gift to her for their wedding day, and of the dreadful act of betrayal when Sophia had murdered him.

They sat together for a long time as he told his story, Rosa nodding with understanding and sympathy. He had travelled a long way through time; it had been a lonely road and one that had almost driven him mad. It was as though he had been locked in a cell without even the company of a jailer. Now he wondered if it was possible for him to settle in here. Rosa's gift of sight was also a gift to him; now at least he would have contact with the living and as long as the bed stayed here, he would have what he needed: someone to talk to. Rosa had rescued him from solitary confinement.

The weather had become settled in the last days of May, warm and dry, and promised an early summer.

Louis had settled into his new home and was an unseen guest who enjoyed watching the household's activities.

The annual spring clean was in full swing in the house. Rugs, carpets, windows and floors were all scrubbed until the house smelt fresh and clean. The chores were divided between the women and they would work until lunch, maintaining the house and gardens. They would rest for part of the afternoon on the days they worked. Those days were long, stretching well into the night, which they all accepted as part of their commitment to the family.

Tuesday, Friday and Saturday were market days in the local town and they were the nights the ladies worked. That pattern was set, it suited Marina and her girls, they worked three days a week. The money they made provided them with all the provisions they needed and sometimes a treat if business had been good.

Louis found to his delight that he was able to move about the house and grounds freely. He liked nothing better than to sit in the garden watching the women work. The hills gave the perfect backdrop to a perfect scene.

Laughter, good humour and the melodies from Rosa, who sang like an angel, made life, or death in his case, as good as it could get.

EARLY SUMMER

Some weeks after he arrived at his new home, there was an incident that made him realise that not only could he move objects in certain circumstances, but also he could reach into people's subconscious by touch.

It happened one evening when Marina and Lucy had retired to bed early and were already sleeping. If a ghost could sleep, then that was what Louis had drifted into away in his retreat behind the curtain of wood.

One minute he was listening to Marina's steady breathing as she slept next to Lucy, the next he was jolted into consciousness by the muffled words tumbling out of Marina's mouth as she struggled to talk in her sleep. Louis could not make any sense of the ramblings coming from her. The half words and cries suggested that she was experiencing a deeply troubled nightmare and was becoming agitated and restless in her sleep.

Louis emerged from his retreat and stood by her bedside, concerned for her. Was she unwell? She didn't appear to have a fever. What could be upsetting her so much to make her so restless? Did the thoughts that invaded her dream come from some problem or was it like most dreams, her imagination running wild?

He sat on the edge of the bed and without thinking laid the palm of his hand on her forehead. It was an instinctive gesture, to check to see if she had a temperature. Then he realised that he wouldn't be able to feel any heat from her, that his hand couldn't connect with her. He felt such a fool but his intentions were good.

Farcical, isn't it? he thought. He was about to withdraw his hand when he felt a strange connection to her. Although he couldn't feel her skin under his touch, the contact between them was allowing him into her mind and dream. He was somehow reading the nightmare she was having. Pictures flashed in his mind and he was conscious of understanding the dream that bounced from her mind to his.

Marina was running on a farm track that ran around the edge of a cornfield. She was following a young man and was desperately trying to catch him up. But her legs felt like lead weights and no matter how hard she ran she couldn't reach him.

She seemed to be stuck in one spot; all the while he was becoming smaller as the distance grew between them. He strode along a track that led to a country house that was surrounded by a high red brick wall and iron gates. The figure of the well-dressed young man had almost reached the gates when Marina's legs buckled under her and she sat heavily onto the coarse grass that edged the field, tears pouring down her face.

"Robert, please come back," she sobbed. "It's our baby, you promised, you said you loved me. How can you leave me? I love you." The words tumbled out of her mouth as she watched him turn and without a backward glance he was gone.

Louis looked down at this poor wretch sitting alone and in distress. She looked about the same age as Lucy, a young vulnerable girl who was in pain.

"Oh my God, what am I going to do?" she cried out through her sobs, misery oozing out of every pore in her body.

She was dressed in a maid's uniform and Louis sensed that she probably worked up at the house. The young man had disappeared into the house but he was too finely dressed to be a servant. Louis could only wonder what or who he was.

Marina reached into her pocket, pulling out a note that was worn and crumpled by constant reading. She opened it, hardly glancing at the words that she knew by heart. She pressed it to her lips, suppressing a sob as she cried out for Robert again.

Whether it was the emotion that woke her, Louis didn't know, but he felt the connection break between them as she stirred before becoming fully awake.

Her face was damp with the tears that she had shed in her nightmare. Now she sat upright in the darkened room with only the faint light from the full moon lighting the bedroom. Her daughter was sleeping soundly at her side and she was brought back into reality as her hand wiped the tears away from her cheeks. She felt vulnerable and so very sad.

"Not again," she whispered to herself. "That damned dream, will it never leave me alone so I can move on?"

She reached over to the side table to find a match to light the candle by her bed; that would give her some comfort for a little time until the dawn came. It was still a few hours away but the darkness always made her feel worse at times like this.

Although Marina tried to settle down to sleep again, comforted by the small light from the candle, she could not dispel the memory of Robert and the hurt that was imprinted so deep on her soul. It was an open sore that had never healed.

It was brought back to the surface by her dream of the man who had deserted her and their unborn child, the same child who lay next to her sleeping so soundly. She had a very bad night with little sleep and when dawn finally arrived she was still awake with an ache that felt like a stone in her heart.

That morning when Lucy woke, she could see the stress on her mother's face. *The nightmares must be back again,* she thought. Every six months or so, they would torment Marina. Lucy didn't know what triggered them or what they were about but she knew they left her darling mother tired and strained. If only her mother would talk to her about them and share her distress. A hug in the middle of the night could be so soothing and settling. But Marina had locked the hurt behind a wall that Lucy couldn't scale, leaving Lucy feeling helpless. All she could do was offer her mother some comfort with a kiss.

Marina was unhappy with the idea of Lucy waking up to find her distressed because of the nightmares. Lucy had once woken up when she was quite small. It was a long time ago but her sweet daughter hadn't understood why her mother had cried so much over a silly dream. She shuddered at the thought but someday she would have to tell Lucy that shameful secret that she had kept hidden for so long. But not now, not yet!

Marina arranged that, for the time being, Lucy should sleep in the next room to her mum so she could sleep undisturbed at night, for only God knew how long these nightmares would go on for.

Over the next week the dreams persisted, returning every night until Marina was too frightened to go to bed to sleep. She hated to relive all the unhappy memories from her past, to see it all unfolding again and again was too much for her.

She felt such a fool. How could she have trusted him? She had believed in every tender word he had spoken to her. Love was such a foolish thing. She vowed she would never trust it again.

She took to staying up until well past midnight, hoping she would be so exhausted that she would not dream. But it did no good; as soon as she fell asleep the nightmare started again.

Marina looked drawn, bearing black rings around her eyes through lack of sleep. She felt weary and downhearted, unable to share the shame and the pain from her past.

Marina's silent guest watched for almost a week as she tried in vain to sleep each night. She thrashed about in the bed, tormented by the frightening vision that visited her. Every now and again she would call out, 'Robert!' It was always the same: 'Robert!'

This can't go on, thought Louis. He had watched her now for six nights. It was funny, he hadn't liked her at first but over the few weeks he had lodged with her uninvited, so to speak, he actually admired her. If only he could find a way of projecting himself into her dream rather than being an observer, he might be able to do something to help her.

The next night she came up to bed tired and afraid, using the nightly rituals to put off getting into bed for as long as possible. She placed an oil lamp by her bed and turned it down low. She needed comfort and the light helped her. She pulled back the covers and crawled into bed, exhausted. Almost before her head hit the pillow she was asleep.

The deep sleep quickly overtook her. Louis didn't have wait too long before the dream started to distress her. He touched her forehead to connect them but instead of just seeing images, as he had before, he pushed his image into her dream.

It was just as before, only this time Louis was walking behind her as she desperately tried to catch up to Robert. He could see that Robert was walking rapidly towards the gate that led to the large house, leaving Marina far behind him. She had been unable to catch Robert and had collapsed on the ground sobbing in her desperation.

Louis stood for a moment, unsure of what to do, but compassion in his heart for her took over and he sat down beside her, putting his arm around her shoulder. She didn't flinch or resist him and he allowed her to sob on his chest until her tears dried up and she became quiet and still.

Her head was still on his chest when he whispered into her ear. "Marina, don't do this to yourself. Whatever happened in the past with Robert is past. You must deal with it and let go." He thought of the irony in his words, but this was about her, not him. He went on. "Think of your daughter, your girls, your family. That's what's real."

Looking at him for the first time, the wet-eyed Marina pushed herself from him, confused.

"You don't belong here," she said. "Who are you?"

"Let's just say I am a friend, a guardian angel, if you will. Let me help you," he replied.

"What's your name?"

"Louis."

"Why are you here?"

"I just came to try to help."

Marina looked desperate.

"No one can help now, he's gone. I'm ruined. How will I survive?"

"All of that is history, Marina, you're a strong adult woman, and you survived. Look, your daughter is almost a grown woman, it's time to tell her the truth. Let go of your guilt and let go of your past."

Marina suddenly felt calmer. Her daughter. Yes! That was right, she had a daughter. This guardian angel, Louis, seemed to understand, he knew her secret and he hadn't judged her.

The landscape was changing as they both stood together in her dream. Her maid's uniform had disappeared and she was no longer a girl but herself again. The field and path that they stood on had faded out and melted away. It was replaced by her own lovely garden, and bright beautiful flowers surrounded her. She could even hear singing somewhere near but couldn't see who was singing so sweetly, but it was all so familiar.

Louis was stood beside her, pleased to see her dream changing before him, and he waved as he walked away, slowly fading as he did until he was completely gone.

He returned to the bedroom and waited. She didn't wake up. Slowly, her breathing returned to a regular rhythm as she drifted into normal sleep. The next morning, for the first time in days, she woke feeling refreshed.

She recalled her nightmare and the man who had comforted her. Was he really a guardian angel or a figment of her imagination?

Whatever or whoever he was, he had put her on the right path and for that she was grateful.

Dreams are strange things, she thought, but she recalled his advice and knew in her hearts of hearts that it was time to tell Lucy all about her father.

Her lovely Lucy was growing up fast. She was already the age Marina was when she had fallen in love with Robert, and look where that had taken her. God forbid that history repeat itself.

She was resolved to face the past. Now she was ready to sit down with Lucy and tell her the secret.

12

Mother and daughter sat together on the chaise longue. Two steaming cups of tea were laid on the small table in front of them. It was a sign that Lucy knew well; whatever her mother wanted to discuss with her was serious. Tea in the bedroom was a clear indication that her mother had some issues that she needed to air with her in private.

She hoped it was not going to be about boys again. What did her mother have against boys anyway? Come to that, when did she ever have the chance to meet boys? Since leaving school the only boys she saw, and that was at a distance, were those she saw when she went to market with Rosa. Rosa, who, she thought rather irritably, watched over her like a fluttering fairy godmother and never let her out of her sight. What she needed was some freedom!

There was one boy – she had seen him on several occasions at the market. He was handsome and he had a wonderful smile. Not that he had tossed a smile in her direction, but she hoped, and although she was shy she had an urge to talk to him. She had heard his friends call him Mark; it was such a nice name for such a nice boy and her thoughts drifted into teenage dreams.

Her daydream was broken when Marina took her hand and brought her thoughts back to the bedroom, the hot tea and the serious talk.

"Lucy!" Marina started, knowing it wasn't going to be easy to talk about the past she had hidden for so long. "I promised that one day I would tell you about your father. I'm sorry I've kept it from you for so long but you have to understand that it is difficult for me to speak about my foolishness and shame. I love you, sweet pea, and no matter what, I hope you won't judge me too harshly when I have finished my tale!"

Lucy was suddenly uncomfortable too. What was she going to hear?

A very subdued Marina leant forward and after a quick gulp of hot tea, she started her story.

Robert had been her only love. She didn't exactly meet him in the ordinary way and she was not his equal, but had she loved him with passion. She worked for his family at the manor house near her village as an upstairs maid, going into service just before her sixteenth birthday; cleaning the bedrooms, lighting early morning fires, changing the linen and generally keeping the six bedrooms, whether occupied or not, clean and in good order.

Their paths crossed every day. He was nineteen, going on twenty, and the favourite of an indulgent father, who had felt a great loss when his wife had passed away. The boy had been only five years old when he lost his mother. Robert was the only boy of four children and the youngest. He was a child born to older parents; his siblings were already in their teens at his birth. The sisters had left their father's home and were married, living with their own families in neighbouring counties. Only he remained with his father.

Marina's mother had instructed her in housecraft, learning how to cook and clean, skills for when she went into service. Her mother had been in service at the Hall when she was a young girl and had worked under the supervision of the housekeeper until she married. Mrs Jones was a good woman and it was through her that Marina was taken on.

All the locals sought jobs at the Hall; His Lordship was known as a good employer, paying fair wages and looking after his staff.

Marina was reassured that she would see her parents often because the Hall was only a walking distance away from the village. She could easily visit her parents with half a day a week and a full day once a month when she was off duty.

Lowered voices had drawn Louis out of his secret world from behind the carving. Louis, who had made himself her self-appointed guardian, who had walked with her in her nightmares, listened intensely. He was eager to find out more about Marina, this woman whom he had come to like.

"I loved him so much, I would have died for him," she confessed with passion in her voice, despite its lowered tone. "I believed he loved me too," she said sadly, but almost to herself. Lucy could feel her mother's hurt as she continued.

She had worked at the Hall for six months before he took an interest in her. At sixteen, she had filled out nicely into a beautiful young woman. Her dark hair was half-hidden under a uniformed white cap enhancing her large brown eyes that shyly looked up through her long dark lashes. She had a small turned-up nose and a pretty mouth that was full of humour when she smiled. The blush on her skin was the colour of apricots and her stubborn little chin made her face pixie-like. None of this had been lost on him.

Robert was incredibly handsome. What sixteen-year-old girl would not be flattered when a young man took an interest in her, especially when the young man was the master's dashing son? She worked as an upstairs maid.

It was one evening when she went to turn down the bed in his room that she met him. Instead of the room being empty as it normally was, when she opened the door he was sat on his bed waiting for her. Bobbing a small curtsey, she inquired whether she should carry on with her duties while he was there.

He nodded. Marina felt slightly embarrassed at being watched by the handsome young master as she turned down the sheets and fluffed up the pillows. She had hardly replaced the feather pillow on the bed when he grabbed her by her waist, turning her towards him, pulled her close and kissed her hard and firmly on her young lips.

She had never been kissed before by a boy. It was a long lingering kiss that awoke the woman inside of her. She didn't know whether to be pleased or offended; a mixture of emotions flooded into her mind.

What could she do? It wasn't as if she had encouraged him to kiss her. Did she have the right to refuse him? What would people think of her?

She was scared of being dismissed and nobody would believe her word against that of the young master.

But when he kissed her a second time, he gently removed her maid's cap from her head, revealing her luxurious thick dark hair.

"That's better, now I can see how beautiful you are." He stroked her cheek and whispered in her ear that he really liked her and that he had wanted to kiss her from the moment he had laid eyes on her months ago.

The arrogance of his first kiss was gone, he was gentle now, and he stroked her hair and cheek, staring deeply into her eyes. He wanted to know if she liked him too. She nodded, averting her eyes to the floor. He took her chin in his hand and lifted her face until their eyes met again. He stared lovingly into them until her shyness melted, her heart fluttered and she felt a kind of magic happening to her. To be held like that by a strong pair of masculine arms was almost like being in heaven. Her legs had turned to jelly and her heart was lost to him from that moment on.

She was besotted; they connected each day by leaving love notes in his bedroom under his pillow. They played a game from time to time where he would sometimes hide himself in a wardrobe and wait for her to come to his room, then he would sneak out and catch her unawares and embrace her. A small flower was left occasionally on his pillow for her to find. What girl would not be impressed by his attention and love tokens? But it was his handwritten love poem that was proof to her of his devoted love and he gained her total trust. At first they enjoyed the innocence of flirting with each other, enjoying those stolen kisses behind the door of his bedroom, sharing the sweet talk that lovers do. But it wasn't long before kisses were not enough. Soon they were sharing an intimate relationship, times snatched from her workload and hidden from the household.

A secret love was so exciting; she had promised him that she wouldn't tell a soul of their affair. He left love notes, instructing her where she could find him in her spare time during the day. They met in secret and the flirtation grew. Kisses no longer satisfied the thirst they had for each other. They met sometimes for a few minutes in his bedroom but they were never totally safe from the prying eyes of the other servants. To guard against being seen by them, they met in the country lane behind the house. They would walk through the fields away from the house and prying eyes, to share their splendid game of love in peace.

They were playing a risky game and they both knew it. If the staff or the family even suspected that something was going on, she would be dismissed immediately and they would be parted forever. But he promised her that on reaching his twenty-first birthday he would have his own money and status in his own right and they would have a life together.

Making love with Robert was the most wonderful and sensuous act Marina had ever known; to be with him was her only reason to live. Robert confessed his love to her and she felt safe and secure. She had destroyed the love notes promising to be with her forever on his instructions, but the passionate poem he wrote, she had kept. Throughout all these years she had been unable to throw it away. It was all that she had left from her disastrous love affair.

Marina held out a crumpled piece of paper to Lucy, who smoothed the paper in her hands before reading it. Her eyes filled with tears as she read the note, penned over sixteen years ago to her mother. Louis read with them.

My dearest love, you are my star
Shining in my darkest night,
If ever I lose my way, my love,
I'll look for your dazzling light.
Your silvery glow, your skin of silk,
Touches my waiting soul,
The rapture that I feel for you
Is a love pure to behold.
No words can ever tell you, my dear,
The deep love I feel for you,
I cannot eat, I cannot sleep,
You fill my dreams all day.
I wait, my love, until the night
When stars come out to play.
I cannot live without your love

And must taste it whenever I can.
In the darkness of the heaven's mass
I seek your delicate light,
I will adore you forever, my love,
My star, my shining light.
R.

A deep sense of sadness hung heavily in the room. Dense clouds had gathered in the sky outside, blocking out the sun and leaving the bedroom in gloom. It was as though the weather was also listening and responding to Marina's story.

Louis knew only too well the sense of betrayal that Marina had faced, he understood the hurt that had squeezed love out of her heart. He could never understand why some people used others and threw them away when they were done with them.

It was touching watching mother and daughter as they shared the memories of Marina's difficult history, reading the crumpled note of Robert's declaration of love together. It made his heart cry out for them.

After a short silence that was filled with oppressive sadness, Marina continued. "We were lovers for a few months when the inevitable happened. I was so excited when I realised I was pregnant. I could hardly wait to tell him. A baby, our baby, made from our love. I thought he would be so pleased and no one could deny our love, even if he wasn't independent of his father. I innocently thought we would be wed and we would be together, just as we planned." Her hands wrung together as her voice faltered again and her eyes were smarting as she held back the tears but continued the story.

Robert was waiting as usual in their special place, with a smile on his face that would have charmed the birds down from the trees. His eyes were full of warmth as he greeted her, lifting her up off her feet and pulling her close. He held her there in an embrace, kissing her with passion before settling her back on the ground.

She looked tenderly into his eyes and told him her good news. The smile disappeared from his good-looking face and hardness crossed it, his forehead creased into a frown and his eyes became cold slits.

He wasn't pleased when she told him. His response was just the reverse of what she expected. His face was ugly with anger and it grew redder and redder as he shouted repeatedly at her, "How could you do this to me?" and "What a silly bitch you are to get pregnant." And worst, he then accused her of sleeping around and denied to her face that he could be the father.

Her world collapsed. Her life was turned upside down. What could she do? Where could she go?

Working in the house and being so close to him gave her hope at first. She thought he would come around to the thought of being a father. He just needed time to think it through. She had given him a shock but he wouldn't leave her like this, he couldn't.

Everyday she tidied his room. Each night she turned down his bed and fluffed up his pillows, leaving a note pleading with him to see her, but there were no more notes waiting in return for her. She still clung on to the thought that Robert would come back to her. He loved her, he had told her so and she trusted him. The weeks passed quickly and were turning into months. It was apparent that he was avoiding her. On the odd occasion when their paths crossed, he simply ignored her as though she didn't exist and she dare not speak to him with the other servants in earshot.

She was scared. If she was found out, God only knew what would happen. Somehow she managed to hide her morning sickness by getting up very early, before the other girls stirred in the attic bedroom, and slipping out to vomit in private, tears filling her eyes with retching and tears of desperation when she was done.

For a few months she was able to work before the baby started to show. She slept in a room with other maids in the house and knew that soon her secret would be out. Sure enough, she was caught letting out her uniform during her time off in the attic. She had sewing needles and thread borrowed from the sewing room. Her body was much more rounded and the uniform was beginning to cut into what was once her waist. Despite Marina's pleading to her roommate, she could not be persuaded to keep Marina's secret and with high moral indignation she reported Marina to the housekeeper. At five months pregnant, she was instantly dismissed from the Hall.

"I hadn't told anyone that I was pregnant. By then I was ashamed that I'd been so foolish, loving a man who had just used me. Now I had no choice but to go and see my parents." The two women sat, their heads coming together as they rested on each other, sharing a moment of support. Marina reached over and squeezed Lucy's hand before continuing. Her face was troubled and speaking almost in a whisper, she frowned as she relived and faced her past once again.

Marina had hidden her pregnancy from her parents but now she had no choice but to go home disgraced and desperate and hope they would be understanding and take her in.

Marina sobbed at the memory of that awful day. Tears she thought she had shed for that distant past were streaming down her face again. It was a sad truth that her parents were shocked, disgusted and ashamed of her. There was no sanctuary, no help for her or her unborn child. She was betrayed again.

Her once-loving parents showed a side of themselves she had never seen before; they were narrow-minded and afraid of scandal. They were more concerned that she had brought disgrace on them than understanding of the hurt and suffering that she was enduring, the hurt that pierced her heart. Her parents had been her hope and they had failed her. It didn't seem to occur to them that the Lordship's young son had used her appallingly and her only crime was loving a man. An illegitimate child, a bastard, in the family was such a scandal that they would rather abandon their own daughter than face their neighbours. Her parents agreed she could stay with them until the secret could not be hidden anymore by the size of her belly. Then she would have to leave, have the baby in the workhouse and return without it.

She was determined that wasn't going to happen but knew that she would be discarded and thrown out of the village very soon. She must have help or she would end up in the workhouse with her baby permanently.

The thought of spending the rest of her life in the workhouse drove her to think realistically about the situation she was in. She must somehow appeal to Lord Parker. He might have some regard for his unborn grandchild, however little it might be, help her to start over and make a future for the two of them.

She was determined not to give up her child, but she could not go to the Hall herself. She needed someone to plead her case, for she would never be allowed to enter the Hall to put her case to the gentleman.

Father John had always been kind to her and she felt she could trust him. The old village priest knew her well; he had baptised her as a baby and given her her first communion, but more importantly, he had already heard stories about Robert when she came to him. He knew of his wild ways and had sympathy for this poor girl.

The workhouse was no place for this sixteen-year-old and he promised to do what he could for her. Sin or no sin, an innocent would soon be born and he knew the workhouse to be the first step to hell. That was not for her or her baby.

Father John was a kind and gentle man, a caring priest that loved his parishioners. He had known Marina all her life, a happy child and an innocent young woman. This world was not so kind to girls like Marina. Most people supposed it was the girl's own fault if she fell pregnant. Somehow the men carried no stigma if they were named and were never judged severely, unlike the poor women who often had to live with the shame of being an unmarried mother for their entire lives, their child branded a bastard, a blow fly and of no account.

Father John knew of one other girl from the village who had been badly used by Robert. That young girl was fortunate as her parents had more sympathy for her than Marina's had.

The priest, armed with the crumpled love poem, went to see His Lordship; he had become a man on a mission. The priest knew Lord Parker to be a good and moral man who had a strong sense of duty and Father John justly appealed to the old gentleman's good nature and encouraged him to do the right thing.

His Lordship was not totally surprised when Father John retold the story that Marina had told him, but his son was his son. He would not have him blamed for a situation that wasn't of his making. He was

disappointed at his son's failings but acknowledged that some of the blame lay with him for being indulgent with him. He found excuses for him and had done so many times throughout his son's young life. His son had had no mother to guide him – what could a father do but his best to smooth the way for him? When the priest showed him the love poem that Marina had given Father John as proof of her relationship with his son, he recognised his son's handwriting and accepted the raw truth. Enough was enough.

Having established that his wayward son had taken advantage of this young woman while she was employed under his roof, Lord Parker felt he had a moral obligation to help her. His son seemed to have no shame or conscience when the old man tackled him about her situation later that day. He had thought his son was a better man than this. He could not and would not condone a marriage between them. After all, the girl was a servant and didn't belong in their world. The old man felt guilty for allowing his son so much freedom and money as to think there were no consequences for any action he might take. Scandal had to be avoided at all costs. Father Brown knew what his son had done and her parents knew, but they could be silenced. He would give the church a little money. As for the parents, he owned the roof over their heads. They would stay silent or be evicted, and he suspected they would not want to deal with the disgrace of an unmarried daughter. Robert would be sent away into the army to learn self-discipline and respect for others. His father believed it would be the making of him.

The old man agreed to make a settlement on Marina and her unborn child, but on the understanding that she would leave the village and no contact would ever be made to either himself or to his son. She accepted.

The amount he provided for her was enough to give Marina a new start, and on receipt of the money she left the district, never to speak to her parents again. She was ready to carve out a new life for herself and her unborn child.

All he had heard saddened Louis. Sitting on the bed listening to Marina, his heart went out to her. Here was a woman in her prime, tear-stained and feeling desolate from having to recount those awful memories of her past. It pained him to think of the loneliness and suffering she had endured making a new life on her own, but he also admired her strength in coming through it all. He understood loneliness and he understood being betrayed by someone you had loved.

How could she allow herself to trust another man after all she had endured? Her heart had been ripped in two. He understood her fear; she would trust no one but herself from then on.

He was feeling that old anger rising inside his breast. It was as though he was carrying hurt for both of them. They were kindred spirits; they had been used badly by selfish people.

The bedroom had become gloomy and cold. The dark grey clouds outside had thickened so much that it felt like dusk, with restricted light coming in from the window. Louis's mood was also affecting the atmosphere in the room. Coldness hung heavily around the women, their breath showing in a white mist.

Marina stood and went to open the door. She shouted down to Rosa in the kitchen for more hot tea; she was cold, so very cold. Lucy found two shawls and both women were grateful for the extra layer of warmth they gave them.

Louis retired into his carved retreat knowing that the room temperature would rise once he had left the bedroom. His garden opened out in front of him; full light fell on him, gone the gloom of the bedroom he had just left. He stood under the tree and looked towards the sun and rolling hills that stretched out before him. He could walk towards them, but not today. He was sad; today he would sit under the tree and dream a little. He sat just for a few moments on the grass, his back propped against the tree, the voices from the room drifting towards his kingdom. Clinking cups meant they were sipping hot tea. He had heard the door shut as Rosa left the room, having delivered a new pot of hot tea to Marina's room.

Goosebumps were standing on the arms of mother and daughter and their breath hung in the air as they breathed out. They were both shivering and pulled their shawls even closer around their shoulders. They assumed that all the emotion had affected them both, not knowing that their unseen guest had influenced the mood too.

For a while mother and daughter were silent, digesting all that had been said and girding themselves for what was still to come. Time passed until all the tea had been drunk and some warmth returned to their bodies. The teacups clinked as they were finally placed back into their china saucers. It was time for Louis to return to the bedroom and share the rest of Marina's story.

Marina leaned forward and started to collect the cups together; it was a diversion to busy herself before she turned to Lucy.

Marina sighed deeply then cleared her throat to restart her tale.

"There's not much more. What I did for us to survive… don't judge me, Lucy, for I'm sure God will do that!"

Lucy threw herself into her mother's arms; her eyes were wet with tears. The two women hugged, loving and consoling each other, giving and sharing strength that was much needed for both of them.

Louis stood behind them and tried to touch them both on their shoulders in an effort to comfort them, before spontaneously kissing each of them on top of their heads. It was another example of the strength of his emotion allowing him the action.

The kiss evaporated into a wisp of cold air that passed from Louis to the women.

"Oh!" said Lucy in surprise. "Did you feel that light brush of cold air then?" she said, touching the top of her head. "I feel as though I have just been touched by an angel."

"I did," replied Marina. "It's as though someone is trying to comfort me too."

She thought of her nightmare dream and the man who called himself an angel, Louis. Was he really her spiritual guardian?

Taking a deep breath and closing her eyes in concentration, Marina continued.

She had bought a brass ring that now rested on her ring finger on her left hand and started her new life with a new identity. With the settlement Lord Parker had given her, she was able to buy the house that they now lived in. When she bought the house it was in a state of disrepair and needed quite a lot of work done to it to make it a comfortable home.

It was not easy and she was afraid to spend the precious cash, so to start with, she only renovated the part of the house she needed to live in; the rest could wait until after the baby was born.

It suited Marina that the house she had chosen was built on the edge of the town; the last thing she wanted was nosy people poking into her business. And they must never know she was unmarried. She didn't have too many neighbours around her and the ones she did get to know were not looking for bosom friendships. By the time she was ready to give birth, she was well established in the district as a soldier's wife waiting for him to return from some uprising overseas.

The local midwife was the only person she saw regularly. Mrs Mullet was a good-natured fifty-year-old who loved a bit of local gossip. And that suited Marina. She needed to spread the word that she was married to a soldier and was waiting for her husband to come back from Africa. She told Mrs Mullet that she had no other family but her husband and she was desperate for him to come home to her before the birth. It was amazing how easy it was to lie when another life depended on you; it was essential for her to be accepted by the locals and no extra questions asked.

Marina was accepted as a soldier's wife but she still largely kept herself to herself. Mrs Mullet kept her up to date with the gossip and the comings and goings of the folk who lived locally. A few kindly people dropped by to introduce themselves, some inquisitive about this young woman, some to see what she was doing to the old house. Marina was very aware of the vulnerable position she was in and played along with the pretence that she had woven to hide her real identity. She was polite but not really forthcoming about any of her previous life. *A liar must have a good memory*, she reminded herself, though at times she was lonely. She was so afraid she might trip herself up and reveal something from her past that it was necessary to keep people at arm's length. Visits from the neighbours became less and less. In the end, she bothered no one and no one bothered her – at least until after her baby came.

Lucy was born in late spring. The few people Marina had got to know through Mrs Mullet came out to the house with offers of practical help. She was brought homemade pies, fresh bread and soup throughout the time she was required to lay in. It was two weeks before the midwife allowed her to return to normal life.

"They were so kind," Marina remembered. "They cooked meals for me. Bringing hot food plated up to help me get my strength back. The lone soldier's wife with a baby living in a dilapidated house needed help." She rambled on as memories came flooding back. "A little help is worth more than pity," she quoted. "It was good, Lucy. I would have loved to have made some permanent friendships with them but I was too fearful to get close. What if I slipped up and revealed the truth, would they have been so kind then?"

Women neighbours came to see the newborn baby girl, hoping for a little cuddle and ready to advise the new mother. The ladies had great empathy for Marina, being mothers themselves, and knew how tiring the first three months would be. With her husband away in the army, they encouraged their husbands to give Marina some of their spare time to dig over her overgrown garden, work that she could not do herself having just delivered her child, and, encouraged by their wives, they set a small vegetable patch with potatoes, peas and beans, leeks and cabbage, ready for late summer for her and her baby. Marina was grateful for the help but was nervous that the lie she was living would be found out. She was determined to regain her strength as quickly as possible and slowly take over from the men and resume her independence.

When Lucy was twelve weeks old, Marina felt the time had come for her to announce that she had become a widow. She recounted with some distress to Mrs Mullet, who still dropped in to check on the baby, that a letter had come from the army announcing her husband's death. She told her that he was killed in action somewhere near Cape Town and that now she was quite alone. Marina immediately dressed in black widow's weeds. It was the custom; everyone recognised that wearing black meant a death had occurred in the family. The few married couples she had come to know came to give their condolences but somehow, because Marina had become unattached, she felt that she was seen with some suspicion. It was strange; the wives suddenly saw this young widow as a threat to them. Young and attractive, they feared she might entice their husbands in some way.

The wives stayed away, no longer visiting, but the men kept popping in to look at the garden and for a cup of tea, if it was offered. She did not encourage them but knew by instinct that some wanted more than friendship, if she was willing. But she wasn't and they at least accepted that. A little company now and again was nice but she knew she must not encourage them. Soon, like their wives, they stopped calling.

The help and friendship disappeared almost overnight but strangely it was a relief for Marina not having to pretend anymore.

Marina knew she had enough money to get by for the foreseeable future but she knew it would not last forever. The innocent teenage girl that she had been was gone. She had had to grow up very quickly in the last year. She had had to deal with betrayal, rejection and the hurt of leaving all she knew behind her and starting a new life all on her own. The young mother must be wise beyond her years, practical, hardworking and ready to face the future with her child. How she was going to earn a living, she didn't know yet, but for now the house must be completely repaired and her baby cared for. For the time being, at least, the future must take care of itself.

When Lucy was six months old, Marina realised she needed help and took on old Tom, an elderly man from the local farm. Too old to work on the land anymore, Tom was a widower with one son. His married son had taken over Tom's job on the farm. It secured them the cottage to live in. Tom worked as a general handyman doing odd jobs for people like Marina, who needed help in the garden and bits and pieces doing indoors. The few shillings he earned gave him dignity and self-worth – there would be no workhouse for him while he could work. Marina was more than happy with the arrangement and Tom helped her for three years until rheumatism got the better of him. By then she felt strong enough to take care of herself and her child.

Marina's struggle started in earnest when Lucy was three years old. The money that Lord Parker had given her was nearly at an end, she having spent the bulk of it putting the house into good repair and providing a roof over their heads. The house was at last refurbished. Now she must look to the future. Her money would not last long. A self-imposed isolation was the best defence she had and until she could find a way to support herself and Lucy, no one was allowed too close; at least, not until fate sent an unfortunate girl to her.

By the time Marina reached her twenty-first birthday she had grown into a radiant woman. She no longer wore black; after four years of pretence, it was a relief to be normal again. She had learnt that life was not fair and her future was in her own hands. She had no skills, had never trained in any crafts. Most women of her age were married with a couple of children or more. With no husband, she must help herself. All the near neighbours knew about the young widow and child that lived in the large house at the edge of the town. There was some talk between them of her taking in lodgers; how else could she survive? Marina had other ideas. There was no way she was going to become a servant again, and neither a maid nor cook for others in her own house.

Her house was now totally refurbished, which had practically cleaned her out of the rest of the money given by Lucy's grandfather. She was lucky in a way; no one from her sort of background would ever have owned property. If all else failed she would have to sell it, if she couldn't work out a solution to secure their future.

She considered her options. Her home situation at the very edge of the town was secluded. She had no training other than cleaning and household chores. There was no work for a woman with a small child.

She decided she had no choice but to trade in the oldest profession in the world. She would never allow herself to be used by a man again. She would use them to make a living.

Over the next few months, she let it be known to the men that she had once refused when Lucy was a baby that she was in business. She selected her clients carefully, slowly building up a clientele that she trusted and who trusted her. She was always discreet and the men who laid their money down knew she would never reveal their names. The house set on the edge of town was the ideal place for the men to come and go without attracting too much attention from their wives or the townsfolk.

"That, my darling, is my story and how we came to be here. Your father and grandfather made me promise that in return for the settlement they gave me, I was never to contact them ever again. I gave that assurance and I will abide by that condition until the day I die." Marina gave Lucy a hug as she continued. "Your father has no idea what he has lost. You, my dear daughter, have completed my life, you are the reason I live." She finished the sentence with a kiss on Lucy's forehead.

Lucy understood now the fears her mother had for her, all those pet talks about boys. Her trips to town always accompanied by one of the 'aunts' and never being left in the company of men. Her mother's history was so horrible that it tied knots in her stomach, but it would never happen to her.

Louis was impressed. What an extraordinary woman Marina was. He wondered why he felt different when he came here. In all the homes he and his bed had been to prior to coming here, he had only ever wanted to stop the bed from being used and he had haunted the buyers to that end. But not now. From the first evening he had stood in this bedroom he was intrigued by this woman who dressed up to hide her real self. He wanted to be part of this family, part of this household. He had Rosa to talk to and six girls to watch over. Perhaps fate had a purpose for him still; how, he had no idea, but there would be no more wandering, at least for the foreseeable future.

Over the next few weeks he learned the stories of the girls that he lived with. The stories only confirmed his high opinion of Marina and her kind heart.

13

THE GIRLS

Nora, Rosa, Emma and Veronica, known as Roni, all worked for Marina. They had arrived at the house at different times over the last twelve years. Marina, with her kind heart, had taken them in when they were wretched and destitute. She was protective, fair and honest and she had taken them all in in their time of crisis. She hadn't cared about their past or worried about their character; all she knew was that they were in distress and she had first-hand experience of how that felt when there was no one there to help.

She had a giving heart. The girls' pasts had injured them badly; she had healed and nourished them until they were ready to face life again.

Marina had told them her story many times and it had inspired them and they sought the strength she possessed. They had become family, sisters sharing a home and bringing up a small girl together.

Now Louis had become part of the family. An invisible force waiting in the background, hoping to share in the years to come, watching over them like a guardian and still learning what he was able to do in spirit form.

Over time he learned of the girls' histories, listening to snippets here and whispers there, and when there were moments of sadness or anger and the sisters shared their stories to help each other.

NORA

Nora had been the first girl Marina had found and taken in.

She had been almost killed by her drunken father and she had dragged herself into an alley, where sadly she would have died had it not been for Marina. Nora's story was as old as time.

Her father worked hard in the local quarry, a hard and dangerous job that caused him no end of anxiety. At the end of his shift he took himself off to the local tavern where he drank until his muscles eased and the dread in his heart was lost in the mist of alcohol.

When he had been drinking he became a mean drunk who became violent but he had never touched Nora. Usually Nora's mother would get a beating if the mood took him. After years of abuse and a particularly heavy beating from which she didn't recover, his wife died. Nora was thirteen years old when she lost her mother and she was obliged to take over the running of the home.

After the shock of his wife dying, George sobered up for about a year. But the grim life in the gravel pits seriously affected him and soon he was back to the bottle. Nora was fifteen when she was given her first black eye. Of course, he was sorry, he didn't mean to do it and it wouldn't happen again. But it did, again and again, each beating getting progressively worse. At seventeen he nearly killed her.

Marina and Lucy had gone into town to the shops. Lucy, the cute three-year-old, was leaving the shop holding tightly onto her mother's hand when she saw a ginger tabby cat across the way in an alley. The cat, which was chasing a fluttering leaf whipped up by the wind, was prancing and leaping trying to catch it until it landed on the ground, only to be moved again by the next gust of wind. The cat stalked the leaf as it moved as though it was a mouse and pranced and pounced trying to catch it. Lucy was captivated by it all and laughed at the tabby's antics.

Before Marina could stop her, Lucy had snatched her hand away from her mother's and was running down the alley after the cat. Marina, close on her heels, snatched up her daughter by her waist, lifting her up and swinging her around, laughing at her little scamp and the fun of the chase. Then she heard a moan.

Nora's moans came from behind some packing cases near the back door of the baker's. Marina's instinct was to ignore the sound at first and go home, but something pulled her to the curled-up figure half hidden between the crates.

Nora's body was black and blue, old bruises under the new ones, cuts on her face and arms where the leather belt, with the brass buckle had been used on her. She had tried to protect her face with her arms but the buckle from George's leather belt had got through. Her eyes and lips were swollen, one eye was closed with swelling and the other was not too far behind it. She had dragged herself out of her home and as far away, as out of reach of her father's hand and his drunken brutality, as she could. She had fallen down there some time during the night and had lain there, just too exhausted to move any further. She lay there not caring whether she lived or died. She knew she couldn't take another beating. She had no place to go but she knew she was never going back to live with him. He would kill her; she'd rather live in the workhouse than be with her father. But the cold of the night and the beating had taken its toll; she could not have crawled another inch.

Marina had never seen such a sight as she saw then. She was shocked. How could anyone do this to another person? Filled with compassion, she called for some help from the local storekeeper, who lifted and carried the semi-conscious girl back to the store. There they called the local carters to carry the poor girl back to Marina's home, where she nursed Nora back to health.

It took almost two years before Nora was ready to reclaim her life. At nineteen, the bonny, rather slim young woman took over running the house and caring for Lucy, who was now five years old, while Marina worked to keep them all. It would be another year before Nora was given the choice as to whether she would like to stay on or go her own way.

Nora had control of her own life now; she was no longer living in fear of her father's hand and if she never saw him again, that would be too soon. She lived a good life with Marina, who was like an older sister to her. She had no urge to leave and she felt safe there with her new family. Soon she would have to contribute to the household's purse. It had taken three years to fully recover from the damage to her body and mental scars. She had been looked after by the generosity of Marina's kindness and she knew she had a debt to repay. And though no pressure came from Marina, the idea of being in control, using men rather than being used, appealed to her, and soon after she joined Marina in the night trade. She was twenty. Ready to face life.

EMMA

After taking in Nora, barely three months had passed before another young girl, a victim of life, needed help.

Emma was begging in the street when Marina first saw her. She looked half-starved – all skin and bone – but had brown eyes as big as saucers that would have been appealing but for the dark rings around them.

Her blond hair was matted and hung like rats' tails down around her shoulders, lank with no lustre, around a face that could be so pretty. The dirty, torn, paper-thin cotton clothes she wore were no protection against the elements. A small bundle hung from her hand; it looked like an old shawl but there was no coat or hat to be seen. Somewhere she had lost her shoes, and she stood on the pavement on the town's high street in torn striped stockings. Her hand was held out timidly in hope of a copper or two.

She smelt! Marina turned her head away from the odour of sweat and grime that emanated from the poor wretch who she passed. She dropped sixpence in the bowl and walked on.

Emma's life had changed dramatically when her father died suddenly. In just six months, her world had turned upside down; she had endured the death of her father and the loss of her home. Her mother, Sally, had taken the death of her father very badly and in her traumatised state she had taken to drinking to lessen the pain she felt. Depression soon followed and Emma was unable to help her.

Her father had been employed as a gamekeeper on an estate near Oxford. The job came with a cottage and Emma had been born there. She had had a happy and secure childhood and loved the estate. Her dad was used to being out in all weather but somehow he caught a head cold that quickly turned into pneumonia. He was in his prime but in one short week he was gone, resulting in her mother and herself becoming homeless. There was sympathy for her and her mother, but the estate needed the cottage for a newly appointed gamekeeper. Her mother was given less than a month to find somewhere else to live. They were evicted from the only home Emma knew. There was nobody to take them in, so what little money that had been saved was used for rent on a small room in a nearby village. Things did not go well for them; her mother tried but was unable to find work for herself or Emma. When the money ran out they were turned out again, but this time they were destitute and took to begging, roaming from town to village in hope of raising enough money for food for the day and to put a roof over their heads for the night. Sally hid some of the money earned from begging from Emma and instead of it being used wisely, it was often used to buy gin.

Her mother was unable to endure the loss of her husband and had taken to drinking herself into a drunken stupor whenever she could. The two of them spent their days looking for work and tramping the road between Aylesbury and Oxford, sleeping under the hedgerows with their bundles when they had no funds from begging, eating when they could – but there were days when they went hungry.

Summer would not last forever. It seemed likely to Emma that the workhouse in Oxford would be their final destination. In the sixteen years Emma had lived, nothing had ever prepared her for the way her life had turned out. Life on the estate was hard; she had helped in the laundry from the age of fourteen, but she had food and warmth in their little home. Now life was a living hell.

It was some time in June when, overcome by drink, Sally had passed out the previous evening. Her breath was still heavy with gin and Emma knew she would sleep until noon. Emma had walked up to the farm, hoping for work for a day or two, but there was none to be had.

That morning Emma had left her mother lying still drunk and dead to the world in a farmer's outhouse. If the farmer or one of his labourers found her Sally would be in trouble, but Emma was unable to wake her. She must go and beg if they were to survive.

Who would give them jobs now? she had thought. The two of them looked like tramps; their possessions had been sold for food long ago. They only had what they stood up in.

Her mother said she was going to change, she'd stop drinking and find work and they would find somewhere to live. But that wouldn't happen; there was no real will for change. Grief and despair were eating away at her mother and Emma knew it. That or gin would kill her.

Neither of them could go on like this. Autumn was on its way and they wouldn't survive through a winter outside on the road. She might get some work if she could tidy herself up. As for her mother, nobody would hire a drunk, not even in the milking sheds or as a washerwoman.

Faced with no alternative, she had little choice other than to take her chances on the streets. Emma had taken to begging in every village and town they passed through. This town was one of the many she had visited, only this time she was on her own.

It was the sound of laughter and jeering that made Marina turn around to see what was going on. A group of boys, high in spirit and low in character, saw a chance of making fun and having some entertainment at the young beggar's expense. They taunted Emma with hurtful words.

Emma was afraid. She drew back from them as they gathered in a circle around her; petrified, she tried to turn and run. One boy sniggered at her discomfort and blocked her path, pushing her back so that she turned to escape the other way, but a large tubby lad blocked that way too.

She had nowhere to go, the boys surrounded her. She stepped slowly backwards until she came into contact with the wall. She sank down and squatted into a small ball, her hands and elbows covering her head, and she made a small moaning sound that only seemed to encourage the boys to be even crueller.

Emma screamed. Who threw the first stone, Marina wasn't certain. By the time she reached the boys, Emma had been struck several times and was bleeding from an open wound on her forehead.

Marina reacted rather than thought about what she was doing. Using a shopping bag and an umbrella she was carrying, she attacked the ring leader around the head and shoulders, beating him as hard as she was able.

The young bully, surprised at the attack, turned and ran. A storekeeper who had seen the attack on the beggar from his store joined Marina, brandishing a broom, swinging it at the rest of the group and catching them on their legs and backsides. Between the two of them they dispelled the youths, who ran away like the pack of curs they were.

Marina, full of compassion, helped the young girl to her feet. Emma was barely able to stand and swayed dangerously back and forth. A stream of blood trailed down Emma's face and, seeing the blow on her head, Marina feared that the girl might be concussed. Who would take care of her? She seemed to belong to no one. Marina could not leave her there in that state and once again, she took it upon herself to take another girl in and nurse her until she was well. Perhaps they could find her family?

But there was no family to be found and by the time Emma told her story to Marina, her mother had disappeared. There had been a search for her, starting at the spot where Emma had left her. But she was gone. Nor could she be found on any of the roads leading in or out of the town. Emma was now quite alone with no shelter, no money and no family. The prospect of her spending the rest of her days as an inmate of the workhouse was a real possibility, and it filled Emma and Marina alike with dread. The young girl was in such a poor state that Marina doubted she would survive six months in that awful institution.

Because of that, she invited Emma to stay until she could decide for herself what her future would be.

Nursed back to health, Emma developed into a lovely young woman. She was intelligent as she was kind. Lucy was three years old and a lively little mite. Emma had taken to her at once and the feeling was mutual. For the next few years, Emma became her nanny and a home help for Marina.

By the time she had reached her twentieth birthday she had developed into a beautiful young woman. Men turned their heads as she walked through the town, admiring her looks. She knew she was attractive to them but her experiences had fuelled insecurities. Being with women she liked and feeling safe in Marina's home with a roof over her head was all she wanted. She had the possibility of earning a good living here with her friends and she would be able to save money for her future. It was the best option she thought she could have.

Marina was delighted; she liked her little beggar, as she thought of her. She would be a real asset to the house and business increased almost overnight.

Two years after Emma had joined the household and when Lucy was five, another two unfortunate girls desperately in need of shelter found their way to Marina's home, almost together. Roni and Rosa had heard of a lady who had taken in destitute girls. Marina, it seemed, had gained a reputation in the small town when she had taken in the beggar girl, and some of the tradesmen who delivered to the house knew something of Nora's plight before that. Marina was generally known to have a good nature but was also someone who didn't mix much with the locals – in fact, she was a bit of a mystery. Some knew her as a young widow with a small child but that was about all. Where she got the money to live on, the gossips were not sure, but some thought she had private means and that was the end of it. Except for her taking in unwanted girls. That was another matter that they couldn't explain.

RONI

Veronica, known as Roni, knocked at Marina's door one evening with a face that had been repeatedly punched and was a mask of black and blue.

Roni's story was like that of so many girls with her background. She was one of eight siblings sharing a two-bedroomed tithed cottage with their parents in a village a couple of miles outside town. With no privacy and no space, sleeping four to a bed, she couldn't wait to get married and move out.

If only it had been that simple. Jake wasn't her first choice but she liked him well enough. Her dad worked with his dad and somehow the two men decided that the young pair would be good for each other! They had been encouraged into seeing each other and soon they were walking out together. Marriage happened as a matter of course but almost from the first night she knew she had made a terrible mistake.

Jake wasn't the kind man she had thought she had married. She worked hard to keep the house clean and the garden planted with vegetables, but it was never good enough for Jake. If the floor wasn't clean enough, he chastised her; if the pantry wasn't tidied to his liking, he chastised her. All too soon, the verbal criticism turned to a slap that increased in severity over the months. In fact, he hit her because it gave him a feeling of power and he enjoyed it. Making love became an ordeal; he would demand his so-called 'rights' at any time, regardless of how she felt. There was no tenderness, no affection, so unlike her dreams of marriage. There was no thought for her in his lust, only his pleasure. It was legal rape.

She tried to leave him and go back home for some protection but her dad sent her packing. She was married now and she would have to sort it out with Jake and make the best of it.

When Jake heard that she had tried to leave him, he felt she had brought shame on him. That was when he openly beat her. Her face and body were never without a bruise, sending a clear message to all who knew them that he was boss in his own house. He could use her just as he wanted. After being beaten as a matter of course almost on a monthly basis, she knew she would have to get out or be killed.

Funnily enough, she had heard of Marina from the storekeeper in town. He had told her the tale of the boys and the beggar girl and how Marina had taken in the young woman. Roni hoped she might persuade Marina to give her shelter for a few days until she could find a way to escape from this monster she had married. Marina did and the few days turned into weeks and then months. As long as her husband didn't find her she would be safe.

Thinking that she was free at last she decided to join the team!

ROSA

Rosa was the last to come into the fold. Marina had first seen Rosa in the market square, sitting on the steps by the town cross. She sat with a bundle of belongings lying at her feet. She was selling corn dollies that she had made from the gleanings that had been left in the fields all around. The market square was full of shoppers, it being a busy market day. In the hustle and bustle nobody seemed to notice her. The noise of shouting from the traders touting their wares around the market stalls was so loud it hurt Marina's ears. Children were running around playing, laughing and enjoying the mayhem; mothers calling, scolding and buying food while their offspring ran riot. The market bustled with all kinds of folk and pickpockets had to be watched out for as they moved among old and young alike. No one stopped or even noticed the girl sat trying to sell her wares, except Marina.

Marina sat down next to her on the steps by the town cross; she was concerned to know where she had come from.

She's an odd one, thought Marina and asked her if she was alright. "You're not from around here, are you?"

"Just visiting."

"Who are you staying with?" enquired Marina.

"I'm not exactly staying with anyone, just passing through really," replied the girl.

"What's your name?"

"Rosa," she answered, but there was fear in her voice. "I can't go back, they just don't understand," she blurted out, almost before she was asked the next question.

"Don't understand what?"

"I— I can't tell you," stuttered the girl. Fear crossed Rosa's face. Her eyes welling up with tears, suddenly the girl slumped into a heap, sobbing uncontrollably. Marina's arm instinctively went around her shoulders.

So I am being called on once again, thought Marina, looking up to heaven and shrugging her shoulders.

Marina knew that Rosa needed help, just as she had done seven years ago. She couldn't ignore this girl.

"Come on, love, I'll find a place for you tonight," she said. "Don't worry, you'll be alright."

The spirits that surrounded them told Rosa that she would be safe with this woman. A guardian angel was standing next to Marina, smiling, and a golden aura framed Marina's body. This woman had a good soul. From that moment there was total trust between them.

It would be some years before the secret that Rosa held would be teased out of her but she, like the others, did tell Marina eventually.

Rosa had always been different. As a small child her parents were highly amused by her talking to her imaginary friends, she had so many. They laughed at the way she so earnestly talked to them and even described them with clarity; the colour of their eyes and hair and the clothes they wore.

She was a small child and it was easy to think nothing of it. Indeed, it was very normal to have invisible friends; many children did. But by the time she was eight, these friends were still around and her parents started to worry.

"She should have grown out of it by now," they confided to each other. "Is there something wrong with the girl?" they asked themselves. Now they questioned her whenever she appeared to be speaking to herself. Slowly the reality of the situation revealed itself.

Rosa's imaginary friends were spirits. Her sixth sense was so highly tuned that spirits of the departed appeared to her. She had seen them all her life and it was quite normal for her to be in touch with them. Unfortunately her parents were not able to completely understand the gift that she had; or curse, depending on your perspective. Not knowing how to handle the problem at first, they just tried to discourage her. That did not work so they took to mocking her, trying to shame her into abandoning her habit. They asked themselves if she could be insane or something more sinister – was she possessed?

By the time she was fourteen and moving through puberty, raging hormones, stubbornness and anger resulted in the church being consulted. A priest came and attended the child. After a brief talk with the young girl, he announced she was possessed by demons.

The experience of being exorcised by the priest was an experience that changed her life. She realised she could no longer be open about what she saw and heard. She was a medium, who must never admit to seeing or hearing spirits again.

Life was tough. Her parents were always watching her, looking for signs that might indicate she was still disturbed. They died in tragic circumstances shortly after she was exorcised. She never spoke of it but she was aware that she must protect herself.

Her grandparents came to live with her but she lived in fear that they would see her in contact with her ghosts, as she was unable to hide her gift all the time. Her biggest fear was that she might be put into an asylum, which was an even more horrific prospect than the workhouse. She had seen first-hand the poor wretches that lived in the workhouse hospital; the girls had lost all their personality and their spirit had been drained from them. Their hair was cropped and they walked head down with eyes diverted to the ground. There were no smiles or laughter. Life was grim and if they spoke, it was only if they were addressed. They were like the living dead. She decided to run away.

Rosa would not go down that road if she could help it, so when Marina offered a roof over her head with no questions asked, she went with her, so advised by her spirits. She sought refuge where no one would look for her and Marina took her on as help for the household chores and garden. Soon her personality blossomed, and with her fear gone she soon found peace.

Cooking and housekeeping came naturally to her, which made the household happy. Though she was never a chatterbox, she was so happy in her new position that the house was often filled with her sweet singing. Her voice was clear and beautiful and she filled the house with a light radiance that was almost palatable. Her spirits were friendly and somehow, now she was settled they didn't pester her as much.

The house at the end of the lane was full. There was no room left and life went on.

For Lucy, the five-year-old enjoyed the growing family. It gave her new aunties who played with her and who sang songs with her. They helped her with her learning. Lucy grew up with her caring adopted aunts. The comings and goings in the evening were a normal way of life to her. The love that they all shared was so precious that no one in the house would risk anything to come between them, no man or woman. Lucy was Marina's love and joy and although she knew that Lucy would soon become aware of the opposite sex, the one thing Marina was sure of was that Lucy would never have to work as she had done and never in that profession.

Marina, to her credit, had not only brought up Lucy but had, in the early years, taken on destitute girls. She had cared for them, fed them and clothed them until they were strong enough, both mentally and physically, to decide where their future lay. The safety and comfort of the house was the only real home these girls had known. Marina worked as a prostitute because she had no choice; she regarded her clients as customers. She ran a business; there was no room for sentiment. Love had let her down. How could she let any man into her heart again? If sex was all men wanted, then let them pay.

Having four young women in her home to help create a comfortable home for the six of them was a blessing and they shared a like mindedness when it came to the profession they worked in. Local men were like bees around a honey pot. But no man got the honey without paying. Over the years, the women made the house possibly the most comfortable in the town, next to the mayor's.

14

LUCY

At fifteen going on sixteen, Lucy found the life in the house was rapidly
becoming boring. There were chores and more chores to do, with the only
breaks from it all being to read her precious books and going to town
twice a week.

Her energies made her restless so when the chores were completed
she would go up to her room and in seconds, her nose would be in a book.
Her outlet and escape was reading. School had whetted her appetite for
it and her mother encouraged her by buying new novels as soon as they
became available; stories of romance and adventure, with so many heroines
like the Bennett sisters in *Pride and Prejudice*. She often imagined herself
as the heroine. A young woman who in her daydreams imagined herself
with a Mr Bingley or Mr Darcy but, the thought never crossed her mind,
she might meet a Mr Wickham.

Lucy was Rosa's little helper around the house and garden; even when
she grew, Rosa still thought of her in that way. In the summertime, Rosa
and Lucy would take any spare vegetables from the plot in the garden to
sell to the local greengrocer on market day in the town. The money bought
meat from the butcher and tea in the tearoom. It was such a luxury taking
tea and Lucy felt so grown up sitting at a table sharing a cake with Aunt
Rosa and sipping an Assam tea.

The small tearoom adjacent to the square was where Rosa would go after the business of shopping. Having someone serve her tea was the highlight of her morning. It was always good to get the weight off her feet, sit and people-watch with Lucy at her side.

Lucy could only go to the town if she was accompanied by one of her adopted aunts and it was usually Rosa. Now that she was almost sixteen, she thought that she was old enough go on her own. Her need to visit the town had noticeably increased and she was eager to show her independence. Rosa was troubled; Lucy was changing from the little girl they knew and becoming a young woman. Rosa saw the way she attracted attention on those trips to market. Lucy was bonny and her natural liveliness was a magnet for turning heads, especially the men. At just fifteen, it was an attention that concerned Rosa because it could be a problem for Marina and the business, Marina would not want extra interest placed on her house and the clients through Lucy.

Lucy was attractive and she was well aware of the looks she received in the town although she was naturally shy.

Lucy had deep auburn hair, which she wore tied back with combs and ribbon; a pair of warm blue eyes, that sparkled with youth; a small, slightly turned-up nose; lips that were full and sensual. Her small breasts and very narrow waist enhanced the fashion of the day but not in an obvious way. When she wore her favourite colour of emerald green it only made her eyes and hair more attractive. Who could fail to notice her!

Mark, the mayor's son, was no exception. He liked what he saw and wanted to get to know her, but to his frustration she was always chaperoned.

Coming to the market twice a week to buy or sell gave Lucy, however brief, a view of life. Living three or so miles outside of the town centre meant she didn't see many young people, not even the ones she had been to school with.

Rosa heard little pieces of gossip that kept the household up to date with the goings on in the town. Having tea also allowed Lucy, with Rosa's permission, a little time on her own, a chance to feel a little independent. Rosa would let her go and shop for small personal things, barley sugar sweets or new ribbons. It gave Lucy the freedom she needed without risk. Rosa realised that being cooped up with her aunts week in, week out, must be stifling for her a lively teenager.

The morning she first met Mark, she had just been and bought silk skeins for her embroidery. She had made some small pillows to fill with lavender, which she planned to embroider with the aunts' names to give as presents come Christmas. She would keep some for herself. Stitching her name on them and laying them beneath her clothes in the drawers of her tall boy, the small packages full of lavender would make her clothes smell fragrant and fresh. Clutching her silks, she was walking back to the tearoom when she literally bumped into Mark.

Seeing her in the market square from the window of his father's shop, Mark saw an opportunity to accidently meet her. She had her head down watching her path when she collided into Mark, staged as it was on the high street. Her package fell to the ground and rolled to the kerb.

"Oh! I'm sorry I didn't see you. My head was in other places. Sorry," he said, smiling sheepishly at her while bending to retrieve her package.

As he passed the package to her she could not help thinking what a good-looking young man he was. She remembered seeing him before at other times in the square and remembered his name was Mark.

She was shy and tongue-tied.

"It's alright," she stammered, blushing as she continued. "Nothing to break, just silk for my embroidery."

As her eyes looked up into his, he saw the bluest of blue eyes looking back. Looking into the depth of them, they reminded him of cornflowers.

"Got to get back to work," he responded. Half turning to go, he said, "I work at the chandler's store. I'm Mark, by the way, what's your name?"

"Lucy," she replied, blushing bright pink, and she was suddenly very shy.

"Hope to see you in the square again, sometime, Lucy," Mark declared. He was as pleased as Punch with the way things had gone and he wore the broadest smile on his face. Her blushes were not lost on him. *She likes me*, he thought. *Well, good, I like the look of her.* And with that he turned towards the store. Before crossing the square, he turned and waved. She was still watching him and at the wave her heart turned somersaults.

When Lucy recounted the chance meeting Rosa shivered involuntarily, as though someone had walked over her grave.

Well, it had to happen sometime, she thought, but she was worried. But for now she would keep her fears to herself. It was obvious that Lucy had found affections for the first time for someone outside the family. How would it all work out? Only time would tell.

The trips to the town had started to become strained. The trips to the teashop were briefer as Rosa felt she must keep a watchful eye on Lucy and stay with her while she shopped. That was not what Lucy wanted; she needed badly to have a chance meeting with Mark, who was all she thought about for much of the day and night.

Lucy scanned the crowds, searching for the tall, dark-haired boy who totally filled her thoughts. Her heart leaped whenever she glimpsed him in the square. She had not been able to talk to him again since their first meeting. Rosa was always there, flapping around her like a mother hen; Lucy could not get any free time. She started to devise a plan to meet him again. However, it was taken out of her hands when Rosa decided that the house needed more candles and oil for the lamps.

"Autumn and winter are just around the corner and it would be prudent to be ready and well stocked," she said. Before any plan could come to fruition on Lucy's part, Rosa ushered them into the store where Mark worked.

Lucy's heart was pounding as they pushed open the stout wood door. The smell of the oils and wax filled the air. The store seemed quite dark coming in from the outside and when their eyes adjusted they saw that shelves reaching from floor to ceiling in natural wood surrounded them. A heavy-looking counter stretched along one wall, the front of it panelled and painted a deep maroon. Hanging lamps for sale covered the ceiling. Amongst them were five that were obviously in use come the evening, judging by the black sooty spots above them. All sorts of items were displayed along the counter: ceiling lamps, table lamps, oil lamps of various sizes, wax tapers, boxes of gas mantles and the latest gas wall lights in shiny black metal, displayed with a sign giving the price of two pounds and sixpence, glass cover extra. The shelves had smaller drawers all along them that were marked with the contents and the prices.

Lucy's excitement was replaced by disappointment as she looked around; Mark was not in the shop behind the counter. Instead, a man sporting a large handlebar moustache stood there.

"Can I help you, misses?" asked the middle-aged man, wearing a white twill cotton apron and showing badly stained teeth from smoking a pipe as he smiled.

"Candles, I need candles," stated Rosa, taking a deep breath to go on.

A door with a glass observation pane in it, that was used to view the shop from the back room, opened from behind the counter and Mark appeared, striding quickly to the man's side.

"I'll take these customers, Thompson," said Mark with some authority.

"Right you are, Mr Mark." He slightly touched his forehead in deference. "I'll be in the stock room if you want me."

"Now then, ladies, what can I get you?"

Lucy blushed, dropping her eyes to her tightly clasped hands that clutched her purse.

So this is Mark, thought Rosa, and although he seemed a likeable lad his aura was indistinct and she couldn't read it. *He doesn't quite know himself yet, she thought, he still has some growing up to do.* How would he turn out? That was anyone's guess. Cold or warm and generous, it was too early to say.

It did tell Rosa that he was immature with the possibility of a temper but he was young and there was plenty of time for him to develop. Then why did she feel nervous for Lucy? Not even her spirits were talking today, only her senses were working overtime.

Although he was talking to both of them, his eyes were on Lucy.

"Twenty candles, please," asked Rosa. "White, ten inches."

Her voice brought Mark back to her.

"Certainly," he replied, beaming from ear to ear, and turned to a shelf behind him where the candles were kept and started to count out the candles stored there.

Lucy was afraid that this meeting was going to end all too soon and suddenly became talkative.

"Aunt Rosa, this is Mark. We met, rather bumped into each other, in the square a few weeks ago, you remember, I told you?"

"Yes, I remember. Hello Mark. You seem very young to be in charge of a store," she said inquisitively.

"I help run this shop with my father, and the store over the other side of the square. You might not know but my dad's the mayor," he added a little cockily, his arrogance showing as he felt the need to impress them.

Rosa knew right enough, the tearoom was such a good place to pick up titbits about local people. But the gossip she had heard about Mark, the mayor's son, was not all good. It was rumoured he was something of a flirt and had broken a few hearts already. Flirty, cocky and a little arrogant – was this the right young man for Lucy?

But Rosa's main concern was how Lucy would explain her life to someone she may meet, her mother and her aunts, what they did and the general comings and goings that went on at home. Rosa shivered. It was unfair but Lucy would have to hide the truth from him and anyone else who came into her life. It was a complication that the women had not foreseen happening so soon in Lucy's life.

Lucy, their joint child, as Rosa saw it, had grown up overnight. Suddenly Lucy's future was a risk; how were they to deal with it?

"The mayor!" said Lucy, shocked. She didn't know.

He was pleased that she was impressed with his status and that she had not tried to snare him because of it. Many of the girls he had met were impressed with his father's position as mayor and so, by association, him. They had tried to use him to give themselves status and he hated that. It was good that this lovely creature was unaware and liked him for himself. He was chuffed and thanked his lucky stars at their meeting in the square.

"I hope we will see you again soon," said Mark as he parcelled up the candles.

Again looking at Lucy, the message was there; the next time she came to town he would be looking for her. She would have to lose Rosa somehow. Maybe she would insist that Rosa had tea while she shopped and then she would make her way to the store.

Knowing he would be looking out for her, she had butterflies in her stomach at the thought of meeting him alone. How could she wait until the next trip to the town? But wait she must.

After paying the bill they left, heading off for the long walk back home. Lucy was unusually very quiet, her head filled full of Mark and romance, dreaming dreams that she hoped would come true. Silence for three miles was three miles too many for Rosa, so she opted for a diversion and getting home quicker.

"Let's see if the carter is going our way today, my back's killing me," said Rosa, rubbing her back. Funny how when she felt stressed she got backache.

Rosa was worried. How would Marina take her news that Lucy was besotted with a boy? Something had to be done.

Louis knew almost as soon as the pair arrived back at the house that they brought trouble with them. Rosa brought it in with her, an atmosphere of anxiety. However, Lucy was in a cheery mood, hanging up her coat before darting up into her bedroom and throwing herself on the bed to dream of what might be, without realising her dreams could never become reality unless he never found out about the house and its secret.

"Marina," Rosa called, "I really need to speak with you."

"Where's the child?" said Marina, coming from the kitchen, wiping her hands on a pot towel.

"It's the child that I want to speak to you about," replied Rosa, raising her eyebrow, making a furrow on her forehead. "She's in her bedroom for now, that will give us time to speak."

"For goodness' sake, you're starting to alarm me, whatever is it?"

Rosa took Marina by the elbow and took her into the garden.

Louis was sat on the old bench by the kitchen. Rosa looked at him directly, noting that he would hear all she had to say. Well, that was okay, she was the only one he could talk to and perhaps he could see a solution that she could not. She shrugged her shoulders and took Marina over to the bench, sitting her and herself next to him.

Rosa had seen Louis from the very first. When he had walked into the kitchen that morning soon after the bed's delivery, she had seen him and had recognised that he posed no threat. In fact, his aura was one of sadness and longing. He was trapped! She knew that. He had not pestered the family; in fact, he had helped, confirming her assessment of him. Marina had confided in her about her troubled dreams and she was not surprised to hear of a guardian angel called Louis.

For the next half hour while the other women were resting, Rosa and Marina shared this new problem, but only Rosa knew that Louis was sharing it too.

"Lucy is not our little girl anymore, Marina. She's grown and we missed it. Under our noses, she has gone from girl to woman without us seeing it. Today she saw the boy I told you about, the one that collided with her a couple of weeks back. I thought it might be a good idea to see what the lad is like so I pretended we needed candles and went to the store where he works. Marina, I'm not sure about him, but that is by the by. The way she blushed and the way he looked at her, they are attracted. How can any young man court Lucy? How can any young man come here? She is bound to be tainted by association knowing what our business is, and he's the mayor's son," rambled Rosa.

Marina knew in her heart of hearts that she had been dreading this day; her girl growing up and needing love, not the sort from mother to child but the physical love of a man. She knew it. She would have liked nothing better than to have had a life with Robert but he had betrayed her. That had been her dream that had turned into a nightmare. Lucy, her darling child, had saved her from insanity and the asylum. She understood longing but more than that, she understood pain. A pain she did not want her daughter to know.

The mayor's son! That was bad news. The mayor was a silly man, full of himself, and an occasional visitor to the house. But her daughter and his son, God! It couldn't be happening and it mustn't happen.

"Listen, Rosa, she's only fifteen, she will have to do as we say. She must not be left on her own when she's in town. We can't encourage them to meet but if we discourage Lucy, she will only want him more. If they do meet, one of us must be there. I can't have him call here lest he suspects something. We must just try to keep them away from each other," she went on, almost to herself.

"I think we should only see our regulars." Nodding to herself, she said, "no one comes in unless we know them. It should not be too hard to keep a lid on this if we are very careful and limit the traffic to our door."

In twelve years Marina had, as well as fixing up the home, managed to save a tidy sum of money. Keeping to the regulars was good; most had been coming for many years and had become more like friends. Enjoying the company of the women and sex without responsibility, the only commitment was to pay for the entertainment. Some even confided their secrets with her.

Marina had been careful to only allow new men in who had been vouched for by a regular client. Because of this rule their client base was small, but the mayor was on that list and they would have to be careful.

No man passed the door by day; only when darkness fell did that house exist.

Lucy had been kept away from the men who visited. They knew of her, of course, even glimpsed her sometimes. She was the widow's daughter but no one knew her personally. Lucy's relationship with the women was as their adopted daughter, they would do all they could to protect her.

Bit by bit, a story began to emerge in Marina's mind, a story that they must get out to the gossips in the town. Most people thought she ran a boarding house for women. Well, now that story would be embellished.

They lived so far out of town that they were usually left in peace. But her daughter had grown and things were about to change. Somehow they had to control it.

15

Marina and Rosa put their heads together and jointly stitched a story. Rosa would tell the story where others could listen and the gossips would do the rest. It was a simple tale and one not too far away from the truth. Lucy lived with her mother and her aunts on the edge of town, her mother owned the house and had private means through the death of a rich relative, making them financially independent, and the aunts worked as casual labour when they needed to. It was a respectable household.

Rosa would let it all slip out when she next went for tea in the town; the waitress was always friendly and they often passed the time of day together. Rosa knew that other ears would be listening and soon her story would circulate around the square.

Marina was in panic mode. She knew she couldn't lock Lucy up but she wanted to protect her, as any mother would. The yearning for the boy would only increase if she did try to put a stop to Lucy going to town.

Better it burn itself out naturally, but please God, don't let her make my mistake, she thought, her memories flooding back to Robert and the biggest mistake she had made in her life. She squeezed back the tears and was resolved to prevent it happening to her daughter if she could!

Mark was thinking of Lucy. It had been two weeks since she had visited the store. The market days on Tuesday, Friday and Saturday had come and gone twice and he had only been able to glimpse her. He had hoped that somehow she would make her way to the shop and to him. He had watched her shopping across the square with her aunt, leaping out of the store to see them, but each time he made his way towards them Rosa detected him and would lead Lucy into the nearest shop where he couldn't follow. He wasn't able to engineer a casual meeting and the disappointment angered him. She was so different from the other girls he knew and he was desperate to be with her.

Young Mark was an attractive nineteen-year-old. He had a strong square jaw with a deep cleft in his chin, deep brown eyes set under hooded lids and a low forehead. He was fairly tall, standing at five feet ten inches, but slight in build; he was still a boy, manhood would come soon and fill him out.

He had enjoyed flirting with the local girls but now he had set his sights on Lucy and sowing his wild oats, as his father had suggested, was definitely not on now. Taking advantage of silly girls was all in the past. They had only wanted to be seen hanging on the arm of the mayor's son but Lucy hadn't known who his father was, which meant she liked him for himself.

He was besotted since their meeting and Lucy totally entranced him with her modesty and shyness. He saw her as a fragile and delicate angel. She had a small beautiful face with a pair of eyes that reminded him of clear blue water. A pure and innocent girl worthy of him and all he had to give. The thought of her was ever present with him and it was driving him insane. He just had to see her, to talk to her, to be with her.

Since serving her and her aunt at the store two weeks ago, he had been unable to think of anything other than Lucy ever since. She would need to be pursued patiently and gently. What he wanted in the future, he wasn't sure; he only knew the stirrings of real passion that had seized his heart. It had never happened before, and what he had in mind for the two of them was nothing less then the raptures of lovemaking, something well worth waiting for.

Louis was very aware of how sad Lucy was. He stood by her bed as she cried herself to sleep. Two weeks had gone by, four trips to town, and she had not been able to free herself of Rosa. Her heart yearned to see him but Rosa had not even gone for tea like she usually did, at least not when Lucy was with her. It was maddening, she couldn't bear it. She had sighted him a couple of times but Rosa had hurried them on into a shop or turned the other way. How she hurt. No one knew how much she yearned to see him.

Marina knew, but couldn't help Lucy. The pain her daughter felt was just teenage love, it would pass – at least, she hoped so. She didn't like to see Lucy with red eyes from crying but was determined that mother love must be tough for the child's sake. Both women suffered and for the first time in fifteen years there was a divide between them.

In one week Lucy would be sixteen, the very age that Marina had learned to love and experienced the magic of physical love. Was her little girl really ready for that? She was still a baby, her baby. How could she protect Lucy from herself?

Louis understood the yearning in Lucy's heart; he had touched her when she was asleep and was surprised by the force of the emotional energies that were pulsing from her; they transported him back with emotion to the memories of his own mortal life. He remembered the feeling of the close warm bodies of Sophia and himself. Spending many hours making love, pleasuring themselves, being as close as any two people could be, becoming one in their passion. One body, one mind.

Time, and only time, would solve this melodrama for Lucy and he wished her well.

MONDAY

When Lucy came down for breakfast on the morning of her birthday, Marina and her aunts were already at the table. They had gathered around the breakfast table with gifts for her, wrapped in colourful tissue paper.

Marina was so proud of her and so scared.

There was a surprise in each package Lucy opened; carved bone hair slides from Rosa, who had sneaked off to town on the Saturday to buy them for her and had taken tea at the teashop to gossip freely with the waitress, just as Marina and she had arranged; while Nora, Roni and

Emma bought her new cotton lawn underwear, cotton that had come all the way from India, in the Empire. Marina's present to her daughter was a new book, *Little Women*, a story of a family of sisters and their entwined lives in America. *Much like our family in one sense and not in so many other ways*, thought Marina when she bought it.

Lucy was so thrilled. For that day Mark was forgotten, or at least pushed to the back of her mind. But tomorrow was Tuesday, market day. When the day arrived her heart was full of hope once again.

The day was bright. Donning coats and hats, Rosa and Lucy set off to town. They had no baskets of vegetables today; today was to be a treat. As well as shopping they were going to the tearoom. The road changed from track to cobbles after a mile, houses becoming more frequent as they walked along chatting as the miles passed. Trees lined the streets as they got nearer to the town centre and once they reached the bridge that straddled over the small stream, they were only a few minutes from the square.

The market was crowded. The hustle and bustle in the square was loud with the voices of people competing with one another. With bread and cheese bought and safely tucked away in the bags, the two of them made their way into the teashop.

A table for two was available by the door and in the window, perfect for viewing the square and watching people. They ordered tea and because of Lucy's birthday they ordered hot buttered teacakes, making it a special treat.

They were chatting when he came in, so they didn't see him until he was there standing by their table. Mark had seen them through the window of the tearoom and decided on the spur of the moment to take a chance. Not knowing just what he was going to say to them, he made his move. Hearing the tinkle of the bell as he pushed open the door, he was met by the delicious smell of baking and newly made bread. Then he was standing next to them, and splurged out the first thing that came into his head.

"Hello, I saw you through the window." He smiled and went on. "I thought I would let you know that we will be taking a stall in the fete.

We will have new scented candles on sale, for the Christmas trade really," Mark continued. "But we want to get in first. I do hope we will see you there."

Rosa was so surprised at his flat-out cheek, she found herself nodding and thanking him for the information.

Lucy's heart had done a double somersault when she looked up and saw him standing there and she was so pleased to see him that she forgot her shyness. Somehow she must get to talk to him alone. Seeing Rosa was nonplussed with his boldness, she took advantage of the situation and asked him if he could help them with carrying a new mangle they were to purchase after tea; anything to have him near for a little longer. Poor Rosa was quite taken aback.

She had been outwitted. The ironmonger was off to the right of the square and Rosa had booked the carter to take them back to the house. If he could just help carry it to the carters for them they would be forever in his debt.

"I would be more than happy to help," he replied, looking at Lucy.

Still in the middle of taking tea, Rosa felt she had no option other than to ask him to join them. Thanking her, he pulled up a chair.

Well, it couldn't do any harm, she thought. *I'm here watching over Lucy. What harm can it do? But what am I going to tell Marina?* His aura today had changed again and Rosa found it difficult to read him. After a few minutes of small talk, snippets of local news, the three of them chatted in natural conversation.

Rosa found he was easy to be with and after a few minutes she relaxed and started to enjoy his company. They chatted about the festival and talked of all the family walking into town to enjoy the fun. The festival lasted a week; it was the highlight of the year for the town.

Mark's father was opening the event. Mark was really keen to have some time off for the opening ceremony; the rest of the week he would have to assist in the store or on the stall. His mother and brother would be expected to help out too. Thinking that he had made good progress in establishing a rapport with Rosa, he asked, "I would like to show you good ladies around the shows after the opening. There should be coconut shies, roll the pennies and hoopla. Say yes, and we can fix a time to suit."

Rosa could not agree to anything without Marina's permission and anyway, she was not sure whether it was right to encourage a meeting.

Oh my lord! Thought Rosa. *This is all happening too fast.*

Answering straight away, she smiled, not wanting to give offence. Then as graciously as she could, she thanked him and declined, saying that all the aunts and Lucy's mother had planned to come into town but at present they had not settled on the arrangements and didn't know whether they would be there for the opening ceremony.

For a moment Lucy had hoped that being chaperoned would have been enough to see him again. That hope shattered, she was bereft. It was at that moment she decided she would find a way to see him; she was sixteen, they couldn't treat her like a child anymore.

If Mark was disappointed he didn't show it. Instead, he nodded and said, "Another time perhaps." He put his hand subconsciously over his trouser pocket. Tucked inside it was a letter he had been carrying around for two weeks, a letter inviting a secret meeting between Lucy and himself. Somehow he must give it to her today.

Leaving the tearoom, they chatted as they walked to the ironmongers. Mark, attentive to Rosa, never once looked at Lucy who walked on his right side. Occupied with Rosa on his left, he slipped the letter into Lucy's hand. Rosa never saw it pass between them.

The ride back from the town seemed to take forever for Lucy, sat up front in between the carter and Rosa, being jostled as the cartwheels turned over the rough road. It was a nightmare.

Lucy could feel the letter deep in her pocket. Touching it gently with her fingertips, she was imagining what he might have written to her and she couldn't wait to be alone and read it.

The mangle they had bought was tied by ropes in the middle of the open cart along with other pieces that the carter would deliver on his way back to town. Reaching home while the weather was still fine was a godsend, and it was a relief when the horses pulled the cart to a full stop in front of their front door. Rosa called to Nora and Emma, who were tending the front garden, and between them and the carter, they negotiated the new mangle through the house and into the scullery next to the outhouse.

Lucy had already disappeared as soon as the cart had stopped. It did cross Rosa's mind that it was not like her not to offer help, but perhaps the bumpy ride had given her a headache. After all, it had been quite a day, meeting up with the boy and the cheek of him. She smiled in spite of herself; he really was quite likeable. Rosa sighed, as it also was a day that she would have to share the event with Marina. How would she take it?

Back in her room with her door firmly shut, Lucy pulled out the letter from her coat pocket, carefully turning it over in her hands, almost afraid to open it. She found her hands were slightly shaking in anticipation. Using her thumb, she slipped it under the buff-coloured corner of the envelope and tore it open. Pulling out the folded letter, she realised that she was quite breathless with excitement as she slowly unfolded it to reveal the neat printed words.

Sitting on the edge of the bed, she couldn't know that Louis was watching her as she unfolded the sheet of paper and started to read.

> *My dearest,*
> *From the moment I saw you I knew we were destined to be*
> *together.*
> *I think of you constantly, remembering the softness of your skin*
> *and your beautiful blue eyes.*
> *I can only hope that you might feel as I do, my darling.*
> *In hope of this, please meet me.*
> *I will wait by the bridge outside the town each Tuesday from*
> *7.00pm hoping you come to me. Please come to me, my love, I need you.*
> *Yours,*
> *Mark*

Lucy fell backwards on the bed, laughing to herself. Her heart was flying; he loved her, she knew it. Clutching the letter to her breast, her face was beaming with light and she felt her heart would burst with joy.

Now she had to find an excuse to leave the house next Tuesday and go to him. Suddenly she pulled herself up. The letter mustn't be found. If her mother got wind of it, all would be lost. But where could she put it? It must be somewhere where no one would find it. Her mother or Rosa would put her clean laundered clothes away into her chest of drawers, so that was out of the question.

The idea of putting it in a book, hidden in plain sight, was the ideal place. No one read novels except her and Jane Austin's *Pride and Prejudice* lay on her bed, ready to receive it. That would be where she would hide it.

Louis was intrigued about what was in the letter that delighted Lucy so much. He had glimpsed it but was unable to read it, but he was aware it was from Mark, the boy that had been the cause of so many tears that Lucy had shed. When he was alone he would find out! He was suddenly distracted by the noise coming up from downstairs.

He had heard the women downstairs laughing, seemingly teasing Rosa about her new purchase.

"You're going to take in washing, are you?" they scoffed. "What are you going to do with all the time you'll have on your hands now you have the newest fangled help?"

Rosa picked up a broom and chased her cheeky friends out into the garden. "Don't think you will be getting off helping me! No help, no clean washing!" But she was smiling too.

Louis loved the laughter and warmth in the house but he hated the way they earned a living and feared for them. Surely the time had come when they could retire. All of them had a little money put by. The physical and emotional scars the ladies had had mostly healed. Not one of them could alter the past, memories would last a lifetime for them, but as time went on the memories came back less frequently. The women were still relatively young, all under thirty-five. Time to find new lives and have their own families, if that was written in their destiny.

Louis moved onto the landing, heading for the stairs, when he heard mutterings coming from Rosa's room and Marina's voice, loud in shock. "The cheeky beggar!"

Passing through the door, Louis was confronted with the two ladies deep in conversation. The chill in the air that came with Louis went unnoticed.

"He really came in and made himself familiar?" asked Marina.

"I told you he did," replied Rosa. "I've told you everything now. I've got to say, I rather like him but I don't know if I trust him," she said firmly. Shaking her head, she went on. "He's immature and over-confident. Lucy could be awfully hurt by him but to see her look at him, well, he could make her happy too. Need I go on?"

Distressed as she was, Marina knew she could not lock her girl up. After all, what was happening was perfectly natural, nature being what it was. Hadn't she felt the same once upon a time? But what were this boy's intentions? She had trusted Robert with her heart and body and he had betrayed her. Was Mark to be trusted?

"What are we to do?" asked Marina, a tear rolling down her cheek. She swallowed hard, trying to stop the sobs that were trying to push up to the surface. "What the hell are we going to do?"

"We watch over her, guard and guide her. The longer we can keep them apart the better. If they are meant to be together, well, so be it, he'll wait for her another year or two until she is eighteen," said Rosa.

Louis nodded in agreement. Rosa was looking at him and seemed to include him in the plan.

However, Louis felt it was time to speak to Marina. He would join with her when she slept that night; he would visit her and plead with her to change her way of earning her living. Today had changed their lives, whether they knew it or not. Lucy was a young woman starting out on life's journey. She should not have to bear the disgrace and dishonour that would come if the secret of the house became known. Marina and the girls must change for the sake of the future. Lucy's life needed to be cared for and planned.

Lucy had put together her own plan to meet Mark. Lucy decided she must go for a walk every night after dinner regardless of the weather. She would pretend to be restless. The aunts and Marina would get used to her going for an evening stroll; by the time Tuesday came around again, going for a walk would be accepted as normal. She nodded to herself in approval. She must contain her impatience until she met him on Tuesday week.

As the evening approached Marina put her fears to one side, it was time to dress up for the part she had played for the past few years as the madam of the establishment.

It had been a pleasant enough day. The weather had kept fine and although a fine veil of cloud covered the sky, it had been warm. Had it not been for the news Rosa brought back, the day would have been perfect. Now the evening meal was over and all cleared away ready for morning, Nora, Emma and Roni prepared themselves for the evening work and their regular clients. Marina too climbed the stairs up to her room to change into the clothes and padding that served as a disguise and hid her true self from the evening world.

As she pushed open the bedroom door she felt weary, a weight lay on her shoulders and she wasn't sure what to do. Lucy was laid on the bed, book in hand as usual. Marina was all ready to speak to her daughter and went quietly over to the bed and touched her gently.

"Yes, Mum, is something wrong?" asked Lucy, looking up from her book.

"Not really, my angel, just that Rosa told me of your meeting in the town with that boy called Mark." Marina went on, "I understand he wanted to meet up with you at the festival in August. I was thinking what was best for you and, providing you are chaperoned at all times, I see no harm in seeing him every now and again. But be very careful what you tell him about us. Most folk would condemn us for earning a living the way we do."

"But you're good people, you don't harm anyone. I can't imagine Mark would judge you. He seems so kind and thoughtful, I'm sure."

Marina cut Lucy's sentiments short. "You're a silly girl who has led a sheltered life; what do you know of life out there? The dishonesty, the cunning, the slyness that men will use to get what they want."

"No Mum, he's not like that. This is not about you. I won't make your mistake." She retorted back to her mum. Flinging herself off the bed, she threw the book down on top of the white damask bedspread in an attempt to make her point, but to her horror she saw the corner of the illicit letter move out from the hardback cover. *God! Don't let her see it*, thought Lucy in panic. Lucy made a grab for the book, pushing the letter back inside the leaf before Marina could see it, shoving the book and its contents back into the deep pockets of her skirt. Relief passed through her body but she was angry too. *Do they think I am still a little baby?* she thought, as she flounced out of the bedroom in a huff.

There is always a slight chill in the air these days, Marina thought as she undressed, laying the pretty print bodice and skirt over the back of a chair. Opening her wardrobe, she took down the black robes from the hook there and proceeded to make herself a madam. Dressed, her hair newly frizzed around her face, hard black lines on eyes and brows, she took up the red rouge and smeared it across her lips. The creature that looked back at her from the mirror hid her nicely. For a long time she had subconsciously hated opening up her home to be used for carnal pleasures. She hoped that when she did go to town, no one would recognise her. Up to now that had proved so.

Louis had seen the transformation many times over the months he had been there. Funnily enough, he always respected her and Lucy's privacy. If he was about upstairs when Marina dressed, he preferred to go back into his own kingdom even though he knew she couldn't see him.

He had watched Lucy's little paddy and seen the letter poking from the book she had thrown down. The letter he had wanted to read was now out of his reach in Lucy's pocket. Perhaps an opportunity would present itself later when the ladies were asleep.

TUESDAY EVENING

Nora was the first down that evening; she could hear Emma and Roni still upstairs getting ready. Marina came next into the sitting room, the room where the ladies waited for the tapping on the side door. The three small client bedrooms were ready, oil lamps lit and fresh flowers from the garden on the bedside tables. Rosa had changed the bed linen. Her working day over, she took herself off to bed.

It was 9.30pm when the first client tapped on the side door. Nora recognised the rhythm being played on the door.

"I'll get it," she said, standing up to let her 'John' in.

She liked this man. For six years he had visited her, a widower whose wife had died in childbirth, leaving him bereft, not only losing his love but also the baby son they had both hoped for. He was kind but lonely. His three daughters were now in their late teens. They helped in his bakery and although they gave him company, he missed making love; 'that closeness and pleasure that can only be reached with a woman', he had said.

He paid Nora well, more than she asked for, and that was a great deal. Nora was his expensive mistress and the only woman he made love to now. With Nora he could enjoy the sweetness of a womanly body without the complications of marriage.

She greeted him with a smile and a light kiss on his cheek. Taking him by the hand, she led him through the drawing room to her room. Once inside the room in comparative privacy, they sat on the edge of the bed.

It had become something of a ritual; he loved to take the combs and hairpins out of her tresses, undoing the coil of hair at the nape of her neck, unravelling the long auburn hair through his fingers until it framed her face and hung loose down her back. Kissing her eyes and cheeks and taking her face gently in his hands, he kissed her long and hard on the lips. Moving her hair over to lie on her left shoulder, he kissed her neck just below her ear, using her erogenous zone to his advantage. She melted against him. He started to undress her; as always at this point, he could feel himself becoming aroused. For the next hour or so they would indulge in foreplay before hitting the climax and satisfaction.

Later emerging from the love nest, Nora was aware that Emma and Roni were at work; both doors were shut and some laughter and jollification had filtered through the walls as 'John' and she were dressing.

Taking the money from the bedside table, she ushered her client back to the drawing room where Marina sat waiting patiently. A glass of wine was waiting, a nightcap to help the clients on their way. A little small talk, a little drink to keep it friendly, and clients would come back, that was Marina's policy.

After showing 'John' out and thanking him for his generosity, saying she would see him soon, Nora came back to the drawing room.

Business was good in the evenings after market day. The market started early in the morning and the men, having stood all day selling their goods, were ready to relax and escape from the hectic day come the evening.

With pockets full of cash and a need to relieve the tensions, the men couldn't think of a better way to do it than have a few beers and a trip to the house on the edge of town. Baker, Butcher, Lawyer, Bootmaker and Corn Merchant could be found making their way to Marina's one time or another, coming to her gate by foot, horse or cart in the late evening. Under the cover of darkness was when Marina heard tapping on her door. These men were the regular 'Johns'; men that had no names, nor families, anonymous and protected in Marina's world. Clients were protected and her girls were the souls of discretion.

There were other houses of ill repute in the town. Men met up with women at the Old Post Inn off the square. Men were propositioned and taken on to shabby houses that were less than clean, solicited by the women in rooms hardly fit for use. These were not for Marina's customers. Her clients were men of substance who valued the discretion that she provided.

16

One such man called 'Richard' was a regular of Emma's and he turned up that night full of himself and bringing with him an old school chum that he knew from way back. Nearly forty years had gone by since the men had last met. They were both in high spirits, laughing at the smallest joke they shared, slapping each other on the back as men do in bonding together. The illegal cockfight in the backyard of the Old Bull Inn that night had brought them more money than they had seen in many a year.

A group of local men gathered after closing time in the yard and friends had joined them. The noise and the excitement that buzzed around that enclosed space, and the good humour that came with a few bottles of beer, raised a further few notches when the cockfights began. The bloody and violent fight between the cockerels, armed with sharp knife stirrups attached to their legs by leather thongs, had proved both exhilarating and very lucrative for them by the end of the evening.

After several fights and seeing the birds attack each other until they were either injured or dead, the sleek black cockerel with the blood red comb stood tall and proud; both men wagered heavily on it and it won. Still excited from the fights and the large sum they had won, they promised to reacquaint their friendship and catch up on all the lost years. They sought to make a night of it with some soft, amiable girls.

'Richard' knew of just the place and after a couple of beers, they borrowed a horse and cart and they found their way to Marina's. Emma had opened the door to the knock of 'Richard'; both men stood on the threshold grinning from ear to ear, looking for the world like little boys. *Fifty-year-olds going on seven*, thought Emma. She almost laughed herself at the sight of them, their arms wrapped around each other's necks, smiles from ear to ear and eager to come in to take pleasure. And although Marina had said they would not allow strangers into the premises, Emma's man was a well-known regular and he vouched for his friend.

The excitement that vibrated around the room was palatable as the two men babbled about their good fortune. They were introduced to Roni by Marina, who then saw fit to let this friend of 'Richard' know that this was her establishment and she had rules. The man was full of affability; butter would not melt in his mouth. Marina was satisfied.

With introductions over, 'Richard' was taken by Emma through the door of the drawing room and up the passage to her 'office', as she liked to think of it, Roni took 'Richard's friend John' to her own pleasant room opposite the one now in use by Nora. Giggling and laughter carried on for some time until at last the couples got down to business.

By then Nora and her man had had a pleasing hour; even she had enjoyed this sweet man. She had lost her fear of men and this man was kind and treated her very well. She had feelings for him that she kept locked up in her heart, and she could not help looking forward to seeing him every week. In her heart of hearts she would not have been unhappy to keep herself just for him.

Bright jade coloured curtains hung in the drawing room, keeping the dark out and covering the small paned window that during the day gave a splendid view of the soft purple-blue hills in the distance. A small table set with six small wine glasses and a bottle of red wine stood waiting to give the gents a nightcap before they left the premises. Two dark green armchairs sat empty each side of a red sofa that held the patiently waiting Marina and Nora. Overhead a large oil lamp gave a warm light to the intimate room.

Waiting in the drawing room, Marina and Nora passed the time talking about new fashions they had discovered in the new issue of the *Lady* magazine. Marina could not read well but loved to see the illustrations of the dresses, hats and shoes in the advertisements.

They sat in comfortable companionship waiting until the business of the night was finished. They waited until the satisfied men came out ready to return home, then they could finally lock up and go to their own beds.

All had been quiet for some time; the night had been slower than usual, it being market day, and the ladies were looking for an early night.

Lucy had come back from a short walk some time ago and had retired to her bed in a much better mood. The walk had done her good; Marina had some misgivings about her going out after dusk, but Lucy had promised not to go far and said that she felt restless and that the night air would do her good. Lucy had returned with a bloom in her cheeks and a smile on her face, much to the relief of Marina, who hated to have disharmony in the house.

It was after eleven and both the women were starting to feel the rigors of the day catching up with them.

Suddenly startled by a half-strangled cry coming from beyond the drawing room, Nora and Marina were instantly alert. The cry came from one of the girls' rooms, then a loud coarse voice was interjected with a sob that came after.

"You bugger!" the man exclaimed. "You bloody whore, I don't pay any bloody woman that sort of money for a f—k."

"Oh my God! We have a rogue," cried Marina loudly, jumping to her feet. "We best deal with it."

Marina and Nora were through into the passage in a stride, just as the door of Roni's room half-opened; she appeared partly dressed and was trying to get through the small opening. Her hands clutched at the door, desperately trying to hang on to it so to propel herself from the room to safety. A man's hand appeared, grabbing her hair and pulling her back into the room by it. Roni screamed again, her hands tearing at his, trying to stop her hair being torn from the roots by this thug.

Louis was at rest. Not that he needed to rest, but somehow when night came it seemed natural to get comfortable and close his eyes. There would be no activity to share during the night; what else would he do?

At the first half-scream he became alert. Had he heard what he thought he had? Perhaps an owl roosting in a tree had made the noise, and for a moment he settled back into the sofa he was on.

The shout from Marina and the scream from Roni brought him to his feet and at a run he passed through the door and was down the stairs in a trice.

Marina and Nora were already in the small bedroom trying to control a man who was bent double over the frightened figure of Roni, her arms defensively over her face, desperately trying to save it from raining blows that struck down on her from her attacker. Nora grabbed his upper arm and Marina his other, but it was like trying to hold down an elephant. They were being thrown to one side like rag dolls.

Nobody felt the blast of icy air that blew through the room on Louis's arrival, seething with anger at seeing a woman being thrashed by a bully. Roni, only half-dressed in white cotton underwear, had taken the foetal position, spots of blood were spattered on her loose bodice. Louis could just see a cut oozing blood over her left eye. The man was like a maniac keeping up a rhythm, beating down on her like a mechanical piece of equipment. She would be badly hurt if this continued.

Adrenaline pumped through the man's half-naked body. He wore no shirt, no shoes or socks; his trousers were caught at his waist by a thick leather belt fastened by a heavy brass buckle. His muscular arms and broad back betrayed his occupation as a manual worker.

A man with no compassion or mercy it seemed, wrapped up in his anger he saw no one but his victim. His strength doubled with each punch that hit on target. All the while Roni curled tighter in a ball, trying to make herself as small as possible.

Louis took the man by both arms, twisting them high up his back, and thrusted him out of the room. The man, who was bent double, was thrown head first against the hall wall with great force. He landed in the narrow passageway in a dazed heap before rolling over and forcing himself up into a sitting position with his back pressed against the wallpaper.

Though no one could see, Louis stood tall over what he regarded as a piece of rubbish laying at his feet and he was ready to do combat again if it was needed.

Marina and Nora were dumbfounded with what they had seen; it just wasn't possible. The air they breathed was icy. Goosebumps stood on their skin and the hairs on their arms also stood on end.

"What happened? That's what I want to know," said Marina in a low and shaky voice. She was almost afraid to speak normally to the white-faced Nora who, having retrieved Roni from the floor, sat down heavily on the bed next to her.

Marina moved to the door, looking down on the man who had his head on his knees, obviously dazed and maybe even concussed.

Checking Roni over, Nora gently helped her sobbing friend into bed, covering her with the light cotton sheet.

"You'll be all right, we'll soon have you cleaned up and on the mend," said Nora kindly.

Noise in the passage brought Nora to the door beside Marina. Two other faces appeared from Emma's doorway.

"God almighty, what's happened here?" Richard looked on the scene in disbelief; his friend sitting totally dishevelled propped against the wall, half-dressed.

Roni had staggered from her bed to her door, her face cut and blooded, with angry bruises already showing on her neck and shoulders. She leaned against the doorjamb looking as though she was on the verge of collapse. Marina moved to her side quickly, steadying her with her arm around her waist, and helped her once more back to bed.

Anger welling up inside of her, Marina responded to 'Richard'.

"Go! Go back into your room, we're seeing to this," she shouted "This devil you brought here has done this to my girl. Get yourself dressed and away. Don't ever come back, you'll never be welcome here again. Emma will see you out."

With that, she gently turned Roni back into the bedroom, calling Nora to go and get the medicine chest and water to treat her.

There was no retort, no answer to Marina. The door shut and 'Richard' quickly dressed, embarrassed and filled with guilt. The elation he had come in with had well and truly dissipated. For the last time, he lay his money down on the bedside table, sadly shaking his head; he would miss Emma. His so-called friend had always had a temper and was a bit of a bully in the schoolyard when they were young. Richard remembered that now, sadly too late for Roni. And now he was barred. The night had not ended well.

Nora made her way back to Roni carrying the medicine chest in one hand and a small bowl of water in the other. She was shocked; they almost never had violent customers. In all the time she had spent with Marina, only a handful of unpleasant incidents had happened and none like this.

She remembered the fear she had had as a girl, beaten regularly until she had fled from home. The horrors of it came flooding back. Shaking herself back to the reality, she crossed the drawing room and stepped up the passage just as the man staggered to his feet. He was shaking his head as though he was trying to clear his mind. One hand was on the wall as he steadied himself, the other firmly on his forehead as he lifted his head and locked eyes onto Nora. His face looked puzzled and then his eyes bulged at the shock of the sight of her.

Nora gasped, dropping the chest, scattering its contents all over the passage floor. She covered her mouth with her free hand, a whimper came from behind her hand at her mouth.

"Marina, it's my dad."

Her face drained of colour. Marina, hearing the chest drop to the floor, had come to the doorway and heard the words spoken so softly. One look at Nora's face and she could see the shock and fear registered there.

George suddenly rallied; his daughter, that little bitch who left him, was here, standing there right in front of him.

"Oh yes! That's right, and in a brothel." He laughed, the sound Nora would remember for the rest of her life. There was no levity there, it was a laugh that froze her blood. She was suddenly rooted to the spot, unable to move or speak and still holding the bowl of water.

"You shifty bitch, so this is where you have been hiding. Quite right, too," he sneered. "I always knew what you were. A bloody little whore not fit to live." He screamed out the words as he lunged for her, his hands grasping tightly around her neck, squeezing the life out of her. The bowl fell and shattered, pieces of pottery flew everywhere and the warm water spilt around their feet, though neither felt it.

Marina was out of Roni's bedroom at the sound of breaking crockery, half sliding on the water, and collided with them, but George's hold on Nora held fast. Marina rained her fists down on George's bare back, trying to divert his attention and make him break the vice-like grip he had on Nora, but to no avail.

Nora's knees were buckling. Her hands were trying to release George's hands on her neck; they dropped to her side as consciousness was leaving her. Her face was turning red and her eyes had starting to bulge as she feebly fought to breathe.

The adrenaline pumped, coursing through George's veins, making him four times stronger than his normal self. Marina could not move him.

"He's going to kill her," Marina wailed.

Stepping forward and taking action again, Louis took hold of George's head, pulling it to one side with his hands, and covered his nostrils and mouth with invisible hands. He pressed as hard as he could and held it tight. This time George couldn't breathe and his head was locked in a vice. He felt the grip on his neck but could see nothing and feel nothing. Gripped by panic, he tried to move the unseen hands that were choking him, releasing Nora as he did.

She fell to the floor gasping for breath. Her eyes were closed but she was still conscious and clutching her damaged neck. Marina was quickly at her side and, half-lifting the girl, she moved her out of the reach of the man who a moment ago was trying to kill her but now appeared to be dancing.

His head was at a funny angle and his face becoming ruddy. Marina was not sure what she was seeing. It was all too impossible, what was going on?

George kicked wildly backwards then forwards, trying to displace this force that was slowly killing him. But George could not see or feel anything that was real. Kicking out his feet, he tried to kick the force that felt remarkably like a man restraining him, but the blows just passed through Louis's ghostly frame while he held on tight, not letting up his grip. As George got weaker, his body became heavier and he was starting to slump into a heap. At that point Louis threw him against the wall with force. George slammed his head against it and this time he slid down, unconscious.

Louis stepped back. Passion had done it again. What had happened was a natural response for most men, but he was not mortal, and it suddenly dawned on him that his anger and fear had brought him as near to being mortal as he had ever been. But in saving Roni and Nora he had exposed the household to his ghostly world. Louis, in the heat of the moment, had forgotten he was a ghost, and even one with powers might not be understood.

He must connect with Rosa.

A shocked Marina took Nora into the bedroom where she sat down shakily on the bed that Roni was occupying. Marina looked at her friends, one beaten and the other half-choked. How could this happen here in her home?

Anger raged in her breast. That bloody man. Life would never be the same in this house now. Fear would come with every tapping on the door.

"Oh! How can I make this place safe again?"

Thank God her girl was asleep upstairs and had been spared the awfulness of the situation.

George's clothes lay where he had discarded them when undressing. Her anger increased seeing them; she wanted him gone and quickly. She bundled the shirt, socks and shoes that belonged to George in a pile then she rifled through his jacket pocket until she found the winning cash that he had boasted about. She took out only what was owed to Roni before replacing it back in the inside jacket pocket.

The money, she placed on the side table, smiling at Roni. She nodded and spoke more to herself than to George's victim.

"You deserve that payment, by God you do." Then she left the room, carrying the clothes out to the passage where George still lay unconscious. 'Richard' simultaneously came out from Emma's room into the passage and they met by the unconscious man.

"Get him out of here," Marina told 'Richard', "before I kill him myself." She turned and gave Emma, who was now stood behind 'Richard', the shoes and clothes she carried.

Grabbing an arm and lifting him under his armpit, Marina indicated to 'Richard' to take his other side and between the two of them, they dragged and half-carried him to the side door. 'Richard' then hoisted him over his shoulder and carried him out to the cart, dropping him none too gently onto the wooden deck.

Coming back to collect George's clothes from Emma, 'Richard' tried to apologise for the awful mess he had inadvertently brought to the house. His plea and apology fell on deaf ears.

Bathed and bandaged, Roni was served with hot sweet tea back in her own room upstairs. It would take some time for the bruises to go but Marina wondered how long it would take before the mental scars would heal. That was anyone's guess.

Marina shivered. Things were not going well. She wondered just what fate had got in store for her and for no reason, she suddenly found herself trembling.

17

When the morning came, Marina woke up troubled. How much sleep she had had was debatable. Questions had run around in her head all night, so many questions that needed to be answered. The strange happenings of the night before could have no logical explanation. What she had seen happen to George just wasn't possible, and yet it had happened. Magic was no answer yet she didn't believe in ghosts, but what else could explain it? She didn't want to believe in the supernatural or magic, but what was left?

Rosa and Lucy had slept through the incident of the previous night. At breakfast the next morning they were surprised that only Marina and Emma were at the table when they came down. Not wanting to scare Lucy, Marina played the whole thing down, but Rosa was aware that Marina was holding back.

Louis also appeared at breakfast, propping up the wall near the table and looking at Rosa with certain intensity. She could see the emotion that showed on his face.

As Marina recounted the story he nodded in agreement from time to time, but she left out the strange happenings that affected George and was careful to keep the information about him being Nora's father well out of the explanation.

There was still much to tell and he needed time with Rosa to keep her in the know. Breakfast over and the table cleared, it was time to see to the house.

It wasn't long after that that Rosa found herself being followed by Louis around the house. She realised that he was looking for a moment to talk to her but she was intent on finishing the chores before finding a quiet place to talk.

Marina also wanted to talk to Rosa and she too followed Rosa, helping as they went through the rooms, it wasn't until the invalids were seen to and Lucy given a few chores to keep her busy that Rosa felt able to get out into the garden and was cornered by Marina on one side of her and Louis on the other.

"Well, have you time to talk now Rosa?" she asked "I'm not going insane, please God, but last evening I—" she stammered, "I started seeing things," spluttered Marina. "He, that man who hurt Nora and Roni, was Nora's father. When we heard Roni scream, Nora and me went to help her. He was beating her but when we tried to help – well! – he was too strong for us and we were pushed away like rag dolls. Then the strangest thing happened. The man George, Nora's father, put his arms up his back and threw himself at the wall in the hallway." She continued, "It was crazy. Roni was hurt but, thank goodness, not badly. This wild man then got up and attacked Nora. Look, let's sit on the bench, I think my knees are going to give way."

Sitting down on the garden bench, she took a deep breath and continued. "Well, as I was saying, you won't believe it. This man went for Nora, screaming at her, he had her by the throat. Lord! I thought he would kill her. Well, what do you think? Suddenly he was doing this dance like kicking his legs. Holding his head at a funny angle and turning red, just as Nora had done when he was strangling her. Then he threw himself back on the wall and knocked himself senseless."

Marina's voice was reduced to a whisper and her eyes filled with tears. "It's not right. It's not. Is the house haunted? Lord! I don't know what to think!"

"Oh, my dear friend," Rosa took Marina in her arms, trying to comfort her, all the time looking at Louis who was nodding, confirming Marina's story and conveying to Rosa that it was his hand that was in all of this.

"Do you remember you told me a story about a guardian angel in your dream?" asked Rosa. She felt Marina nod against her.

"Well, it may seem far-fetched," said Rosa, "but do you think he could have stepped in to help?"

Marina sat back. Her face had a puzzled expression across it as she looked back at Rosa.

"Do you really think so? My guarding angel?" she said hopefully.

"I don't know, really I don't, but what other explanation could there be?" Rosa answered, but she was looking beyond to Louis, a pleading look upon her face. What else could she say?

Marina was happy to grab hold of an explanation, however far-fetched. Any explanation was better than the alternative that was madness. Nora had seen it too. They couldn't both be going mad, could they? It was some comfort that they had both seen the happening together and the thought of some sort of guardian was the only explanation. She suddenly relaxed.

Louis smiled. It was a good outcome. If he was recognised as a guardian angel that could help Marina and the family from time to time, that pleased him. It meant that for the first time since he died, he had become part of the family.

Marina had decided to put away her disguise; her padding, the rouge and heavy eyeliner. Since the episode with George and Roni, it seemed she was under a false assumption that by playing it tough she would have no trouble in her house; it clearly was not the case.

Life would never be the same after the attack on Roni. The door was firmly closed to all visitors for the time being. It took over a week for the ladies of the house to settle down after that dreadful night. Life in the house carried on but without its usual laughter. They all were really stunned by the events and a dark brooding affected them all.

Roni was laid up in her bedroom; her nerves were shot. She burst into tears at regular intervals throughout the day for no apparent reason. She was in a state of shock from what had happened to her and what could have happened to her. The thought overwhelmed her as she thought over and over again that she could have been killed.

The money she had been able to save might just be enough to open a tearoom like the one in town. If she stayed here, she realised she could be putting her life at risk again. Her future was unsure. Finding a secure solution was now in the forefront of her mind. Now she must plan ahead.

Nora was nursing a bruised neck and had a very husky voice from her damaged throat, but her throat was the least of her concerns. Her brute of a father had found her after all these years. Fate was so unkind. Now he knew where she lived and he had tried to kill her. His hatred for her terrified her the most, but the question was would he come back for her and try again?

Her experience of last night was something she couldn't make any sense of. How she had survived being strangled and been rescued from her father's attack was a mystery. One minute she was fighting for breath and on the verge of oblivion, the next she was released and it was her father who was fighting for his breath. He was dancing like a hanging man before crashing into the wall unconscious. It was as if some outside power had taken charge of the situation and saved her from the hands of her murderous father.

Had God intervened? She wasn't religious and believed in nothing, at least until now. It seemed there was no other explanation, so for now she would just be grateful to a higher power that had helped her, a power that she really didn't understand.

There was nothing she could do but wait and see if her life would change, and for the time being she must stay put until she thought through all the implications that last night had brought. But change was on the way, she could feel it and it frightened her. Her life had been good here, but had the time come to move on?

There had been no trips to town for two weeks now. The market days came and went. It was only when provisions started to get very low that Rosa decided to go into the town.

When Lucy realised that Rosa was off shopping to the town, she was very keen to go too but all the pleading in the world fell on deaf ears. Rosa declined her company.

"You're needed at home to help your mum and Emma with the chores; after all, they're two pairs of hands light with Nora and Roni being unwell."

That didn't stop Lucy trying once more to change Rosa's mind, but the look on Rosa's face and her shaking her head told Lucy she wouldn't win and she accepted Rosa's decision.

The ache in Lucy's heart wouldn't go away. She had been suffering for days; she was so desperate to see Mark even if it was only at a distance. Rosa had guessed the reason for Lucy's insistence and would have none of it.

Slighted and discontent with Rosa's firmness on the subject, Lucy decided to make her own arrangements and immediately planned to slip away after supper and see him. The eager words of his letter seared into her memory and she would meet him by the bridge and they would be alone. She was already trembling with excitement at the thought.

The day was never-ending. She scrubbed the kitchen table and floor in the morning soon after Rosa had left for town, but it was hot. The garden looked so inviting bathed in the sun, the grass shimmering emerald green as a light breeze tried without success to cool the day down. After a quick bite of bread and cheese for lunch, Marina agreed to Lucy working in the garden with the express order to tidy up the vegetable plot and pick beans and carrots for the evening meal. How lovely it was to be in the sun. She wore her straw hat with the deep brim to protect her head from the heat and it shaded her eyes from the glare of the sun.

She had been working for about an hour when she first heard it, a sort of funny hissing sound coming over from behind her from the beech hedge that surrounded the garden.

Pisssss. There it was again. Looking up, she could just see the white of a handkerchief and part of a hand showing above the beech leaves.

"No, it couldn't be, could it?" she said to herself, her heart racing and forgetting all the warnings from her mother about strangers and men. She moved quickly and quietly over to the spot where she had seen the hand, hoping that it could only be one person.

Louis was half laid out on the garden bench; he had been watching Lucy at work for some time. She was a lovely young girl and a credit to

Marina. Strong both in body and spirit, a willing hand to work hard for the benefit of the household.

The sound caught him by surprise when it came. After the second time he heard it and saw the fluttering of white, he was fully alert. Suspicious after the commotion of two weeks ago, he was on his feet immediately and moved over the lawn quickly, following Lucy to the spot where the noise had come from, and stood beside her. She felt a chill in the air at once but supposed it to be the breeze passing through the branches, or maybe it was because she was standing in the shade of the hedge.

The hedge was at least three feet wide. From its main structure the branches leafed only on the outer surface, leaving a clear view to the other side if one pulled the leaves to one side. The branches did not want to give and she struggled but her force on them rewarded her, for the face looking back through the hedge was Mark. She felt quite giddy. Happiness filled her heart. Here was the man she constantly dreamed about.

"Mark, what are you doing here?" she said in hushed breath.

"Aren't you pleased to see me?"

"Yes! Of course. Yes, but you shouldn't be here. Someone will see you."

"It's been over two weeks since I've seen you. I have waited for you at the bridge. Are you sick?"

"No. No, not at all."

"I saw your aunt in town today alone. When I saw you weren't with her, I— well, I was worried!"

"Really?" Lucy smiled. "You were worried about me?" Her heart lifted with the thought that he really cared for her.

"I managed to get a few hours off so I came out to try to see you." Mark was surprised at himself; he had wanted to see her but until that moment hadn't realised how much. All this was new to him; he was pursuing a girl! All his adult life it was he that had been pursued by the opposite sex. "When I saw you in the garden it was such a relief," he said wistfully.

"You have to go," pleaded Lucy. "If mother comes out and sees me talking to you, it will mean trouble. I'll meet you tonight after supper at the bridge. Promise." Putting her fingers to her lips, she blew him a kiss.

"I'll be waiting," replied Mark, smiling back at Lucy before turning and quickly walking away.

Well, well, thought Louis, *what do I do? Young love so tender should be cared for, on the other hand what kind of man is he? Lucy wouldn't fall for just anyone, but just how well does she know him?* The two questions needed answers. He would watch Lucy carefully and maybe it was the time to find that letter that Lucy had hidden.

Supper was a quiet affair. Rosa was back late from town, which meant that supper was later than usual. Roast chicken and fresh vegetables from the garden were eaten in silence, except for Lucy who injected some warmth around the table. She was the bright star in the gloomy kitchen. Only Marina noticed Lucy bolting her food down; she was glad that Lucy had a good healthy appetite. It never crossed her mind that her daughter had an appointment that she wasn't going to miss.

"Going for a bit of a walk, Mum," called Lucy from the hall, pulling on her boots, coat and hat while her mother still sat at the table with all the ladies. "I need to walk off some of that dinner, back soon."

Before Marina could answer, Lucy was out the door, slamming it behind her.

"Well, would you believe it? She eats like a horse and then needs a walk," remarked Marina, feeling somewhat out-manoeuvred by her daughter. She hadn't even said goodbye.

Lucy's face glowed as she walked down the road in the soft sunlight, knowing that each footstep took her nearer to Mark. Each step seemed lighter as she walked to the bridge and to their secret meeting place. There would be daylight for at least another two hours, which would be plenty of time to meet and get back home before dark. Passing the few houses on the outskirts of town, she made her way down the broad dirt track avenue that was lined with trees until it ended abruptly, making way for the irregular cobbles that started the road that led into the town centre.

Streets soon appeared on either side of her. Small terraces of cottages built in local stone with thatched roofs and small yards lay on both sides of the cobbled road. Soon they gave way to larger terraced houses with long gardens that were dug over. Vegetables grew in abundance everywhere she looked and each home had a midden that held an ash toilet. Women were out laughing and talking to each other as they took in the washing that had dried in the hot sun that day, children were still in the streets calling each other, playing Whip and Top, Hop Scotch and Tag. The sounds were generally unfamiliar to Lucy but they were sounds she liked. Sometimes she thought that her home was too quiet.

There was an excitement living in a town and she carried that thought along with her as she walked on.

The bridge was not far now with the canal and all its barges and narrow boats. It carried all manner of goods from London to Oxford.

A figure was leaning against the stonewall looking down into the water, distracted by the continuous traffic below.

She was almost beside him before he looked up. He heard footsteps on the narrow pavement and he straightened up, his face breaking into a wide grin when he saw the owner of them.

Lucy suddenly became shy; the excited young woman that had walked almost three miles on clouds was face to face with her dream man. What did she do next?

Lucy was tongue-tied and flustered but Mark took charge of the situation. Gently taking her hand, he pressed it to his lips while looking in her eyes with such caring and affection that Lucy's heart did a double somersault.

"Shall we take a turn on the tow path for a few minutes?" asked Mark. Not waiting for an answer, he guided her towards the steps that led down to the canal.

"I can only stay a few minutes. Sorry, but I have to be back before dark." Resisting his arm, Lucy took a step back to the balustrade of the bridge, her hand clasping the decorative banister.

"You're right, of course, and rather than being late back, I'll walk home with you now," said Mark gallantly.

It was important to get to know this girl; when and where they met didn't matter, just so long as she learned to trust him.

On the walk home they talked of their likes and dislikes, their hopes and dreams, future wishes, but Lucy was careful not to talk about her 'family'. She kept to the story Rosa had told. Fear, for the first time, crept into her heart and instinct told her that honesty would destroy anything that might develop between them.

The last half-mile from home, she insisted she walked on alone, promising that the next market day she would see him, albeit chaperoned. And while he wanted to be alone with her, if that was all that was available to him at this time then so be it. Time was on their side. To rush her would be a disaster.

Before he left her, he gently took her face in his two hands, tilting it up to kiss her forehead, nose and finally her mouth softly, pushing his passion back into his depths, fighting the urge to go further. He must not frighten her. Her love was worth waiting for; better that she gave it freely than he took it in lust.

The walk back to town was strangely lonely for Mark. That, too, was a new experience for him. He had always enjoyed his own company, never needed people, was always self-sufficient. Did he really need Lucy? Was she the one?

She could not remember walking the last half-mile back home; she could only think of the magic of the moment of his kisses. He smelt so good, his hands were strong yet gentle and she could still feel his touch on her face. She arrived home while it was still daylight. Coming into the house, Marina was waiting for her in the drawing room.

"Had a good walk, sweetie pie?" asked Marina. "It's a warm night, let's hope we can sleep."

"I'm off to bed, Mum. I walked almost to town and now I'm tired. See you when you come up," answered Lucy, giving Marina a kiss as she passed her, striding to the stairs. She didn't want to say anymore or share any of the ecstatic feeling she was reeling in. What she needed was her own space, quiet to sort out these new feelings that assaulted her body and mind. Was this what it was like to feel love? She had new longings in her young body, ones she didn't understand.

Marina said nothing more. She had seen that look on Lucy's face and knew it well. It rekindled the memories of her young past; a seed of uncertainty entered her heart and she prayed to no one in particular.

God! Not more trouble, please. She's been out a long time. Could it be she had met him? Not wanting to accuse Lucy or face the unpalatable truth, Marina let her fears go for now, aware she must be more vigilant from now on.

The door opened quietly. Only when it shut did Louis realise Lucy had returned. The girl was slumped against the door looking as though she couldn't move, her eyes closed, her face flushed. She looked for all the world to be in a place where no one could reach her. Suddenly she threw off her coat and hat, twirling around in a small dance as she made her way to the bed. As she went, she picked up her book off the nightstand. The letter was tucked in the front flyleaf. Taking it out like a precious object, she held it to her bosom before opening it up to read again. The room was already growing dark. The night was closing in; the sky, once a delicate blue-grey, was turning fast to pink and grey. Soon it would be dark.

The night lamp was by the bed on the nightstand, ready and waiting to be lit. Raising the glass, she turned up the oil and when it was ready she lit the lamp. Replacing the glass, she adjusted the flame until it gave her the light she needed to read Mark's letter again.

Lying on the bed directly in the lamp's light, she read the words over again. Louis, stood by her side looking over her shoulder, was also reading the letter. He was amused; this letter was a perfect example of what a girl would want to receive as a love note. The question was, was it genuine?

Genuine or not, the happiness Lucy exuded was real enough. She had an extra lightness about her, anyone who knew her could see the change.

And even though she had promised herself to only see Mark in company, love, being what it was, was already driving her to recklessness. The need to feel him close to her again was overpowering, and the memory of the kiss burnt into her soul. She needed to taste his lips again soon.

Mark was politeness itself each time he saw Lucy with her aunt on market days in the square. Whatever deep desires they had for each other were suppressed; only when their eyes met did they reveal the feeling they shared.

The days passed, quickly rolling into weeks and before they knew it, it was September and the autumn fair that Mark had talked about was upon them.

In spite of herself, Rosa liked Mark. Her foreboding about him was swept away by his charm and the ease with which he conducted himself.

By the time the autumn fair arrived she would have no qualms about allowing Mark and Lucy a few minutes alone together. Perhaps it was time to reacquaint herself with the teashop. It seemed such a long time since she had had the opportunity to engage with the waitress and listen to the tittle-tattle as she watched the world go by.

Two days before the opening of the festival, the square became a hive of activity. Many stalls were erected around the square, looking very stylish with bright stripy bunting decorating the front of them. A platform was built for the opening ceremony and it was draped with three large Union Jacks. All was ready; come Saturday, the fair would start. The town council would be up there looking impressive in high collars and dark suits, the mayor in the centre dressed in his regalia, his badge of office and the gold chain with the heraldry of the town emblazoned on it. The white swan was the emblem, dating back to Anglo-Saxon times when Buckinghamshire was known for breeding swans for the crown. A large field behind the square that was used as a cattle market would also be used for the main events. That too was decorated with bunting at the gate and small Union Jacks pinned to some of the animal pens. It was empty now, but sometime soon the farmers would bring their livestock in with feed and water, ready for Saturday and the start of the fair.

SATURDAY

The September festival was always crammed with many people coming in from the outlying farms and villages. Farmers' wives brought cheeses, jams, butter and cream to sell on their hired stalls.

The day that everyone had worked so hard for had arrived. The town crier held forth with great gusto while ringing a large hand bell before announcing the mayor and inviting him to open the event.

The mayor obviously enjoyed hearing his own voice and ignoring the heavy sighs from his audience, went on and on until at the end of a rather lengthy speech he cut a red ribbon and announced the fair open.

Mark stood with his family in front of the podium applauding. Mark always found his father rather embarrassing on these occasions; he could be so pompous, yet he was proud of him at the same time. The family had not always had position and wealth. His father had started with so little but with hard work and with some luck he had built up two good businesses.

Marina, Lucy and Rosa had arrived mid-morning. The opening ceremony had just started and they quickly became part of the crowd around the podium.

Lucy could see Mark standing right at the front with a lady and young boy. *This must be his family*, she thought. He must have felt her eyes on him for he turned around and their eyes met. Both faces broke out into broad smiles, though Lucy, still shy, dropped her eyes immediately. No other acknowledgment was made. The lady on his right turned to see who had caught her son's attention and seeing Marina, Lucy and Rosa somewhere at the back of the crowd, saw fit to nod in recognition but with no warmth and lacking a smile. She quickly turned back to the podium and paid all her attention to her husband.

When the ceremonies were over, Mark would have two hours free before he was expected to take his turn behind their special stall filled with distinctive candles; beeswax candles, carved candles, scented candles and the very latest in fashionable oil lamps.

A band made up from the stallholders swung into the rousing tune of 'Daisy Bell' with fiddle, trumpet, drum and banjos. The spectators were soon caught up in the music, quickly tapping their toes or clapping their hands in time to it. The atmosphere was festive, relaxed and happy. Lucy forgot all about her shyness as she clapped along with everyone else.

The music of musicians sounded all around the large space and Morris dancers in their fancy flowered hats, with their sticks and whirling their pigs' bladders, danced the traditional old movements from a time so long ago that no one remembered where they came from.

The Punch and Judy man had arrived with the crocodile and the policeman puppets to entertain the children. Everyone of the children would shout at the antics of Punch; they would have a good time.

The fair lasted for seven days and the locals got together to show off their skills. Everyday was filled with different events: contests of sheep shearing; sheepdog trials; choosing the 'best in show' of the birds, poultry, dogs, and foods, each section and class judged by the people who were deemed to have the knowledge on such matters; horses, plough equipment and new inventions designed to make life working on the land easier; the sales of cattle, bloodline stock, sheep and poultry; as well as prizes for the best vegetable in show. The selling of seeds, corn and the like went on over the week, as well as the town's shopkeepers trying to make a living by the side of the temporary stallholders.

The music played on. Marina wanted to look for new boots and Rosa was determined to have morning tea at the teashop. Lucy had a few pennies to spend on herself and though she went with Rosa for a quick drink, Lucy was allowed to shop on her own for ribbons to trim a straw hat that needed a makeover.

Mark found her looking at lace and ribbons some thirty minutes later at a stall just two stalls away from his father's. The stall was strung with a strong line of string at shoulder height, tied from one end to the other with reels – some small, some large – hanging from it. Each reel had a different type of lace, ranging from narrow broderie anglaise to collar lace. Ribbons of every colour were side by side, looking glorious in a rainbow-like chorus. Underneath, laying on the wooden counter, were crochet hooks and threads, bone buttons, hook-and-eyes, wools for darning and cotton reels for sewing; everything for making and mending in the home.

The stall assistant wore a navy dress with a deep lace collar in white. While she waited, her fingers worked at a piece of crochet making a border lace as she waited patiently for a customer.

Lucy stood before the stall totally absorbed with the choice in front of her. She didn't hear Mark as he came up behind her.

"The red ribbon would suit you," he whispered in her ear, winking as she turned her head to see the person that belonged to the voice. He passed behind her, indicating with his head for her to follow him.

"A yard of the red, two inches wide, please," Lucy said, pointing to the ribbon in the centre of the line. She half-watched the lady pulling off the red ribbon, measuring it as she did. After cutting the required length she wrapped it in clean tissue and handed it to Lucy.

Once her purchase was safely in her pocket, she pushed her way through the crowd in the direction he had gone. Some stalls were protected from the weather by covers, top, back and sides in tarpaulin, and as she edged her way to the outer stalls a hand came out and gripped her arm and pulled her into a side opening that hid them from the milling crowd.

Mark stood, grinning at her. Lucy crossed her heart with her hand.

"You scared me," she said accusingly.

His arms encircled her, holding her tightly to his chest. He kissed her on top of her head.

"Missed me?"

"Maybe a little." Breaking his grip, she pushed back from him.

Taking her hand, part dragging her along after him, he turned, making his way out from the square.

"Come on, let's take a little walk, no one will miss us – thirty minutes! Promise!" That innocent lost look was on his face, eyes pleading, and a lopsided smile melted her heart.

"Let's get away from all this," he pleaded.

She made up her mind and without saying a word, she squeezed his hand in agreement and followed him out of the square.

The streets were empty beyond the fair. The hustle and bustle was merely a murmur in the background as they made their way towards the grand union canal and Queens Park. Turning into the park through heavy iron gates, they headed towards the bandstand right in the centre of the park.

Benches were placed around the stand for people to sit and enjoy the music when it was played on weekends and late summer evenings. They made their way to a bench in the sun and stopped, then sat down.

"Missed me?" he said again, cheekily.

"Not for a moment," she teased.

His eyes were on her as he took her face gently in his hands, kissing her forehead, nose and lips just like before, but this time the kiss was strong, lingering and passionate, broken only when she pulled away.

His arms went around her and again his mouth sought out her lips, bringing them down on hers with such a passionate force it took her breath away. He wanted her now more than ever. How was he to bear the longing? He was eager to woo her, love her, but he knew if he moved too soon she would be afraid and he would lose her.

It was almost a good thing that he was due back at work within the hour; it would at least concentrate his mind away from thinking of Lucy.

Her body reacted to his kiss, strange stirrings that she had never felt before. Her thoughts flooded in. She was aware of wanting to feel his lips on her neck and feel his love. It was almost too shocking to contemplate.

Was that normal or was she a wretched creature who was no better than a slut? She stopped there; her thoughts frightened her. Her aunties and her mother, was that who she was comparing herself to? My God, what was she thinking? How could she ever speak of it to her mother, how could she ever tell Mark the real truth? Suddenly she felt trapped in a web of lies that she could not see a way out of.

Holding her as he did, she longed for the day to stand still. *Please let the moment last.* For a while they kept the world at bay until the town hall clock chimed and brought them back to reality.

Their brief encounter was over. Mark would be in trouble if he wasn't back on time and Lucy could well have been missed too. They made a promise to each other to meet up as often as they could over the period of the festival.

Quickly they retraced their steps back to the throng. They shared a quick hug and a brief kiss before parting company and both went back to play the roles they were expected to play, looking innocent, but their hearts were flushed with young love and were in turmoil.

They were gone for no more than half an hour. Fortunately neither had been missed and when Lucy caught up with her mother, Marina was completely distracted and as pleased as Punch with her purchase of new boots. She showed Lucy the soft brown leather ankle boots that fastened at the side with several small buttons and stitching as fine as you would get in Oxford, or so the assistant in the shop had told her.

Happily, they met up with Rosa in the teashop and Lucy showed them her new ribbon, only Rosa remarked that she had been quite some time for such a small purchase but it passed unnoticed by Marina. For the next hour they became part of the milling crowd, eager to see all that was on offer, including the candle stall, where Lucy bought a particularly beautiful rose-scented carved candle to decorate her bedside table. The lady whom Lucy had taken to be his mother was standing with Mark behind the counter. He didn't introduce her to the lady and he seemed slightly embarrassed; nevertheless, he was friendly, unlike the woman who watched as he wrapped it with care and handed it to Lucy.

"Will we see you again over the week?"

"I do hope so, it's all so exciting, isn't it? I would especially like to see the dog trials on Monday. Then the games on Wednesday. Could we come again soon, Mother? It's only once a year, please," begged Lucy.

Marina smiled. It was exciting and for her young daughter, who lived a quiet life away from the busy town, it must seem something of a huge party with daily events going on.

"I'll think about it. Not every day, mind, but you should see more of life."

And so it was agreed. Lucy was beaming from ear to ear when she caught a glance from Mark. Smiling, he gave her a wink.

18

Mark made sure that his lunch breaks always coincided with the time that Lucy was shopping in the square, leaving Marina and Rosa at the teashop drinking tea and listening to local gossip. There was never much time to share but they snatched a few precious minutes together and that was all that mattered to them.

Lucy always bought a little something to take back to the tearoom to show her mother, hiding the real motive of her movements.

Mark and Lucy would steal away to the park or onto the towpath by the canal. It wasn't private but they felt it was safer being away from the square, sure that neither of their families would discover them, and for a few precious minutes they could be together.

They shared their likes and dislikes, books, their hopes for the future, all the things that mattered to them, but by some sixth sense she never spoke about her mother or her home.

When the fair finished at the end of the week they had no choice but to go back to meeting in secret. But both of them knew that their meetings at the bridge would only be for a week or two, the nights were closing in and an autumnal feel was in the air.

Heavy dew was in the grass both morning and evening and soon excuses to go out in the evening for walks would be looked upon as suspicious by Lucy's family. They realised that soon they would be unable to meet.

Mark's desire for Lucy increased daily. He was becoming desperate to find a release for his passion. He could not and would not touch her; she was the most pure girl he had ever known, a virgin, and he knew she was not ready for the full extent of a man's love, yet he had needs that would have to be satisfied or he would go mad. The idea of marriage was in the forefront of his mind, but she was so young and how would he tell his father he wished to wed? And how would her mother react when he asked for her hand?

By mid-October there was a real change in the air. Summer was gone, the sun had weakened, there was a real chill in the evenings. The fires were lit in the hearths and the smell of wood smoke escaped from the chimneys. The smoke drifted, curling lazily above the roofs and wrapped its self around the shedding branches of the trees that were losing leaves. They were turning yellow, gold and red before slipping away from the branch and falling to the ground. Dark nights and dark mornings would not help the pair; market days were the only time they could see each other, but now they were never alone. The smell of her hair and her skin stayed with him, kisses were only a memory. His body ached for her. What could he do?

It was sometime later that he heard of a high-class brothel on the very edge of town. It was out of the way, and very private. Colin his cousin had described his visit there and that he had slept with a lady who knew how to please a man.

That's what he needed, a release from these lusting desires. Who would know? What harm could there be? His cousin was a regular and would vouch for him. Colin was his cousin and friend and the only person he could confide in, he would understand his torment.

Mark had spoken to Colin about Lucy, the girl he was very fond of. He admitted that nothing had happened between them and he was still a virgin. Mark's birthday was coming up at the end of the month and on October 29th he would turn twenty.

Colin could see the frustration that Mark was going through and thought it was high time that Mark was made a man. Colin's present for his birthday would be to take him to the house on the edge of town and introduce him to a real woman.

Three months had passed since Roni had taken a beating. Louis could still feel some fear drifting about the house and although there was some normality, it was apparent that there was still a certain nervousness in the air.

Business had resumed, though visitors were kept to a bare minimum. Marina chose to only open the house to cover the expenses that they needed for the household and the girls decided who they entertained. Louis was always on hand now, wandering the halls when they were working and Marina had reassurance from Rosa that the guardian angel who had already proved his worth, was still around to protect her and hers.

From then on, Roni only saw her regulars. She would not risk herself again. She was uncertain how long she would stay with Marina and work in the house but this was hard; this was the only real home she had ever known and she wasn't sure whether she was brave enough to face the world alone.

Emma, who was as bubbly as always, decided that she was a good enough reader of character to know whether a man was good-natured or bad, and firmly believed that most people were kind. Anyone could be in the wrong place at the wrong time.

Nora's neck was no longer bruised and the soreness had gone, but her fears were still real. No matter how much Rosa reassured her, Nora could not really settle down to life in the house. She had thought she would never see her father again after she dragged herself from him fifteen years ago. The safety and shelter she trusted was destroyed in the few minutes when her father discovered her at the house.

Even the information that Rosa brought back from town concerning George didn't help her anxiety. Rosa had met 'Richard', the unfortunate man who had brought George to the house the night of the beating, unexpectedly in the town. He had told her that George had been badly concussed by the blow that knocked him unconscious and by the time they had arrived back to town, George had had a seizure. Not knowing what else to do, 'Richard' had taken him to the infirmary in the workhouse; a terrible place but at least there was a doctor who would look at his injuries, and while the money that he won lasted he would have help. After that he would be on the parish poor list, God help him. George was now laid up in the hospital, unable to move his arm or leg on his right side, and had lost the power of speech. He had become an invalid who was dependent on charity and others just to live; he would not trouble anyone else in what was left of his life. It was some relief for Nora knowing that but it didn't dispel her fears. Her fear of the unexpected was all-consuming; the 'what if' it happened again with another client? It preyed on her mind, it was that reason that Nora took the decision not to avail herself for clients anymore; the only man she was happy to see was 'John' the widower. He had always been kind to her and was shocked to see marks on her neck when he visited shortly after the incident. She didn't tell him the full story – how could she? Her own father brutalising her was humiliating. She was so ashamed, it was as though she was in some way to blame for George's meanness.

The fact that Nora had been hurt deeply concerned 'John', something he had not expected to feel. He had grown fond of her over the years but he had always thought of it as a business arrangement rather than a personal one.

It would seem he was wrong. Their relationship changed for both of them; they both felt it, yet fear of loss of independence and vulnerability held them back. John increased his visits to twice a week to see Nora. They talked, drank tea together and generally put the world to rights on his visits. Sex had become more intimate and sensual between them. A new bond grew between the two of them. Nora started to see her future away from the house but maybe not too far away from John. Owning a tearoom like the one in the town, if she could find one, would give her a fresh start. A tearoom with living space above it would be ideal. It would be the start of a new life for her and more security and maybe she could have a new name. If only she had the courage!

Colin and Mark met up at the Post House Inn a couple of weeks after Mark's birthday. It was one of the oldest pubs in the town, built in Tudor times, and it was reputed by the landlord to have been visited by Henry the Eighth and Anne Boleyn after their marriage, not that Colin cared, it was just somewhere to drink.

It was a noisy and well-attended public house just off the cobbled square. In celebration of Mark's birthday, the two of them joined the crowd and enjoyed more than one locally brewed beer in the bar. The room was smoky. A mist of tobacco smoke hung over the heads of the smokers as they pulled on the clay pipes filled with cheap tobacco. They sat on stools drinking their beer from pewter tankards, and if their smoke was not enough, smoke belched out from unseasoned wood on the fire from the inglenook fireplace. It sent eye-smarting smoke into the room, though the patrons didn't seem to notice.

Colin was ten years older than Mark and still a bachelor. He enjoyed his freedom to the full. He would see Roni tonight, this being Friday, and he would take his little cousin with him. Later that evening a carter would take them out to the house and Mark would enter as a boy and come out a man. Mark was nervous and uncertain about how the night would turn out for him. His sexual adventures had been with girls of his own age and they had never gone beyond a certain point. He wondered if this trip was really what he wanted. His nervousness was apparent to Colin, who could not resist teasing him.

"Ready to test the equipment then, cousin?"

"I've been there before, Col," he said boastfully.

"Really, are you sure? I'm taking you to be with real women, not girls." Laughingly, he slapped Mark on the back.

"One more for the road?" Colin said, raising his glass to his mouth and finishing off his drink.

"Get them in, lad, then let's be off."

By the time they left the pub it was already nine in the evening on a very cold and dark November night, and they were well on the way to drunkenness.

The carter was already in the square waiting for them. The young men climbed aboard dressed in heavy woollen overcoats and woollen scarves to protect them against the night air and they settled themselves on the tailgate, ready for the adventure. They were laughing and joking as the cart took the road out of town as per Colin's instruction. Driving along the road in the dark, the houses got fewer as they travelled towards their destination.

They were bordered on both sides by large trees. Their huge branches hung over the road, reaching out towards them almost menacingly as they rode along that night. Stars shone brightly in between the branches of the trees and a ring of white surrounded the moon, announcing a possibility of a heavy frost before morning.

The ride took a little over thirty minutes. Mark was puzzled in his near-drunken state because the route seemed familiar to him, *but all roads lead somewhere*, and he dismissed his thoughts and joined Colin in men's talk for the rest of the journey.

Even in the dark he was sure that this was the road he had taken in the summer to see Lucy. Thank God it was night; if they happened to go past the house where she lived he wouldn't be seen.

When at last they drew up at the bottom of the short drive that led to the side entrance of the house, he was completely confused. It looked very like Lucy's house but he must be mistaken, this couldn't be where Lucy lived. The night was playing tricks on him.

Paying off the carter with a decision to walk back to town later, they walked the few steps up the path to the dark sturdy door that kept so many secrets behind it. Colin, in a confident mood, knocked at the door with his usual knock. Roni was waiting in the drawing room when she heard it. She was expecting him, he always came on Fridays, but she was surprised when she opened the door and saw a handsome young man standing next to Colin.

"Well now, who have we got here? Come in, come in, get out of the cold. So lovely so see you again, Colin," welcomed Roni.

"Roni, this is Mark, my cousin."

Mark was already colouring up. He thought Colin was great and he looked up to him in many ways. Colin was always ready for a laugh but after a glass or two Colin could be a bit loud. Not wanting to be embarrassed by him because of this being his first time in such a house, he found his voice.

"Nice to meet you," he blurted out, proffering his hand to her.

She smiled and said gently, "You've not been here before, have you?" Taking his hand, she led him to the sofa. "Sit, make yourself comfortable, tell us about yourself. Emma will join us in a minute. You'll like her."

Colin followed, sitting down heavily beside Roni, his arm moving quickly around her shoulders. He kissed her cheek. She looked into his eyes and saw a raw longing in them.

"Look, Colin, you know the rules, no one is allowed here unless approved. Now, this nice young man hasn't been here before. I need to know who he is?"

"You're right! Yes." He stood up and bowed towards her and in a loud voice announced, "Meet Mark, eldest son of the mayor and recently become another year older. This is my treat for him to meet a real woman, just like you, but you're mine." He giggled like a schoolboy, happy and full of himself, and sat down heavily on the sofa having finished his statement.

Emma had quietly come into the room and sat on the armchair. She had heard Colin's introduction. The young man in question was looking over at Emma. She was petite and pretty, with a womanly shape emphasised by the laced corset she was wearing under her bodice that was nipped at the waist. The full skirt stretched tight across her stomach but fell in pleats, with a tiny bustle at the side and back when she stood up. Her brown eyes were deep and rich, complementing her blonde hair that was piled up on her head and fixed with pins. He started to think how it would feel taking out the pins and allowing the hair to fall around her naked body. Excitement gripped his stomach and a heat of arousal filled his loins.

Roni looked over at Emma. Unspoken words passed between them. Roni nodded and Emma nodded back. It was the signal that Mark was accepted.

Mark had said very little, his fears from earlier forgotten for now. What he wanted and needed was release from this pain of passion. Emma was so lovely, even if she was quite a bit older than him, and he was ready to feel her body next to his. The urgency was overtaking him. Emma stretched out her hand and indicated for him to come with her.

She stood waiting for him to join her. Her eyes on his, she found his hand and slowly she led him across the drawing room and down the passage to her room. They were closely followed by Roni and his cousin Colin who passed through the door opposite to them, already kissing as the door closed behind them.

The room Emma used was dimly lit with a small oil lamp on the bedside table. The heavy velvet curtains were closed to keep out draughts from the window but the room was very cold. Usually it was warm and cosy, but the small fireplace that normally held the coal fire had only grey ash from the night before.

"Oh dear! What was I thinking? I forgot to lay the fire for tonight." She shook her head in disbelief. "Sorry, Mark, we will have to use my other room. It's not normal but we don't want to freeze, do we? Whatever you do, please be very quiet – we don't want to disturb anyone, do we?"

"No, of course not," he said, not really understanding what she meant.

"Follow me." Grabbing his hand she pulled him through the door across from the drawing room, picking up a small lamp on the way. Looking carefully around, she put her finger to her lips, indicating silence, and crept up the stairs with him, turning into the second room on the landing.

Mark saw they were in a much bigger room, decorated with blue and pink wallpaper, pink velvet curtains at the window and a homemade patchwork bedspread of multi colour on the bed. The room was much more personal, definitely a woman's, and so much nicer than the one downstairs. A well-lit fire behind a guard threw out welcomed warmth around the room. Two armchairs sat by the fire and a sheepskin rug lay between the fire and bed.

Emma moved over to the fire and started to undress. In a stride, Mark was beside her.

"No, let me," he said.

Emma stood in the warmth of the fire as Mark, with slightly shaking hands, began to unbutton her bodice. Removing it revealed the white cotton shift and corset that held her fulsome body. Her breasts, high and full, rested above the corset. His finger ran lightly over her neck and down to the V in her cleavage. Her face was near with a small smile on her lips when she took him by surprise and kissed him hard on the lips.

Together they removed the laced corset, freeing her body to his hands. His lips moved to her neck and breasts while his hands undid the hooks on her skirt, loosening it until it dropped to the floor. Standing there on the rug, he proceeded to strip her completely.

His hands reached up to her hair, pulling the hairpins out one by one. Her hair tumbled down around her face and reached down her back, almost to her waist.

"God, you look so good," he said, touching her breast while pulling her to him.

"You too," she said, and started to relieve him of his clothes. Soon they were standing naked together in front of the fire, touching and kissing until they found themselves laid on the rug. Mark was at last free to explore the lovely body of Emma.

She taught Mark the meaning of real foreplay and for the next thirty minutes, Mark felt the rise and fall of passion in him until she took him to the climax he had dreamed of.

The two of them lay entwined for a few more minutes until she gently pushed him so he rolled onto the rug beside her.

"Are you alright?" she asked; it was his first time, after all. With a deep sigh, Mark pushed his hand through his hair and answered, "Never better."

Still nude, Emma sat up and getting to her feet, held out a hand to encourage Mark to stand. She took him over to the bed. She had noticed that men needed time to recover after sex. A few minutes of rest would fix him up. While she dressed, Mark closed his eyes, cat-napping for a minute while listening to her dressing and moving in the room. Then she was by the bed, leaning over him.

"Can I get you a drink?" whispered Emma. She smelt so good and he was surprised that arousal was not far away again.

"Please," muttered Mark, his eyes still closed.

"I'll be a few minutes. Be dressed when I get back, will you? I've got to get you back downstairs unnoticed." A small grunt sounded from the bed, acknowledging her instructions.

The door shut quietly and her footsteps could be heard walking away. It was the custom of the house at the end of business to give the client a small drink before he left the premises to find his way home. She would bring one to him.

Emma went downstairs to the drawing room. It was empty; Roni and Colin were still in the guest room down the passage. She would have to wait for them to come out, which could be some time, so perhaps it was a good time to have a small brandy herself, she thought. Settling herself on the sofa with a glass of amber liquid, she laid back and closed her eyes, resting for a few minutes before going back with the brandy for Mark.

Mark lay for a few minutes on the clean white sheet, thinking about the last thirty minutes; it had been so good. Emma knew how to pleasure a man, that was sure, and physically he was satisfied, but he also had feelings of guilt. Somehow he felt he had let himself down. If Lucy ever found out... No. That was too much to think about. He rolled off the bed and found his clothes by the fire. It was dying down now; soon the room would be cool, but not yet. He slowly pulled on his clothes, thinking Colin would be waiting for him downstairs. He must find his cousin; it would be a long walk back to town and he wanted to clear his head.

Sitting on the chair putting on his shoes, he had a sudden overwhelming urge to get out of the house.

"I must get out of here," he muttered to himself, crossing the room to the door in an instant.

He opened the door into the dark hall and strode out, then he froze in shock as the door opposite opened, revealing the silhouette of a figure. He stepped back into the doorway, not wanting to be seen, but let out a gasp as Lucy walked out into the passage, the light of the room revealing her face as she came alongside the doorway in which Mark stood.

Shock and disbelief froze him to the spot.

"What in hell's teeth are you doing here?" Mark spat at her. Lucy couldn't believe her eyes. How could Mark be here, in the house? Then the realisation hit her; he had been with one of her aunts.

She turned back towards the bedroom but he was too quick for her and caught her arms, pushing her into the room.

"Oh! I see it all now. You were making a fool of me. Me! The mayor's son. How many people know what this place is and what you do here, sweetness?" he growled at her.

Lucy was shaking her head, trying, wanting to explain but to no avail, he couldn't hear her.

His head was spinning. The aunts looked after her, that was what she said. He had just been with Emma. What a fool he had been to think that this girl was special.

"Oh my god, what was I thinking?" A cry left his lips from deep in his soul and a black rage came down upon him. Seeing nothing but this deceiving vixen in front of him, a hate that he could taste rose like bile from his stomach. How many people knew and were sniggering behind his back? He had a relationship with a whore's brat and, worse, probably a whore herself. He was blind to any reason or explanation from Lucy as he pushed her further into the room and threw her onto the bed.

In an instance he had locked the door and placed a chair under the handle to ensure that no one would be able to force their way into the room. No one would disturb them now. The hate was growing in his heart.

Lucy was dazed and shocked at what was happening. She was trying to sit up on the bed while pushing her hair from her face.

"What are you doing here?" she asked timidly. She was anxious, she had never seen him like this and fear was ready to take over, she was on the edge. "Please, Mark, let me explain."

Explanations were useless in the blind rage that was racing through his veins; even his face had changed from a young man to a distorted mask of menace.

A second later he was upon her, knocking her back flat on the bed. Sitting astride her, he pinned her arms above her head. The weight of his body squeezed the breath from her and fear flooded in. His face was inches away from hers, threatening her, his eyes were huge in their sockets and pupils dilated. His breath smelt of stale drink that added to the discomfort. She still could not quite believe what was happening to her. This was Mark, the man she dreamed of every night, the one she longed for every day. How could he be here doing this? He must listen.

She opened her mouth to speak but her words were laboured because of his weight on her.

"Mark," she whispered, "let me up."

He responded by grabbing both of her wrists and holding them together, pining them down. He was so strong and he placed his free hand over her mouth. Leaning forward, he whispered back.

"You'll not tease me anymore, I will have you. I had thought of us together, maybe even marrying, but you bitch, you deceived me. You're a whore's brat, destined to be a whore yourself, if you're not one already." His smile was so cold it became a slit of disdain. This smile she didn't know, his loving smile she remembered was gone, now it curled at the corner of his mouth, making his face cruel and full of mockery.

"Now, my little petal, I'm going to deflower you."

Fear suddenly gave Lucy strength and she tried for the first time to fight him off. Pushing her body with all her strength, she tried to dislodge him.

If only she could get her hands free, but he was too strong. She would not be a pawn in his game to be used and thrown away. Somehow she would fight him for her honour.

Still sitting astride her, he repositioned himself, holding her legs down while half-lying across her. He looked around the room, searching for something to bind her with and to gag her; she mustn't be allowed to cry out.

A silk stocking lay across the bed along with the red blouse and a matching scarf. A red and black print skirt lay across the chair by the bed, ready for the morning. *She would be going to Saturday's market in those*, he thought, *looking out for me to make me look an even bigger fool than I am already.*

He reached over, grabbing the scarf, thus releasing her hands. They came up and clawed at his neck and face then tried to remove the hand that still covered her mouth. His skin was left under her nails and red weals were already showing on his skin.

He seemed oblivious to her fighting him. Driven by some demon that lay in his soul, he took his hand away from her mouth, trying to gag her, but she struggled, moving her head away from his hand. She managed a strangled scream before he held her once again. The scarf was finally secured in her mouth. He tied the knot behind her head so tightly that it tore her hair from its roots as she struggled to resist him.

Too afraid even to cry tears, she knew that she was going to be raped.

19

Since coming to Marina's home Louis had learnt to live a life in his own ghostly way. It was certainly not has a mortal nor fully spirit.

The nether world he had left behind when he died was in the past, it was a place that he didn't want to dwell on anymore.

He felt a sense of purposes now living there even if his abilities were limited. Limited as they were, they had been good enough to save Roni and Nora, though they didn't know he was their saviour.

Rosa had called him a guardian angel, and Marina had accepted that, he was their secret, the unexplained help that came to the rescue when the family was in danger.

He had learnt to admire Marina. Her bullishness hid a kind heart that she protected from all except Lucy, whom she loved without question.

Louis moved about the house and garden, not intimidating or interfering with their lives. He could still enjoy the smells and sounds of life. The kitchen and garden were his favourite places to be in, although he couldn't eat or drink, the smell of roasting meats, freshly baked bread almost made him salivate.

His range of movement was limited to the house and grounds. It was as though a magic circle surrounded his bed, giving him space to roam, but not unlimited. With so much life happening in this house he needed no more than he had.

Louis was in the kitchen enjoying the smell of freshly baked bread that Rosa had just taken from the oven it was her custom to slice a little off the crust and butter it; she loved warm bread even though it often give her heartburn. He was enjoying the scene before him when he heard the stifled cry. It was not loud. Rosa seemed not to hear it but the sounds and smells seemed to be heightened in his spirit senses.

The cry came from upstairs, possibly from Lucy's room. Moving quickly he was upstairs, passing through the door of her bedroom and saw to his horror a scene he could never have thought possible.

Mark was astride Lucy, gagging her with a scarf. How could this be the young man who he had seen through the beech hedge a few months ago, the man who had written such a pleading letter to Lucy? How could it be the same man who seemed unaffected by this frightened girl?

Louis was sickened by the spectacle before him, his anger welling up. He tried to push Mark off Lucy but his hands passed through Mark's body; he tried again with more force, but again he failed.

He remembered back when he had died, trying to clutch the bed sheets with the same desperation and panic that hit him now; somehow he must find a way to help Lucy.

There was something else happening in the room. He could see a grey shadow flitting around Mark body and the smell of evil was growing. The grey shape was growing and it became darker. It had become almost black, the shape evolved into an outline around Mark's body before Louis saw it enter Mark. There was only one explanation Mark had become possessed by a demon.

The smell of evil grew stronger. It was obvious to Louis that the demon was being fed on Lucy's fear and on Mark's anger. An evil force that was too strong for him.

Anger and emotion had been Louis's tool before. He remembered the vase he broke when he arrived at the house and stopping George had been the result of inflamed anger at George's treatment of Roni and Nora. Louis hated bullies, mean-spirited people who inflicted hurt on others weaker than themselves.

Louis used his memories of his past to build up anger in his mind, he had to harnessing that power, and he needed to do it now. He had to stop this.

Even now, Mark was tying her wrists together with her own silk stocking from the bed. He had forced her into sitting position and had managed to tie her hands behind her back, his body serving as a weight to stop her from trying to escape. Lucy was exhausted from fear and straining beneath his body weight.

"This was not how it was supposed to be. God help me," she prayed, shutting her eyes. Unable to help herself, she handed herself over to her maker.

Lucy could feel his brutish hands touching her neck and shoulders, finding the hook-and-eye at the collar of her bodice and opening it up. Next he tore the buttons off her bodice one by one and ripped the top open, forcing it off her shoulders and down to her elbows.

Finding the straps of her under garment of fine cotton, he ripped them apart, exposing her young small breasts. The sight of her breasts excited him even more, he felt the power he had over her. It was exhilarating. She was no longer Lucy. She was no longer anyone. She was his to do with as he pleased and it pleased him to feel her fear.

Once again Louis tried to stop Mark. Louis had wrapped his arms around Mark's chest and tried to pull him off her. Mark's intention to remove her clothing from her slight body was stopped for a moment when a cold and vicious sensation went through his body. Goosebumps ran down his arm as Louis gave it one more try.

Someone just walked over my grave, thought Mark.

For a moment Mark stopped what he was doing, but the mindless thrill he was enjoying called him back to the moment and he ripped the garment from her. Louis had failed again.

Sobbing now, Lucy was unable to cry out because of the gag. She sagged against the pillows and mentally gave up.

Louis didn't understand it. It should have worked. In his anger and frustration, he pushed over a nearby vase from a table, scattering water and flowers everywhere. Mark merely lifted his head to see where the noise came from before carrying on molesting Lucy.

Louis tried to move the bed, hoping to shake it so hard he would stop Mark and bring him back to his senses before it was too late. It didn't work; Louis could see a black mist stretching out from around Mark, it was becoming thicker as the fingers of evil invaded the room.

Louis knew that whatever it was, it was too strong for him to defeat on his own. Could Rosa help? Could her spirits know the answer in fighting a demon. He must find her. She must listen to him.

Down in the kitchen Rosa and Marina were having a nightcap. Bread was made for the next two days, plus a Victoria sandwich cake and scones.

They were chatting together in the quiet of the kitchen, sat in front of a warm fire relaxing until Louis suddenly appeared in front of Rosa.

She was startled; he had never done that before and when they spoke it was always in private. She was taking a sip of her drink when she looked up at him.

"Rosa, come with me, help me," he pleaded. "Lucy life is in danger. Mark is in the house upstairs. He has her bound in her bedroom and he's in a blind rage, I fear she may be raped or even killed by him."

Rosa dropped her drink, spilling the warm milk and brandy over the table and down her skirt.

"Oh my God!"

Marina turned towards Rosa, startled by her and seeing shock on her face, she asked, "What is it?"

"Quick Marina, upstairs now. We've got to get to Lucy." Marina didn't question her order; something was very wrong, and they moved in unison to the stairs, mounting them as quickly as they could up to the bedroom.

Louis had already disappeared and was back in the bedroom standing by the bed. Mark was beyond reach now, an evil veil of black surrounded him and it had become his aura; Mark was gone.

Lucy struggled under the demon's weight. His delight in her suffering was apparent. His mouth was on hers in spite of her gag. Laughing, he kissed her neck, moving slowly down towards her breasts. Each kiss was another invasion on her senses and body.

Louis was beside himself with anger. More dark mist appeared in the room where he stood, though neither Mark nor Lucy saw it.

The room grew dark and cold, the mist and the demon became one absorbing more evil through Mark body.

It was enough to strengthen Louis's anger and give him the momentum he needed. Taking the side of the bed in his hands, he heaved it up; the sudden movement caused the bodies to tip from the bed, with Lucy landing on top of Mark, her full weight landing across his stomach, winding him.

Rolling off, she tried to stand on her shaking legs and somehow she moved towards the door. Her mother and Rosa were calling from the landing on the other side of the door and were banging on it to be opened.

Blood started to flow back into her arms; lying on them had put them in cramp, making them painful and useless.

A cooling breeze passed across her face. Her gag loosened and there was a slight tug at the stocking that tied her. She could feel movement between her wrists; the tie was slackened, the silk loosening more each time she pulled her wrists apart. She couldn't know that Louis was expending his energy on freeing her, she just knew that hope had returned to her.

Louis's next task was to move the chair from under the door handle to stop it from barring the way in. But there was still the problem of the locked door, though the key was still in the lock.

Mark was half-sitting. Finding strength, he came up on one knee, his hand holding his stomach, his head bowed down, resting for a moment. When he finally raised his head and looked across at Lucy, his eyes were the colour of blood. Louis knew then for certain that a malignant force had taken over Mark's body completely.

From a half-crouching position, Mark lunged forward, taking Lucy by surprise and taking her feet from beneath her.

The hammering on the door by clenched fists had no effect on him. He never heard them. The spirit inside Mark would not be stopped easily.

Lucy's bodice had been torn from her and her skirt lay in tatters. She looked pathetic and frail lying on the floor as Mark once again straddled her, but with her hands that were now free she punched and pounded any part of his body she could reach. He responded by winding the poor girl with a punch into her solar plexus. In pain and desperate for this terror to stop, Lucy would have screamed if she could. Now tears poured down her face.

Mark moved his leg, forcing it between hers.

Oh God! she thought. *Will nothing stop him?*

Forcing her legs apart, he groped to free her of her drawers. She was still fighting him but to no real effect. Mark, tired of Lucy attacking his body, resorted to half-strangling her. His hands were around her neck, her eyes throbbed and blackness invaded as she slowly lost consciousness.

Invaded by evil, Mark was unaware of what he was doing. All the lust, anger and guilt he felt at seeing Lucy in the house, had given this depraved and murderous spirit demon a way into his soul.

Shouts and cries came into the room from the landing.

"Louis, what's happening? Come here, please," called Rosa.

He debated. Could he go and leave Lucy like this? If he left, she might die; if he stayed, he was not sure if he could fight both spirit and mortal.

Rosa was on the landing with Marina, both were as white as sheets. As Marina continued to beat on the door, Rosa stepped back when she saw Louis pass through the wall.

Rosa had felt the evil behind the door; the air felt thick and heavy and there was a smell that clawed in her throat. It was the same smell that she remembered from years ago. Rosa had always seen spirits since she was a small child. She heard them and lived with them every day. She was nine when she was confronted by a disturbed spirit that was able to move into a mortal body and feed on the victim's emotions for a short time. The owner of the body did not seem to be aware of the possession until the spirit left. Rosa had watched as it had used her father.

Was it back? The same demon that appeared soon after the priest had tried to exorcise her?

He had, instead of closing down the gateway and barring her spirits to her, opened up another gateway, a gateway of evil from hell and because of it her parents had died. They had interfered with her spirits and her gift and let loose the demon's lust for violence and death. It had forced her father to kill her mother and then himself that was all she knew.

She had sought to banish the evil through her gatekeeper and force it back into the netherworld. She thought she had. Only now this was happening, so like the past; could it be the same demon?

"Louis, he's here."

"Who?"

"The spectre that killed my mother and father."

"How?"

She offered her hand and put his hand on her forehead; her memories were all there. She showed him thoughts of the past. A man was pressing the life out of a middle-aged woman, limp under the man's hands that were around her neck. Then Louis saw as she died a black shape emerged from the man, fat and gloating. It moved overhead to look down on its victim, watching the man coming to his senses and looking down at the woman, wondering what he had done. His wife lay dead at his feet. A loud moan escaped from the man's open mouth. Falling to his knees, he lifted the woman to him, rocking her back and forth in grief. "What have I done?" he sobbed in disbelief. The spectre, feeding on the negative emotion, actually grew in size. Rosa had seen it all hiding behind a chair. That night her father took her to her grandparents. She never saw him again.

Rosa communicated with Louis by thought, not wanting to alarm Marina anymore than she was already.

"Louis, to fight this demon, you must fight like with like. Merge with Lucy and fight it with spirit and flesh. Lucy will not fight you. Be quick. Save her."

Louis understood but this was a strange request from Rosa, but he knew from the vision that he had just seen there was no time to question it.

Back inside the room, Louis could see Lucy's hands were instinctively on his hands at her throat. Moving to her, Louis merged with her before she slipped into a faint. Her limp body surged with renewed energy and strength. Louis drove his fingers through Lucy's fingers and into the demon's eyes with as much power he could muster.

The shock and pain it caused to Mark and his occupant momentarily stopped the attack, giving Louis all the advantage he needed. With a mortal body to use, he quickly brought a fist to Mark's stomach and a rabbit punch to the neck. Dazed for a moment the demon fell with Mark to the floor in a heap. Louis stood in Lucy's body over the stunned man. Lucy's booted foot connected to Mark's groin and he doubled up in agony on the floor; another kick in the small of his back and one in the head finished Mark off. The evil within Mark waited for the physical body of his host to recover sufficiently so it could strike again.

The awful din from the fight could be heard in the hallway. The group waiting there had beaten the door until their hands ached, shouting to be let in but with no response. Now they were standing stock-still facing the door, from behind, which the dreadful sounds still came. The anguish of only hearing and not being able to see what was really going on inside the bedroom was pure agony, especially to Marina.

Colin and Roni had arrived on the landing with Emma. The noise from the bedroom had penetrated the whole house. They had to do something. It was Colin who suddenly turned and raced down the stairs, leaving the others staring at his disappearing figure. He ran through the kitchen and out into the garden, where he had seen the pile of logs used for the kitchen fire. Surely there would be an axe nearby. There it was, lying on its back on top of the woodpile, waiting for him to pick it up and carry it back up the stairs to attack the door.

The door of the bedroom shattered and splintered under the attack from Colin. His arm reached into the bedroom and pulled the chair away from under the knob releasing the door. As it opened, the family from the landing poured into the room led by Colin, who was still carrying the axe. The smell in the room was overpowering, a stomach-churning smell that almost stopped them in their tracks. Instead, it was the sight of Lucy standing over the prone figure of Mark that brought them to temporary halt.

Mark's face turned towards the interruption in the doorway, his face twisting into a malevolent smile, his eyes bloodshot and narrow.

The demon realised he had lost control of the situation and left Mark's body, dissipating into the air and moving out through the walls to God knows where, taking the foul stench of evil with him.

Mark was left lying bent double on the floor, dazed and in pain, exhausted, his anger gone. He was in a state of wretchedness, not knowing what had really happened.

Colin was the first to reach the battered couple. Marina, just behind on his heels, caught hold of Lucy just as Louis decided it was time for him to leave her. Louis made his exit, leaving Lucy to slip to the floor in a semi-conscious faint. She would have bruises on her body for days to come, but she would live.

Marina tended to her child. Colin could make no sense of what he was seeing; his cousin lay in a foetal position, battered and dazed, while a young slip of a girl stood over him. What the hell was going on?

Louis knew she had not been raped but the experience of what happened tonight would live with her for many years to come. Would she, like her mother, relive this night in her dreams? He hoped not.

Once Marina had dragged the bedspread from the bed, she was at Lucy's side and down on her knees. She wrapped it around her girl, tears of fear and relief rolling freely down her face. Rosa brought water from the large floral jug and a flannel, gently dampening her forehead, bringing her around. Emma followed with smelling salts. Lucy soon regained consciousness and gladly lay in her mother's arms, feeling safe for the first time since seeing Mark on the hall landing. She shuddered. Suddenly she felt sick as the memories flooded back. Tears were welling up in her eyes, then the burning hot tears rained down her face. Betrayed by the one she loved, how could he? Shock and relief waved over her.

The nightmare was over.

Colin stood over Mark's prone body wondering how the hell that slip of a girl had managed to floor his cousin. What had happened? Lucy was half-dressed, her bodice lay torn and tattered on the floor. Her modesty was protected from the eyes in the room by the bedspread that was wrapped around her now but it didn't cover the angry red marks that ringed her neck like a necklace.

Colin couldn't believe that Mark was capable of this, yet it was all there in front of his eyes. She was bruised and marked; his cousin was guilty of trying to strangle her. He hoped that was all. He prayed Mark had not tried to rape her.

She had certainly fought back, but how did she overpower him? It was impossible and yet Mark lay at his feet in the foetal position. The axe still hung from Colin's hand and the shattered door confirmed it was no dream.

Disgusted and ashamed, Colin threw the axe to one side, grabbed the jug from Rosa and poured its contents over the prone figure.

Somehow Colin dragged Mark to his feet, out of the room and down the stairs, collecting their outer clothing on the way, and out into the night.

The night sky was clear. It was cold and a frost was already gathering on the dead leaves and grass on the roadside. Even the trunks of the trees sparkled from the light of the full moon. The disk of white light had a halo of frost around it; it was going to be a very cold night and they had a long walk ahead of them.

The silence was deafening, only the occasional hoot from the owls out in search of food interrupted it.

Mark walked slightly behind his cousin Colin, the high spirits and laughter from earlier were all forgotten, his head was trying to cope with new conflicting memories. Mark struggled as he tried to put together what had happened. All he could remember was seeing Lucy in the light of the doorway as he left Emma's room. He remembered the anger he had felt at her for being in the house and catching him upstairs where he had… but no, no, that wasn't right. She had lied to him, that was it. He had pushed her back into the bedroom, he remembered that and straddling her on the bed, and then nothing. A big fat blank. But then… yes! He remembered. He was seeing things happening in a nightmarish vision he was having, but it wasn't him, was it?

Yet he was hurt, his head and his back felt as though they had been kicked, and as for his nether region, walking was difficult.

Colin was devastated. He had brought Mark to the house to taste the delights of the physical love of a woman. He had been euphoric when they met at the inn. It was supposed to have been a rite of passage for Mark, the moment of making Mark a man. Now all there was were questions.

Which way to turn? Did he try to keep it quiet? Could he keep it a secret? Keep it within the family? Who needed to know? On the other hand, would Mark do this again? Was Mark lost to a touch of madness?

Colin was disgusted by Mark's lack of repentance. He had not even tried to talk about what had happened and no apology had been uttered to him about the evening.

They had walked for perhaps a mile when suddenly he rounded on Mark, stopping him in midstride with a threatening hand clutching fast on Mark's collar. Colin's face was flushed with anger.

"Are you insane? What the hell do you think you were doing back there, attacking a young girl and leaving marks on her throat, are you mad? I took you there to make you a man." Emotion stopped the words being spoken; he gulped and wiped moisture from his eye before he finally said, "Not to make you a murderer or a rapist."

With that he released Mark and started back on the journey with his head down and his hands pushed well into his pockets. It was better that they were there than punching Mark's face because that was what he wanted to do.

Mark was dumbfounded; he remembered hands being around Lucy's neck. *Oh my God.* He remembered the tearing of her bodice and her small breasts. He saw it all! He watched it happen but he was a bystander. He didn't do it.

He caught up with Colin and suddenly a floodgate opened up from Mark. He talked non-stop on the way back but it was all gibberish ravings to Colin. Mark insisted that he had been taken over by something. That was what had happened. It was none of his doing.

Yes, he was angry, she had tricked him and made a fool of him. He had really loved her and he had put her on a pedestal, she was so special to him. What had he done? But it wasn't him, not really. It was as if he was watching but not actually doing the deed. He was taken over. Yes! Yes! That was it, taken over. But by what?

"Listen, Colin," Mark said, pulling at Colin's arm to slow him down." I met Lucy weeks ago in town when she was with her Aunt Rosa. We have been seeing each other in secret ever since. I really liked her, loved her and wanted her. I didn't know she belonged to that household, she never spoke about her family, I only knew she lived with her mother and her aunts. I never suspected her aunts were, well, you know. It really wasn't me, Colin, it really wasn't. I really don't know what happened. You just have to believe me," Mark pleaded, trying to explain.

He was ashamed and confused when he had seen Lucy on the landing, then his anger took over. All his desire for her became lust, anger and hate. The combination of his powerful emotions had started the whole sorry mess, but still somewhere along the way, his memory would not bring to the front his murderous attempt on Lucy's life. It was as if another person's eyes, hands and body were using him as a puppet.

Colin shook his head.

"There was only two people in the room, Mark. You and that young girl," responded Colin. The rest of the journey was travelled in stony silence.

The road back to the town seemed to go on forever in the freezing cold. It did nothing to help the two young men talk things through. Neither one of them wanted to think of the challenges that lay waiting, at the end of their journey.

"What are you going to tell your father?" asked Colin, standing outside the mayor's house.

"I'll tell him the truth."

"What do you mean by that?"

"Look, Colin, I know you don't believe me but I really don't know what happened. I was coming out of the bedroom, Emma had already gone downstairs. As I opened the door, the door opposite opened at the same time. Suddenly she was there. She shouldn't have been," he started to sob. "It was such a shock. I remember pushing her back inside the room. I was so angry.

Then she said something but I wouldn't listen. I thought she had betrayed me, played me for a fool. When I pushed her on the bed and straddled her I was only going to frighten her. God! I was furious, livid in fact, and then suddenly it wasn't me anymore. It was me but wasn't. Lord, I can't explain."

It was very late and they hoped they would not disturb the household but as it happened both of Mark's parents were up waiting for him to come home.

The first thing Mark's mother saw when she greeted him was the red scratches running down his face.

"Mark, what on earth has happened to you?" Not waiting for an answer, his mother turned to Colin.

"You were supposed to be taking him out and looking after him, what's happened?"

She went to hold him but he flinched as she took his head in her hands, she felt a large bump on the back of his head.

"You've been assaulted," she said, stepping back from him, "Paul, Paul, come here. Mark's hurt."

Paul came out of the study and walked across to where they were standing in the parlour. Colin took the lead and pushed forward, stopping Paul in his tracks.

"Uncle, I think we need to talk about this in your study, in private, please."

Colin ushered Mark and Paul back into the room that his uncle had just left, leaving his aunt stood in the parlour, open-mouthed, not understanding why she was being excluded from the meeting that was bound to be something to do with her son's injuries.

In the mayor's study-cum-library, Paul sat himself behind the large mahogany desk and indicated to the two men to take the chairs in front of it.

With his hands clasped and resting on the leather top, he sat back and prepared himself for what was to come. Paul was horrified when he was confronted with the story. There was his position to think of, what would the councillors say if it all came out? He had to think of a way to contain the scandal and help his son.

His eldest child had assaulted the young girl and almost committed murder, though he could not remember doing it. The men talked into the early morning, going over the story and picking it to bits, trying to find the truth. But Mark did not change his version of what happened. He kept repeating, "it wasn't me".

A doctor was called and visited Mark the next day. The three men went through what had happened the evening before almost minute by minute for the doctor. But the doctor had no answers, he could not explain any of it; Mark seemed a perfectly normal young man. His eyes were clear, there was no temperature, his blood pressure was normal, there were no fits or seizures in the family.

"Perhaps the drink in some way turned his mind or maybe his encounter with the lady of the night had disturbed him, all that pent-up frustration and need. Who knows what happens to the mind when it's under stress?" the doctor mused. At the end of the consultation it was decided that Mark should go into a sanatorium. The doctor presumed Mark had had a moment of insanity and that he must be watched in case it returned.

Mark agreed to it. He was frightened; how could he have done what Colin said he had to the girl he loved? His memory of the evening was still incomplete; however, he accepted that he was the only person in the locked room with Lucy and he prayed that there would never be a repeat of what had happened. The doctor signed the papers of his admission to the hospital and it was settled that he would pack up and go immediately to a private clinic in the neighbouring town of Whitchurch.

His mother found it particularly difficult to understand why he had to be hospitalised. She argued with Paul that she could look after him at home and nurse him until he was well but she was overruled. Paul told her that Mark had suffered a fit and had fallen down, hurting his head and scratching his face in the process, and that he needed to be monitored by experts. Not knowing the real truth, she unhappily agreed that he would be better off in hospital.

The red-bricked building that housed the clinic was set in its own grounds. Private and secluded, the large manor house was surrounded by lime trees and set with formal gardens that could be used by the patients who were deemed well enough to use them.

It was expensive. Paul was a wealthy man who was determined to get his son well and have him returned home. The room that Mark was given was comfortable but secure. It overlooked the gardens and he was able to watch his fellow patients, wrapped up in warm winter clothes, taking walks in the cold November sun, their faces ruddy from the cold air and their breath a white mist, matching the stiff, crisp white frosted grass that they walked upon.

Mark had a male nurse to see to his needs and also to observe him; the doctors wouldn't take risks in case he became violent. He settled down to the routine of the clinic. Everyday he talked with doctors and a psychiatrist, who talked through his fears and mental condition. He was given all the standard treatments for mental instability. The medicine only made him lethargic and sluggish. After a time he refused to take any more; without it he quickly returned to his normal self. The doctors were coming to the opinion that he was quite sane and they had no idea what had caused him to have that bout of madness.

Mark's mother was distressed at the thought of her precious son having to stay in hospital. The family honour was at stake, Paul and Colin partly to protect her from the truth but mostly to protect themselves, had thought up a suitable story to hide behind. If she ever found out about the house at the edge of town and the visits her men folk paid there, the family would be destroyed forever.

The madness of his son's actions that led to his internment in the sanatorium must be kept a secret. Because of Mark's illness he would remain there until the doctors agreed to his release. Paul knew had it not been for Colin breaking down the bedroom door and getting Mark out of there, that his son might well be waiting for his turn on the gallows.

The mayor knew Marina; he had been once or twice to her house in the past, but the house was now a threat to him and his wife must never find out about his indiscretions. The house must close and the women gone. The episode involving his son must never get out into the public domain. He decided that they, Marina and her girls, must leave the area as soon as possible.

20

That night in November would never be forgotten by any of the household. How could this have happened to them in their sanctuary? The place had protected them after their experiences of cruelty in the world outside. That night was a catalyst for the women and a crossroad for Louis.

It had taken almost a month for Lucy to heal. The bruises of black and blue turned yellow then faded. Her wrists and neck were still sore for a time. But everyday she grew stronger and her injuries finally healed until only the memories were left to haunt her. And they did. Love had betrayed her. Mark, the boy she loved, had attacked her and he had destroyed her hopes. Now she was only left with hate and shattered dreams.

Now, on top of everything else, her mother had told her they would have to leave their home. It was the only home she knew. She had spent sixteen years growing up there in a happy environment and the thought of moving made her nervous. But perhaps a new start would be good for her, given what had happened.

To start over would be difficult but Marina's strength was to always deal with each problem that came along. She would say you couldn't deal with what might be or would be or could be, only what is. And the situation was that the mayor would not allow them to live in this town anymore. Although Mark had been the perpetrator of the attack, Marina and Lucy would have to pay the price.

Marina had received a letter from the mayor giving her the choice of moving or going to jail for running a house of ill repute. What a pity that most of the councillors had been clients one time or another, including the mayor. And although some of the councillors had sympathy for Marina and the girls, it was better that the women were encouraged to leave the district.

The house felt unhappy. The sadness the family felt increased each day as they wondered what sort of future lay in front of them. They felt so utterly powerless. How could they stand up to the men who made the laws and ran the town? It seemed a huge injustice that they must pay for the crimes committed by Mark. It seemed it was always the weak and powerless that suffered when so-called justice was being metered out. But this wasn't about justice it was about saving face. The mayor had a reputation he could not afford to lose and he would protect it no matter what the cost was to them.

Breakfast around the kitchen table was subdued. It was 7.30am and still dark. The weather had been cold and damp for weeks. A heavy frost lay at night and the damp drizzly days were still hanging around, it was December and there was little sunlight.

It was as though the damp from outside had penetrated the house and seeped into the kitchen, affecting the mood of the ladies eating there. In two weeks it would be Christmas, though no one felt like celebrating.

It was Emma who broke the silence.

"I've been thinking, we can sit here and be miserable or we can enjoy the time we have left together. Christmas is in two weeks – let's get organised, make some chains to hang, cheer up the place. We can't do anything about the weather but we can do something about our mood. And we can at least celebrate that Lucy here is recovering well."

"You're right," said Marina. "We should be thankful." She put her arms round her daughter and hugged her.

Lucy was looking so much better. A month ago she looked so fragile, pale and bruised. Now the colour was back in her cheeks and her eyes and hair shone with health again, hiding the agonies that were going around in her head. But she would keep that to herself for now. She was nervous and needed company most of the time but she kept up a pretence in front of her family, knowing how they worried for her. Night was the worst. When she shut her eyes, when she hoped that sleep would take her to a place of rest, was when the memories returned in force. Did she really feel safe in her own home? She wasn't sure, but her mother and her aunts tried so hard to help her feel secure, at least in company she could smile again. Time was what she needed. Trust in others would be an issue for a long time but she would recover. Yes, she would! That much she promised herself.

"Yes, let's," Lucy agreed. Keeping busy always helped. "We could all use a lift of mood."

A new air filtered around the room. Louis, who was standing watching the group, found a smile growing on his face too. Relief coursed through him. His ladies, as he thought of them, had turned a corner; their healing had begun. He sat down to watch this new air of resilience and optimism that was filling the room. It was as though the sun had just appeared from behind a cloud and filled the room with warmth and light.

Looking at Louis across the kitchen smiling at the group, Rosa felt the lift in the room too. Suddenly she found her voice and *While Shepherds Watched their Flocks by Night* flooded the kitchen. Her voice was clear and melodious and for the next thirty minutes a number of well known carols were enjoyed around the table.

Roni and Nora felt their moods lift and found themselves laughing, amused at the thought of eating breakfast while singing carols.

"Well! This is just what we need," smiled Marina, joining in, though singing was not one of her gifts and the off-key notes she sang made the ladies at the table double up with laughter.

Louis sat in the corner. He was caught up in the new atmosphere that bounced about the room, humming the tunes of the carols as best he could. Christmas might be fun after all.

COLIN RETURNS

The ladies were sat in the drawing room, talking and planning the way ahead.

It was December 21st, the shortest day, and it was already growing dark though it was only 3.30pm.

"Should I light a lamp yet?" asked Nora.

"Good idea," answered Marina, "I hate dark nights and short days. While you're up put some more coal on the fire, will you? There's a love."

Nora was halfway to the door to get the lamp when there was a tapping on the outside side door.

The women were surprised and a little stunned; no one had come to the house and knocked on that door since that awful night in November. No one was welcome. Business had ceased. No one moved or spoke until the knock came again, this time a fraction louder.

"Who is it?" shouted out Marina, moving quickly and standing behind the door.

"It's me, Colin. Can I talk to Roni?"

"She's got nothing to say to you."

"Please, please, I've come to see you all to apologise, only I didn't dare come before now. I feel so responsible. Please let me talk to Roni, if only for a minute."

"Go away, the house is closed."

In almost a whisper he pleaded, "Please, I'm not here for business, I only want to talk. To know how you all are. I'm sorry for what my uncle is doing to you. It's not right. I've tried to talk him out of driving you away but he won't listen to me." He raised his voice in desperation. "Please, I must talk with Roni."

"Must you!" retorted Marina, looking over to Roni. "Do you want to talk with him?"

Roni nodded. She was rather uncomfortable knowing how Marina felt, but she had always had a soft spot for Colin. She had from the first time she saw him, her heart had leapt and a thrill had rippled through her body. For her it was beyond physical attraction, she loved him. Their weekly meetings had been special to her though she never spoke of it to anyone. Her dreams she accepted as just that, dreams that could never come true, dreams that made her feel foolish at the unrealistic nature of them.

"You have five minutes," said Marina firmly, opening the door and feeling the cold rush of winter air come into the room from outside. Colin, cap in hand, stood nervously on the doorstep.

Marina turned away, muttering, "Shut the door behind you." Looking at the others but speaking to the couple, she said in an equally firm voice, "We better go into the kitchen and leave you to talk. Five minutes and you're gone." Marina left the room, followed by the others, leaving Roni and Colin standing looking at each other, not knowing what to say.

It had always been so easy when he was a customer. Now he was a visitor he was tongue-tied.

He was just a man who wanted to see the woman he missed. All the many times he had visited her, he had never asked the question why he had to come back each week to be with her. He had valued his freedom, never thinking he would ever want to be settled with one woman, but the thought of her being out of his life forever, gone from the area and never seeing her again had hit him hard and he didn't like the thought of it at all.

"Look Roni," he said, taking her hand, "can I come and see you every now and again until you leave?"

She grabbed her hand back defensively. "Really! You know I am not a working girl any longer?" Her eyes starting to fill up with tears, her emotions were confused and overwhelming her. Colin looked so downcast as he answered in a faltering voice that she felt sorry for him.

"Yes, and I'm so sorry for bringing this on all of you. If I hadn't brought Mark here—" He stopped mid-sentence, unable to speak. He had brought him so it was his fault, his burden that he had to live with. Roni and the rest of the family were being turned out of their town, being made to sell up and move on.

His fault, entirely his fault, and he felt so guilty.

Roni could feel the anguish he was feeling surrounding her as well. She was touched by his obvious sympathy for her and her adopted family and the plight they were in. Reaching out to him, she reminded him.

"If you hadn't been here, Lucy would have died," she said quietly. She touched his shoulder in a gesture of friendship. "You should remember that, you saved her by breaking down the door."

Colin welled up. His eyes were watery as he gulped, trying to keep the tears back. He didn't want to be disloyal to his family but his uncle was wrong to punish this family. His feelings for Roni were strong at that moment; he knew he couldn't live never seeing her again. Why had it taken something so vile, so rotten to make him realise it?

He had never questioned why she did what she did. He was selfish and conceited; he had never thought past his own pleasures. If she gave him the chance he would get to know all about her, including her past, and maybe they might have a future together. By coming here tonight he hoped that maybe he had taken the first steps to make that happen.

Marina made an appearance back in the room; she seemed to fill it with fearful energy, stating in a stabbing tone, "Your five minutes is up! You should be gone."

"May I call after Christmas? Please." He looked to Marina then Roni. "Just to see how everyone is," he pleaded.

"That would be nice," Roni replied before Marina could refuse.

Setting his cap firmly on his head he left quickly before any more conversation might deny the arrangement that Roni had agreed to. Marina was left open-mouthed. When she recovered, slowly shaking her head, she said "I hope you know what you're doing, Miss."

Roni hoped she did too.

Whether it was seeing Colin again or not, she didn't know, but Lucy's memories of that night and Mark returned in full force.

History repeating itself, thought Louis, as he watched the girl toss and turn, the bedclothes becoming tangled with her body; she would get no rest tonight. It reminded Louis of the time he intervened when Marina was troubled with nightmares.

Should he try and intervene? Faced with that choice, he remembered too having to invade her body to save her life. No! He would wait; she should not have to endure further confusion by waking and maybe remembering more of that night than she did already. Marina, as always, was waiting in the wings to soothe her daughter's night terrors, calm her and try to normalise life for her. She would do more for her daughter than he could that night.

Christmas Day and Boxing Day had come and gone. For a brief time, the household had enjoyed the Christmas spirit, knowing that this was the last time they would share it with each other in this house. The house which had been their home and refuge for so long.

It had been a diversion for the ladies. Louis, the only bystander, watched and enjoyed the energy that moved about the kitchen over the Christmas period. It was perfect to him, a picture of what a family should be.

A feast had been prepared; a goose roasted to perfection served with vegetables from the garden store and Christmas pudding, black and full of dried fruits, steamed for hours, spilling its rich aroma out into the kitchen. Louis's senses were overwhelmed, the smell evoking memories from his past. And for a moment, just a moment he felt the anger and the despair of his existence, this half-life he lived, sharing but not being part of reality. He pushed the feelings quickly away. Self-pity never helped.

He looked on the smiling faces of Marina, Lucy and Rosa laughing and eating around the kitchen table and relaxed; he had made a difference to their lives.

At the end of the meal Rosa proposed a toast. As they raised their glasses she said, "Happy Christmas everyone. Grateful thanks to our guardian angels, wherever they are." Looking directly at Louis, she nodded. "May they continue to look after all of us."

"Yes, indeed," agreed Marina. Louis knew then that he was valued.

It was a new year and a new start for the house. It was exactly seven days later when Colin's rap on the door was heard again. Colin's weekly visits resumed. At first, only Roni was happy at his return visits to their home; to say that the atmosphere was a little strained when he appeared was an understatement. But he was determined to win the women over and grow a friendship with them. Little by little, his warmth and sincerity had an effect on the ladies, reducing the walls of protection they had put around themselves to rubble, slowly letting him into their lives. They had a sort of understanding and a bond from that miserable night in November but total trust would have to be earned, and it was not so easy to come by.

Life was going to be uncertain and scary for the lone women once they went their separate ways but change would come regardless and they had no choice but to face whatever came. The relationship between Colin and the household was very different after just a few weeks he had become a friend and it was obvious that he was a changed person.

A great void had been left where once Mark had been. It was supposed to have been a rite of passage to make him a man. What a fool he was, believing in that. Now he knew better; as if sex could make a man. Love, however, was a different case. He had lost Mark's companionship and was not prepared to lose Roni's. Becoming friends with the women and helping them in moving on were his top priorities, plus slowing down his vindictive uncle in his plan to get rid of them. Mark was Colin's friend and cousin, they had been like brothers throughout their lives; Colin didn't know how he would fare without him, but for the life of him, he still could not understand what had got into Mark that awful night.

The mayor had given Marina extra time to sell up and move on, whether through Colin's influence or not, she didn't know but she was grateful. It gave Marina the time to put together a plan to find a new business and put the house up for sale.

Neither Nora nor Roni had fully recovered from the terrible night when George had attacked both of them, plus they carried the extraordinary episode of Mark's involvement with Lucy in their minds. Unsettled they both accepted it was time to move on and find a safer way to earning a living. Each of them had managed to save a substantial sum over the years so that both girls were able to plan new futures for themselves. And plan they must before they had to leave the home they had shared with Marina.

Mark's stay at the hospital was for much less time than originally thought. By the end of January he was declared fit. Mark felt fine he had had no fits or bouts of violence in the three months that he was there under observation. The doctors could find nothing wrong with him and they released him as fully recovered. Too many memories of that November evening had returned while he was convalescing. The awfulness of his actions truly disgusted him.

The England he knew was at war. Many of his friends had already gone to fight the Hun. The government had said the war would be over by Christmas but Christmas had come and gone and there was no end in sight.

He felt the call of duty to go and fight for his country. He at least would be helping his country and perhaps he would find some peace in his mind for what he appeared to have done to Lucy and her family.

Colin had told him of the scene he had encountered when he burst into that bedroom. Of Lucy lying half-naked on the floor, bruised with red weals around her neck. Now he remembered and he had to live with the nightmare both awake and when he was sleeping. Lucy was the girl he loved, he could never live with the guilt of it or the loss of her. War was welcome; he would die there or come back a better man.

For the short time before being drafted into the army he stayed at home, he had been tempted to write to Lucy, begging her for her forgiveness. He explained that the doctors had said that he had been temporarily insane; there was nothing else that could explain his actions.

> *Dear Lucy,*
>
> *I'm writing this before I go to war in France. I can't tell you how distressed I am at the wrongs I have done to you. My only explanation is that I had some temporary madness (according to my doctors). It's only now that I fully remember what happened that night. I am so ashamed. Please, I beg you to forgive me if you can.*
>
> *I may not come back from the war but if I do, I hope that somehow I can make it up to you for all the distress I have caused. I will always love you.*
>
> *Mark*

When Lucy received the letter, she tore it into small pieces and threw it into the flames of the fire.

"That's where you belong, Mark – in hell!"

21

Marina replayed that November night over and over again in her mind, the terrible attack on Lucy. She remembered standing on the landing hearing the noises from behind the door and fearing for her daughter, being locked out of the bedroom, hammering on the door with her fists and Rosa at her side in that hall landing. At one point, Marina was aware Rosa was in conversation talking to an invisible God-only-knows-what. It was just before Colin acted and broke down the bedroom door. When it opened, Mark was prone on the floor. Lucy seemed to be in a trance before she also fell in a heap on the floor.

What had happened? Could Rosa explain it? Marina hoped so. The right time arrived one day after lunch. Nora had gone into town determined she wasn't going to be driven out and was looking for a property to start a tearoom of her own, Lucy and Roni had decided to take a rest and were in bed and Emma was busy sewing a new skirt in her room.

In the quiet of the kitchen, Rosa and Marina finished the washing up and cleared away to make the table ready for the evening meal. The weak sun from the garden shone through the French doors, catching Marina's eye; she had a sudden urge to be out in the cool fresh air.

"Fancy a turn around the garden?" she asked, looking at Rosa.

Rosa felt stifled in the dim light of the kitchen too and with a nod of her head went and opened the doors. As she stepped out through them, the cool air hit her. Turning her face to the sun she stood for a moment feeling the gentle warmth on her. Her garden was as it always was in February, without colour but tidy. Only a few leeks were left in the vegetable plot and by the summer, someone else would be tending it. A lump came to Rosa's throat. This part of the house was hers and she would sorely miss it.

Marina's arm came around her shoulders, tenderly moving her forward onto the grass towards the bench. She instinctively knew the sadness Rosa was feeling.

The bench was in full sun. The frost that had settled there in the morning had all melted. There was a comfortable calm between them as they sat together. They had shared thoughts and secrets together throughout the years and cared for each other as sisters would.

Without needing to watch her words, Marina asked the question she had held on to for so many months. "Rosa, I'm puzzled. That night on the landing when Lucy was attacked, I remember you acted strangely. It seemed you were talking and giving instructions to someone just before Colin and Roni came to help." Her emotions were racing back as she pictured the scene again in her mind's eye. Swallowing hard, she continued, "What happened, Rosa? Can you tell me?"

The pain of growing up with this gift she had had reflected badly so often in her life that she was not at ease sharing her experiences, but with Marina it was different; she had an open mind and had never judged her. That said, how could she tell Marina that the demon could have been the same as the one that had killed her own parents?

Despite the sun, a shiver went down her back; she was deep in thought for a moment until a ghostly touch brushed her shoulder lightly.

"You must tell her what you know, Rosa, she deserves that." Louis's thoughts seeped into her mind; she knew he was standing behind her.

The time appeared to be right to tell Marina all about Louis, the guardian ghost and friend of the house who, to her certain knowledge, had prevented murder at least twice. He had also helped Marina through a period of malaise and troubled dreams where the past had almost consumed her.

"I can only try," said Rosa. "First I have to confess that I have been keeping something from you. Louis, your guardian angel, is a ghost, trapped here by his life's blood that was caught into the wood of the bed you bought."

Marina was stunned. "What are you saying?"

Rosa put her finger to Marina's lips and, shaking her head slightly, continued. "Let me finish. On that evening you are asking me about, Louis came to me in the kitchen. He was desperate to help Lucy and had been fighting Mark in spirit, but he knew he was losing the fight. The trouble was, Mark was not actually himself. When we got to the bedroom door I could smell an odour, a thick smell of decay. It was a smell I knew from long ago when I was a girl; the smell of evil and death, brought by a demon that feeds on misery, anger and hate.

"Mark somehow became its puppet; it invaded Mark and he became possessed. The demon was in control and Mark was not the person we knew. The spirit inside of him was using him and feeding on Lucy. It prolonged Lucy's agony for as long as possible before it was ready to kill her. That way it could feed, all the while growing and become stronger.

"Louis told me that Lucy's life was slowly being drained away. He was fighting but he was a spirit, whereas the demon that was inside Mark's body was using Mark to do its will. Louis needed a physical body to fight it. I told him he must use Lucy's body, that it was the only way to save her. Louis blended his spirit into her body. He did not harm her in any way. He became her strength, she was his limbs. Together they defeated the evil."

Marina was shocked and pale with the news.

"So you are telling me that I brought the ghost into the house when I bought my bed, and that this ghost saved my Lucy?"

"In a word, yes."

"And he's here?"

"Yes."

"I've never believed in ghosts," whispered Marina. "This Louis, where is he now?"

"Stood behind us."

Marina turned and looked behind her. She could see nothing and she smiled at her foolishness. "But of course, he's a ghost."

She was so grateful that her eyes became watery as they filled with tears and impatiently she wiped away an escaping tear from her cheek with the back of her hand. She badly wanted to thank him for saving her daughter, but she felt slightly awkward smiling at an empty space. If only she could see him.

She looked over Rosa's shoulder at the spot where she thought he might be; for a split second, a thin shadow seemed to appear, blotting out the sunlight for a moment, only then it was gone. As if he knew what she was thinking, she felt a light brush on her cheek that was like the fluttering of a butterfly – cold, yes but a kiss that warmed her heart.

"If you can hear me, thank you," she said, with some modesty. It was clear she was in his debt, but how could she repay a ghost for what he had done for her?

She had not feared him. It was Louis's turn to smile. She was grateful and he felt her acceptance of himself into this extended family.

Louis liked this woman more each day. She was strong, kind and cared for the family she had brought together, despite all the hardships that had come with it. She wouldn't have changed any of it.

It was true that he was appalled when he first saw her bidding for his bed. Dressed in that awful disguise, she had looked and acted like someone from the gutter. He should have known better than to judge her; had he thought about it, there was more to her than met the eye. Anyone who appreciated his work and loved crafted wood had taste and style. From the very first day he spent in the house when she shed her disguise, he had found her intriguing. Since then he had come to admire her resourcefulness and her big heart, for it was a beacon of love that was shared in the household.

She wants to see me, thought Louis and he wondered if there was a way.

The conversation carried on between the women.

"In truth," Rosa went on, " I doubt if Mark comprehends what happened to him. I knew when I first met him, that he was conflicted with an incendiary temper that once lost so would his reason. But he had a good sensitive side too that disappeared when the evil spirit used him."

"Are you saying that Mark was innocent of what happened? I just can't believe that."

"No! Not exactly. I'm saying it was Mark's eruption of anger that allowed the dark force to use him. I can only conclude that the shock of seeing Lucy and the fact he had just left Emma filled him with guilt that turned to anger. And remember, we had told him a story that he had believed. Seeing Lucy here and realising her aunts were working girls must have been something of a shock, he must have felt betrayed and rage followed."

"But why Lucy? He loved her," interjected Marina.

"Love and hate are the same coin, just on different sides. Both powerful emotions, so close they sometimes cross."

"But where did the evil spirit come from? Our home has always been so full of love and care. I really don't understand."

Rosa sighed as she replied. "Who knows, Marina? From the walls of the house, from the trees, I don't know. The demon only needed a gateway to get here from wherever it came from and that gateway was Mark's fury and hate."

"I don't know whether to feel sorry for him or not. If he was possessed then he wasn't really Mark." Marina stopped and a great sigh escaped from her lips. "But what he did to my girl…" She stopped again; there was no need to say anything further. Her pain for Lucy was obvious and when a tear trickled down her face she felt a ghostly hand wipe it away. It stirred an emotion in her she had not felt for a long time and she was not sure she was ready to feel it again. He was a ghost; how could she possibly care for a ghost?

Later, the household heard through Colin that Mark had been killed in the trenches in France. *Another young man killed for what?* thought Marina. She felt sadness for his family, especially his mother. All Lucy felt when she heard was relief. Now he would never be able to touch her again and because of that knowledge, some of the fear she held deep within her disappeared.

Louis was standing in the drawing room watching as Colin gave the house the news. He was clearly upset. He sat down with the ladies and gave them all the details. His cousin was dead; the telegram had come that morning to his uncle's house. Colin had seen the mayor with shaking hands holding the paper with the bitter message. Unable to cry in front of his wife, he had shut himself in his study and cried silent tears. Colin's poor aunt was beside herself; she had taken to her bed with a tonic to calm her nerves but she had no restraint and the cries of anguish could be heard downstairs. She allowed her tears to flow, hating her husband for not sharing their grief together. What she wouldn't have given to have Paul's arms around her and cry together for the loss of their dear son. Colin confessed that his aunt now feared for her youngest boy Simon; he had reacted with passion and anger and was eager to avenge his brother's death against the Germans. Colin's aunt was praying that the war would soon be over, before he was old enough to enlist. She could not take the pain of the thought of losing both of them to war. Colin also felt anger but it was tempered by some hidden relief. Because of a heart murmur, he had not been called to fight. His body had let him down but maybe it had also saved his life.

Lucy's face betrayed her thoughts. Louis understood. Her poor young body had been injured; her natural trust in people had gone and she no longer felt secure with strangers.

Her eyes filled with tears but the tears she shed were for herself. She wondered if she would ever trust a man again. In the night, when she was restless, Louis would join her in her dreams and would try to soothe her. His heart went out to this very young woman who was barely more than a child. She had dared to love and lost.

In the struggle when Mark attacked her, she remembered she had tried to appeal to him but his eyes were filled with madness, the pupils coloured black and the whites bloodshot red. Eyes that were Mark's, but not Mark's. She couldn't reach him, she tried and tried but he wouldn't listen, she had given up hope of staying alive. How she had fought him off at the end she didn't know. She remembered a slow blackness overtaking her and then a sudden surge of energy that raced into her body. She knew she was dying slowly but her limbs suddenly had a life of their own; they thrashed about, attacking Mark, hitting him, kicking him, even though she knew she was still very weak and faint. The state she was in, her actions just didn't fit. How could she have fought Mark when she was on the verge of collapse? Rosa said her natural instincts for survival had kicked in but a part of her mind didn't accept that and she still questioned it.

Only a few nights ago, Louis had stepped into a nightmare she was having. She was restless and sobbing in her sleep. When he laid his hand on her forehead, he was transported into the nightmare that troubled her. She was surrounded in darkness, curled up into a small ball on the floor. Several pairs of huge eyes pierced the blackness, staring down at her. They were much larger than the size of normal eyes. They glowed red and black, the way she remembered Mark's had done that awful night. Hands, large and rough, were reaching out towards her, dozens of them touching, prodding and nipping her as she tried to hide herself, crouching and becoming so small that she wouldn't be seen. Louis took her hand that protected her head, with his other hand he lifted her face to his, giving her a smile to give her assurance, and he pulled her up to her feet.

He brought light into her dark space and the eyes and hands faded one by one as the light reached them. She was soon standing next to Louis being bathed in soft light that was growing steadily brighter; she saw the room that she stood in was Marina's. The carved bedhead with its sun over the tree of life was glowing and was sending its bright rays across the room to her and Louis. Walking towards the bed, they found that the Garden of Eden surrounded them, the flowers came to life, the leaves on the tree murmured in the breeze she felt on her face. She was no longer afraid.

This gentleman was here to help and she could see from his eyes his kindness; there was no threat in him. They walked a path that wended behind the tree, passing all kinds of bright beautiful flowers she didn't recognise, but the perfume that came from them but it was quite heady; it lifted her spirits as she walked on the path. They were walking away from the garden now, towards purple hills and a grassy plain. The path became wider and split in two, the left side of it becoming stony while the path on the right side was still bordered with blue cornflowers. The flowers continued on the right but on the left, the stony path was developing into a rocky, uneven, unfriendly trail. Without warning a huge arch appeared before them. It stretched from one path to the other and connected them both in the middle on a narrow strip of land. Within the arch she saw two open doorways. Light spilled out of the door on the right but dark shapes moved in the left-hand doorway and she could hear wails and shrieks that were muted but nevertheless audible from that space; noises that made her stomach turn. Some fear returned. As they got nearer, the shape of a man appeared to be standing in the centre of both entrances. He was struggling but she couldn't see who with. Coming nearer she saw it was Mark. She tried to turn and run then but Louis held her firm.

Lucy, be patient for another minute, then you can go. The words were heard but not spoken. She looked at Louis; his face still read kindness. All right, she would stay for a minute, but only a minute. She looked towards Mark again. This time she could see his struggle. He was between two spectres, one an angel shining so bright that she could only just make out his outline, and one a dark moving mist that shaped itself like a man before half-dissolving and reshaping itself again. The dark spectre was using all its strength to pull Mark into its dark world, while the guardian or doorkeeper of the light was trying to take him into the light. Mark was in purgatory, a halfway place between heaven and hell. A place where there was no peace. Mark's memories plagued his mind and tears of uncontrollable grief poured down his face. His guilt was pulling him to the dark side and his hope was pulling him to the light. He was trapped in between the two, lost by his guilt and needing forgiveness.

Lucy was without pity. She looked at him. She had loved him but he had betrayed her, it was that simple. She was indifferent to his plight. It was of no interest to her now. Whatever he got by way of punishment he deserved, she would cry no tears over his plight.

Louis was saddened by her response but understood. They turned and walked back through his garden, back to her room and her bed. She would sleep now, but only part of the nightmare was gone. Sometime in the future he would try again to give her the chance to forgive, for what she was holding on to would only get more destructive as the years went on. Hate would damage her soul and take away some of her light.

FEBRUARY 1915

Nora was the first to leave.

The winter was cold and wet, much wetter than normal; the walks to the town left Nora worn out. Searching for a place to rebuild her life was not going as well as she had hoped. Every vacant shop she had been to see had either been too small, didn't have a kitchen or didn't have living accommodation above, which was crucial to her plan. She had scoured newspapers every day for the last two months, ever since the New Year.

Time was running out for Nora. Marina was due to take up the new post at Easter time in two months; she must find a place soon or she would have nowhere to live.

It was a serendipity moment when she accidently bumped into John on one of her trips to town. They had got on so well for so many years and she had missed their time together.

Everything had changed and the relationship they had had was lost. Then here he was, on the same street, looking at her with his gentle eyes. Her heart skipped a beat, she suddenly felt shy. He took her by the hand and invited her to have a cup of tea with him.

Down the road was a little teashop, set back off the road on the corner of a quiet side street. Inside were half a dozen tables and a counter with a glass case. Delicious buns, cakes and sandwiches were displayed under glass domes. Hot steam rose from the kettles that sat on the hob waiting to be used for coffee and tea. The lady who was in charge came across as soon as they sat down. Three other couples were enjoying the homemade cakes and were happily engaged in deep conversation. The atmosphere was warm and calm in the little shop. How envious Nora felt looking at the lady who stood waiting with notepad, ready to take the order from them. This was just what she was looking for. How long would it take for her to find what she so desperately needed to make a fresh start?

For today at least she settled back and enjoyed John's company. He had missed her as well and for the next hour they chatted just as old friends would have done; there was no tension between them. John settled the bill when they were ready to leave and they arranged to meet there again the following week.

It had been so lovely to meet John again. She had hopes that they would remain friends and, if she was very honest with herself, she hoped for even more.

She spent the rest of the day walking around the town hoping to find premises, but there was nothing. Her walk back to Marina's was long and gloomy. Only the thought of seeing John the following week kept her from being completely dejected.

The week sped by and she found herself walking to town on a chilly but sunny day. They were to meet at eleven and she had given herself plenty of time to walk the few miles into town.

There was peacefulness all about her and it gave her time to think and, because she was something of a dreamer, it also gave her time to hope. Hope for her future. This time she was sure she would find those premises she needed.

Her thoughts turned to John and their meeting up for the second time. *He must really like me*, she thought. After all, he had been quite insistent on meeting again.

She was quite sure in her own mind that the sex thing was a thing of the past and that now they could get on with just being themselves, and they would get to know each other in a completely different way. After all, he had always been the perfect gentleman and had treated her with thoughtfulness and generosity.

When she arrived, the tearoom was half-empty. For a minute she felt panicky; he wasn't there. *Don't be silly, Nora*, she said to herself. *He could just be held up, it doesn't mean he's not coming.*

She settled herself down at a table for two near the window. The owner was busy serving another table and as she waited for her to attend her, for the first time Nora really looked about her, surveying her surroundings with a critical eye. Apart from the glass counter, which was bright from the effect of the cakes, buns and sandwiches on display, the rest of the interior was dingy. The walls sported quite a dark shade of brown paint, there was a plain wooden floor and the few tables were all covered with large brown checked oil cloths.

If it had been my place, she thought, *I would have had white walls to reflect the light from the window, blue gingham tablecloths and a vase on every table holding a single seasonable flower.*

"Hello Nora." The voice of John cut into her daydreams.

She nearly jumped out of her skin.

"Oh my goodness! You startled me, I was miles away."

"So I see," said John, pulling out the chair and sitting down opposite her. He put his hand into his pocket, found a penny and laid it in front of her. "A penny for your thoughts!"

"Oh, it was nothing really. I was just imagining what I might do if I owned a place like this."

The conversation eased naturally into Nora's aspirations and hopes about finding a tearoom like this. To get away from her past and make a new start. She needed a shop with accommodation and she must find one soon.

Time was running out. Marina was packing up and in a few weeks she would be starting her new life in a neighbouring town. Nora had been looking for many weeks but nothing she had seen had been just right. Either the rent was too much or there was no accommodation, or it was too far from the main streets to attract the volume of customers she needed to give her a chance to be successful.

It's funny, thought John, *in all the time I have spent with Nora, in all the conversations we have had, never once have we talked about her hopes or the circumstances that brought her to 'the house'!*

In an ideal world he would have liked to have met her in different circumstances, somewhere very respectable so that he could have introduced her to his daughters, but that could never have happened. However, if she ran her own shop… He paused on that thought, not ready to think further. At least, not yet!

He must not rush into anything. For now, he would continue to see her for tea now and again and see how they both got on. With that in mind, he invited her to tea the following week there in the tearoom.

John was already sitting at a table when she arrived. She had been so distracted seeing him there that it was only when she entered the shop that she noticed the notice on the door. Her heart leapt; the shop was up for let, enquiries within.

John passed the shop every day on his way to his office. He saw the notice go up midweek and had already engaged the present owner in discussion, declaring an interest on behalf of Nora.

Butterflies turned in Nora's stomach. Was this the break she had been waiting for?

John explained it all over their cup of tea. She could sign the papers within the month and she would have her dream come true. Was fate taking a hand in helping Nora? Was the door of opportunity opening? Had fate deliberately brought her here? She hoped so. If she could afford the rent and there was accommodation over the shop, she would be set for the future.

22

A NEW START

Marina was busy sorting out the furniture. Some would stay in the house when it was sold and some she would take with her when she left. She had managed to find an inn in the neighbouring town of Broadford that she could buy and run, and make a fresh start with Lucy. She had no connections with the small town and with a new surname, they would be able to make a new life there.

The Pack Horse stood alone on the corner of the main street. An unmade road not much more than a dirt track ran down the left-hand side of the pub, it led to a row of dismal dwellings where the local farm workers lived. The pub's entrance was across the corner of the building, touching both the track and the main road, serving as an entrance for the residents of the poor cottages equally with the residents of the white thatched terraced cottages, named after the old Queen Victoria, that lined the main road. They were set back from the road, sporting small well-tended gardens filled with spring flowers that were almost ready to burst open and show their colours, it being March.

Directly opposite the pub was Home Farm, the hub of the town, employing many people whom Marina hoped would frequent her public house. The farm served the community with milk, butter and beef, as well as producing vegetables according to the season. Marina would be able to buy all she needed from just across the road to make her new venture work, for her pub would serve food as well as ale.

Marina had realised the inn's potential when she came to view it just after the New Year. The Pack Horse had had a good reputation, and the landlord had served the community well until he made a decision that cost him his health. Marina heard the story through the agent on viewing the property. It had been an unfortunate choice on his part, made that night some months ago when he had taken it upon himself to intervene in a drunken brawl in the road outside his pub. Two brothers, well known for becoming aggressive after drinking, had set upon each other after a silly argument, which neither brother could remember the thread of, when they sobered up the next day. Too late for the landlord, who had tried to separate them, he had tried to get between them pushing them apart to stop the fight. Sadly the brothers were no longer even aware of the world outside. In the heat and fury of the fight they were immersed in, they turned their anger and fists on the landlord, beating him until he fell and then, not being content that he was down, using their heavy booted feet on him until he was unconscious. Only when the patrons saw him drop, as they watched from the safety of the pub doorway did they rush out and desperately drag the brothers off the injured man. Only then did they become aware of just how injured he was. It would be a long time before he would recover from the beating and his wife and children no longer felt safe at the inn. His wife made the decision to take him back to the village from where they had come from, back to the extended family they left behind. It was for the best for all concerned. What had been a disaster for them became an opportunity for Marina.

Marina had lost none of her sharpness in business or the need to survive in the world. She feared the future for Lucy. Never in her wildest dreams had she thought that any harm could come to her baby, her daughter, because of her need to provide for them the way she had. The workhouse had never been an option for them, once the old lord gave her money to provide for the grandchild he would never openly acknowledge. She had to pretend that she was a widow to save her daughter from being pilloried and labelled a bastard. It had been her job to protect her and she had, until Lucy met Mark. No one could have foreseen what happened to Lucy or the consequences that had ultimately brought Marina here to the Pack Horse.

The Pack Horse had lain empty for some months and the place was in a disgusting state when Marina stood in the doorway and surveyed the squalid room. Light from the open door caught the speckles of dust mites that had been disturbed from the sudden waft of air into the room. With a key in one hand, her other hand placed squarely on her hip, she surveyed this place that was to be her new home. In the dim light that came from the dirty windows she could see layers of dust covering the whole room. Cobwebs dangled like fine lace from the beams above her head. *How quickly the spiders took over,* she thought to herself. The inn had been vacated rather quickly two months ago and it looked like it; no one had bothered to clear up the place. Chairs, stools and small tables were scattered around the snug bar. The floor still had the sawdust on it that had been spread there from weeks ago. The smell of sour beer still hung in the air from the discarded tankards at the back of the counter; they still held small quantities of the foul brown stuff.

Lord! Thought Marina, *it'll take a month of Sundays to get this place up and running again.*

"However long it takes," she said loudly to herself. This was a new chapter in their lives; she would roll up her sleeves and face the task.

Marina cleaned the bar area and one small room at the back of the building, ready for Rosa to sleep in. Rosa had agreed that she would take up residence a couple of days before the main move. Someone would have to be there to receive the new supplies that they would need to start up the business. Rosa would set up the kitchen and make it ready for the breads and soups that they would offer as part of the new venture. Food would be available, alongside beer and spirits once they were open.

There was still so much to do: meeting with solicitors, reading and understanding the legal papers before signing them, seeing bank managers and just general juggling to make the move from one lifestyle to another.

It was March and they were ready for the move. Moving into another town and making another life for herself and Lucy was nerve-racking.

Her family of girls that she had loved so much had split up now. Nora had found her teashop and was busy building a new life for herself with support from John.

Colin and Roni had moved to Oxford, away from the narrow minds of his uncle and family, she would never be good enough for the family but she was good enough for him.

Emma, who had always been adventurous sailed east as many people had to find a new life in America and Marina hoped she would find happiness there. Her girls, her friends, had found new paths to follow and she hoped they would find good new lives wherever they went.

Her dear friend Rosa wanted to move with them and both she and Lucy were pleased about that. Rosa who was sensitive and talked to spirits. Who had befriended a ghost that had saved lives, a spirit who lived with them and would move with them. A spirit, according to Rosa, that was trapped in between worlds and was connected to Marina's finely carved bed.

March was one of those months when the weather could be warm, even promising that spring was just around the corner, or wild and ferocious with snow, ice and driving rain. Today the skies were grey and there was a bite in the wind as men moved backwards and forwards, in and out of the house that had been home for many years, loading the van with all Marina's possessions. For the past two weeks, Marina, Lucy and Rosa had travelled daily over to what would be their new home to clean and prepare the rooms for this very day. Old furnishings in the pub had been taken down; curtains washed, dried and re hung; rugs and carpet squares lifted up then hung over washing lines and beaten until not one speck of dust was left in them.

And here it was, moving day. It was with a certain sadness that Marina and Lucy walked around the empty house that was no longer a home, just a shell that had treated them well. It was the kitchen and the garden that they would miss the most, the gatherings around the kitchen table for breakfasts of porridge, hot buttered toast and laughter. They had enjoyed the long days of summer in the garden with the girls. They had sat on soft cushions that covered the bench in the early evenings, sipping tea together, surrounded by flowers that gave off a heady perfume. They would miss that and the friendship they shared for all those years.

A lump stuck in Marina's throat. Taking Lucy's hand, she moved her towards the front door to turn the key in the lock for the last time.

The snow had gone from the streets where it had laid for a week, the weather had warmed up a little and, although grey skies were predominant along with a gusty wind that tugged at your clothes, no rain clouds were in sight. It was fine enough for moving.

They moved on a Tuesday. Marina, being Marina, was determined for the pub to be ready to open to the public by the end of that week. And so it was.

True to her word, she opened the doors of her inn the morning of the fourth Friday in March and hoped that this new venture and new home would be good for all concerned, but especially Lucy.

THE PACK HORSE

Rosa was already living at the Pack Horse. It had been agreed with Marina that she would go first and live there so that she was available to receive new stocks of food and ale in readiness for their opening. That had all gone well.

Rosa scrubbed the kitchen down until every surface shone. The wooden tables were so clean that you could have eaten a meal off the surface. The day of the move came quickly and by late afternoon the van had delivered and was gone. The plywood crates were stacked in the various rooms, clearly marked on their sides with their contents, ready to be unpacked and put away. All the furniture was standing where it would stay for as long as Marina lived in her new home. Emptying the crates and setting up the bar would take a couple of days. First of all, the drinking glasses and tankards must be washed and stacked on shelves that stretched over the bar. That was at the top of Marina's to-do list. Crockery and utensils that were only to be used for the pub meals would be cleaned and stored in readiness for use. Everything would be in order for the opening in two days' time.

Marina's new bedroom was set at the back of the pub overlooking a garden that was not as big or as pretty as the one she had left, but it had potential. Once they had settled in she would see to planting bulbs and seeds to bring it to life.

Her bed stood bare at the wall that faced the window she was looking out of. She had come up to make the bed; one job less for later when she knew she would be too exhausted to tackle it. She turned, looking at the mattress that lay askew across the slats. Her eyes rested on the box holding the linen that was waiting beside it.

"No time like the present," Marina said loudly, moving over. Reaching to pull the mattress straight, she saw the stains left by Louis's blood.

Oh my Lord. A chill shot down her spine and her hand flew to her mouth, smothering the words that were on her lips. She couldn't understand why she hadn't seen those marks before. What was it that Rosa had said about the ghost? He was connected to this bed somehow, she remembered that. Now seeing the stains that were half-hidden under her mattress they suddenly unsettled her.

He must have died on this bed. She thought, before saying out loud in shock. " Oh my God, is he always here?" Questions came that she had never thought of before. It looked like blood. Yes, it must be blood. Was he murdered? When? How? The questions were left unanswered for now; she would be sure to ask Rosa questions later.

Dismissing the thoughts, she shook out the linen and made up the bed ready for the night. With so much to do before bedtime, having a bed ready to drop into at the end of the day was a must.

Louis was laid on the chaise longue watching and listening to Marina. He understood her fears. Yes, he was there all the time, but what she didn't know about was his kingdom behind the curtain of carved wood. She didn't understand that the choice wasn't his. He was a prisoner, his life's blood kept him tied to the bed he died on.

Thank God he had his place of refuge somewhere to hide. A place made by him for himself, his retreat, his den. After all, they both needed some private time.

He already missed the girls he had lived with for so long. They had gone their own ways to live new lives in other towns. They never knew it, but they had given him purpose, a reason to be. In his limited way he felt that he had been something of a guardian to that household. Now he felt lost; a great uncertainty hung over him. He had no control but to follow wherever the bed was taken. He hoped that by moving with the family of three to this new place he would find a reason for living this half-life he was burdened with, but only time would tell.

SETTLING IN.

A haze of white smoke and a strong smell of stale tobacco hung heavily in the bar above the heads of the darkly garbed men who were sitting at the small tables, pulling on pipes or puffing their Woodbines while enjoying a pint.

The snug, as they called it was dingy. Snug it was named and snug it was. The small windows hardly gave any light to the room and because of the black beams on a low ceiling there was nothing for daylight to bounce off. The ceiling had become yellow with nicotine, the result of many years of smokers using that bar.

The fireplace sported a black beam that served as a mantelpiece. It was decorated by several horse brasses, which had been tacked along the face of it. Oil wall lamps sat against the distempered wall, leaving trails of dark sooty marks above the neck of the glass shades. The marks reached up to the ceiling but despite the décor there was a good feeling to the place.

Decorating it was just another job on the list for Marina to do. Not that the men sitting at the tables even noticed the ceiling; they had come into the Pack Horse to escape their harsh life for a short while, to forget the back-breaking work most of them were committed to doing every day just to feed their families and to keep a roof over their heads.

Every night the regulars came to drink in her bar. It was true that some called on the way home. But mostly men would go home, wash off the day's grime and eat with the family before slipping out for a pint before bedtime. It was an opportunity to meet up with the lads and have a bit of a natter. For a couple of hours they were able to share a tale, exchange a bit of gossip, have a grumble about life, even give vent to anger at the unfairness of those who have and the have-nots; resentment or anything else they needed to get rid of could be talked about over a pint.

Marina had heard it all before, catching snatches of their conversation as she worked behind the bar. These men were not so different from her clients from her former life. Friday night was her busy night for the customers to let go of the tensions of the week. A night to have a game of darts, skittles or draughts, and if a little betting was going on on the side, no one objected. Except perhaps the wife, who stayed at home worrying, caring for the family, hoping that her man would not stay out too long, come home drunk or return in a bad mood if luck hadn't smiled on him. But most of all her fear might be that he would spend more money than they could afford on drink.

The fact was that some men couldn't resist the drink or a little flutter. The thrill of the game and the hope of winning took over and robbed them of all the common sense they might have had, leaving most of the men with pockets much lighter than when they came. Marina tried to keep an eye on what went on, feeling for the wives at home, but she had a business to run and food to put on her table as well. Mainly the atmosphere was good-humoured and that was the way Marina would keep it.

The snug was a place where these men could feel at ease and at home. The small wooden tables were stained a little with the product on sale, but this only gave character to them. Three-legged stools stood on rather an uneven flagstone floor and rocked rather dangerously in use, but the customers didn't come in for comfort or the design of a serviceable seat.

As the weeks passed it became obvious to Marina that she needed a man to help out around the inn. Most tasks were within her scope but she found out very quickly that she needed more muscle and a strong back to tackle the heavier work. The men that frequented the pub were unlikely candidates for the position. They were altogether too familiar with her. She, as landlady, had to be friendly back, but she knew they would not take orders from her easily.

No, it isn't practical to have someone from the neighbouring streets working for me, she thought. She had no intention that her past life be revealed.

Rosa and Lucy would not let anything slip out deliberately, but accidents happened. *No! It is better to hire an outsider, someone like ourselves,* she thought. Gossip spread so easily and folk had a habit of exaggeration; she would not risk their personal information becoming local tittle-tattle.

Fate took a hand about a month after Marina made that decision to hire male help. A young man came knocking on her door early one morning looking for a job.

The three women had not been up long and they were having breakfast in the kitchen. It was Sunday morning, the Saturday night shift was always a late finish and it being Sunday meant they could have a late start. The ladies were thankful they wouldn't need to open up until noon and they were enjoying lingering over their tea and toast.

The door-knocker sounded loud and urgent as the noise of it penetrated down the hall to the kitchen.

"What on earth…" moaned Marina, "Who can that be?" Smoothing her hair down with her hand, she got up, stepping briskly to the door, ready to give whoever had disturbed their breakfast a piece of her mind.

When she opened the door she revealed a tired-looking young man standing there on her step. He was not what she had expected to see. Suddenly, all her irritation at being disturbed from her breakfast disappeared. She became attentive, looking him up and down, assessing him. He looked as though he could do with a good meal and a bath and his clothes would not have hurt from a good washing in a tub.

Times were hard. So many young men walked the country looking for work and this poor beggar was just one of them, thought Marina.

"Have you got any work for me, missus? Anything at all?"

His eyes, the colour of forget-me-nots, pleaded with her, but the tilt of his chin still showed an independent soul.

Marina looked at this dark-headed youth and recognised the look of someone who was nearing the end of his tether. A silent desperation oozed out of his pores, she could feel his soul screaming for help. She knew despair, knew desperation and she knew at that moment she couldn't turn him away.

Over the years Marina had become a good judge of character; even so, she was aware she was taking a risk taking him on. There would have to be rules and she would have to set him duties but maybe, just maybe, this was heaven sending answer to her prayer.

"I have need of an odd-job man as it happens; heavy lifting, decorating and occasionally keeping argumentative customers apart. Do you think you could do that?" asked Marina.

As though a weight was lifted from the young man's shoulders, he suddenly looked taller and a huge smile lit up his face, a face that was transformed. He looked positively handsome.

"I'll do anything you ask and more," he replied.

"Well! I better know your name then."

"Luke, missus."

"We need to sort out wages and somewhere for you to sleep, but right now, Luke, you need food and a hot bath, not necessarily in that order. Come in and I'll introduce you to the family."

As they walked along to the kitchen she wondered why she seemed to have the knack of attracting waifs and strays into her life. It had always been females up to now, this time it was a male. She hoped she had done the right thing.

She need not have worried. The man she hired scrubbed up really well and before long, she realised that his assets were not his only strength, but that he also had a good head on his shoulders; he was business-like and honest. God had smiled on her the day he had sent Luke to her door.

So many things slotted into place after he arrived. Having a man living in made the place seem safer, more secure and the customers more respectful somehow.

He was a gentle man in many ways, kind and thoughtful, hiding an inner strength that he could draw on when needed. Maybe because of that and working close with him every day, Lucy became attracted to him. Despite the scars left by her past, she became ready to move on in her life and she was aware that Luke liked her too.

Watched over by Louis, the attraction he could see they had for each other was more than he could have hoped for. Lucy would heal now and he thanked God for it.

23

Exploring the pub after moving in Louis walked into the snug bar. Every table was occupied and his first impression was that the snug was very busy. The dress of some of the men was a little old-fashioned, not too dissimilar to what he was wearing. Had he looked more carefully, he would have noticed that some men did not have a glass in front of them. But what had struck him as he entered was how most of the men turned their heads to look directly at him.

My God, thought Louis. *Can they see me?*

As if to answer the unheard question, a bearded guy to his right greeted him with a nod and offered a seat at his table with his hand.

"You new here?" he asked, head to one side in inquiry. "You look as though you've seen a ghost!" He laughed at his own joke and started an avalanche of laughter amongst over half of the men seated there.

Noticing the man's clothes properly, Louis realised that the man and himself wore similar clothes, clothes fashioned in the last century. Incredibly, he realised he was in the mixed company of other ghosts and mortal men in the snug of the Pack Horse.

All the men sat at tables around the fire with glasses of ale in front of them were mortal, the rest were ghosts. The snug could be cold but somehow tonight it seemed colder than usual to the regulars. They had no idea they were sharing a room with past patrons and when Billy came in and sat down on a chair already occupied by a ghost, another bout of laughter erupted from the spirits. Billy appeared to sit on the knee of a well-rounded ghost who dissipated through him, leaving Billy chilled. He shivered, exclaiming how cold it was in the snug, colder even than outdoors, and how someone had walked across his grave.

The ghost of a past tavern keeper was put out by Billy and abruptly disappeared through the floor in a bit of a huff into the cellars below, which were his favourite haunt.

"Well, young man, are you going to answer me?"

Louis was tongue-tied; it had been so long since he had a face-to-face conversation that all he could do for a moment was nod in an idiotic way and stammer the word, "Ye— yes."

It transpired that these souls situated there in the inn, unlike Louis, were there by their own choice; they had not gone forward through the light that had appeared to them at the moment of their death. They hadn't passed to that unknown place beyond. They had not wanted to leave the world that they loved and knew so well. They visited the inn that had been their retreat and refuge during their lives and they had chosen to stay around it, still enjoying the sounds, the sights and the smells. And if they were a little mischievous from time to time – a chair moved as a mortal sat or a drink falling over – it amused them, but they never hurt anyone and they had each other as company. There was no such thing as time in their existence; they were there in the pub or not there, choosing to move about the inn or back to where they had spent their mortal lives, wandering the streets in search of what, they were not sure. No malice came from them. Louis could feel no emotions from them at all. They were just wandering souls without purpose. Louis soon learned that they were not good company. Their childish mischief targeted at men who couldn't see or feel them seemed disrespectful to him. It was more disappointing for Louis as he had hoped to find companionship in their company, but they never stayed in one spot for long and often had no memory of a former meeting. There was no time, no forwards, no backwards, no memories, just a vagueness of being, a shadow and nothing else. At least Louis had Rosa to interact with and the family to watch over, so much more than those poor souls.

The first twelve months had passed quickly.

"A whole year gone and March here again." Marina nodded as though she was agreeing with someone. Louis stood at her side. He wondered if she was aware of him. He couldn't tell.

Marina was happy, the family had settled in well, including Luke, who was as much a part of the family now as one could ever be.

The days and weeks ran into one another in a gentle monotony, the locals accepting these outsiders as their own. Though the work was hard, Marina was enjoying her new life.

Her one regret was her distrust of any man who paid her a compliment or showed her attention. She loved being a landlady; she could spread her affection among her customers without commitment, but lately she had started to have longings and although she was happy, she had to admit something was missing in her life.

Lucy was so much better now. Her nightmares were a thing of the past. Marina suspected that Luke might have something to do with her new self. Laughter came easily and the light in her eyes shone out whenever she was near to him.

He is a good man. Lucy could do a lot worse than love him, Marina thought.

Could it be because Lucy was settled and Marina was not worried for her anymore that she was more aware of herself? Certainly Rosa thought so. Rosa noticed a subtle difference in Marina when they talked together; some of the inner walls that had protected her over many years were coming down, she was opening herself up, which could only be good. Marina had never been able to focus solely on herself but now she was much more in tune with herself and her surroundings. Rosa and Louis loved her; she had a heart that knew no boundaries. Yes, she could be wary, but underneath that protection she held a caring that reached out to everyone she knew.

Rosa did what she always did, seeing to the daily chores, feeding the family with her nourishing food and giving common sense advice to problems. That was her contribution to Marina for taking her in when she was in dire need.

She only used her spiritual sense to converse with Louis. She was well aware of the other spirits coming and going but they were not trapped or in need. More importantly, the family were not in any danger.

Louis lived through the daily workings of the inn, visiting the snug to listen to the men passing the time of day. How it reminded him of his past life in his village so long ago. People didn't change; fashion did, hairstyles too, but people were concerned with their lives, their families and their working conditions, all the same topics he had talked about with his friends over a pint.

The work for the women and Luke started early morning and it would be late in the evening before they could stop. Only after gently easing the last customer out of the building could they could fall into bed for a few hours' sleep before starting all over again the next day. Weeks passed quickly for the extended family and during the past year they had worked hard. The inn had been refurnished and decorated; now the inn felt like a home.

In the quiet times between lunch and evening Marina had started to question Rosa more about the ghost, the so-called guardian angel that had intervened in the attack on Lucy. It was almost two years since that awful night. She had promised herself she would talk about him but if she was honest, she was too scared to broach the subject with Rosa. She had tried not to think about him and because she had been so busy setting up the business, she had been successful.

But now it was different. During parts of the day she had time on her hands, her mind would wander and her imagination would be troublesome. Was he near? Was that a draught from a door or was he passing her? Clear memories of when she first brought the bed home were in her mind. A draught in her bedroom when the window was closed. Was that him? The butterfly touch on the top of her head when she told Lucy about her father. Was that him too? It was getting to the point where she was starting to mistrust her judgement. Nervousness was getting the better of her.

Rosa had repeated the story that Louis had told her; his wife had betrayed him, just as she had been betrayed by Robert, but he had paid for his love with his life. It was largely because Rosa saw her worrying that she suggested she try to be more open to energies that the natural world held. She even encouraged her to talk to him.

Over the weeks and months that followed, Marina tried hard to reach out beyond the linear boundaries of time and into the ethereal realm beyond.

It wasn't easy to believe she was getting it right but every now and again she was sure she could feel him near. She relied as much on the physical reaction of her own body as her sixth sense, like the hairs on the back of her neck standing on end or the goosebumps she felt on her arms or the icy spot she could feel in a warm room. Were they all clues to where Louis might be?

The more she linked to where she supposed Louis was the more she became anxious. She had become very unsettled at bedtime, knowing that his blood was trapped in the bed she slept in, the bed that had trapped his soul. What had once been her pride and joy, her beautiful carved bed, had become a source of worry. She tried to think of him as her guardian angel who was not around to watch her every move during washing, bathing and dressing but as much as she tried, the thought of him being there made her edgy.

The feelings she held would only grow if she didn't face her fear. As she lighted a candle on her bedside table, she decided to tackle the problem head on. She had felt a chill in the room when she entered. It was August and had been a rather warm day. Now, as she closed her curtains, she could see a clear night sky and a three-quarter moon with just a hint of haze around it. Had the temperature dropped like a stone or was Louis near?

She changed into her nightdress and sat on the side of the bed and started to braid her hair. The candle she had lit flickered with her movements, casting shadows on the bed headboard. She stood and pulled back the bedspread but instead of getting into the bed, she sat on the edge again, smoothing her nightdress in a nervous gesture. Her eyes followed the motion of her hands but didn't really see them moving.

"Louis," she said in a small thin voice, "if you are here, I need to talk to you." Although she felt rather foolish, she continued. "Please let me know

I'm not talking to myself." *What a fool I am,* she thought. What on earth am I doing?

Then the candle went out.

Louis had withdrawn into his creation that was set beyond the screen of carving when he heard her calling to him.

In an odd way, he had tried to normalise his existence by developing a daily routine set around the workings of the pub; active during the daylight hours and withdrawing at night into the world he had created. The carved headboard was no longer a place of wooden images created under his hand; It was his refuge that no one knew about, not even Rosa and certainly not Marina, how could she know about his world of imagination. If Marina had known about it she wouldn't worry her head about sharing her private space with him, she would know he had his own space where he escaped to every night.

It was a pity she couldn't see his world it would be good to share it. If he had a one regret it was that he had not seen fit to include a dog in his carvings. He berated himself; if only he had carved a dog laying under the tree in its shade, he would have had companionship in his private world, a friend to sit with, a friend that would him give unconditional love. How he would have appreciated that over the years.

Marina's softly spoken voice had drifted into his world, bringing him out into the bedroom. He was intrigued; she had not spoken to him directly before on her own, she had thanked him once but that was in Rosa's presence.

He moved quickly and snuffed the candle out. Marina was sat in semi-darkness with only the gas lamp from the street giving some light in her room. She whispered, "You are here, aren't you?"

He had such high esteem for this lady, who after all the knocks life had thrown at her had not lost any of her femininity or her open heart.

What is this all about? He wondered. He settled himself on the bed beside her. Having no bodily weight, he made no creases or indentation to indicate he was there.

Marina felt the hair on her neck rise and a little chill slipped down her left arm.

"You are here, aren't you?" she asked once again, getting up and relighting the candle.

"Yes, I'm here," he answered. His cold breath lightly passed across her face and she shivered slightly.

She had an uncertain look on her face and sitting down again, she fingered the hem of her nightdress, not quite sure whether she should go on.

The candle flickered again and her eyes went straight to it as if expecting something to happen.

"Okay," said Louis. Knowing now exactly what she expected, he killed the flame with his finger and thumb.

In the half-light a smile played on Marina's lips.

"So you are here," she said, and somehow she felt that in the semi-darkness what she wanted to say would be easier.

For the next half-hour, Marina explained just how she felt now she was more aware of his spirit being around her. That not knowing where he was in her home, her inability to see him like Rosa could, left her anxious. She tried to impress on him just how grateful she was for saving not just her daughter but also her girls in the old house.

He could understand that she didn't want to be spied on but she must understand that through no fault of his own, he was caught in a situation and trapped by death to this bed they were both sat on.

Louis was rather amused; there she was trying to make arrangements to save her modesty. After all these years, why now? She couldn't know he had never spied on her or Lucy but why had she become so aware of the situation now? He decided at that moment he must settle her fears. He would reach into her dreams that night and show her his world, the world he retreated to – never her bedroom.

Back in his private world, Louis waited for sleep to come to Marina. He was delighted that she had made contact with him, knowing that when the time came they would be able to walk though his world and talk to one another completely and without constraints.

Laid in her bed, night thoughts were keeping her awake. Old emotions that had been buried so long had surfaced. Since opening herself up to

Louis, she was very wary of the feelings that emerged from her inner self and she had no intention of letting them grow. This was a strange relationship she had started to share with Louis. It was the first time in many years that she had shared her thoughts with a male. Did a ghost count? Surely not. He had helped her back when nightmares plagued her and she relived her abandonment over and over again, when her heart had been smashed into so many broken pieces. She had determined then that no man would get near to her again, she would never go through the pain and heartbreak that a love affair might bring. Sitting on her bed talking to a ghost, sensing him but not seeing him, was a little crazy. If anyone saw her they would have her packed off to the lunatic asylum in a shot.

He had put out the candle, hadn't he? She was starting to doubt herself. She groaned. She had ended her speech with a very formal goodnight, thinking she had dismissed him. What if he hadn't really been there?

Her thoughts rambled on until tiredness from the day's work finally caught up with her and she fell into a deep sleep. She was not conscious of the kiss Louis gently placed on her forehead as he bent over her bed, or of him taking her hand in his. There was a strong connection between them. Louis knew he had the power to enter into people's dreams just as he had with Marina all that time ago.

Now he wondered if he could take Marina into his world in a dream state. It would be good to share his world with someone, someone whom he admired. Wouldn't it be wonderful if that could happen?

Holding her hand, he entered into her unconscious self. She was still wrestling with the meeting they had just had and was not surprised to see him. In her dream he took her hand again and, without a word, indicated for her to move towards the bedhead. He could feel her soul rise up and meet his. How easy it was for them to walk into the carved picture and beyond, past the heavily laden tree full of ripe fruit. She could feel a spring in the grass between her toes as she walked barefoot up a small mound that led to the meadows.

Still hand in hand, the two of them walked towards purple hills that appeared low on the horizon. The sun shone brightly without giving any real heat, but she wasn't cold. The sun shone every day in his world; there was no winter, only summer, and the sky was the colour of cornflowers. He reflected again on just why he hadn't thought of carving swallows to fill the empty sky.

Walking together, they headed in the direction of the stream. The light made the water sparkle as it ran swiftly on below the meadows, flowing fast, making a soft sound. It struck Marina as odd but then she realised that she was in some sort of a dream, only it felt so real. They had walked in silence until Louis stopped and suggested they sit and talk. She was in her nightdress and barefooted, sitting in a meadow with a ghost. How could it be real?

Any shyness there might have been in the real world was gone; here they were a couple who were connected by history, a couple who had loved and lost, who understood hurt and real loneliness. The comfort they felt sitting side by side was truly magical. How easy the words came.

For the first time Marina was able to see Louis's face clearly. She remembered when he had visited her in her dream and she had confused him with a guardian angel. Now she could see a handsome young man with a beautiful smile and a manner that was totally charming.

Over the years Louis had learned all about Marina's background; now he wanted her to know about himself. Here was an opportunity for Marina to know the truth; his history, his death, how he was murdered by his wife Sophia, how he had loved Sophia and was seduced by her beauty and her willingness to marry beneath her station. He had believed that they were soul mates. He had married her despite fearing that the difference in their social standing would be an obstacle. As a craftsman he could not provide the diversions of trips, parties and the wardrobe of clothes that she was used to. She had been loved but spoilt by her father in his eagerness to compensate for her not having a mother. Louis had believed with all his heart that she wanted to be with him above everything, that she would learn to accept a different lifestyle. But the novelty of being a craftsman's wife had soon wore off; the new life she had with him never lived up to her expectations. Envy and jealousy had eaten into her shallow soul and that led to his death.

Now Marina saw the pain in his eyes. *My God, he has been hurt as much as me.* Her heart felt it might burst with pity, compassion, sympathy; a whole myriad of feelings overwhelmed her. She touched his face gently with her fingertips, brushing away what might have been a tear from his eye. He looked away but she brought his face back to hers. They were just two souls brought together by fate. Wouldn't it be wonderful if they could help each other to heal?

She looked into his eyes and he into hers. It was as though they were being pulled together; his arms were about her shoulders, drawing her into his chest. She wanted to be held. It was such a long time since a man had held her. She allowed her body to soften and melt into his, trusting him. *Perhaps the healing from all the hurt has begun,* she thought.

They lay back on the spongy grass, her head resting on his shoulders, her eyes still in contact with his. Something happened between them that Louis never thought possible. It was as natural as breathing. The tenderness in their eyes awoke a longing that brought their lips together and they shared a long passionate kiss. Feelings that had been suppressed for so long could no longer be denied. They were overwhelmed by a need to be with each other.

My God, is it possible… thought Louis, *that a ghost could love a mortal?* Here they were and it was happening, there in his own kingdom.

Locked in each other's arms, just enjoying the closeness of their embrace and feeling totally at peace, another uncanny thing happened to Louis: he fell asleep under the blue sky in that silent meadow.

When Louis awoke she was gone, back into her own body, asleep in her own bed, resting and filled with comfort from the dream she had had. Louis realised that to keep her with him, he must not sleep, that it shattered the dream state he had created and she could only live in it if he was awake.

When the morning came, Marina's worries were gone. She knew that Louis shared her world respectfully and had his own world to live in.

227

Last night, on his invitation she had entered his world and shared more than just conversation. She had come alive again, not ever realising that she had locked her heart and all her love away deep down in a corner of her soul. Today she surfaced, letting go of the barriers she had hung on to, awake to the new possibilities that life could bring. Sharing a kiss with Louis was something she hoped to share again with him, very soon.

'The heart wants what the heart wants.' That old saying went around and around in her head. She couldn't deny it, her heart was so full she felt like dancing and singing and most of all, she wanted everyone to feel as good as she did. The truth was she couldn't tell anyone, except perhaps Rosa, how she felt; anyone else would think her mad. But for now it would wait until she was sure of just what she was feeling.

The only question was how she got through the day. The chores and the customers became secondary to her impatience for the night to come. Would he come to see her again? She really hoped so. She remembered being drawn to him and that long lingering kiss and she felt her heart leap. A smile on her lips almost caught her off guard and she found herself blushing. Her breasts heaved and a large sigh escaped from her. Night could not come quick enough.

She need not have worried. Walking through the inn as he usually did every morning, Louis stopped to watch her work. He saw charm in the way her trim body moved and her clothes hugged her, enhancing her curves. And he saw that her beauty was more than skin deep.

He still could hardly believe the unexpected gift he had experienced during the twilight hours with Marina. Touching her soft warm hand, it was as though the warmth of her life's blood passed through into his pores, warming his cold body and awaking those instincts he thought had died with him.

Last night when he took Marina into his arms, all his human emotions were awakened and he became aroused; he could almost believe that he was alive again. At least he knew that within his world he could act as any normal man would and no longer as a ghost. Holding her and being held had been a truly beautiful moment. Her hair smelt of lavender and when he touched her skin it felt like silk. For whatever reason, in his kingdom, he was able to touch and feel and when they kissed it was a revelation, leading him to hope that there could be much, much more they could share together, even the special act of lovemaking. Tonight they would be together again.

Neither of them were disappointed. When Marina got into bed that night wearing her best muslin nightdress she was a little embarrassed; she had taken care to choose something pretty. The lace trim on her neckline showed off her white soft skin that glowed with good health. It also emphasised the gentle slope of her shoulders and the discreet V between her breasts. Yes, she wanted him to admire her the way she admired him. He was such a nice-looking man. He was maybe in his thirties with dark hair and dark eyes. It was the tender look in his eyes as he looked into hers that made her want to love him.

Uncertainty suddenly hit her as she corrected herself. No! He wasn't a man, he was a ghost, an ethereal being that she couldn't see and could only guess when he might be near her. *Is it really possible to fall in love with a ghost?* she asked herself. She already knew the answer as the room grew colder and her heart fluttered just at the thought he might be there. Marina snuffed out the candle on her bedside table by the bed. Knowing that she couldn't be with him unless she was in a dream state, she snuggled down under the blankets and waited for sleep to come.

Excitement and longing were so strong within her that it took longer than usual for her to surrender to sleep. When she did, Louis was waiting. Taking her hand, they walked once again into his kingdom that was always summer and always blessed with light and sunshine.

In his perfect world they had nothing to fear, no busy bodies, no one to interrupt them. That quiet place, that little piece of Eden he had created years ago for a love that betrayed him was all forgotten now. With the green grass under his feet and the sun shining on them both, this new Eden he found after his death was no longer a headboard made from wood, but a gateway to his sanctuary. He was with Marina in a place made for them both to be together, and he rejoiced in it.

Both of them had been denied love for so long that this new experience was like being under a magic spell. It lifted them to new heights as they touched and kissed, hardly daring to go further and taste the forbidden fruit of their own bodies. Days later, when at last they did come together in love and in their dream world, their souls met in perfect ecstasy; a true definition of soulmates.

24

Days, weeks and months passed with Marina becoming more beautiful as time went on. The sparkle of youth came back to her face and though no one could account for it, the household knew that something was going on in her life. She had a secret that she could not even share with Lucy.

Lucy had noticed the difference in her mother. What had brought about the change didn't really matter; it was good to see her mother full of smiles and full of extra energy. There was a lightness in her being that she had never noticed before; certainly all the time she was growing up with the aunts her recollection of her mother was one of a business-like manner in all she did in the house. Here at the inn she had a business head too but somehow she was softer.

Lucy and Luke got on very well, sharing chores and a bit of banter every now and again. At first when he came to live with them she was very wary. Oh yes, she had understood the business needed a man to help out, but she had thought her mother quite mad to give a job to a ragamuffin who just turned up on her doorstep desperate for work. Now she knew better; her mother's judgement of people was usually good and her soft spot for helping others made her who she was. Luke was loyal and honest, he gave his best every day in the inn, he was clean, bright and respectful, and Lucy had become quite attracted to him.

Her battle with nightmares of Mark and herself was over at last; he did not intrude into her dreams any more. She felt strong again. She was almost twenty and like any young woman of her age, her thoughts were about finding a man to love and having her own family.

For almost four years Luke had worked for Marina. She had accepted him as one of the family almost immediately after he turned up on her doorstep. Like so many others that were unemployed he had walked for days looking for work. Without a proper craft he could only expect fieldwork or odd jobs to keep him fed.

He blessed that day that Marina had taken a risk by taking him in and employing him. It was a kindness he could never repay but he could work for her and pay her in kind. She had saved him from the workhouse or the parish relief; he had kept his self-respect and for that he was eternally grateful.

Marina had been giving him more responsibility lately; he was practically running the pub.

It gave Marina immense gratification giving Luke more responsible duties around the inn and seeing him rise to every challenge she gave him. He had taken on more and more of the everyday running of her inn and it was good to hand over some of the responsibilities and delegate.

This capable young man had grown from the vagrant he had been when he appeared on her step into a trustworthy assistant. He was an intelligent person but had never been given a chance in life before he came to her. She guessed that, like herself, he had to take whatever job was going, but that if he had been given the opportunity and support, he could have been whatever he wanted to be. You couldn't choose your parents or what station you were born into, she knew that to her cost. Very little was known of his background, save that a stepfather had been the reason he was on the road; some massive row had caused the split in the family, giving him no choice but to leave. By leaving he was lost to his mother and his siblings, but he knew that at least there was one less to feed in her nest and that must be of some relief to the family pocket.

Now his duties included the ordering of stock, cashing up on a night, keeping the ledgers in order and hiring help to serve and clean the place. He was a natural people person and seemed to get the best out of people, whatever he asked of them.

And so the years passed. Marina happily reined back her contribution into the business. Her comfortable existence made the years happy ones and when Lucy and Luke came to her for her blessing to marry there was not a happier person on the planet.

Marina and Louis were as happy in their world too, given the restrictions of the situation. Their love flourished. He watched over her during the day, his eyes were everywhere and any trouble was often diverted by telling Rosa what was happening in the bar rooms. Night was the time Marina watched over him. Caring and loving him with all her heart and sharing what she could with him was her job. He had spent many years without hope, without joy. He had had only a half-life for so many long years, but now she could at least be real for him in her dreams and his reality.

INFLUENZA IN THE SNUG

John from home farm was the first casualty of the outbreak of flu. His son had just returned from the army unit based at the top of the hill outside the town. Father and son decided to have a gill together after his dad had finished work.

It was his usual habit to call in at the snug after getting the cattle in from the fields. That night was no exception. His eyes had ached most of the day so when the headache came he was not worried; eye strain at his age was not unusual.

It was warm in the snug. The fire was low but still gave off quite some heat and there was a slight smell of burning ash and soot from the chimney. Most of the regulars stopped talking when he walked in to call and greet him in their own friendly way.

Marina was behind the bar, waiting to serve him.

"What will it be, John?" she asked, smiling, her head tipped to one side waiting for his answer.

"The usual, Marina, if you please." He looked around and saw his son already sat with a drink in front of him.

"And how are you today, John?" Marina enquired politely.

"I'm not at my best and that's for sure, getting old I expect, eyes and head aching and my legs don't feel too good either," he groused.

"Get that into you," she said, passing his ale to him. "You'll feel better," she said, hoping it would cheer him up.

Without warning, John sneezed. It was so unexpected that he didn't have time to pull out his handkerchief. It was just as Marina was picking up the money he had put on the counter.

"Oh my goodness," she said in surprise.

"Sorry Marina, I have been sneezing on and off all afternoon."

"Could be hayfever or maybe a summer cold." She smiled but was not too happy at the thought of catching a cold from a customer.

John paused for a moment.

"I expect it's hayfever, that would account for my eyes being the trouble they are." He turned and crossed to where his son was waiting for him. He was seated at a small table near the hearth and pointing to the stool he had kept free for his dad. The drink secure in his hand, John walked over to join his son.

Two weeks later, John died of pneumonia and half of Marina's regulars were down with influenza, but the most distressing thing was the way it had spread, taking the very young and the very old. The cottages where the farm labourers lived were a breeding ground for sickness. Damp rooms, little sanitation, poor diets; the poor souls had little natural protection from illness. No one could afford a doctor; at best they were paid twenty shillings a week. The families with several children could only buy medicine from the pharmacists, but it was often no better than coloured and bitter water that did nothing to help.

It started with a dry throat. Her sinuses felt raw when she breathed in and the back of her eyes ached along with her neck and shoulders.

It was probably only a cold. The illness that had taken over in the town was striking the working-class families hard. She felt so sorry for them; most didn't have a chance. It had always been as it was now, that even the slightest illness could be fatal for the weakest of them. If not death then it could certainly be life-changing; a bad chest would leave some strong men as weak as babies for the rest of their lives.

Thinking as she did, she responded by shrugging her shoulders. *God, they ache,* she thought. She might have come from working-class stock but through destiny she had made something of herself and she learnt from others' mistakes. One thing was sure, she had always put nourishing food on their plates and had always maintained that 'strength comes through the mouth', making sure her family and herself ate well.

The trouble was, at that moment she really didn't feel too good. *Better have a hot toddy and an early night.* Rosa or Luke would finish her shift. Besides, the pub was quiet with the illness sending people to their beds. And that was what she needed right now, to lie down in a warm bed, wrapped in blankets in a dark room. *That will stop my eyes from aching so much,* she hoped. Picking a whiskey bottle from the bar, she went up the passage to the kitchen where she found Rosa tidying up after the evening meal.

"I've got the most awful dry throat and such a bad head," she said, reaching up to a shelf to take down a tumbler. "There's only Billy in the bar and I guess he will be leaving soon, can you cover for me? I need my bed."

Rosa nodded; it wasn't like Marina to ask for help, she must really feel unwell.

"Have you a temperature?" Rosa asked, concerned.

"I don't think so, though I don't feel myself."

"Get yourself to bed, tomorrow you might be better. I have some honey and lemon, I'll make you a hot drink and you can put a drop of that whisky in it. If nothing else, you'll sleep well. Look, why don't you go up and I'll bring it to you?" suggested Rosa.

"What would I do without you?" Marina asked, suddenly emotional.

"You would do fine," smiled Rosa, reaching out to give Marina a hug. "Off to bed, now. I'll be up in a minute."

But she didn't sleep well; her nose and head throbbed and the morning light that poured into her bedroom hurt her eyes. It was six in the morning and she felt worse, not better. She had had a restless night. Sleep had been sporadic; with the heat her body had generated causing her to throw off her covers as her temperature rose, and then, cooling down too fast, she was shivering with cold, unable to get warm. Getting up was difficult but it was time to start her daily routine. Her joints ached along with her head and legs, her arms didn't seem to work properly. Moving was a struggle.

I just need a hot cup of tea and an aspirin. Once I get going I'll be fine, she thought.

Louis was very concerned. He had watched over her all night, watched her toss and turn, and when he attempted to join with her but couldn't he realised that she was ill. Her whole body was fighting an invisible force that had invaded her, denying them from being together.

She dressed with effort and somehow managed to get downstairs. Rosa was already in the kitchen with the fire lit and the kettle singing. Steadying herself, Marina practically fell rather than sat in a chair at the table, holding her head in both hands to support the weight and carry the pain. Her hair was straggled from sweating in the night and the dark rings around her eyes told their own story.

"What on earth do you think you are doing?" asked Rosa. "You should be in bed."

"I thought I might feel better if I got up," replied Marina.

"Well, you thought wrong, back to bed with you. I'll bring you a tray and let's not see you down here again until you're well."

Marina smiled a thin smile and nodded. Using the furniture and the walls to support herself, she somehow managed to get back up the stairs and cast off her clothes letting them drop where they fell, vowing that she would see to them later. Gratefully she pulled on her crumpled nightdress from where it had been thrown on her quilted bedspread before climbing into her unmade bed, sighing with relief.

She was so pleased that she had insisted that Luke and Lucy moved out when they had married. Those lovely precious granddaughters of hers were out of the way of this dammed illness. Tilly, short for Matilda, and Sarah were her pride and joy. Lucy's family had come quickly; they had been married four short years and had two children already. Living at the other end of the town, in the posh part, as the locals hereabout thought, she hoped would give them some sort of protection from this outbreak of flu. Luke would be arriving shortly to open up. All would be well, she just needed to sleep.

When the breakfast tray arrived she had already fallen back to sleep.

Well, thought Rosa, *sleep will do her more good than food, but I do wish she had drunk something.* She left quietly, meaning to return with lemon water in a jug for the bedside table.

Marina slept for most of the day, waking with a mouth that felt as though it was filled with sand.

Thank God for Rosa, she thought as she reached for the water waiting for her on her side table. Just the action of putting her arm out of the covers made her shiver. She had to admit to herself she must have a temperature. The water eased her throat and thirst but only made her feel colder. She must eat; how else was she to get better? The sleep had helped and she felt strong enough to get up. A smell of chicken soup came up from the kitchen and she suddenly felt hungry. It had been almost twenty-four hours since she had eaten.

It's no good, I've got to get up, she thought, but when she tried to put her feet on the floor her legs just didn't want to support her. She sat on the edge of her bed pulling a night shawl around her shoulders to keep out the chill while trying to decide how she was going to get downstairs.

Rosa heard her moving about upstairs and, going to the bottom of the steps, shouted up that she would bring her food and to stay were she was.

What a relief, thought Marina, and with effort swung her legs back into bed and laid back on the pink embroidered pillow cases that Lucy and her embroidered during the long winter nights, just a few months ago.

The soup was hot and nourishing and she was glad her stomach was full, even though it had strangely tired her out eating it. Sleep was calling again.

Rosa was glad to see an empty dish when she returned to the bedroom to collect the tray she had brought up earlier. She left Marina sleeping soundly, closing the door sincerely hoping she would be well come the morning.

Luke was behind the bar but customers were scarce. The bar help hadn't turned up. *Just another victim of this damn flu,* he thought and sure enough, the barman's wife called in later that night to confirm he was ill. It was hardly worth opening up for the trade they were doing. People were going down like flies on a cold day. He was worrying about taking the illness back to his family; coming into work was one thing, risking his girls' health was another. This area of town was particularly hard hit with the flu. Nearly all the families were suffering in the neighbouring streets and the numbers were getting larger everyday.

The night was particularly bad for Marina. She woke in the early hours. It was still dark though the birds had started to sing their dawn chorus. Her head felt as though it was going to burst, her temperature was raging. She was desperate for water but could hardly move. She feebly tried to call out to get Rosa to help her.

Her voice was so weak that hardly a sound left her mouth. She must get up, get help. She forced herself out of the bed. In her struggle to get help in the half-light, the side table fell over, hitting the floor with a crash. Marina followed it, crying out involuntarily as she hurt her shoulder on impact.

Rosa woke with a start and rushed to Marina's room. She did what she could to nurse Marina for the rest of the night. In the morning she would call out the doctor, but for now she helped Marina back into the bed, helping her to sip water and using cold wet cloths on her forehead, trying her best to reduce the heat in her friend's body.

The doctor could only confirm just how sick Marina was and that there was little he or anyone could do but wait and hope. He did, however, decide that they could do with some help and a nurse would come to help out, especially at night.

Luke turned up as usual next morning. Lucy had wanted to come and see her mother but on Luke's insistence she agreed that the children must be her first concern, so she stayed at home and waited for him to give her a report on her mother's health. When he did come home, the news he brought was not good and for the first time in her life, Lucy feared for her mother's health.

Luke was not sure of the risks he was taking coming backwards and forwards from the district so laid low, but his common sense told him he should be prepared to close the inn until the danger of spreading the illness passed.

The decision was taken for him a couple of days later when Rosa complained about a headache and that her chest felt tight and was restricting her breath. She had been taking cod liver oil, a tonic that was supposed to protect against illness. It hadn't helped, nor had a well-known brand of pills that were supposed to cure everything from flu to cancer. The inn was closed and Nurse Rowen was called to live in and care for the two sick women.

Marina's temperature raged for the next few days. When she did surface from the semi-conscious state that she was mostly in, she could hardly bear to open her eyes. At times the ceiling spun above her head, moving and spinning until she felt bilious. Even when she closed her eyes against it she could still feel the movement, she could not escape from it. She hadn't eaten for days and sipping water was such an effort that she had no desire to drink. She only wanted to rest.

The rattle in Rosa's throat when she breathed was distressing. What was worrying was the speed with which the illness attacked her. She was propped up on many pillows in her bed supporting her body into a sitting position. Her face was grey except the two high spots on each cheek. The greyness of her face against the white of the pillows showed just how gravely ill she was. The cough was deep and obviously hurt her when she had an attack, which was frequent; it racked her poor body and left her breathless.

Louis was beside himself with grief as he watched the two most precious women in his ghostly life slip more and more towards death. There was nothing he could do. If only he was mortal, if only he had hands that could hold and a body that was strong he could help. If only.

Marina's sheets were wet with sweat. Her nightdress clung to her body. Louis was full of dread; he was losing her, his beloved Marina.

He had tried so many times to link with her but her mind was in turmoil; hallucinations were taking her on journeys that he could not join, dark places of heat and fear.

In a strange way Rosa was at peace with herself. Ancestors were around her bed at the end and they invited her through the gateway between worlds into the light, and she was ready. Her chest had hurt so much when she breathed, her body had felt so heavy and leaden; now she felt light and comforted by those around her. She knew that Marina, her dear friend, would come soon and they would be together again.

Louis watched the life drain out of Rosa and a light too bright for him to look at appeared above her head, a ghostly shape rose from out of her body and she was quickly absorbed into it. All that was left was the vehicle that had carried her soul for all her years. Grey, empty, still warm, but Rosa was gone.

Louis was distraught. How could he tell Marina? Did she need to know? Her fight for life was still on a knife's edge. Knowing about the loss of her friend would surely take her down further.

Nurse Rowen had rushed out to get the doctor when she realised that Rosa was slipping away; she would be back soon.

Louis stood by Marina's bed looking at the very sick woman, the woman that he loved. Her pillow was wet with sweat from her hair. Her dark locks fanned out and framed the face he had kissed so many times with passion. He tried to link with her, touching her hand and stroking her forehead, but she was down deep in a world he couldn't reach.

He feared for her. Now that Rosa had passed, was Marina next?

He couldn't bear to think about it. For the last six years he had loved with all his heart. Marina, Rosa and he had shared an understanding and sympathy for each other; he couldn't lose it.

Rosa knew him, could see him and converse with him; Marina and he had a physical love in a dream state in his kingdom. Without them he would no longer exist again. He prayed that his wonderful woman would recover and come back to him.

The doctor arrived with the nurse. He could hear them climbing the stairs and going into Rosa's bedroom. He heard low voices coming from it and he sensed the scene they had met. Death was a sorrowful thing and he decided to see for himself their reaction to it.

With great respect, the doctor took the wrist of Rosa to find a pulse; he shook his head, looking at the nurse. Moving the pillows to lay Rosa flat, he crossed her arms across her chest and covered her face with the sheet. He would call the undertaker when he went back into the town, but now he would check on Marina as he was here. A few people had passed on during the night. He had been called out several times and was dog-tired. Night was always the worst; it was funny how many went at four in the morning. That was the time of death, he was sure of that.

"We best see Marina now, there is nothing left to do here."

Picking up his bag and followed by his nurse, they both moved along the landing to Marina's room.

"She's not good," confided the doctor, looking at his nurse, "but she's clinging to life somehow. As least there is no chest infection; she might just make it."

Collecting his belongings, he left the room, again followed by his nurse. She would see him out and then grab a little sleep for herself. Her night had been hectic too.

Louis was relieved to hear what the doctor had said and resolved to stay by Marina's side for as long as it took to see her recover.

The day passed without Marina surfacing from the semi-conscious state she was in. He willed her to improve and for a fleeting time in the late afternoon he thought he saw some improvement; she was less restless and seemed to be sleeping normally. The nurse had popped in and out through the afternoon; she had wet Marina's lips but there was no response. She had seen this all before. The poor woman was slipping away.

It was in the early hours of the morning that Marina startled Louis by asking him to hold her.

She could see him! That had never happened before; only when she was in a dream state was she able to see him. But there she was, imploring him to hold her, something he could only do in his own kingdom.

How could he manage to comfort her now? He moved to her side and sat on the bed. Gently he put his arms about her, not expecting to be able to hug her, but as if in answer to his own question, he could.

His heart was tearing from his chest. He guessed that she was leaving this world; how else could she see him and how else could he hold her? She touched his face, caressing his lips with her finger.

"One last kiss Louis, I love you so much," she whispered. He kissed her with all the love he possessed. A light opened the gateway above their heads. For a moment Louis thought he could go with her and they would spend eternity together on the other side. The light brightened. It became so bright that it blinded him; it was then that he felt her slip away from his arms and pass through the gate.

At that moment, her earthly body slipped through his arms, falling back into the bed, his bed. Her spirit had gone and he hadn't been able to go with her. Once more he was a ghost living in a void with no voice, no hope and no one to comfort him.

He returned to his kingdom behind the façade that he had made, back to the kingdom that was empty of life. A sun that gave no heat and a landscape that grew nothing. He walked by their stream and remembered the fun times he had shared with his beautiful Marina, paddling and splashing. Overcome, he sank onto the bank and sobbed. There was no one to hear him. This half-life was agony.

Through the pain and torment of living without Marina, he resorted to sleep. He slumbered, unable to face the living death sentence he was bound to. Nothing mattered anymore.

Lucy and Luke survived the epidemic. Half the town had been touched by a death in the family. Lucy lost two members but her children were unaffected. That would have been just what her mother would have wanted for her. Luke went back to running the inn and for a while Lucy thought of moving back to live there, but there were just too many memories and too much sadness that surrounded the place, so in the end she stayed where she was. She did sell the bed that her mother had died on. Her mother had loved it so and, despite its beauty, there was just too much sadness attached to it. She was glad to let it go.

The bed was sold many times over but Louis slumbered, keeping himself to himself behind the wall of carved wood.

25

HOME COUNTIES

Her small-boned body was curvy without being overweight and her bright brown eyes shone with intelligence. Her small nose was slightly upturned and she had full lips and a generous mouth that often broke into a beautiful smile. Her face was framed by lush chestnut-coloured hair that fell to her shoulders and graced her elegant neck.

Katie had felt so special at being able to go to college and then on to university. No one else in her family had had that opportunity in their lives, not her dad, not her uncles. A decade ago a woman expectation was no more than serve in a shop, become a nurse or be someone's receptionist. Her mother, whom Lucy thought was a wise and intelligent woman, had never expected more in her life than to have a short occupation after leaving school before marrying and having children. That was normal for families like hers and if her mother had a secret longing to be more than a wife and mother, she had never spoken about it. Bringing up children was an important role for women in her mother's generation, it was an invaluable job which sadly was generally undervalued by society now.

Love and security, guidance, moral values were the true lessons a child learnt at their mothers knee, enabling them to grow into responsible members of the community.

Katie's dad called her mum the managing director of the family business. And she was. It was her mum's knee that she went to for help, for both the physical and emotional problems she had. Dad was there solidly in the background, but Mum was her friend and someone she could tell anything to.

She had had a happy childhood but now she was a woman with a hunger for life and she must satisfy that driving force within her. She was ready to face the world just as her mother had taught her to do.

Her older brother Phil had left home years ago opting out of further education after school. He wanted to work, earn money and be independent. He decided to work in the car industry and was taken on as an apprentice. It had been the right decision for him, cars and motorbikes were his passion. He was a fully trained mechanic and lived in Oxford and worked at the Ford plant to build a career.

Now it was Katie's turn to find independence. More women were going on to be managers, directors and the old idea of a woman staying home was being rejected by her generation. The old stereotype that men thought a woman should be was changing fast. Katie looked at the new opportunities that were out there for women; her generation were seen as go-getters, a new force of energy in the workplace and she wanted to be part of it.

She thought seriously of her future and knew she wanted more than just an occupation. She wasn't marking time until she married, she didn't intend to let a marriage rule her life what she wanted a career. At that moment in time it wasn't her inclination to give it all up for a man, at least not yet. Should Mr Right come along – well, she would see.

The workplace had begun to open up for women; places at the top were no longer exclusive to men in the business world, but it seemed you had to be stronger and better than a man to get to the top. There was an exciting future for women like herself willing to study hard and get out there in the mix of industry. Women were becoming lawyers, solicitors and doctors, and she, like many other young women, was looking at the possibilities of having a profession for herself.

Moving away from home had been an emotional wrench for Katie. She remembered the excitement of when she receiving confirmation of her place in the university of her choice. It was intoxicating and frightening at the same time. She was nervous about going to live in halls with strangers. Although she got on well with most people, there were some people that were not, for whatever reason, easy to live with. However she got on well with the opposite sex, men loved her bubbly personality and generous spirit.

THE CELL

Her small car was packed with all the possessions she would need for this new chapter in her life. Her university was a couple of hours' drive away and she had to be there by 9am to be shown the living quarters that would be hers for the first year. It was a week before term started; new students were allowed a week to settle in. She had to get used to the layout of the buildings, meet the tutors, buy study textbooks, find the dining room and meet other students who would be in halls with her.

The stairwell of concrete led up to the fourth floor. The railings and banister had seen better days. The room she had been allotted was on the second floor.

Her heart sank when she saw the tiny room that was to be home to her for the next year. Little light came from the one medium-sized grimy window and it was badly in need of a good clean and a dressing up with new curtains. Sometime long ago, the bare wooden planked floor had been stained with dark varnish; now it was worn into light patches and scuffed by the soles of the many shoes that had walked in and out of that small room over the years.

She was dismayed. Her room at her mother's house was so cosy and clean but it was no good complaining, this was to be her place for twelve months and she better get used to it. She had passed that Scandinavian store as she drove into the university complex – it was just down the road. She could buy a cheap and cheerful rug that would hide the offending floor, and cheerful curtains to brighten up the room. It might not be too bad after all. The walls had been painted magnolia a long time ago and were no longer bright but a grey-yellow in colour. *Will I have time to repaint?* she asked herself.

The bed she had been given to sleep on was horrifying. It was narrow with a three-inch-deep thin stained mattress lying on top of the slats. She shuddered at the thought having to sleep on it. Well, that was never going to happen, she wouldn't even use it for a dog mattress if she had one. She also needed a rug and curtains to make the room habitably. But where was the money to come from to buy a new mattress as well as a rug and curtains? Perhaps her mum would help out? The grant she had been awarded wouldn't last very long if she spent it unwisely.

As the old adage stated, there was scarcely enough room to swing a cat, if Katie stretched out her arms sideways and had she been a larger individual, she might have been able to touch the sidewalls of the room – well, nearly. One thing did please her, the room had an old desk in it that sat under the window it was somewhere to study in peace and store her books.

Once Katie had made some improvements to the room, she would settle in. Her mum had arranged to meet her at lunchtime in her room and was shocked at the pitiful space her daughter would have to live in for the next year. Her mum had packed some cleaning materials in Katie's car along with some other provisions and took the matter in hand. Together they cleaned the room thoroughly before going out to shop with a list of items they would buy to spruce up that dismal room.

Katie and her mum drove off to the multiple store just up the road. The store, well known for its clean-cut designs and easy-to-build furniture, had everything a home would need and then some. They bought new curtains in a white and yellow floral design, they would certainly brighten up the room, a small patterned rug and a new single mattress with a mattress cover. They brought their purchases back to the offending room and quickly installed them. Amazingly, the small room was brought to life. It shone. Now it was clean and bright, it smelt good and looked good. Standing back Katie and her mum were satisfied with their work and Katie was ready for her first night in The Cell. It was an affectionate nickname she decided to call her small room. It was still small but it was now a room she could live and work in.

The Cell had seen a lot of action over the years and could have told many a story about its past occupants. This was her first year in halls; everything was new and a little nerve-racking but she would hold her own with whatever was thrown at her. She would come out of the other end with the qualifications she had come for, that she was sure of.

Tears and laughter and frustration had been part of the fruits of that first year, and a small diversion with a young man had been emotionally draining. It hadn't lasted. Tom was from the same working-class background as hers and she liked him well enough, but it soon became apparent that his ideas about women were old-fashioned. He had wanted to put her in a box and label her. He had even suggested that it was pointless for her to study and getting a degree because she would marry and have a family and all her education would be wasted.

Tom was tall, dark and handsome; any other girl would be happy to be with such an attractive man. But Katie saw his raw ambition and feared that he wanted a woman who was intelligent and attractive to be an asset to his career. Any push or drive she had for herself would be squashed if she stayed with him. Her life would be unfulfilled, her ambition forfeited for the sake of his. That wasn't in her plan for the future she intended for herself.

She enjoyed studying and expanding her knowledge, and she was determined to be a success at whatever she did in the future. Her dream of becoming a manager in a large organisation was why she was here working in her Cell, studying business management.

She had been homesick to begin with during the first few months at university, it had not been without some uneasy moments. It was such an entirely new experience being solely reliant on oneself, and it took a little while to adjust to it. Going out with Tom had certainly helped to begin with; he had been there to share this new experience with her and she liked having a boyfriend, but when she decided to break up with him it hurt. She knew that they walked separate paths and they would never survive as a couple.

After she had finished with Tom there was a sadness about Katie, so noticeable that when Janet passed her open doorway, she invited Katie back to her room to offer some sympathy over a cup of coffee.

Sympathy is fine except when you are trying to be strong; the kind words from Janet just opened up the hurt and Katie couldn't help but shed a few tears. She had enjoyed Tom's company, now there was an emptiness in her life. She had brought it on herself but that didn't stop her sense of loss and pain.

Janet, wiser than her years, assured her that it was for the best, that college romances were common but they rarely lasted and that Katie would get over it given time. Katie sincerely hoped so.

The first year had in many ways been enjoyable despite the long hours of study. She had met Janet who, like herself, was hungry to make a place for herself in the world. They got on like a house on fire and had become firm friends. Janet wanted to become a journalist and, like Katie, was one of the new breed of young women who intended to succeed in this man's world that they were competing in. The girls often worked together in the silent comfort of companionship in one bedroom or the other, sharing cups of coffee and burning the midnight oil.

On occasions it had been difficult to study, especially so when it neared the end of the term. There was important exams that they had to pass to continue on their courses. Janet and Katie were working late most nights and concentrating was difficult with the other students on their landing making lots of noise. The parties to celebrate the end of the year had started early and their fellow students were partying night after night with drink and loud music. Katie appealed to their neighbours, asking them just to turn the music down a smidge, but she only got verbal abuse and taunts about being a swot back from them. Just as Katie and Janet were committed to study, these students were the exact opposite; committed to having fun and boisterous with it. In the end, earplugs were the only answer.

Katie was deeply incensed by them but it didn't matter, they didn't care. She had no idea when they studied or if they studied. She had a difficult time believing that they were serious about getting a degree, but only time would tell. What she did know? She intended to get the best degree she could.

In the blink of an eye, the first year came to an end and the friends celebrated the successful finish to their freshman year with a bottle of wine over a Chinese supper. It was a cheap and cheerful way to end the term.

The two girls had become close friends. Similar in temperament and humour, they decided that rather than find separate lodgings for the following year, they would find a place to rent between them and share the next three years together until they graduated.

They had a little time before they left the halls and they spent it searching for somewhere to live come September. They scanned the noticeboards in the halls where they found addresses for rooms to rent, but when they viewed them they found them wanting. It would seem that some landlords who rented to students had a low regard for their tenants when it came to looking after their property, which reflected in the scarred furniture and décor of those shabby rooms.

It was normal for students to find their own living arrangements from the second year onwards outside of the university halls. The girls ideally wanted to live within walking distance from University as the cost of having to buy bus tickets was extra expense that neither girl wanted to have.

They spent a great deal of time walking the familiar streets around their college, trying to find that property they would share for the duration of their life at university, eventually turning to the estate agents in the town. It turned out that they were not too helpful either and often the student accommodation on their books turned out to be shabby, dirty and expensive; too expensive for just the two of them. Sharing with other students would have to be considered, but with who?

They had walked for hours up and down the streets that were lined with Victorian houses clutching pages of information on rented properties. More through luck than good management, they found a small side road where a small group of more modern houses had been built in what might have been the back gardens of the Victorian ones that stood behind them. There was a rent sign in front of a large semi probably built in the late fifties. This could be just what they were looking for.

Rooting through the papers they were holding, Janet squealed with delight when she found the house in question and pushed the details of the semi under Katie's nose. They almost ran back to the estate agents to see if they could view the property that day.

They were in luck. The house in question was empty and the owners were working overseas and would be away for the foreseeable future. To have tenants for three years was more than acceptable, according to the agents. A very agreeable young man found the house keys and took them back to the house to view inside.

It was just what they were looking for; clean, not badly furnished, with a good-sized kitchen and living room plus a dining room, and three large double bedrooms and a good-sized single. There were loos upstairs and down and a lovely bathroom with a coloured bathroom suite of avocado and a shower over the bath. It was just what they wanted; everything was right except the rent. It was too much for the two of them. They had to find another couple to share the cost.

Katie was pretty sure that her dad would be able to find the money to pay the deposit they needed to sign up. With their grants they could manage if they could find someone to take the third bedroom. And Dad would get his money back at the end of the let, wouldn't he? This was it, they knew it, but who would share? They agreed to see the agent the next afternoon; that would give them enough time to speak to Katie's dad over the phone and plead their case.

A few yards on from the estate agents they passed a coffee shop. The smell of roasted coffee permeated out on to the pavement and reminded them they were thirsty and ready for a break. Still clutching the house details, they turned around and went back to the door, walking into the café to talk more about this exciting development.

In the brightly painted café they sipped black espresso coffee and rested their aching feet while pouring over the details of the letting contract the agent had given them to read.

At last they had found a house that was just what they wanted, but they didn't know of anyone to share with and didn't have anyone in mind to ask. They were mindful of their neighbours in halls, who were more concerned about partying than studying. There was no one from that crowd they would ask. They wanted like-minded people to share with, those who would contribute and not take. But who? It all seemed too impossible to put something together by the next day, but they were desperate not to lose the house.

The excitement they had felt was starting to fade; it was being taken over by a sense of despondency as they sat looking at their half-empty coffee cups and an image of the house that was just out of reach. The bright café seemed not so bright anymore.

Sat at a table towards the back of the café, but within earshot, was a couple that Katie knew slightly through the university. They were mature students she had met on her course who, it seemed, had changed track. They had both worked in what had become dead-end jobs going nowhere and with no real prospects. It had been a tough decision on their part, but they decided to go back to college to retrain to kick-start their careers.

Katie looked over to them and gave them a smile and a nod in acknowledgement, then realised that they seemed to be sorting through estate agents' pages of lettings too. Katie pinned her ears back. She could hear their conversation; they were having trouble finding a place to live too. The couple were a little older than Katie and Janet, maybe thirtyish and well turned out in smart modestly-priced clothes. They had always seemed nice in the casual conversation she had had with them during the meetings in the common room.

Katie leaned across to Janet to whisper across the table to her.

"Do you think that couple would be interested in a share with us? I know it's a bit of a risk as we don't know them that well, but listen – we could ask them to join us, say, for six months; that would be plenty of time to see if we get on together. If not, we will have time to find someone else to take their place." She ended with a shrug of her shoulders and looked expectedly at Janet, waiting for a response.

Janet looked over at the couple, thinking about what Katie was suggesting. She knew them by sight too.

"They look nice enough, but look – let's talk to them and see how it goes."

Katie eased herself over to the couple's table with a smile that greeted old friends. In a non-threatening way, she introduced herself properly.

She explained that Janet and herself had overheard their conversation, and that they too were looking to rent.

"It's a minefield, isn't it? Everywhere we've looked that's reasonable in rent, the place is a dump. Look, if you are interested in joining me and Janet at our table we may find a solution for both of us." The couple agreed to talk to see if there was mutual ground to solve the problem of a place to live.

Moving extra chairs to Janet's table, the four ordered more drinks and spent some time in small talk getting to know each other better. Jim and Olivia were easy to get on with, and after an hour together they reached an agreement: they would take a six-month let with Katie and Janet and see how they got on.

By the end of the afternoon all questions were answered and everything was agreed to go ahead. Katie's dad was only too pleased to have his daughter housed in suitable accommodation and agreed to supply the deposit. Come late September, in a short seven weeks, they would have somewhere to live. A house that would be a home for the next three years.

SETTLING IN

September came quickly. It all worked out well; they had all managed to move in without any disagreement on the choice of bedrooms. Katie was relieved to have a good-sized room she could study in, so unlike The Cell. A place to call her own and personalise it in a way she wanted. It had to be comfortable and bright and somewhere she could shut herself off if need be from the distractions that invariably would be present from time to time. She gathered up her personal belongings from her parent's home that included the rug and things from her desk that she had had in The Cell.

She took an old-fashioned wooden trestle table that she rescued from the back of her dad's garage; that would work well as a desk for her for the time being. A table lamp, personal computer and small printer were laid out neatly on it when it was seated in front of a large double-fronted window, which flooded the room with light. It was all so different from a year ago and her claustrophobic Cell. She now had a dressing table, a small walk-in closet and a double bed. She could make tea or coffee when she wanted right there in her room.

The large kitchen was the gathering place to exchange gossip and it was where they ate, unless by necessity they needed to make a sandwich to take back to their rooms while studying. The group became very good friends over the three years they spent together, but Janet was the special friend Katie would share much of her life with on campus.

After years studying business management, the petite and beautiful Katie had achieved a First. When the ceremony came and she was gowned in the black robes, she was proud to line up with the other graduates to receive the temporary blank parchment wrapped in red ribbon. The degree certificate would come through the post to her in a few weeks. Her parents sat through the ceremony with all the other parents, clapping as each student received their scroll. When Katie's name was read out they could not have been prouder; she was the first one in their family to receive a degree and her father could be forgiven for wiping a little tear from his eye whilst smiling and clapping his hands until they were sore.

The photographs that were taken on that unique day would be on show for the world to see on their sideboard forevermore. They shared a special lunch in an upmarket restaurant to mark the event. What a treat; the food was delicious and it made a special memory for them all. The event would stay in Katie's memory forever and she basked in her own self-importance for a while. Enjoying the adoring looks her parents gave her, was embarrassingly good.

It was all too good to be true. She felt she had arrived from one journey but her real journey into the future was only starting.

After the euphoria of the success in gaining a First and being on cloud nine, the high point soon became a low point. She had believed that her degree would be a passport to a good job; after all, that was what her teachers had told her, a ticket to quick employment and a good salary, but that assumption was quickly dismissed. She had applied to a whole host of companies but had not been offered a suitable position at any of the retail multiples she had hoped would take her on in one of their graduate schemes.

She had many interviews and they seemed to go well. She had dressed for the part and appeared full of confidence, making sure she looked smart, modern and reliable. But she soon found out that making her way into a man's world was not going to be easy. She had had high hopes of success at first, until the letters of rejection started hitting the mat at the rented accommodation where she still lived.

The let still had a few weeks to run before she would have to move out. Janet had been lucky and had landed a job on a local paper somewhere near Watford. She had already moved out, along with Jim and Olivia, who had returned to the town that they had come from. They too had quickly found work. She was so happy for them but being on her own made the failure of her interviews seem worse, somehow.

With no prospects in sight, her course finished and only a month of lease left to run on the rented house, she had no choice but to return home with her tail between her legs, to live with her parents until she could find a job.

Her parents were kindness itself but that only made her feel more of a failure. She felt she had let herself and them down. After all, they had supported her in so many ways through her studies, not least the twenty pounds her mother would give her here and there when she was hard up.

And how was she paying them back? She was living off them again with no prospect of a job anytime soon. Of course, they never said anything; in fact, they seemed to be pleased to have her home, they said they had missed her light and loving nature and the energy she brought into the house.

But Katie wasn't happy. It wasn't being at home that caused her unhappiness – she loved her parents. It was that dreadful feeling of failure that hung over her head. She must get a job and get one soon.

Any job would do. She could not bear the thought of her parents thinking her a failure or having to support her for any length of time. Not that they would say anything, they were too good for that, but she felt she had let them down and her self-esteem was at that moment at a very low point. It seemed there was a shortage of jobs for women in management. It was still a man's world out there and women were still not taken seriously. Old barriers were slow in coming down.

Home was the only place to go until she could find work. To have a few home comforts after university was a plus, and a place to hide until she felt strong enough to find her place in the world. She would have to take an interim job until she found the place that was for her.

After six months of marking time at home, Janet, her good friend from university, unexpectedly called Katie on the phone.

Janet had been working as a journalist with the newspaper, covering fashion and health matters, for almost seven months. She was settled in Watford but was ready to move into a house that she had found to rent. The paper she worked for was looking for someone to work in telephone sales, selling advertising space to companies and the general public and, knowing Katie was looking for work, Janet had recommended her to her employers for the vacancy.

"Wouldn't it be great to share again?" Janet had said with enthusiasm.

Katie rather thought it would, only the job at the local paper was not quite the move she wanted, but it was an opportunity that might lead to a solid future. It was a chance to be independent and it was a new opportunity to prove her worth to herself again. After some thought, she gratefully took the offer with both hands.

26

The three bedroom terraced house that Janet had found was in reality two doubles and a box room and was only partly furnished. But it was only a couple of miles away from the offices and you could walk to them if you needed to.

The two of them giggled like schoolgirls when they put the key into the lock of their new home and opened the front door; it so reminded them of the years they had spent studying together, but this was a new adventure to share and they were naturally excited. They walked around the rooms looking carefully at all the furnishings they would be responsible for, any damages they would have to pay for – but they were pleased to admit that the fixtures and fittings were in pretty good shape. Nothing to report to the agent, no chips or scratches; they could see nothing to worry them.

It was only when it came to the bedrooms that they were faced with a small problem. Both were a good size and well decorated, but only one had a double bed in it and the other, a single fold-away.

Janet had not argued when Katie insisted she should have the double bed; after all, Janet had invited Katie to share with her and had found her a job. They could have tossed a coin for the bedroom with the double bed but Katie had said quite firmly that in all fairness, Janet should have it, and Janet didn't disagree.

With Janet now owning the largest bedroom and double bed, Katie moved into the other double, having settled for that narrow little fold-away.

The low Z bed reminded her of the bed she had had in university in the room she'd nicknamed The Cell. It too had been narrow with a thin mattress, but at least this was clean and it would have to do until Katie had earned a few pounds so she could buy herself a proper bed.

Settling into her new home and new job was easy. Janet and herself were good companions both at work and home and the days passed into weeks and then months. The people who were employed by the paper were like a huge family and the newest arrival was soon adopted by the other members and brought into the fold.

Katie's temporary job, as she thought it to be, was going well. The space she sold for the paper was not too expensive and the management gave her wriggle room on the sales, with offers and discounts to help to sell the space that was available. She was good at her job. She was naturally at ease with people and had a pleasant phone manner that made her especially good as she canvassed customers selling the advertising space in the paper. As the advertising space in the paper was quickly bought up week after week, the management noticed her. The revenue she brought into the paper was not insubstantial; all the credit was given to her and her persuasive tongue.

She was also a great favourite with the staff, with her bubbly personality and kind nature; she always had a smile for people, she was a positive influence and she was always ready to help out when it was needed. As the weeks passed into months, her abilities were seen and rewarded and she was invited to head up the advertising section. The job came with an assistant and she was in charge of designing the layout for the advertising. Her assistant was a pleasant young man who had the gift of the gab, and the advert space was now being sold between them. The eager young man was keen to make his own mark in the job just as she had, but he had the added ambition to be a journalist just like Mike, a man he admired who worked on the paper.

Mike Devilian, the sports reporter, noticed Katie when she joined the paper. He was taken by her large dark brown eyes, and the shine on her chestnut hair that hung softly around her face. She was petite at five feet three, and her shapely frame was always well dressed and was enhanced by the modern styles that she wore.

Mike had a roving eye, he always had. *What could be better than to have an attractive bird hanging on my arm?* he thought, and she was certainly attractive. He needed to be seen with attractive women, it boosted his self-image and, in his mind, his credibility with his colleagues and friends. But he had a secret. For most of his adult life he had lived with an anxiety that lay tight in the pit of his stomach, knotting and churning when faced with any problem, though no one would ever have known from his cool and charming exterior. He was all lightness and confidence itself, the life and soul of the office party, happily laughing at all the jokes and moving round the room appearing to be only interested in the person that he was conversing with at that moment in time. He appeared to be a good listener only occasionally his eyes betrayed him by scanning the room for the next person to impress.

It was at such an occasion that he met Katie. They were both immediately attracted to each other. His Irish father and Italian mother, both sadly deceased, had given him a youthfully boyish look. He had black hair and blue-green eyes set into a sculpted masculine face with hooded eyes, high cheekbones and a classic Italian nose, with a full sensual mouth that made him something of a head-turner with the ladies. He was almost six foot tall, thick necked and broad across the shoulders. You could see that he worked out; his legs were strong from playing all types of sport and they moulded to his trousers as he moved. There were not too many women who didn't notice him. Muscles rippled under his white open-necked shirt that was tucked into his slim belted waist at the office, with his sleeves rolled up to below the elbow; one could see at a glance the strength in his arms. Mike was considered to be available, unmarried and fair game for all the single girls.

Though Katie was interested in finding a boyfriend, Mike was not exactly her idea of an ideal man. He was handsome and he knew it and she wasn't sure just how trustworthy he might be. Her ideal man would have values, intellect and ambition. Mike was, however, as she found out later at the Christmas bash, fun to be with, and she was attracted to him in a physical way.

It had been the spring when Katie had moved in with Janet. Months had passed and Katie was still sleeping on the Z bed. Now it was December and the pre-Christmas parties were lining up in front of her, the office party being at the top of the list.

Dressed in a little black dress she had bought especially for the event, the party was in full swing when Katie arrived at the office. The main office, a fairly large room, had been allotted for the fun and games that evening. It could have used a lick of paint but in the subdued lighting and with Christmas decorations it didn't look too bad.

Fellow workers were already enjoying the party, drinking beer and listening to the music from a music centre that someone had brought in. They were busy letting their hair down, dancing, drinking and waiting for supper to be served; it was being provided at the paper's expense.

Katie entered the noisy room decorated with old-fashioned homemade paper chains that were hanging down from the ceiling. They were stuck in position with sticky tape and it looked as though someone had used an entire roll to make sure it stayed in place. At each joint across the ceiling the chains were held in place with drawing pins, plus a sprig of mistletoe was hanging there, waiting for the unsuspecting – or otherwise – victim to be kissed under it. She eyed them up. *I will have to avoid those sprigs,* she thought to herself as she crossed the room to meet up with Janet. Too many of the men were passed their prime and smelt of stale tobacco or beer or both. She didn't relish the thought of being caught by one of them, even if it was the Christmas do.

There was a smell of hot spicy Indian food coming from a corner of the room where foil cartons were stacked alongside white dinner plates. A group of serving ladies were chatting as they set out the supper on trestles that were covered in paper tablecloths decorated with snowflakes and robins. *Hardly Christmas fare,* thought Katie, but it was the 'in' food these days, perhaps she would try it. The smell of beer lingered in the air and she noticed the men seemed to have large pints in their hands while their female companions sipped cream sherry or a light champagne Perry in small glasses.

Someone had moved all the desks to one side and up against the walls, clearing a square space in the middle of the room. The music centre was blasting out Elvis Presley from two speakers and a couple moved in time to the music, valiantly working hard at having a good time. The rather robotic dancing looked stiff, even rigid, in that small space. With all the banter that was going on in the room, it had become a very noisy place. Janet and Katie were having difficulty hearing each other over the din; everybody, it seemed, was talking in raised voices, including them.

The whole atmosphere had changed from that morning when the office was getting ready to go to press. All the staff had been busy finishing off their columns under the watchful eye of the editor, who was striding around the office chasing everyone up. The deadline was imminent and they were putting in place the finishing touches to the local weekly paper. The hustle and shouting from the editor to everyone in his sight was now in the near past.

Christmas was coming and the office would close down for a few days. The employees would be sharing the festivities with their families, seated at cracker-decorated tables eating turkey and plum pudding with brandy sauce. Tonight was the preamble to it.

The room was filled with warmth. Smiling, friendly colleagues were stood in small groups laughing at old jokes that they had probably heard before while enjoying a glass or two of their preferred tipple. As Katie passed Mike on the way to the bar, he took her by the waist and gently led her onto the floor, holding her tight as the music changed to a gentle ballad. She didn't object. She had noticed him months ago; he was handsome and charming but had something of a reputation with the ladies. The slow tempo of the music and the closeness of his body stirred feelings in her that she had not experienced for some time. There on the tiny makeshift dance floor, she felt a new chapter of her life was opening up to her. Excitement welled up inside her as she looked up into the handsome face and saw the passion in his eyes. Could this be the start of a meaningful relationship, one she could lend her soul to? She rather thought it was and she could.

27

MARCH 1970

The Old Colonial Store stood in the high street of the small market town in which Katie lived. It boasted three floors of new and antique furniture and goods.

Each floor was dedicated to different sorts of merchandise; bric-a-brac, ceramics and small bits of furniture on the ground floor; wardrobes, beds, tables and chairs on the second; and carpets and soft furnishings on the top floor.

Katie had gone there to find bits and pieces for her space in the house she was renting with Janet. She was interested in picking up a bargain and was looking at goods that were second-, third- or even fourth-hand as she wandered through the store. She was sure she would find some trinkets at a reasonable price.

Having found a couple of matching vases and a set of eggcups, she decided to climb the stairs to the second floor to see if she could find a modestly priced bed.

The second floor opened out in front of her through the fire door from the landing. It was badly lit and her eyes had to adjust to the gloom. The furniture had been crammed in without any order; it looked as though the pieces had been dropped into any available space regardless of bulk or size. Somehow she would have to find a path through the maze that was set out before her. Beds were squashed in between wardrobes, tables and chairs. But she would not be put off; she was determined to see all of them. Today she hoped to find one to replace the dreadful Z bed she was currently sleeping on.

Trying to avoid bumping her knees on the wooden obstacles as she squeezed her way through the maze to look at all the beds, she made her way towards the far wall at the back of the large room. She was quite disappointed at the utilitarian quality of the beds. She was surrounded by cheap white vinyl padded headboards with buttons on low single divans and cane headboards with mattresses that lay on narrow-slatted bases. There was not much in the way of comfort on those narrow beds and they were definitely not what she wanted. The lighting got steadily worse as she moved towards the far wall; the electric lights and small windows were no help as she fought her way through the stores stock searching for a bed.

Why her eyes were suddenly drawn to the back of the room she would never know. Her eyes lighted on a large headboard that was half-covered by a dust sheet. She moved towards the double bed that was half-hidden under the greying dirty material.

Moving carefully through the furniture to the back of the room, she could make out carving under the fabric on the extraordinarily large headboard that sat proud above its slatted-based frame. Her fingers clutched at the cloth and moved it to one side, revealing a picture that was instantly recognisable, a story as old as time itself. There was the tree of life and Adam and Eve.

"Oh my God, its beautiful!" she cried out loud, then looked around embarrassed at her outburst, but thankfully there was no one around to hear her on that floor. Automatically, she reached out to run her hand over the wood. How warm it felt under her touch. No rough edges caught her fingers as she ran them through the grooves that the tools had made so many years before. The wood had been sanded to a satin surface and her fingers slid over the tree heavy with fruit and onto the figure of the man, moving up to his face, tracing the strong lines of its profile. The bed seemed to talk to her, as though it had been waiting for her to come and claim it for her own. She must have it.

What woke him? He didn't really know. Was it the drapes being removed, revealing that dim and dusty room he hated so, or was it the sound of a woman's voice that had brought him out of his cocoon of self-inflicted sleep? It was a voice he seemed to recognise.

He had slumbered for years, off and on, never fully awake, for it didn't matter what year it was or how many years had passed, when he surfaced from his sleep the despair was just as raw as it had been when he had lost Marina.

It was necessary to block out all emotions. He was trapped again in this netherworld, so lonely now he would have killed himself if he were able. The light of the gateway to the next existence had been denied to him. How he wished he could have passed on with Marina. He was glad he could protect himself in sleep, from the pain that seemed as bad now as when the flu had taken her. Grief was an emotion he wanted to submerge and hide so deep in his soul that feeling it again wasn't an option. Twice the bed had been sold and he had been disturbed to endure the anguish of it, he had been forced to haunt the purchasers and through his groans and bad humour the bed had been returned to the store, where he could sleep out the misery he felt. Now once again some wretched thing or person had the audacity to wake him and disturb his rest.

He felt rather groggy; he resented being brought back to the surface of his pain. The dimness of this prison he was locked in was made all the worse by his eyes seeing his surroundings. Dim electric light bulbs and the light from small dirty windows that were way down at the other end of the dingy room did not hide the badly made and damaged beds that surrounded him.

His eyes did not really focus at first; staring out into the badly lit room only made him squint with an effort to see. As his eyes adjusted, coming back into focus, he was shocked to see a face peering at him through the veiled wood, looking not at him but at his carving.

His heart leaped and tumbled in the shock of recognition, for the beautiful young woman who appeared to be staring back at him through the headboard had the face, albeit younger, of his lost love Marina. He was stunned. It was as if an electric shock was passing through his body.

How could this be? Could she have been reincarnated and fate was at last being generous to him? Was he being allowed a second chance to love by the gods that be? Questions rattled around in his head. Somehow he had to be part of her life. Was he encountering Marina all over again? He hoped so. He couldn't lose her a second time; somehow, he had to be with her.

It was a pity that she probably wouldn't have any memories of their time together in her last life, if indeed she was the reincarnation of Marina. He must find out. He would have to introduce himself to this lovely young woman.

The headboard was somewhat dusty even though it had lain under a dust sheet. Almost without thinking, Katie pulled out a clean hankie to free the carving from the light film of dust that lay on it.

She was immediately stirred by the scene in front of her and gently moved her fingers across the wood, caressing it and marvelling at the fine quality of the work. She had never seen anything like this before and doubted that she ever would again.

She had only been looking for a bed to replace the Z bed and fit nicely into her bedroom but here was a piece of art and she was convinced that it had laid here half-hidden just for her to find. This extraordinary discovery was meant for her, her alone, and she must have it.

The price tag was tied to a slat; it hung down under the bed. Her hand reached down and lifted up the white label. She was shocked to see a price that was well beyond her means at this moment in time. It seemed such a desperately high price that her heart sank with disappointment. She wanted the bed so badly, yet how could she afford it? Touching the carved tree under her fingertips and feeling the sensitivity of the wood, she looked with a loving eye, taking in once again the beauty of the scene. Feeling the warmth of the wood under her fingertips she smiled a sad smile, turning away, accepting the loss. A strange feeling overcame her; a light cool caress touched her delicate neck, moving her hair in the breeze that came from nowhere. It was as though someone had opened a window and a spring breeze had swept through the room, searching her out. A shiver went down her back and goosebumps stood on her arms. That old saying 'someone is walking over my grave' came to mind. She turned to see where the draught had come from but there was no window open in that dismal room.

She was stopped in her tracks with an overwhelming desire to buy the bed, whatever the consequences. No! It was more than desire; it was as though the bed was demanding her to buy it.

How could she afford it? Yet she wanted it so badly and she must have it.

He knew that she was the one to take him and his bed away from this dusty and miserable existence. The thought that he might be involved in her life excited him; a prospect of hope that he could hold on to. He saw from the look on her lovely face and the sensitivity in her eyes when she admired his work, that he would be able to reach her mind. He felt her touch as she caressed him through his spirit in the wood. Already he felt in close harmony with her spirit. He saw the disappointment on her face when she read the price tag and he was afraid might lose her.

Emerging from his retreat to stand by her, he used all the spiritual power he could muster and touched her shoulder. He leaned towards her and gently moved her hair back from her face, kissing her lightly on her neck. Whispering words in her ear, Louis begged her to buy the bed; he knew he needed to be with her. He encouraged and pleaded in a silent thought and positive energy that left him and entered her. There was no language barrier between them; thought and feeling was all that was needed to communicate from his ghostly spirit to her mortal soul.

She decided she would have the bed if she could persuade the owner of the store to make a deal with her. Hire purchase, or at least paying for it by instalments, had occurred to her and it might be the best way to go forward. Now she just had to find the owner of the store to make that all-important deal. It never occurred to her that he might say no.

Katie found an assistant wearing an old tan-coloured coat walking slowly across the floor with a sheaf of papers in his hand. He appeared to be checking the stock, ticking off items on the papers as he went. She asked where she might find the managing director and he directed her to the owner of the store. His office was situated one flight down.

She practised her speech as she descended the stairs and made her way to the back of the store where she could see an office. Through its open door, a seated figure was half-hidden by the back of the large swivel chair that he was sat in. She took a deep breath and knocked on the door with purpose.

His back was towards her as she looked into the room; he appeared to be hiding in the small office that was the size of a shoebox. Papers laid on every available surface and they were piled high in front of him. They were sharing the same space with a half-eaten sandwich, which still sat in its cellophane container, marked with a supermarket brand and a price of £1.00. A half-finished mug of strong tea was standing next to an ashtray that was full of cigarette ends. A row of several mugs that were mostly empty looked as though they had sat there for a few days waiting to be washed. One still had a milky skin that had set itself on top of the dregs. *What a mess,* thought Katie, looking at the litter that sat on the surface of what had once been a rather splendid roll top desk. The tabletop of the desk was inlaid with green-tooled leather but where she could see it, it was badly ringed by previous visits of hot mugs with wet bottoms.

A squat little man sat in the high-backed leather winged chair that seemed much too big for him.

"Well?" he said in a bored and distant way as he responded to the knocking. His small round head nodded as he swung himself around to see who had entered his sanctuary, who had disturbed his concentration from the list he had been checking before the knock on his open door.

Looking through the thick lenses of his spectacles, his eyes lit up. They moved over Katie's body, looking her up and down, approving what he saw, a smile curled onto his face. A pretty girl was always welcome in his office and this lovely creature scored ten out of ten.

His hand stroked his near-balding head in a nervous gesture and it appeared to Katie that the initial indifference had suddenly been replaced with an intensive interest and his smile had become a leer.

The name on the door had read Mr Slimann. She hoped the name did not reflect the nature of the man but, judging by his leer, she would have to leave her opinion of him until after she had negotiated with him.

So with a deep breath, Katie recited her proposal to him, the one she had practised on her way down to meet him. She told him how she had fallen in love with the carved bed and went on to persuade him to let her pay for it in instalments.

It would take several months, and she would only take the bed after her final payment. The smile on his face grew even wider. What she didn't know was that Mr Slimann was keen to offload the bed as soon as possible. That was as long as he didn't lose money on it. It had been sold twice and returned because of some strange happenings, so the purchasers had said. He hadn't seen anything untoward himself but his assistants had also experienced strange feelings and noises around it. That was why it had been put at the back of the room on the second floor. He had paid a goodly sum for the bed in a moment of madness thinking he would make a good profit on it, but the profile of his customers didn't fit its style, it was not the usual stock he would buy in to sell and most of his customers were not looking for anything so elegant. It had been a foolish moment when he bought it.

Someone would have to have a pretty large bedroom for it to look right in it. Here was a girl willing to pay the full price for it, albeit over a period of time. He rubbed his hands together with glee and drew up an agreement there and then. The first payment was due on the first of the month with a deposit of twenty pounds securing the purchase. He happily called an assistant to his office to put a large 'sold' notice on the bed. Both Mr Slimann and Katie were overjoyed with the outcome; both were getting what they wanted.

Over the next five months Katie visited the store, taking her payment with her on the first of each calendar month. She always spent some time on the second floor sitting on the slatted frame, looking at and touching her purchase, sometimes even spending her lunch hour eating her sandwich perched on the edge of the bed. She felt comfortable there, even among the dusty and, frankly, dirty room. She could not explain the urge that pulled her into the store; it was as though she was magnetised to the bed, it seemed to call to her. The thought was so irrational that she tried to dismiss it when it occurred, but try as she might she always succumbed to it.

On August 1, Katie walked into the store and made her way up to the tiny office of Mr Slimann to pay the last instalment.

Mr Slimann had agreed to deliver the bed free of charge and she was eager to make the arrangements, not least because she could at last say goodbye to the Z bed, the bed that she had laid on since moving in with her friend Janet. She was so excited at the prospect of having a good night's sleep on a mattress that she could stretch out on. She had already bought a good sprung mattress; it had already been delivered and was sat in her room awaiting the arrival of Louis's masterpiece.

The details of the purchase were completed and delivery was for the next day, Saturday, at 10am.

Thank goodness she would not have to see the slimy Mr Slimann again. He reminded her so much of Uriah Heep, that awful character created by Charles Dickens. She felt Mr Slimann undressed her with his eyes and his clammy handshake and damp hands unnerved her so much so that she had to wash her hands immediately after meeting with him.

Saturday morning arrived. The sold notice that had sat on Louis's bed was removed by one of the two burly men who had come to deliver the bed to Katie's home. Old woollen strips of blanket were wrapped around the legs while a large blanket covered the ornate headboard. The two men, used to removal work, expertly separated headboard and footboard from the base. Covered and protected, they lifted the bed out through the building into the warm August day, and Louis with it.

Louis had not seen a blue sky or the sun for years. He was happy to be moving out of the miserable store and on to a new chapter in his ghostly existence. He marvelled at how far the world had come from when he was mortal. In his century, a horse and cart or a carriage had been the mode of travel, if you had been lucky enough to be able to afford them. For him and for many others, walking was the only mode of travel. Most people stayed in and around the village or town they were born in, only travelling to find work and then only within walking distance of their home. In this century, the noise in the streets was alarming; metal four-wheel carriages called cars careered up and down the wide black painted road, and even the sky had transport in it. In the time he had spent with Marina, these modes of travel were just being developed. Now, people could get on public transport and be taken to the destinations that appeared in writing on the front of the vehicles called buses. Goods were ferried in large enclosed metal lorries. The world he knew had moved on in leaps and bounds. People of this time seemed to be always on the move and were busy, busy, busy. Bicycles, so unlike the bone rattlers of Marina's day, were gone. Sleek colourful bicycles sped down the road with low curved handlebars, making the cyclist look uncomfortably squat as they rode along. Everyone appeared to be in a hurry.

The long skirts and long sleeves that Marina and the girls had worn had been abandoned long ago and the style of dress that some of the modern women wore appeared unseemly and quite brazen. Some modern women appeared to be dressed in only underwear and quite unashamed of it, while other women seemed to copy men in their dress and wore trousers. He was quite bemused by it all. It was something else he must adjust to. Time had moved on and he recognised that he was out of step with this era, but he would learn.

Katie was very happy; after the Christmas party her friendship with Mike had taken off. It had developed into a loving relationship that she had not really expected. The last eight months had been spent talking and learning about each other and she felt now that they had a mutual respect that would sustain them as long as they stayed together.

Mike's bedsit was in a large Victorian house on the edge of the town. It was the place they shared time together in, and it looked out onto a park where the two of them would walk on a pleasant summer evening. The old house had been fashioned in dark stained natural wood panelling; the doors and staircase were very grand but terribly old-fashioned. The panelling that skirted the hall and up the stairs made the hall dark and gloomy, but it was perfect to hide the lovers in its dim light when they climbed up the stairs to their haven. A deep-pile wool carpet in large floral pattern laid on the hall floor and up the stairs, cushioning the footsteps of the couple as they crept up to his room. They had no wish to upset his landlady, who was a little old-fashioned when it came to allowing the opposite sex into the bedrooms for any length of time. She liked Katie well enough and she often became deaf when she heard the front door close rather more quietly than usual on Friday nights. She remembered when she was young and had forbidden desires. Mike was fearful that he might upset the old lady; the rent was low and it was near his job, it was too convenient to lose. So the two of them were always mindful of Mrs Brown, who lived below him.

Mrs Brown lived on the ground floor and after her husband died, she let out her bedrooms to two male lodgers to supplement her income. She liked having company in the large house; it made her feel safe.

Mike's room was large enough for a small settee, a coffee table, a wardrobe and a three-quarter-sized bed that was pushed up against the wall in a corner of the room. A small door led off into a small cubbyhole that passed for a kitchenette. It held a sink with hot and cold water, a square wooden table, a kitchen drawer unit on which sat a Baby Belling with a two top ring hob and grill. An old-fashioned kettle that whistled madly when it boiled sat on the hob ready for use. Mike was not a chef and didn't think beyond boiled eggs or something on toast.

Most Fridays the two of them could be found sharing the small bed in his room, it was warm and comfortable and his strong arms felt so powerful as he held her. His lips searched for her neck, pushing back her soft chestnut hair down onto her shoulders, moving down and down until he found her round firm breasts, his lips searching for that hard proud nipple. Lying there under a spell of excitement and expectancy, desire and passion stirred in her belly. There was an urgent desperation that clutched at her; she wanted more and needed him to fulfil her needs. He needed her touch too and she knew how to please him. It made him feel so alive to have her fingers gently caress his body until his manhood became large and stiff. When at last he could bear it no longer, he took her, the rhythmic movement becoming more urgent until the climax came with quiet moans, leaving them happily clinging to each other as they came down from the height of passion.

Hunger surfaced after making love and cheese on toast, washed down with hot coffee, was their favourite Friday supper.

Christmas to August had seen Katie blossom into a confident young woman and although Mike and Katie were lovers no one at work knew except Janet. Of course colleagues gossiped and speculation was rife about them after the Christmas party last December but after dating for a few weeks they decided that they would keep their affair to themselves not wanting to mix their private life with their professional one. The gossips could gossip, they would soon get tired of seeing the two of them at work, appearing to be totally disinterested in each other, thus having nothing to talk about. Gossips being gossips would soon move on to juicier targets.

So to the outside world Mike still flirted with all the women he could while she worked hard at building up a career within the paper. The one thing they never did was to make love in the house where Katie lived with Janet.

Katie was doing well; she seemed to gobble up everything that was thrown at her, nothing was too big for her to tackle. She was bright and knew how to handle people in a fair and even-handed way. Her business degree started to become useful and not just in seeing to her section, for she understood the business overall and became something of a trouble-shooter, helping out in areas that were not strictly under her job description. But the editor was more than pleased and it kept his little band of workers happy, and that kept him happy.

But Mike's job was not giving him satisfaction anymore and he seemed to be at a crossroads in his life. He loved Katie in his own way and he could see that she was doing well at work but he was getting bored with the same old things that he was reporting about week on week. Of course, he loved sport but this small town never seemed to produce any really big sporting events or personalities. He dreamed of working on a bigger newspaper in a large city and flying off to cover some exciting game abroad; the world cup, the Olympics. Anything that would give him a bit of excitement, an adventure away from this insignificant town. Most of the time he sat in pubs drinking with the local rugby team, listening to their reminiscing of their past glory, singing bawdy songs and making dirty jokes, and he recognised he was looking at men who were running out of steam fast and soon would be over the hill.

Other times he would be standing on the side lines of a football match watching kids attempt to beat their opponents, egged on by their braying parents who shouted a tirade of insults at the opposition, encouraging their young to foul an opposing player. Those parents wanted the win much more than their children did and Mike didn't want to be there. Where was the spirit of sportsmanship? And though he loved Katie and she satisfied a need, there was still emptiness inside of him, one that he couldn't fill. He couldn't rest. He was constantly in an anxious state and he was turning more and more to whiskey, that amber liquid, to escape his life. It made him relax and helped him to sleep.

When the alarm went off at the usual time, Katie rolled over, reaching out to the small clock that was sitting on a low bedside table. With her eyes still half-shut, she managed to turn off the ringing before the urge to throw the damn thing across the room became too great. She turned over, stretching out to ease the stiffness in her back that the Z bed caused. Suddenly smiling to herself, she raised herself up on one elbow and shouted 'yippee' out loud. Today was Saturday and her wonderful bed was due to be delivered.

Janet shouted from the other room. "Hey, you all right?"

"Couldn't be better," came back the reply. "My bed is coming at ten this morning and I can't wait."

With breakfast over and the Z bed folded up and hidden away in the closet, Katie cleaned the room thoroughly before sinking onto the settee. The room was now ready for the delivery. It was time for a well earned drink and Katie sat enjoying a hot, steaming milky coffee drink that had been handed to her from Janet, who came and sat beside her with a serious look on her face.

"I wanted to talk to you," said Janet. "I have some news. I applied for a job two months ago with a magazine in Leeds. Well, I had a final interview on Thursday and they offered me the job yesterday. It's an offer I can't refuse. Better pay, a car and, best of all, I'm going as the beauty and fashion editor. I'll have to work a month's notice then I'm gone," she said, shrugging her shoulders. "I know this is a surprise and you'll have to find someone else to share with," she added. "I've loved being here sharing with you, but it's time for me to move on. You do understand, don't you?" The look on Janet's face was a mixture of caring and sadness and though Katie was shocked, she knew her friend had to find her own way in life just as she must.

"I'm so pleased for you, Jan, I'm sure I will be able to find someone to share," Katie replied. Deep down she wondered if Mike would be interested, though it might be a step too far for him. She didn't think he was ready to commit. No, not yet. Still, she would mention it and watch his response.

The chimes of the doorbell brought her back to reality. It was five to ten and the bed was here.

Louis had spent a very uncomfortable time in a white van loaded with many items due for delivery at various addresses. The smell of exhaust fumes and diesel filled the van, along with cigarette smoke from the man called Pete who was giving directions to Larry the driver. The road was appalling; there were potholes that made the van lurch one way then another, moving the furniture in the back, making the ride as unpleasant as it could be. Had he not been a ghost he would have been crushed. The one bright spot was having windows in the back doors, allowing Louis to see the countryside as they passed on their way to Katie's home. Louis could see cows and sheep in the fields, Heavily leafed trees and hedges and borders filled with wild flowers and weeds lined the roads. Not that it mattered; he just drank in the sights and enjoyed the confusion of colours as they passed at a speed that was not recommended for such roads.

At last the waiting was over. How many times had she visited him in the store? Nine or ten times. Each time she seemed more beautiful than before. Not that she really knew she was visiting him; no, but without her knowing, there was a connection between them, he could feel it and he needed to make her realise it too but without frightening her. He knew only too well how people reacted when faced with a spirit, even if it was friendly. He remembered their first meeting and the gentle kiss he had placed on her neck. She had touched the exact spot afterwards; she had felt it, he knew she had. How to proceed was the question he asked himself. Well, time would tell.

The van took a bend too fast and a chest of drawers passed through Louis like a knife through butter. The furniture moved back in place as the van levelled off down the straight road. The headboard was safely wrapped in old blankets to protect it from damage, not that the driver of the van seemed to care one way or the other and at the next bend the cargo moved yet again.

They were now passing rows of houses with neat, trim and tidy gardens.

"Third house down on the right," called out Pete in a loud voice so that Larry could hear over the top of the engine and the radio that was singing out from the local radio station. Pulling over to the curb, Larry stopped the van with a jerk, miraculously straightening up the furniture in the back once again. Light flooded in as Pete opened the back doors he threw the tab end of his cigarette to the ground and stepped on it. Pete climbed into the van to help just as Larry appeared, having just rung the doorbell to let Katie know they had arrived.

Katie opened the door to the two deliverymen with a smile and an invitation to take the bed up the stairs to her lovely clean bedroom.

Sliding the bed pieces from the van, the two men took the bed inside the house, carrying it up to Katie's bedroom, not knowing that they carried Louis as well.

The men from the Colonial Store built the bed in record time, even unwrapping the mattress and placing it on the bed frame, ready for Katie to make up. Katie's face glowed. Why this bed meant so much to her was a mystery to her, she only knew the comfort it seemed to give her and the pleasure she got in just looking at it.

A new mattress cover was waiting to be pulled over her new mattress. Two new crisp white double sheets were waiting, still in their cellophane packets, on a chair by her bed. New pillows and cases lay on the bed with a light, thin duvet and a bedspread of lilac and gold quilted squares. She knew that they would finish the look of her bed and her room. She stepped back to admire the bed that sat majestically in her bedroom and was pleased with what she saw.

Louis was very pleased too. He liked the room he was now a part of. The cream-coloured walls were adorned with family photos and small prints of multi-coloured landscapes. A large window looked out onto the green grasses of the garden, where he would be able to roam and watch the world go by in this row of terraced houses. Best of all, he was with his darling girl at last.

28

Louis had spent many years in that dimly lit room in the Colonial Store, fretting and grieving for the loss of Marina and Rosa. They had been so important to his existence but over the last five months he had had regular visits from a beautiful girl whose name, as yet, he still had to learn.

He had come to the wrong conclusion when he first saw her, in believing that she was the reincarnation of Marina, the woman he had loved so much. His loss had been great and he was in desperate to be part of this girl's life and love again. He wanted to have some kind of existence, instead of living a miserable life trapped behind the wooden curtain he had made such a long time ago.

For five months this lovely girl had come to see her bed and unknowingly visit him. She was sensitive; he could see that by the way she touched the carving so carefully and the way her face lit up when doing so. She stroked the wood so tenderly, tracing her fingers over the objects, talking to herself as she did. Questions poured from her. Who had made this wonderful bed? When was it carved? Where did it come from? What was the story behind the scene of creation? Were those profiles of the man and woman based on real people? He heard them all. If only she had Rosa's gift he could have given her the answers directly, but she wasn't Rosa. Given time he would have to find a way of answering those questions.

Sometimes she had come just to sit on the slatted frame, sometimes she would have her lunch with her; it didn't matter, she came because after each payment she owned a little more of the bed and he was a step nearer to being with her. Five months had come and gone, and he and the bed had finally been packed up and delivered to the girl he had come to feel affection for.

But he wasn't complacent about the situation, he knew she had an earthly life in the modern world and at this present time, it didn't include a ghost that wanted to know her. It also occurred to him that perhaps she was in a relationship with someone. He hadn't thought of that while he was still in the store. Well! He should think about it now; she was, after all, a beautiful woman and she may be in love.

He would have to tread carefully. He wanted to know her and her to know him and although he knew a mortal relationship was impossible, he thought of the meaningful relationship he had had with Marina through the dream state they shared. Circumstances were different but it could happen again.

He was coming to terms with ideas that deflated him somewhat. A mortal and ghost in a fruitful relationship, how stupid. He cursed under his breath. Here was the girl that he seemed to have waited for through the space of time. After all the long years in limbo, only going to where the bed was purchased and watching mortals busy living their lives, while life passed him by. He longed to reach out to her, to learn about her for he already knew that he loved her.

She was a modern woman who was so excitingly different from the women in his time. But he could not intrude, he would give her space and privacy and he would be satisfied with just being there for now. At last he had new horizons, he would be able to roam in the new space of the house, and he would try and enjoy this new modern world and learn all he could about it.

Katie was attempting to pull a cover over her new mattress when Janet stuck her head around the open doorway. Seeing Katie struggling because the cover was a tight fit, she scolded.

"You should have called me. Here, let me help," said Janet, crossing over to the new purchase in the bedroom.

"Thank you, Janet. I thought you were busy."

"Never too busy to help you," Janet replied with a smile on her face. Together they tugged the fabric on elastic until it was nicely tucked under the new mattress.

Well, thought Louis, *I know the name of one young lady at least, that must live here.*

The new sheets were still in their packets of cellophane on a chair by the bed. When Janet turned to pass a packet to Katie, she saw the bed fully for the first time.

"Oh Katie, I see what you meant when you said you had bought a very special bed; it's extraordinary."

A smile crossed Louis's face. *Thank you, Janet,* he thought. *Katie — what a lovely name for my darling girl.*

The girls quickly made up the bed and finished off the look by throwing the gold and lilac brightly patterned patchwork quilt over the duvet. Both the girls stepped back to admire the newly dressed purchase. It looked amazing.

"Tell you what," said Janet keeping her face straight, "I'll swap you rooms."

"Not a chance, you cheeky thing," was the reply. Katie could hardly wait for the night to come and bedtime.

Katie's first night in her newly bought bed was a joy and her soul sang. Lying between the crisp white sheets she stretched out, sighing a sigh of contentment. Her arms reached above her head, touching the warm wood, feeling the edges of the carving under her fingers. She rolled over onto her stomach and saw the story played out as she scanned the delicate tool marks before her eyes. Her fingers played lightly over the tree of life and traced along the edges of the man. Adam, as she thought of him, was strong and broad-shouldered; he stood with his hand outstretched, reaching across to the love of his life, Eve. A sudden wave of sadness touched Katie's heart but only for a moment. Was she the love of Mike's life? She loved him but how much, she wasn't sure, and she wasn't sure about the strength of his feelings for her. The scene of the lovers had sowed new doubts in her mind about him. She shrugged her shoulders. She wouldn't allow this moment to be destroyed by sad thoughts; after all, somehow she knew that she was at the start of a new and wonderful chapter of her life. Turning the light off, she snuggled down in the bed and felt secure and comfortable before quickly drifting into sleep.

Her ghostly sentinel, her new guardian, stood looking down on her sleeping figure. He had a smile on his face because love filled his heart. The emotion was enormously strong and he had the overpowering desire to kiss her. She would not feel it and she would not know he was there; that didn't matter. He bent down and kissed her on her cheek. She turned over, maybe disturbed from the ghostly touch of his lips, he wasn't sure. Katie's soft white shoulders were exposed to the now cooling room. Reaching over her still form, his hands clutched at the white sheet. He had been able to move solid objects in the past, usually when his emotions were at their strongest; maybe he would be given the same gift now through love. Hardly daring to hope that he would succeed, he purchased the fabric with his hands and covered up her delicate shoulders from the cold.

Deep relief washed through his body; so love too had a positive effect. He felt at that moment that he would be able to protect and care for her, this woman he loved.

In reality, he knew he was still a ghost. She would be afraid if he tried to contact her when she was awake; his only option was to try and reach her when she was asleep. It was a method he had first used when Marina was suffering from nightmares so long ago; he had placed his hand on her forehead and he had shared thoughts with her. He had used it before and knew it to be a gentle way to reach and communicate with people. When the time was right he would contact Katie.

It was a week later that Katie dreamt of a Victorian manor house and garden. There was a ten-feet-high red brick wall surrounding it and internal walls that separated one garden from another. It grew vegetables, flowers and fruit trees and had a carp pool, and it even had an ornamental maze within the gardens. Somehow she recognised herself as one of the gardeners in her dream. She was tending the soft fruits and vegetables that were laid out in immaculate order in beds and borders all around her. She could see flowers, the multi-coloured blooms in vast displays set in a six-feet-deep border that stretched out from the red walls. She could smell the fragrant scent from the roses that lay alongside the bushes, and from the white and pink peonies giving off their own heavy perfume. Then she was setting down straw under the strawberry plants to keep the heart-shaped fruit from spoiling on the wet earth.

Wood smoke wafted through the air, catching her unawares after the scent of the sweet-smelling flowers. She turned, looking towards the point in the garden where the source came from. She was curious. The strawberries could wait and she wandered down to a path that led towards to a fairly large garden shed. From where she stood halfway down the path, she could see through the open doors and into the dimly lit interior. There was an outline of a man working inside at a bench. A small brazier stood by the doors of the shed, its smoke curling up into the air before the breeze sent it flowing towards Katie once more.

She was moving slowly towards the shed now. The figure inside was growing more distinct at each step she took. As she neared the open door, she could see a man carving into a large curved panel of wood. The man half-turned and tossed a handful of small wood shavings into the fire; she could hear the crackling as the wooden bits shrank and twisted in the hot flames, sending off another waft of sweet-smelling smoke. Now standing at the open door, she peered inside, waiting for her eyes to adjust from the bright daylight to the dim interior. The man stood with his back to her; he was totally absorbed in his labour. She moved a little closer. Now she could see his hands engaged in the delicate work there on the curved headboard. With a small mallet and chisel, he was carving the man that stood next to the tree of life. He had not yet started on the woman, she was only marked out, but Katie recognised it. It was hers; this was the bed headboard she had just bought. She called out hello to him but he didn't turn to her. She wanted to see his face. Who was he? She wanted an answer to one of the question she had asked herself so many times in the store, but as she moved towards him a dreadful ringing bombarded her ears. The noise was overpowering but it didn't seem to affect the man at his work, where was the noise coming from?

Katie woke up, slamming her hand down onto the alarm clock, turning it off but at the same time knocking it sideways, causing it to go flying. It passed through Louis who was at her side and landed on the rug.

"Damn and blast it," she said loudly, dashing from her bed to retrieve it, hoping it wasn't damaged.

It was already seven o' clock and time to get up.

She felt puzzled and cheated, but not alarmed. Puzzled because the dream she was remembering, she seemed to be part of. Cheated because she hadn't been able to see the man who was carving her precious headboard. She shrugged. It was obvious that her preoccupation with the carving the night before had manifested itself into her subconscious, hence the strange dream. Oddly though, she felt that the man was not really a stranger and she really wanted to see his face. Perhaps she knew him in another life. She laughed at herself, turning her mind to the present, and started to get herself ready for the day.

August was passing quickly, soon to become September. She had no more dreams of that colourful garden and the man that carved; reality was more pressing, for with each passing day the thought of Janet leaving brought heaviness to her heart. They had been friends for so long and the month passed so quickly. Soon Janet would be gone and Katie would miss her dreadfully. The last week of the month was the worst. Janet spent her time packing and talking about her new job and even though Katie knew it was right for Janet to go and pursue her ambition, she felt put out. She would have to find a person to share the house with, someone whom she could trust and get along with. It was sad that the month in which Janet had worked her notice had passed in the blinking of an eye. She missed her already, for they had had such fun together and been as close as sisters could be over the years. But now it was time to face up to the problem that was looming before her: finding someone to share her home, someone she could get on with long-term, someone who she would have to find quickly to help pay the rent and utilities. But who?

29

With Janet now working in Leeds, Katie needed to find a new friend to share the tenancy at her home. The obvious choice was Mike but she was not sure she was ready for that sort of commitment. True, they had a good physical relationship – more than that, she thought she loved him in her own way – but there was something that made her nervous about completely trusting him with her body and soul.

As the weeks rolled by, she realised she had to do something fairly quickly. She knew that time was running out, along with her bank balance that was shrinking at an alarming rate. She had still not found anyone who she felt was suitable to share and live with. Almost in desperation, she decided to take the plunge and invite Mike to sub-let his flat for six months and come live with her on a trial basis, knowing that he still had his old place to go back to if sharing did not work out. It was also the time when the two of them admitted to having a relationship to their fellow colleagues. No one would believe anything else once they were living together.

He would have to square it with Mrs Brown but as luck would have it, the young assistant of Katie's at work was looking to move out of his parent's house and rent himself. Both Mike and Katie could give Mrs Brown a reference on his behalf. It was settled and sealed over the next weekend.

Her two-bedroom and box room home was soon littered with the trappings of Mike's lifestyle. A squash racket stood propped up by the door, while the dark green balls he used in the game were placed either on the radiators or sat on a windowsill; apparently the rubber had to be kept warm so they were always ready for the game. He played matches several times a week at the local club.

Then there were the golf clubs that almost jumped out at her when she opened the door of her downstairs closet where she hung her outdoor clothes. It really irritated her and she wondered why it bothered her so much. She had loved her space, everything in order, a place for everything. Mike was fun, he had a wicked sense of humour and now he was living with her he could even cook a little when pushed; it was, however, a great pity he did not seem to know how to clean up after himself. He seemed unable to cook a meal without using every pan and dish she owned in her kitchen. The mess that she had to clean up after him was bad enough, but worse, she had to praise his cooking as though he was earning brownie points. But on reflection, she enjoyed his dabbling. And he shared the rent and at times she shared his bed. She did really like him, but love? Perhaps that was something she wanted to feel, but she could not quite convince herself now he was living with her. Was he her Mr Right?

It was strange, she could not bring herself to invite him into her bed. Somehow it just didn't seem right. Her bedroom with her special bed was sacred and not to be shared.

It was always the same routine at the weekend. Katie and Mike would work together doing the household chores, but each alternate Saturday when they were not working for the paper, they shopped together, buying something special for supper. It was a time to relax, get dressed in old comfortable clothes, cook the meal then settle themselves down in front of the TV. Later, after a bottle of wine that had been shared between them, it seemed the most natural thing in the world to make love.

Moving towards Mike's room laughing in between the kisses, comfortable and with full stomachs, they were happy and relaxed from the wine. The stressful week was behind them; they only had to think of themselves. They were ready to give pleasure to each other. Later in the evening, feeling rosy and content, Katie would make her way back to her own room. Mike didn't seem to mind her leaving him; in fact, he made a point of saying that they both would get a better night's sleep if they slept separately. And if by chance a football match or sport were on TV after their lovemaking, he would get up, grab a beer and watch it. Back in her room she would hear the television go on, then she would settle down under her covers, sometimes with a book but mainly she would be ready for sleep.

Sleep had never been a big priority in Katie's life; she was always busy, there was never enough time in the day to get done all she wanted to do. Sleep seemed a waste of time until she bought the bed. She couldn't explain it, but now night and sleep had become a pleasure she looked forward to. The comfort she got from the bed was important, but most of all she enjoyed the dreams she had.

It was strange how she was repeatedly seeing the same dream, albeit in more detail each time. The dream seemed to be playing out a story. It was one she wanted to know more about. The man whose face she had not been able to see was still a mystery, though she thought it might be a subliminal image of Mike; the overall shape of the man's body could be his, apart from the hair that was tied back in a leather thong.

Over the last few weeks she had had several dreams that could only be described as an induction into another life; the dreams sometimes seemed more real than reality. She had the first dream a few days after the bed arrived. On the second occasion she dreamt of the man; she was watching him carving but this time she was viewing him from across a room. Another woman sat watching him as well. She was dressed in costume, or so it seemed, but then as Katie looked around the room she could see that it had no electric lighting and the usual consumer goods that belonged to her world were absent – no telephone, no TV, even the decoration was the kind you would find in old pictures in a museum. The man too was dressed in garments that belonged to a different time. How far back in time she didn't know; his breeches were black, finishing below the knee and laced at the side over thick knitted hose. He wore a loose waistcoat and full-sleeved shirt; how it fastened, she didn't know – only his back was visible. They were in a room, part workshop and part living, with a door going off to the right of the large window. Sunlight streamed through the glass onto a workbench that had an array of tools belonging to a carpenter on it. The headboard was propped up and firmly fixed so he could work on it. The young woman was laughing, her dark hair pinned up and dressed with ribbons. Katie could see her bright blue eyes sparkling as she stood up and moved towards the man. As she reached his side, her hand slid around his waist, and on tiptoe she tried to distract him by kissing his neck. With her other hand she loosened his hair and ran her fingers through it.

The tools in his hand were discarded to one side as he turned quickly to the woman paying him such affectionate attention. His hands sought her body and he was not rejected but encouraged by her throwing her arms around his neck and accepting his mouth that was so impatient to find her lips. The kiss was long and hard, passion would surely follow, but like in all dreams she was taken somewhere else. The dream became muddled and quickly she seemed to be back in the room staring at a completed headboard before the scene slowly faded. The dream was gone and Katie still had not seen his face. When she woke she felt utterly cheated. She remembered his back was broad with strong powerful arms and his hair was dark and curly. That was all she could remember, except she saw the passion that existed between the couple. She thought that perhaps making love with Mike had had an effect on her; the brain was so complex, wasn't it?

By October, the dreams that invaded her nights were starting to affect her.

She was coming to the realisation that what she originally thought, that Mike was the subconscious source of the dreams were wrong. More was going on but she didn't know what.

The beautiful gardens that she had been part of when the dreams started had gone. She was no longer a gardener; instead she had become a voyeur watching a love story play out that was repeated and expanded in each dream. The woman, who was clearly the man's lover, was definitely not her and the man may be of a similar build to Mike but clearly this person was not him. This man was an artist, a maker of beauty, sensitive and responsive.

Katie recognised that she had started to believe that the manifestation of her imagination had assumed a real persona and she had started to believe him to be real, and that the bed was somehow telling her its history.

One dream she had recently experienced had really frightened her. She was back in the room where she had seen the couple making love. However, this time it was late, sometime in the evening, she thought, and the man with dark curly hair was asleep. He lay on his stomach. His head was half-hidden between his arms, which were cradling his head, and the pillows were scattered like cushions across the bed. Above the man's head was the headboard that he had been working on in so many of the dreams; it was finished and it dominated the furnishings in the small room. The carving stood out in relief, the Garden of Eden filled with fruits, vines and all manner of nature, the sun streaming down on the grasses, and standing on either side of the apple tree were the completed figures, holding hands, in a garden made for lovers.

As she stared at the scene, she was reminded about the feel of the wood under her hands as she had traced the outline of the man back in that dusty store. For the first time she connected with the man, this man who had so much talent and skill that, even though she couldn't know him, she admired him and surprised herself as she was moved by emotion. She cared for his sensitivity, the graceful lines of his work and had she known him, she thought she would have liked him a great deal.

Her attention went back to the bed. She was suddenly cold and very uncomfortable. Hairs at the back of her neck and arms had risen. She felt a moment of panic.

As Katie looked at the sleeping figure, watching the steady rise and fall of his body as he breathed deeply in a dreamless sleep, she was suddenly aware of the dark-haired woman standing in the doorway. Her hair and clothes were bedraggled, as though she had been out in a storm. Her clothes looked damp from rain and the look on her face froze Katie's blood. The woman's eyes were bloodshot, red-rimmed from crying; her mouth was twisted into a grimace and pure hate and anger emanated from her body.

Walking over to the bed, she stood over the inert figure, her hands taking up a pillow, and for an awful moment Katie thought she was going to smother him. In obvious anger, the woman threw the pillow across the room before she darted back through the doorway.

Moments later the woman returned. In her right hand she held a large kitchen knife; her left hand was moulded into a fist, it was almost hidden in the folds of her dress. Madness shone from her eyes as she moved forward to the bed. Raising her armed hand above her head, she thrust the knife down into the back of the sleeping form. The knife plunged into his back and the rise and fall of his chest ceased, his breathing stopped; there had been hardly a sound from him and death must have come in an instant. Suddenly sanity hit the woman and she recoiled back from the realisation of what she had done.

A silent scream etched around her mouth as she turned and ran from the room, leaving the prone figure, his nightshirt covered in blood, blood that was seeping down into the fabric of the bed frame and soaking into the slats that held the mattress he lay on.

Katie awoke in a state of shock. She felt sick to her stomach, her head ached and for the life of her she could not understand her reaction to what was simply a nightmare. But it had seemed so much more than that; it had been almost as though she had observed and witnessed a real murder.

Getting up, she made her way down to the kitchen. Mike was snoring and in a way it was comforting knowing he was there. *Why do nightmares make you feel so insecure?* she thought to herself, knowing there was no answer. Making herself a cup of tea with a heaped spoonful of sugar, she drank it down sitting at the kitchen table, waiting until she began to feel more settled.

It was only a nightmare, after all. She supposed that wine and making love with Mike had brought on this erotic dream; at least, that was what she tried to tell herself. Feeling calmer, she climbed back up the stairs and into her bed.

For the second time that night she drifted into sleep. No dreams invaded her mind and she woke the next morning completely refreshed.

Time: that relentless invisible line that has no beginning and no end, a measurement made by people to give them order in their lives.

Time was no friend to Louis. He had been caught in a place where there was no measurement, only days and nights that were joined together in pain. He had had an urgent longing to be free from his netherworld since the death of Marina. Now he had been rescued from that store and was residing in Katie's home, the urgency had changed; he no longer wanted to be free, now he wanted to be known.

It was October and ten weeks had passed since he had arrived there with his bed. In that time he had shown Katie part of his life through her dreams. It was only now that she seemed to understand that the dreams he was sharing with her were much more than her overactive imagination stimulated by her life. She was seeing his life, his history and, yes, his pain.

She didn't know yet about his longing to know her and he was still unsure about how he was going to introduce himself to her.

In the time he had lived there, Katie's best friend Janet had moved out and Mike had moved in. He had known that Katie would probably have admirers but it was still an uncomfortable truth when Mike moved in and took over Janet's old room. Even he could see the powerful attraction between the two of them. Mike was handsome and full of life. Together they posed an ideal couple. It did not sit well with Louis; he had no right to be jealous but somehow it was impossible not to be. She was so beautiful and he was so lonely.

Was the time right to interrupt her dream, put himself into it and introduce himself to her? Would she finally put two and two together and understand he was a friendly ghost that was living with her?

He knew she had had a fright when he had showed her his death; he had followed her downstairs and sat with her until she had calmed herself with hot tea and was ready to go back to bed.

Earlier that night she had been with Mike, making love in his room. He could hear them exchanging sweet words of love; the sighs and the moans of passion were still in his head. When she had come back to him and his bed, he watched her settle down and drift off to sleep. He had touched her forehead soon after and was transported into her dream, where he told her the story of Sophia murdering him. She had woken up in shock, shaken and frightened. He hadn't meant that to happen.

He had tried in his own way to make her realise that she had not just bought a bed but a ghost as well. A ghost who not only had feelings, but who wanted to live in the present.

Louis found his emotions oscillated from love to anger on a daily basis. The woman he loved was often in the arms of this man that now lived with her. He knew he didn't have any rights to her. What the hell, she couldn't even see him. Nevertheless it hurt.

By visiting her in dreams, he had tried to show her something of his previous life and hoped that through this method she might at least learn to know him. Rosa had been able to see him; some people have that gift of sight and he knew he had connected with Katie while he was still in the store. If there was this mental link, he felt it was very likely that Katie would be able to see him if only she would open up her mind.

She was asleep. He looked down on her lovely face, her skin so soft and relaxed in sleep, her hair splayed out over her pillow and hiding part of her face. He moved the tendril of hair to uncover her ear. He could tell her things while she lay asleep; he whispered to her that he would tell her his story, taking her through the years until hopefully she would realise that the man she was seeing in her dreams was an entity, not alive but not dead. Hopefully she would come to see him just as Rosa had done.

He already sensed that she was intrigued by the dreams he had initiated. He had loved Marina and although he could not have had a mortal relationship with her, he had truly cared for her right up to her last breath. If only the light that joined this world to the next had been for him as well he would have been spared the last few years, but that was not to be. He had grieved with a pain that he wanted to forget and spent years locked away in his hand-carved domain in self-imposed exile. Now he was here with a lovely woman who he was determined to get to know and for her to know him. Loneliness had almost consumed him, driving him towards madness. Then he had seen her, talked to her, whispered words, and she had responded. Meeting her in her dreams was his only path to connect with her and he would use any and all methods to do just that.

30

It was her favourite day of the week, the one day that she didn't need to set the alarm. Katie loved Sundays. She could wake naturally, come around at her own pace, make a cup of tea and crawl back into bed to drink it at her leisure. To keep her company, she would enjoy listening to the music on the radio until she felt guilty enough to get up and seize the day.

Mike would already be up and gone down to the sports club, already enjoying his usual game of squash, and he wouldn't be back for ages. Katie snuggled down under her covers in her bed and started to think about her strange dream.

Really! Why was she dreaming about this couple making love and then the woman committing a murder? Could it simply be that her relationship with Mike had influenced her dream or was it that new TV series, that costume drama set in the last century, that had heightened her imagination, or perhaps a bit of both? Either way, the first part of the night had been unsettling and she was glad that after a warm drink in the early hours she had managed a sound night's sleep after all. But it was strange that the dreams she was having were always around a carpenter whose face she never saw and the carved bed she now owned. Those were the only dreams she remembered having. Odd indeed.

Lazily she raised her arm above her head, her hands touching the wood. It was so sensual under her touch that she turned onto her stomach and, resting on one elbow, traced the relief of the man carved there with her finger. It was one of many times she had done it. Was there some sort of connection?

She heard the phone ring from somewhere in the living room. It brought her back to reality with a start. "That will be mum," she muttered out loud whilst flinging the bedclothes back and dashing barefoot out of the bedroom to answer the phone.

"Hi, Mum," she said with certainty and then laughed at herself when she heard the familiar voice of Janet calling her from Leeds, saying "Oh, really?"

For the next forty minutes the girls exchanged news and gossip alike and when it was time to say goodbye, Katie reluctantly put down the phone onto its cradle, realising just how much she missed her good friend who now lived and worked so many miles away. Having a girl friend to talk to was something she missed; one could not talk to a man in the same way as to another woman. She had touched lightly on the subject of her dreams, or rather nightmares, but in truth Janet didn't have an explanation for her dreams either.

She had hardly put the phone down before it rang again. This time it was her mum and she was still in her nightdress.

"Hi, Mum," she said, "how's everything with you?" Every call from home or from Katie started with the same sentence. It was good to hear her mum's voice and she did miss her old life to some extent, but since she had worked for the paper her confidence had grown and she enjoyed her independence. She was concerned that her parents were in good health and able to cope for themselves and, regardless of the truth, they always told her they were okay and not to worry about them. But she did. They had not been too happy to hear that she was sharing her home with a man but recognised they were rather old-fashioned in their views. Nevertheless, every call included a need to be reassured that she had made the right decision. Twenty minutes later, she finally finished the call and dashed back to the bedroom with a pair of the coldest feet ever. Pulling open her sock drawer, she donned a pair of socks that she called the Wicked Witch of the East socks, ringed in coloured stripes, because they reminded her of the film *The Wizard of Oz*.

The morning had almost gone and she had made no progress in readying herself for work on Monday. Usually Sunday was a combination of washing and ironing and getting lunch. Sunday came and went so quickly; how she wished she could hang on to it and somehow stop time. She was on catch-up now and the next hour saw her rushing through the chores, finally allowing herself a lunch of soup and crackers at about one thirty. She had just finished the washing up and was drying her soup dish when she heard the key in the lock. He was back later than usual and she wondered if he wanted some soup; he must be hungry after all that exercise.

"Honey, I'm home," he called with a laugh in his voice, shutting the door behind him by giving it a push so it slammed as it contacted with the door jam.

Mike dropped his games bag and racket on the floor and kicked it to one side, attempting to stride from it, but he had hopelessly misjudged the amount of beer he had put away and he wobbled for a moment before steadying himself by grabbing the back of a nearby chair.

Oh God, thought Katie, *he's come back worse for wear*. She feared he must have had a liquid lunch in the squash club bar. It always made her cross when he came back to their home smelling of booze.

Letting go of the chair, Mike swaggered towards her in a boyish manner, a grin all over his face. It would be so easy to have an argument with him right now but really she knew she had no business judging how he spent his recreation time. They weren't married or engaged and although they lived as a couple they were still free to pursue their own paths.

Mike looked at that moment like a seven-year-old who had been caught with his fingers in the cookie jar.

"Aw, don't be cross. I just had a few little drinks. I won my matches and I just had to celebrate a little." His voice was high-pitched, almost a whine, pleading his case to her. The silence from Katie was heavy with disapproval. Crossing the room in an ungainly manner, he was beside her in seconds, moving faster than she would have thought possible given the fact that he had tottered rather than walked and his speech was slightly slurred.

"Give us a little kiss then," he begged, his face just inches from hers, blasting her with breath that would have melted plastic. She automatically turned away from him but he caught her in a powerful grip by her shoulders, turning her back to him. He towered above Katie and she was more than aware of the powerful strength that held her, a strength she could not oppose if he became angry.

"Play nice, Mike," she said, reaching up to his face and gently tapping him on his cheek.

"Aw, come on, one little kiss for the victor, eh."

"Not in the state you're in, your breath smells like a brewery," she retorted.

He pulled her towards him, holding her tightly in arms locked across her back. No matter how she wriggled she was fastened tight and she could feel his excitement growing, manifesting itself in the bulge in his pants growing harder as his body touched hers.

This was not good, not good at all.

His lips sought hers but she turned her face away, her lips out of his reach.

"Let me go, you're hurting me," she demanded in a raised voice. "What do you think you're playing at?"

"I just wanted a little kiss," he said rather sulkily, letting her go. "Just a bit of fun. I thought you might fancy a successful man to take to bed."

She laughed out loud. Almost as she did, she recognised it was a mistake. He was drunk and, like most drunks, was easily offended.

"Are you laughing at me?" shouted Mike, grabbing her wrists and holding her in a strong grip. This time he was really hurting her. "I could have my pick of women like you, and don't you forget it," he sneered.

Katie's face was screwed up and she was biting her bottom lip, trying not to let him see she was hurting and frightened.

"Let me go," she pleaded. She was suddenly cold, her skin prickled with goose bumps as she fought her fear. Her instincts had kicked in; he mustn't see her fear. Then almost immediately something strange happened.

What brought him back to his senses she didn't know, but the mood changed suddenly. Mike muttered under his breath something she couldn't quite hear, but it sounded like 'I have the hand of death on me', which made no sense to her, but suddenly he released her from his grip and stepped back from her.

Her wrists were ringed red where he had held her and fear was now replaced by anger when she inspected them.

"If you want me to want you then don't come home in a drunken state," were her parting words as she escaped up the stairs, retreating into her bedroom, locking the door behind her, feeling secure now that there was a stout wooden door between them. She was struck by the thought that there was a bully hiding in Mike that came out after he had downed a large quantity of drink. She didn't like it!

Louis had not been privy to Mike's homecoming but became aware that things were not quite right when he heard raised voices in the living room, and so came to investigate. He walked in as Katie was complaining that Mike was hurting her. He could sense her anxiety and didn't like the way Mike was gripping her.

Louis shook his head sadly. He watched Mike behaving like a schoolboy who was taking his bat home because he had lost the game. Dutch courage was a name for it, but getting drunk never really helped to boost one's confidence or, if it did, it disappeared and evaporated at the same rate the booze did as one became sober.

Katie seemed to be in control of the situation and he had no intention of interfering until she laughed. A red haze appeared like a halo around Mike's torso; it was a ghostlike haze that only Louis could see. He had seen something like this before and knew that anger, rather like a volcano, was ready to erupt. Rage was building up in Mike, a rage that could explode; Mike may not be able to control that anger. He had lunged and grabbed Katie's wrists; now she looked to be in distress and there was fear in her voice.

Louis moved swiftly behind Mike and laid his hands on Mike's shoulders. The cold that Louis conjured up seeped through Mike's clothes, feeling icy as it touched his skin. Then Louis whispered in Mike's ear, "Let her go, Mike, or by the devil's tail I'll take you to hell. I am the hand of death."

It had the desired effect; Mike released her rather quickly. Louis removed his hands and followed a relieved Katie back to her bedroom, leaving Mike rather subdued in the living room, wondering what sort of devil had spoken to him – or was the voice just the result of one too many jars at lunchtime? He just didn't know.

Trying to avoid each other whilst living in the same house proved to be something of a challenge. However, the game was played and during the coming week they only managed to bump into one another once at work during a coffee break.

Although neither acknowledged the other as they sipped their coffee sitting at different tables, Mike was under no illusion from the frosty look on Katie's face that forgiveness was not about to happen anytime soon. He wasn't about to let the situation just run on; he sought to find a solution that wouldn't antagonise her further. So when an expensive arrangement of her favourite flowers was couriered to her desk on Thursday afternoon, four days after the event, she couldn't help but smile and forgive him.

There was a miniature envelope stapled to the wrapping paper, from which she drew out a handwritten card in Mike's spidery writing. It read 'So sorry, won't happen again, M'.

She hoped in her heart of hearts that he was sincere; after all the unpleasantness that he meant the words printed on his card.

It would be really great to get back to some normality in the house. She had been getting up and starting out to work before Mike was out of bed just to avoid him and it was becoming a pain. The worst thing was arriving home and having to grab a bite to eat on the run and make her way straight to her bedroom to eat it, effectively shutting Mike out of her life. Consequently she had become something of a prisoner in her own home. That was something she did not want to prolong.

She had not slept well at all the last four nights, locking her bedroom door but still sleeping lightly, listening out for him. What she expected him to do she wasn't quite sure, but the trust she had had in him had definitely been damaged. It was with great relief that that evening she didn't feel she had to hide away from him. In reality, he did not come back to the house until late and she was already tucked up in bed when she heard the door open. She didn't acknowledge his arrival, not wanting to engage in any conversation at that late hour. Tomorrow was another day, but for tonight she would sleep well.

31

Normality returned on Friday night with a surprise for Katie.

Even before she had put the key in the lock she could detect the aroma of cooking emanating from the kitchen. The smell was mouth-wateringly delicious. As she moved through the dining area towards the kitchen she saw the table had been set. Another surprise.

A green salad was sitting in the bowl waiting, with wooden salad servers propped up ready for service. Green olives filled with garlic, her favourite, were also sat next to some Italian ciabatta bread with a dip of olive oil and balsamic vinegar already mixed. Her stomach rumbled in anticipation. An opened bottle of Chianti and two elegant wine glasses were next to her best dinner plates and the small bowls for the salad were all laid, ready for dinner. She was impressed!

Mike had pulled out all the stops and had shopped on his way home. He knew that Katie would be returning home later than him that night – she always did on a Friday – and he had managed to slip out of work early in readiness to make a meal for the both of them by way of an apology, and maybe for him to eat humble pie. He had bought minced beef, tomatoes, fresh basil, onions, garlic, pasta and a large quantity of Cheddar cheese, which was even now cooking in a moderate oven, just waiting for Katie's return home from work.

Mike popped his head around the kitchen door and saw a look of approval on Katie's face as she looked up from the set table.

"Hi, Katie." He had that little-boy look again on his face but mixed with a mixture of anxiety and penitence.

The night before, Katie had arranged the flowers that he had sent her on the coffee table. She went over to them and picking up the vase, she carried them over to the dining table. He could see Katie was placing the flowers he had sent her on the table as a central decoration. He nodded towards them.

"You like the flowers?"

"Of course I do. I'm sorry I missed you last night I wanted to thank you. They are lovely and set the table off, don't you think?" Not waiting for an answer, she carried on. "What are you cooking? It smells so good."

"Lasagne, with a bottle of good red wine to wash it down. I hope madam approves?"

Katie laughed. "Madam is very impressed, I didn't know you cooked Italian. And madam is very hungry. Do I have time to wash before dinner?"

"Fifteen minutes to go, mi lady," said Mike, touching his forelock in pretence of being subservient.

"Lovely. I'll be right back."

By the time the bell pinged on the oven, Katie was back. She felt clean and fresh, her hair was brushed and her teeth were cleaned and she was relaxed for the first time in nearly a week. She felt good.

Mike, she noticed, was also looking good. He was wearing a new polo shirt with smart jeans; the look was smart casual and there was not a mark on him from being in the kitchen – she always managed to spill something on herself when she was cooking. Then she saw the apron screwed up on the counter by the cooker. That explained it.

The bell pinged for the fourth time before Mike donned the oven gloves to open the oven door, revealing a beautiful brown-topped cheesy lasagne, which he carried carefully over to the dining table, placing it on thick place mats between the two set places.

Discarding the oven gloves, he then offered a chair to Katie, sitting her down and flicking a napkin onto her knee before serving them both a good-sized portion of the rich pasta.

The flavours of the meal, washed down with the full-bodied Chianti, set the mood for the evening. For the next hour the two of them tucked into the food, talking occasionally in between mouthfuls, enjoying the informality of the evening and a returning friendship.

When Mike tried to apologise again, Katie put her finger to his lips saying, "It's forgotten, let's not talk about it again." He nodded, gratefully accepting her wish to put the whole incident behind them.

By the end of the meal they were good friends again, enjoying each other's company in the way they had when they first met. Their laughter and humour had made the evening pass in a relaxed and intimate way. They shared the clearing up, carrying the remains of the meal back into the kitchen. The washing up was shared with a great deal of humour too. Katie washed the pots, Mike was drying, but Katie occasionally splashed him in a playful way. It was such a relief to be friends again. When Mike came up behind Katie, catching her on the waist and turning her around to him and kissing her none too gently on the lips, she responded to him. After downing the last of the wine, Mike led Katie to his bedroom. He was forgiven and trust was restored; things were back to normal.

Katie crept back to her bedroom in the early hours of Saturday morning, carrying her clothes in a bundle under her arm. She had left Mike sleeping and taking most of the bed. The wine had been excellent but booze had the nasty habit of causing snoring, and Mike had been snoring like an old steam engine when she left him. As she crawled into her lovely bed she felt uncomfortably cold, even allowing for the fact it was early morning; it felt like the middle of winter. She had had a lovely evening and felt good. Life was going to be sweet again, that she didn't doubt. But right now she was frozen and shivering as she pulled the duvet up around her ears, snuggling down deep under the warm cover. She waited for sleep.

Louis was agitated. The wonderful aroma from the kitchen had floated up to the landing and into the bedroom. It had drawn him out of his sanctuary and downstairs to the dining room. Katie had obviously just arrived home and was putting a vase of flowers onto the prepared table; a smile was on her face and she looked pleased to see Mike. How different from a few days ago when he had rescued her from Mike's drunken advances. Part of him was happy to see that she wasn't afraid and wasn't in danger from Mike, but he was worried. Would she really be that gullible and not recognise that leopards do not change their spots? Whatever made Mike tick would come to the surface again, he was sure of that.

He had watched the couple eat and flirt over the meal, the bottle of wine relaxing them and stealing away any reserve that common sense might have on them. He could see where the evening was going and he hated the thought.

He watched the two of them enjoying all the things he could not share in, all the things he wanted to share with Katie, but he was trapped. His situation was hell. He still had to reach her; she was still unaware of his presence, but he promised himself she would know him soon.

He watched with sadness as Mike led Katie from the kitchen through the dining room and up the stairs.

When they disappeared behind Mike's bedroom door, he returned back to his own domain with a longing in his heart and emotion that was tearing him in two.

Later that night she was back curled up in his bed, with a certain glow about her; sex had been good, that was apparent. Illogically he felt betrayed. He was trying to contain his anger but as always when he was angry, an icy cold atmosphere followed in response to his emotions.

How was he to tell her that he was here, standing by her bed, carrying a love that he wanted to share with her?

He was sure now that this lovely girl was not the reincarnation of Marina.

Yes, Katie looked very similar to his Marina, his love who died in his arms all those years ago. However, he knew now that it was because of his profound grief that he had grabbed at the notion that she had been reincarnated. He wanted the chance to start living again in his private kingdom with Katie, just as he had done with Marina's during her lifetime. However limited that might have be, it was so much better than the empty void he lived in now with no one to interact with.

But living here was not the same. Marina's house had been lively, full of activity and happiness and sadness alike, but every day was different and eventful. He joined in through Rosa and was instrumental in keeping the house safe for the girls.

His position here was even lonelier than it had been stuck in the store, except for the weekends when he could observe Katie and Mike. And although it was good to have company to watch, he was no nearer communicating with Katie.

He respected her as a modern woman in a modern world, a world that he scarcely recognised, with machines that allowed voices and music to be projected into the room and turned on and off at will with a switch, and a box that had a glass window that played moving stories of people, plays and something called movies with actors who had an odd English accent. A world where women were comfortable wearing trousers instead of long skirts, and who worked full-time and still ran the domestic side of their lives. And where sport had become so important that, it seemed to him, it had become a religion.

Louis could see that modern life held few restrictions and men and women lived together out of wedlock; no one seemed to care. Getting married and sharing lives together didn't seem to be a condition on which one had children anymore. Women were educated, leaving school at fifteen and going to colleges and universities.

The news came on the box at ten o'clock every night; it was the one time when Katie sat down to catch up with the outside world and, unbeknown to her, it was where he learnt about her world, a world still fraught with tragedy and unjust situations, just as it had been in Marina's time and his own.

Things had been much simpler in his era but there was always change, developments and new inventions, and with change there was always a price to pay as every century would bear out.

His thoughts came back to the sleeping figure wrapped up in the warm quilt. He didn't see what she saw in Mike. He was a shallow individual who would never grow up. He would always be childish, a little boy who always wanted the biggest and best for himself. Louis had seen many men like him; weak characters who habitually blamed others for their own failings. Grudgingly, he had to concede that he had a sense of humour when he was on form and he had a kind side as well. Drink was Mike's problem; it changed his personality from being an affable young man to a bully. It was obvious that drink had become his crutch and that he needed Dutch courage to face life.

The possibility of Mike losing his temper when he was with Katie made Louis shudder; he had seen the haze of red when Mike's anger was at the point of breaking. He was unpredictable when he drank and Katie could be in danger.

Concern replaced his anger when Louis looked down on the sleeping woman. Her dark hair was spread out on the pillow and only her forehead and her eyelids peeped out from under the soft quilt.

No one will hurt her if I have anything to do with it, he thought.

The past few months living in Katie's company had given him time to learn about her. He found her to be clever, strong-willed, affectionate and kind, and she had a willingness to work hard to achieve her dreams; all the qualities that his own dear Marina had possessed to survive in the world. And although it was a very different world that Katie lived in, it nevertheless was one she worked in to live and to live well.

He waited. He was good at that. Soon she would be immersed in a deep sleep, then he would introduce her to his netherworld, his retreat, his kingdom.

Her breathing had become steady and deep, the breath was long and relaxed, an indication that at last he could start this journey with her.

He placed his hand on her forehead, just as he had done to Marina so many years before. He had gone into Marina's dream state to help her with the nightmares she suffered; at least, that was how it started. Later they were able to use the skill to become lovers.

This time he was doing it for himself. He wanted her to know of his existence, he wanted to touch and know her. His fingers rested on her skin and he delved into that part of her mind that controlled her dreams. It was an empty void, a blank canvas waiting for him to paint a picture for her.

He brought her consciousness to him and into an extension of her bedroom, a scene he could use that was familiar to her. She would be comfortable in her own surroundings. And so his dream with her started. She was sitting in her bed, looking curiously at the man who stood beside her. She wasn't afraid of him and somewhere in the back of her mind she felt she knew him.

He held out a hand, greeting her with a smile. She smiled back, not quite sure what to do next. He half turned, indicating that they should go towards the dim light that was appearing behind her.

"Oh! That's who you are," she said in a slightly surprised voice, recognising his form from her previous dreams. That faceless man who belonged to her dreams was now beside her and in her bedroom. Of course it was a dream, just like before.

His hand extended towards her and she took it, looking at this strange man that stood before her dressed in the old-fashioned but familiar clothes that she had seen before in her dreams; the full gathered shirt, half-covered by a short black waistcoat laced up at the back, breeches that finished on the calf, black cotton stockings and strong working boots. His handsome face was framed by dark hair that hung in a short tail, tied back in a leather thong.

What a strange dream this was, to be sure. She was sat in bed in her bedroom holding the hand of a man, and a light from somewhere behind her was getting brighter by the minute. Her body was casting a long shadow down on her patterned quilt.

A sudden urge came upon her; the eyes of the man were almost pleading some action from her, she must get out of bed and follow him. Her legs swung out from under the covers as she flung them back to one side, standing to reveal the floral nightdress that reached her ankles. Not exactly the sort of dress to hike in, though why she thought she might be in for a walk she didn't know.

The bundle of clothes she had dropped by the bed before she tumbled into it, were still laid there where she had dropped them. She reached for them but they were gone. She realised she was already dressed in them. *Dreams do that*, she thought. Her feet were cosy in her fur slippers and she was all set to go.

They were side by side now, watching the light growing at an incredible rate. The spread of it began to take over the room and for a minute she felt panic. She must have unconsciously reacted by tightening her grip on the hand she was holding.

"Don't worry, everything is fine," said a voice in her head. Was it his voice or her voice of reason? She didn't know.

Her bed was gone, the room was gone, and the light was now all around her and the dream man who stood beside her. It took a few seconds for her eyes to adjust to the brightness of the light, then as her eyes came into focus she looked into the centre of the bright opening. A recognisable landscape started to appear.

The apparition of light had grown around them, coming to a stop when it reached their feet. The light changed its character, becoming sunlight that was warm and gentle, kissing her face as she turned it to the sun overhead. Where was she? Just then she had more questions running through her head than answers, but the man started to move into the sunny landscape, still holding her hand, and she was guided on to follow him.

Soft grasses were flattened underfoot as the two of them walked with purpose up the green bank towards a tree that she felt she knew well. She realised that the spread of the tree was huge as she walked towards it. The sunlight had a dappling effect on the grass as it shone through the branches and leaves.

What a lovely tree to rest under, thought Katie.

"Later," said the voice she had heard earlier. She looked at his face. He was smiling though not directly looking at her. He had heard her thoughts and answered her. Was that possible?

Her focus went back to the tree. What an extraordinary tree it was. It was her tree, the tree on her bed, the one she had traced out with her finger so many times before. No, there was no mistake. This was her tree from her headboard. The tree was laden with different fruits; apples, pears, pomegranates, plums, oranges, even grapes grew happily there. Their vines attached to the branches with the ripe plump fruit hanging down from the lower limbs. All you needed to do was to reach up and pluck the fruit and eat your fill.

A sandy path appeared that stretched up around the tree and carried on down into a small dip before continuing to run through the wide cool meadow that stretched out in front of them. They stopped under the tree to survey the whole of the vale; the sun was caressing her face with gentle warmth as she looked up into a pure cobalt blue sky and then beyond.

What a beautiful place this is, she thought. She could hear water running by close to where they stood. She couldn't see a stream but guessed it lay somewhere beyond the meadow. It almost sounded like music as it played its way over what she thought might be pebbles and rocks. It could only be that to make such a delicate clear crystal sound in such an idyllic spot.

She cast her eyes further over to the horizon and could just see a small dwelling half-hidden in a dip; only the top of a whitewashed walled cottage with a grey slated roof showed, the sun giving the white of the cottage a sparkling glow.

Trees in the distance were tall and mature and beyond them a small range of purple-blue hills stood up proudly, finishing the perfect picture before her eyes.

She was still being held by the hand, though very gently, by this rather old-fashioned guy wearing a gathered shirt and breeches. His hairstyle belonged to a bygone age and she couldn't quite see why he was in her dream; then she remembered he was the carpenter in that other dream she had had. It was all coming together now. How wonderful it was to see the carved world she loved so in a realistic setting – how real it was and how beautiful. She would not be sad to have this dream again.

"Do you like my world?" The voice was in her head again. He was looking down at her. The face she saw was strong and handsome; his square jaw was masculine and his full lips were set in a gentle smile, but it was his eyes that seemed to be talking to her.

They were sad yet full of longing, there was kindness there and grief, there was history looking back at her, history that she was not quite sure she wanted to know.

"Do you like my world?" The voice was more urgent now but still in her head.

She found herself nodding in agreement to the question, still gazing at his face. She hadn't seen his lips move and yet it was him that had spoken, wasn't it?

That is the trouble with dreams though, she thought, except this really didn't feel like an ordinary dream. But of course it was a dream; she had seen him before. She gulped, remembering the scene in which he had died, murdered by a woman with a knife. She felt slightly panicky but the smile on his face as he looked down at her settled her apprehension and a calmness passed from him to her through their clasped hands.

He moved behind her without releasing her, passing his arm across her body and locking his other arm around her waist. She was held in a new warmth and security. Strength emanated from his body into hers that was so sensual that she felt aroused. They were now connected and his lips hovered near her ear.

"My name is Louis, Katie. I have been waiting to meet with you."

"Why?"

"Because I loved you before you were born. I lost you and you found me and now I love you again."

She struggled to one side and looked up into his brown eyes, her hair flicking down over her face as she did so. His one arm released her so that she was now facing him.

His statement unnerved her. Her eyes were wide with anxiety. Whatever could he mean?

His fingers took the tendril of hair and he sensitively moved the offending lock off her face and tucked it behind her ear, at the same time bending forwards and kissing her lightly on her cheek. A thrill passed through her as his cold lips touched her warm skin and a hot sensation bolted though her body.

There was no doubt about it, she was having an erotic dream.

"A dream! Do you really think so?" said the voice that was back in her head.

How did he know what I was thinking? she wondered, but came back to the same conclusion that dreams were always muddled up. This just had a little more focus, that was all.

She felt him sigh. It was wearisome and sad, but he took her hand more firmly and moved back down the path from where they had come, out from the sunlight and into a darkness set in front of them. But as the light got dimmer behind them she realised they had returned to her home and were back in her bedroom.

Louis had realised that he must be careful and take a slow path to get her to know him. It was frustrating; he held a heart brimming over with love for a woman who didn't know him, a woman he felt he had loved for eternity. She would have to learn not just his history but about the man himself. So slowly it must be; if not he might lose her completely. His voice was once again in her head. "Goodnight, my darling girl."

He left her curled up under the duvet sleeping soundly, everything back to normal, before returning back to his retreat and sitting under his tree, listening to the bubbling of the water and thinking how good it was to have had her in his kingdom, however short the time had been. He had held her and he had felt her respond to him. He was now sure it could happen, it would happen; they would be lovers in this new age he was living in.

32

Mike was up with the larks the next morning, no hangover marred the day and he was full of energy and satisfaction. They were back on track; his relationship with Katie was back where it was before the bust up and the sex they had shared last night had never been better.

God, I'm good, even if I say so myself. He was no fifteen-minute man; when he made love to a woman, she knew it. He congratulated himself once again on his sexual prowess.

He had slept well, the sleep of the innocents. Nothing had disturbed him and now he was ready to face the day. Life was good. You couldn't beat it, a good meal, good wine and good sex – that was what life was all about. It had been a masterstroke making that evening meal last night.

Debora, a fellow worker from the office, had been so helpful with advice when he mentioned the problem he was having with his girlfriend. It had been Debora's suggestion to make an evening meal for Katie. It had been a great suggestion to get the wheels back on.

He had always thought that Debs had a soft spot for him. She wasn't bad-looking either, although he had never thought of her as a possible date. He saw her in a different light now she had been terrific.

He thought back to the previous Thursday when she had seen him sat alone drinking coffee and looking 'like a wet week', as she put it. It wasn't like him; that's why she had come over to him and shared a coffee with him. It was then that he confessed to his boorish behaviour and that he was at a loss to know how to make amends to Katie. Admitting that Katie and he were together.

"I didn't mean it, you know, it was the drink talking," he had explained.

Debs had all the answers: send Katie flowers with apologies and make her a meal she would really appreciate. Italian was always her favourite food when they dined out. *How hard can it be to knock up some pasta with a meat sauce?* he had thought. Mrs Brown, his ex-landlady, was a whizz cook; a quick phone call to her and taking a few notes was all he had to do. He was practically home and dry.

It had all worked like a dream. He was back in Katie's good books and there he intended to stay. He hummed a tune while he made himself instant coffee and slammed a couple of slices of bread into the toaster. He groped in a cupboard to find the Marmite and took butter from the fridge. He needed to put some fuel in him before he met up for a match down at the club.

A few minutes later, the toast eaten and the coffee drunk, a very happy Mike dashed out for his morning sport. He would not be coming back today tanked up – he had learnt his lesson, at least for now.

Louis had heard Mike get up. Katie was still sleeping when he left the bedroom. He hoped she would remember him when she woke. He followed Mike down the stairs and watched as he made himself his breakfast. The tune he was humming was familiar; it must have been something he had heard from the 'telly', as Mike called it.

Most evenings after returning home from work, Mike and Katie settled down and watched television programmes. Rather than miss certain shows by sitting at the table, often they ate their food from trays resting on their knees.

Louis didn't fully understand this 'television'. One programme in particular was devoted to a street in the north of England. He recognised some of the character types, but in this street most of the people were at odds with one another. Every week there would be another dispute between them. He had lived mostly in harmony in his village in Yorkshire and had never seen such disharmony among this community.

His heart had warmed to hear a northern accent, albeit not his county, but he felt uncomfortable acting like a voyeur, watching folk who didn't know they were being watched. Coronation Street was an interesting but unpleasant place to live but perhaps the people would get along eventually, he thought. Only later did Louis realise that he was watching a play, a drama, and not real life. It was something of a relief, though he felt foolish for not recognising that it was entertainment.

His thoughts wandered back to Mike and his humming. Music in this century was very loud and noisy but he had to concede it had a beat and the rhythms were very catchy. But that was not why he was watching. He wanted to learn about this age he was now part of.

Mike was a modern man, who lived, dressed and worked in a very different world to the one he had left behind. It was also unlike the time period he had lived in with Marina. The television had showed Louis machines of this new age; machines that washed clothes, cleaned carpets, cooked meals, dried clothes, and there was even a tea-making alarm clock that woke you up and made tea for you at your bedside.

The only horses he had seen were for racing and the mechanical coaches carried people now. Many people had their own individual vehicle, which he supposed meant that people in this century were very rich; in his century, only the very wealthy owned their own carriages. He had arrived at Katie's home in such a vehicle and he still remembered the noise and the awful smell that came into where he was standing.

He had heard Katie talking to her mother on the telephone that sat in the hallway; he had only known the post for carrying messages, but he remembered the telegraph and the telephone from Marina's time, though the design of the phone now was very different. Mike had used it the night before and had written down the words Mrs Brown had spoken from some miles away.

There were so many new inventions in this time that amazed him. Something else that interested Louis was the way men dressed now. The clothes looked so comfortable. He had always cared about his personal appearance and was very stylish in his time, even if he was only a craftsman. His wife came from society and insisted that 'clothes maketh the man,' showing the village just how fashionable the pair were. In this world, the clothes he wore were plainly from the past.

Louis was hugely aware that, compared with Mike, he belonged to a different age. His hair was far too long and it was tied back in a tail; Mike's hair was short to his collar. Mike's clothes were close-fitting and lightweight, and they looked easy to move in, not like the ones that he wore; his were worn for practicality and warmth. These modern people didn't seem to worry about getting dirty or being cold. Indeed, everything they needed seemed to be right there in their homes, all you needed to do was push a few switches. Life was much easier.

But that wasn't the point. He wanted to appeal to Katie, to make her see him not as a dream, not even as a ghost; he hoped she might see him as Marina had, a soul trapped in a netherworld, but a world she could share with him if she could learn to care for him. That was his hope.

He looked again at Mike wearing a short-sleeved top with a V opening and small collar. It was not tucked into his trousers, the way he wore his shirt. His trousers were long and came down to his ankle, showing white socks and a shoe made of canvas. *Well, Mike isn't going to have to walk through muddy roads the way I did,* thought Louis as he looked at his thick leather boots. He wanted to look like Mike, only he didn't know if it was possible to alter his appearance.

For now he would bide his time. Louis would learn what he could about this time. If he could not change his appearance, he could at least teach himself to be a modern man by listening and watching everything on the telly. He had learnt to move things; how hard could it be to switch the telly on during the day and learn from it? He was determined to look like and be what he thought Katie would find attractive.

33

Four weeks passed without anything unusual happening. Life was back to normal.

In many ways, she and Mike were closer than ever. There was only one small thing that bothered Katie; once a week she would have that recurring dream with the carpenter. She was taken into the landscape portrayed on her bed headboard, he called her his darling girl and they strolled through the meadow and down to the stream. She was warm and happy in the dreams and he had whispered his name to her: Louis. The dreams seemed more real than reality at times. She would wake up and almost be disappointed that she was back in her bed in her room.

Mike's career was going nowhere. Katie, however, had been promoted and was now a grade higher than him, salary-wise. Envy started to eat at him. It was obvious that the bosses thought more of her than him.

He had been passed over again. He would have liked to run the sports section but no, it didn't seem to matter that he had spent the best part of ten years working for the damn paper and had only been promoted the once.

Old Bob – *What's his name?* – was retiring in three months. That job should have been his by rights, but instead it had gone to Jim. Well, okay, Jim had been with the paper for almost as long as himself but, well, he was younger than Mike. Age should count for something.

Mike had started to resent the paper and some of that resentment had started to rub off regarding Katie. Her abilities were undeniable; everything she touched seemed to turn to gold for her. He thought he ought to move on, get a job in a new town and start over; he might be appreciated then.

Well, he would get around to it soon, he promised himself, but the truth was that he was afraid; afraid of change and afraid of the uncertainty it would entail. And what if he moved and was no better off? Could he risk all he knew? Life was not so bad and it could be really good with Katie when they were close. Well, she didn't always see his point of view but women were like that, weren't they?

When she told him the news of her promotion, it changed things.

He envied her promotion, though he didn't want to admit it. It was a bitter pill for him to swallow. That was the moment he started to feel differently towards her. How well he remembered how she had come to him full of excitement with her good news, expecting him to be pleased for her. Why her and not him?

These feminists were everywhere these days, using their sexuality to get the jobs that should go to the guys. After all, when the babies came, it was the men that had to support their little families. These women never thought about that, did they?

He kept his feelings to himself. On the surface he had hugged and congratulated Katie, and invited her out for dinner. At least they would both be able to have a drink or two and she would be in such a good mood that sex would surely be his dessert. At least that would be some compensation.

Mia Casa was their favourite Italian restaurant. Luigi, the owner, had become a friend over the many months they had frequented his business and his food was always tasty and such good quality that they almost always over-ate.

Tonight was no exception. The meal of meatballs and spaghetti in an excellent rich tomato sauce was particularly good and they had been supplied with paper bibs in case the odd rogue drip stained their clothes. Now with full stomachs, they watched the waiter taking away the soiled plates before returning quite quickly with the dessert menu, but tonight they waved it away. Mike concentrated on finishing the wine while Katie pondered slowly, turning the liquid in her half glass of wine, on whether she should share her strange dreams with him. She was interested in what he might make of them and now that dinner was over, Katie decided she would.

He tried to smile through her colourful narrative but just what was she chattering on about? Some guy whose face she couldn't see and then could and all that talk of a carved bed, that sod of a bed that he wasn't allowed to lay in. It was okay for his bed to be used as a sex playground. Well, that was all right by him, a man's needs must be met.

Katie saw the change on Mike's face; she knew that look, he was going to sulk like a small child because the conversation wasn't running the way he wanted.

But she wasn't going to be put off and asked him outright.

"Don't you think it's very strange to dream a series of ongoing dreams? Has it ever happened to you?" she enquired, looking over the flowers that stood in the middle of the table. *Why do they do that?* she thought, and in an irritated gesture she moved the vase to one side for a better view of Mike's face. "No, really Mike, I would like an answer, what do you think?" She tilted her head in an enquiring mode while picking up her glass that Mike had just topped up with wine.

He had not forgotten himself when pouring and was at present on his third glass. Katie decided not to say anything but had begun to wonder if he had already had something to drink before they met up. He was looking rather ruddy, his cheeks were red with high colour and there was that look in his eyes that she had seen before. She hoped it was boredom and that she was mistaken in thinking it was intoxication. She didn't want a repeat of the situation she had had to face just a month ago.

Mike pulled a face, taking a gulp of wine before he spoke.

"A series of dreams – no, never. I expect you are just having an anxious dream or nightmare. Personally I never remember anything unless it's a nightmare. Come on, drink up," answered Mike, reaching across the table to take her hand and giving it a squeeze. "Let's get back home and cosy up."

She withdrew her hand rather quickly, realising Mike's intention in his statement. *Is that all this man has on his mind?* she wondered. Up to that point, she had genuinely hoped they would make love rather than have sex. To share love with someone she cared about would have rounded the day off nicely, but now she was offended. How could he take her for granted like this, thinking that sex would be automatic? Sex was so different to sharing love; at least it was for her.

She sipped her wine but the enjoyment had gone. She was deep in thought. The evening had not gone as well as she thought it would.

Mike downed his glass in one gulp then, pushing his chair away and standing up rather unsteadily, threaded his way around the tables, crossing over to the till to pay for the meal.

It appears dinner is over and now I'm expected to pay the piper, thought Katie, sipping the last of her wine before standing to collect her jacket. *Well, maybe I won't be willing to pay up. Let's see how he behaves when we get back.* She hoped she wasn't misjudging him but he had a track record now. All she wanted was to be loved in a tender and meaningful way. She didn't want fifteen minutes of rushed drunken sex that served him but demoralised her.

The drive home had been torturous; she had insisted on driving and had taken his keys from his pocket on the way to the car. She was now very sure he had been drinking before she had met him at the restaurant. She guessed he had got there early and had a couple of whiskeys before she arrived. The last thing she wanted was for him to be breathalysed or, God forbid, an accident when he was behind the wheel. Fortunately he had not argued when she took the keys.

She had had maybe one and a half glasses of wine. The rest had been downed by Mike; not enough to make him difficult when they got back, but with the spirits, she suspected that might be different matter.

She already knew that things would be difficult when they got back to the house because of his actions in the car. His hand had already moved onto her knee and was slowly moving up her leg towards her crotch. She slapped him, removing the offending hand and asking him what the hell he was playing at. She was trying to drive through the town without seeking attention from the traffic police.

"Oh, come on babe, I fancy you rotten." His boozy breath hit her with his words.

"Tough, Mike, safety first," was her reply. It was obvious that she would have to find a way of handling him once they were home. She suddenly regretted ever inviting him to share her home. Drink changed him and he had promised just four shorts weeks ago never to do this again.

Louis heard the key in the door. She was back late tonight. He supposed that she had been out for a meal, probably with Mike.

Well, why not? It was Thursday, almost the end of the working week. She worked so hard and she deserved some relaxation. He remembered his old habit after a hard day when he would stop off for a tankard of ale, meeting up with his old pals. How long ago was it?

He was brought back to the present by the raised voice coming from Katie. "Take your hands off of me." The voice was coming from beyond the door, which was only partly open. Katie pushed it fully open and entered the house in a rush.

"You're drunk and I don't want you," she shouted at Mike, who was following her in.

"Saving yourself for that fellow in your dreams, are you?!" he laughed, but it wasn't a happy sound that came from his mouth. Mike closed the door with a back kick, slamming it shut with a bang.

"Come here and stop playing hard to get." He grabbed her by her shoulders and spun her around to face him. He sported a large grin and had that look on his face he had used so often, that little-boy look. He embraced her, tightening his arms around her slim body so she was unable to move.

His breath was foul; the Italian food laced with garlic, three quarters of a bottle of wine and the rest he had drunk in secret was a combination that was show stopping.

"Get off me, you rotten drunk, who do you think you are?" she retorted, struggling to free herself.

"I'm in charge tonight, love, we have to celebrate your promotion, don't we?" he asked. It wasn't what he said but more the tone in which he had said it that bothered her. She was suddenly more frightened than annoyed. The situation was getting out of hand; she must change her tack and take control.

"Mike, darling, I've been in these clothes all day. I have to get cleaned up and change into something more attractive for you." She smiled, looking up at him, no longer fighting in his arms. She leaned against him in a kind of submission.

"There's a good girl," he said, releasing her, and playfully slapped her bottom quite hard as she turned to go up to her bedroom. She climbed up the stairs with Mike following behind. When she reached the landing she turned to him, holding up her hand, indicating for him to wait.

"I'll just be a minute," she smiled before dashing into her room, slamming the door shut and locking it tight with a key. As a further precaution she propped up a chair under the door knob to make doubly sure he couldn't get in.

With her back to the door, she could feel it shudder as he rained down blow after blow on it from his fists, while at the same time demanding to be let in and for her to stop playing about. It didn't go on too long, perhaps a few minutes, before he gave up. It was obvious to him that she wasn't going to play his game the way he had planned it.

"Have it your own way, you silly bitch," he called out at the door, giving it one final blow before he shrugged his shoulders and walked away.

"You don't know what you're missing," he shouted back over his shoulder. There would be another time and he wouldn't be fooled again. He regarded her as a little tease. She had practically promised him sex, hadn't she?

Louis was relieved that Katie had been able to deal with the situation this time, but what if that idiot should try it on again? She might not be able to stop being assaulted or even the unthinkable, raped, by him. He must go. This man was not to be trusted either sober or drunk; there was an unstable streak in him. Surely Katie must see that.

The awful truth was that this was Mike's home. He lived with Katie. How Louis wished he didn't. He frowned; he was worried for her.

He remembered dear Lucy, Marina's daughter, so innocent, who was abused, attacked and almost raped by a boy she trusted. But for his intervention, it would have happened. It had taken years for her to recover fully and he simply didn't want Katie to be subjected to that or risked in anyway. But what could he do, a ghost? He felt so impotent at that moment.

Katie sat on her bed looking down at her shaking hands; she was relieved to have escaped the silly man's advances. It was the drink again, it was a repeat performance; like Dr Jekyll and Mr Hyde, Mike had two sides. Mike had changed. She reflected back over the past month. He was not as caring or gentle as he had been when they had first got involved. And although he often had a glass of wine or two in the evening, he never seemed to need more. He certainly hadn't got drunk in front of her and she wasn't sure why he had drunk so much tonight. Had something upset him to make him drink the way he had?

It occurred to her that he had been hoping for a promotion. Was it today that he would have heard? He hadn't actually said when he would be told. Had he been turned down and not told her, was that the real problem?

She still couldn't excuse his behaviour tonight, regardless of whether he was carrying rejection or not. It wasn't her fault he behaved so badly. But then she thought, *Oh my God, if he didn't get the promotion he wanted and I did – Lord, that would hurt; and now I've rejected him as well.* She shook her head slowly, not knowing what to believe, but he had brought it on himself, hadn't he? *Would he have hurt me?* She shook her head, not believing it, but a little niggling doubt stayed with her.

The evening had spoilt a good day and that saddened her; she had so wanted to share her happiness with him. But she wouldn't be put down. She had got her promotion and she was proud of it, and her parents were proud of it too. They were as proud as Punch when she had phoned them with the news. She would go on and prove her worth. She tossed her head defiantly, staring at her reflection in the mirror on her dressing table. Her fingers danced through her hair as they always did when she was worried. Smoothing her hair, she pushed it back into the bob around her face.

She frowned. Who was she kidding? What was she going to do about Mike? His behaviour had been appalling. She wasn't a sex toy; she had feelings and she had loved him. What had gone wrong? Her face screwed up as hot tears that she had held back since leaving the restaurant suddenly flowed down her cheeks. Disappointment and resentment were released with the tears, dissolving the tension and hurt she was holding. She threw herself flat on the bed and cried into her pillow until she could cry no more, and she hoped that the morning would bring the answers she needed.

Louis stood at the end of his bed, watching the sobbing figure; anger was building up inside of him. Why couldn't he comfort her? If only he were mortal, he would sort that man out and care for his darling girl.

He heard Mike's footsteps as he walked away, going down the stairs to the living room. Perhaps his anger would serve a purpose tonight after all. He passed through the chair and locked door and followed Mike downstairs.

34

His feet could be heard as he plunged down the stairs in great haste, muttering under his breath as he went.

Drunk! She doesn't know what drunk is. Well! She has blown it, thought Mike angrily. So he had got pissed off at being passed over and he needed a little drink for consolation, anyone would, wouldn't they? And just because she had been promoted, she wasn't going to lord it over him. Oh no. That wasn't going to happen. Grudgingly, he had to admit she was good at her job and probably did deserve it.

He had made a mistake coming to live with her; they had got on better when they lived separately. Unfortunately she was his landlady now and that meant she was in control. Things had not been the same since he came here; he couldn't be himself anymore and since he got drunk the other week, she had insisted he 'toe the line'. Hers not his. He wasn't a child, was he to be punished indefinitely?

She didn't understand the pressures he was under and that bloody editor was the same, telling him to lay off the drink when he was working. When he went out to report on a match, no matter what sport it was, he was obliged to buy the lads a drink afterwards and they responded by giving him extra gossipy titbits.

He would never get that sort of information from a straight interview, would he? He nodded, he could see it all so clearly now. He was just doing his job and should he drink one or two extra tots, well, that was how it was. One needed to be fluent and relaxed when writing the copy for the paper.

Cricket clubs, rugby clubs, football clubs were all the same. He always found that sitting at the bar sipping a small malt was a good way to engage the barkeeper. The barkeeper was the fountain of all knowledge in every club he had been in. They seemed to know everything that went on in it. It wasn't enough just to report on the game; small personal data about a local premier player was a good pull for the paper. He just needed a break, something to get his teeth into. If only he could get a scoop, someone like George Best, who was something of a hero to him. He had all the women he could have and enjoyed a little drink – well, a lot of booze, he admitted to himself, his thoughts becoming melancholy. But then George had wrecked his career. He was a good example, a brilliant footballer and a modern legend but with a flawed personality. Well, he wouldn't fall into that trap. If only he could get a scoop on someone like that, it would surely make his name and raise his profile. The editor would love him.

But he knew his meeting up with the great and the good was his fantasy. His reality was, in the main, monotonous and frustrating. It was a daily serving of the dull local matches.

"God, I could almost write a piece without seeing a damn match," he muttered.

He headed for the sitting room and the cabinet that held the drinks and glasses; he opened the doors wide and grabbed a handsome crystal whiskey tumbler and a three-quarter bottle of single malt. He moved quickly to the settee and fell heavily onto the cushions. He put his boots on the coffee table in front of him.

"Sod her," he said loudly and he reached over and grasped the top of the bottle.

The screw top came off easily and he poured himself three fingers of the amber liquid before tossing half of it down his throat. It made his throat sting; it was fiery hot when it hit his stomach. His face twisted with its contact.

He raised his arm in a mock salute towards the ceiling, holding the malt whiskey in his hand. "Goodnight mi lady. Bitch," he added to the derisory toast.

A few years ago he thought he had the best job on the whole planet. The paper covered all the local news in his town and the surrounding villages. The football and cricket clubs played at county level and at first, he was content with reporting them as he saw it. Rubbing shoulders with team members excited him; he felt like one of the boys. But years had passed and he was still waiting for a star to rise from one of the clubs, a George Best, someone who would help to elevate him with the excellence of his reporting skills at the paper.

He almost had an addiction in his desire to report sport. When he was younger, his appetite for any game that involved a ball was always foremost in his mind. It came before everything. He was a man who lived in a man's world; women had their place and it certainly wasn't on the golf course, cricket field or football pitch.

His thoughts became verbal and he was contented to talk to himself. "God forbid those conniving little loves who are challenging men in the workplace, to ever be able to encroach into sport and spoil the male world."

He sighed to himself and helped himself to another swig of the amber liquid. He was starting to feel the need to lie down but he would finish his nightcap first. He sighed again, his emotions dropping into deep melancholy.

"Well, that won't happen anytime soon, men will always be the stronger sex, won't they? Only men have the stamina to play these beautiful games. At least that reserve is sacrosanct." He contently nodded to himself in self-agreement.

"God, I must get to bed while I can," he said out loud. The whiskey had not only hit his stomach; his whole body was now fighting the effects of it and it wasn't winning.

Steadying himself by holding on to the arm of the settee, he pushed himself up from it, one hand still holding the glass of whiskey which he drank as he stood up. Unsteady now, he nearly fell backwards to where he had just been sitting but managed to balanced himself at the last second, placing his glass with a shaking hand very clumsily back on the table.

"Oh! My head, it's spinning," he uttered unclearly. His free hand was now holding his head as he walked with great difficulty towards the door.

He was trying to leave the room and avoid the obstacles of furniture that barred his way. The furniture was both a hindrance and support as he used his hands to help steady his passage because his legs would no longer obey him.

From a chair Louis sat watching the drunk and incapable man. *This guy is so stupid*, he thought.

Louis watched his gait as he walked towards the doorway. Mike looked like a sailor trying to navigate the deck of a ship in rough seas.

The doorway appeared to be too narrow for Mike to get through as he crashed into the door, hurting his shoulder on the way. He swung his whole body forward, lurching to grab the banister with both of his hands, before hurling himself up the stairs to his bedroom.

Louis followed him, smiling in amusement at the pathetic vision in front of him. What did Katie see in this man? Perhaps after tonight she might question that herself.

The stairs were something of a challenge for Mike. One step up and one step back, he was making no headway at all in the challenge to reach his room. In desperation he resorted to dropping down on all fours and, using both his hands and knees, he climbed up what seemed like an impossible incline.

By the time he reached his room he was feeling very unwell, and the room was not exactly still when he threw himself onto his bed with a groan.

He even admitted to himself he had been stupid drinking with the lads at lunch. That and a couple of whiskeys before he met up with Katie, red wine with the meal and his nightcap were not mixing well. But rather than blaming himself, he blamed the editor and his disappointment at being passed over, and Katie. Why was she a success and not he? No, it was her fault too. She had to have some of the blame. She had rejected him as well; that's why he had to have a little comfort and resorted to booze.

His stomach was heaving, doing double somersaults. *God!* He hoped he wouldn't throw up. Laying there, he knew that standing was definitely not an option and he feared he would never reach the bathroom in time if he did vomit. If he could, he would try to sleep it off. He closed his eyes, hoping that his stomach would settle.

Louis's entrance to the bedroom brought a serious chill to the room. Laid on his belly, Mike opened his eyes at the sudden drop in temperature. He was freezing but was unable to raise his head from his pillow. His arm groped about on the surface of the bed as he tried to find the edge of his duvet to pull it over himself.

Louis had other ideas as he watched Mike's feeble attempts to grab the quilt cover. He would teach him a lesson, knowing that in his present angry mood he had the power to move objects and hold fabric. He caught hold of the duvet and held it fast, not allowing Mike to budge it even an inch. No matter how much he tugged at it, it remained where it was, which had the desired effect of frustrating Mike.

"Oh, sod it!" came the slurred words from Mike as he gave up on it and lay still.

But Louis wasn't finished with him yet. As soon as Mike had given up the tug of war with Louis, Louis lifted the duvet up and threw it over Mike, covering his head.

"God, how did that happen?" said Mike as he struggled to free his head from the duck down cover. He turned over onto his back, still struggling.

A further surprise was waiting when he reappeared from the duvet. Mike was confronted by his travel clock floating in front his eyes; it was levitating over his head and then when it came level with his ear, it burst into the loudest ringing that the alarm could muster. A shocked Mike flapped his hand out to catch hold of the offending object, but it moved quickly away from his outstretched hand, still ringing a shrill sound. A moan came from Mike's throat, his eyes following the clock, but his head seemed pinned to the pillow. He couldn't move. He resorted to pulling the duvet back over his head to deaden the sound that was penetrating into his brain like a jackhammer from his clock, the clock that should be sitting on his bedside table.

His heart was already racing through the amount of alcohol he had put away that night, and it was increasing even more now through fear.

Was he seeing things? Did he have the DTs? Was that ringing real or was he imagining all of this because of the drink?

Louis turned off the alarm and settled the clock back where he had found it. A face reappeared from under the duvet with a look of utter relief on it. How good it was to have silence back in the bedroom. Mike's eyes were closed; he was feeling very sick, his head was spinning and the ceiling was spinning. God, he felt rough. His hands were holding his head, trying to stop the movement of the revolving room but it didn't help.

Louis kicked out at the bed, his foot hitting the mattress with some force. The bed moved well on its castors and travelled some way across the room.

"Oh my God," Mike's voice was full of fear. "What the f—k's happening?" He was a wreck and Louis saw it.

Louis couldn't resist shouting in his ear. "By the devil's tail, I'm watching you, Mike. Treat Katie with respect or you'll pay for it."

Louis had wanted payback for the way Mike had treated Katie that night, that irascible and belligerent man needed to be taught a lesson, but now the only thing that Louis could see lying on that bed was a weak and frightened drunk.

He almost felt sorry for Mike. Louis turned away from the pathetic figure lying there holding his head in his hands. His eyes were shut tight, the pallor of his skin was a sickly grey and any minute now he would throw up. It was time for Louis to leave and let this apology for a man stew in his own juice.

Feeling sorry for Mike soon disappeared as he left Mike's bedroom and he reminded himself that this chauvinist of a man was responsible for the maltreatment and bullying of his Katie, his darling girl. If Katie had not managed to escape and lock herself in her bedroom Mike might have forced himself on her, and that couldn't be forgotten or forgiven.

Back in her room, he stood looking down at her sleeping figure dressed in night attire. He could see the stain where the small damp patch made by her tears had dried on her pillow. Mike's threatening attitude had upset Katie and that made him angry, but his overwhelming desire to hold her in his arms and comfort her was stronger. He took her hand and immediately she was transported with him back to his retreat.

She was back in the dream. She was sitting under the spreading tree and the sun was pushing its rays of warmth and light through the leaves and branches onto her skin. It was such a comfort to her. But even in her dream state she felt the echoes of the day and felt exhausted, drained of all emotion and very sad.

Louis sat next to her and felt her sorrow touch him like a cold hand clutching his heart. How badly he wanted to enfold her in his arms and love her. Impulsively he reached out and wrapped his arms around her, pulling her towards him so that their bodies were touching, close and intimate.

Feeling protected like this was a new feeling for Katie but that was what she felt. She was so comfortable in his arms that her spirit was lifted immediately and all the sadness and anxiety just melted away.

His head bent forward towards her ear and he said almost in a whisper, "Oh, my darling girl, how can I make you understand just how much I love you?"

His deep voice was earnest and when she looked into his eyes they confirmed the truth of his words. Katie felt love flowing into her heart; here was someone who she could trust. What a pity that her dreams were better than reality. And this man who had become special to her was only a dream, but at least she could respond to him; after all, a dream couldn't hurt her so she might as well enjoy a little love in the arms of her comforter.

Her lips cut off his next sentence as her mouth pressed hard on his in a passionate kiss. No words were necessary. Their bodies were close, stirring their basic instincts; they clung together, both in need and both reaching out to each other. The kiss became kisses and the heat of passion began to take over.

They needed no rugs or cushions. The cool grasses became a bed for them to lay on, Louis with his 'darling girl' held tightly in his arms, sharing a treasured moment of love together. Katie on her part felt closer to him emotionally than she felt for any man she had ever known. She was ready and very willing to be loved, and the expectation of making love burned in her breast.

He felt her move even closer to him, if that was possible, and he wanted her very badly. He took her chin with his hand, turning her face up so he could look into her eyes. He saw her longing; he was put in the position of making a very sensitive choice for the both of them. He was hesitant in moving forward to fulfil their desires by making love to her. Before he was willing to commit to an act of love, he wanted her to realise that he was not a dream, that he was a soul trapped between worlds. She needed to know that, so that when they finally made love it would have a real and proper place in their lives. He wanted her to know that she was involved with a spirit and that he wasn't just a figment of her imagination. He sensed that she still believed that she was only dreaming and she thought that he was only a projection of the anxiety that she felt because she was living with a man who was unreliable, a bully and a chauvinist.

But here she was, her body was soft next to his and she smelled so good. If he wasn't careful, his need for her would overtake his self-control.

He kissed her forehead, lips and finally her neck and her whole body responded. Her arms, already wrapped around him, became noticeably tighter, his hands slid lightly over her body, gently exploring her back and waist and moving slowly towards her breasts.

Dressed in the thin light nightdress, none of her body was hidden from him. Her breasts were pert and her nipples were proud and hard. His body was also responding and it was now or never to step back and wait.

He whispered in her ear, "Now is not the right time, I'm sorry, my darling girl. Soon, I promise soon. When you truly believe in me then we can truly be together." He kissed her hard with all the love and emotion he could inject into the kiss.

His eyes were moist as emotion took its toll, and with sadness he took her back to her bedroom and her bed, hoping that she would not be too hurt at the decision he had made for the both of them.

Katie slept fitfully for the rest of the night with other dreams that invaded her sleep. The next morning she woke up tired and depressed.

She was vaguely aware of the waking dream she had had. As she became conscious she had sudden recall and with sadness she remembered Louis and the tenderness he had shown her.

Why, oh why, couldn't Mike be like the Louis of her dreams? Her heart skipped slightly when she recalled the passionate kiss she had enjoyed with him. What was it he had called her? 'My darling girl.' She liked that; how different to Mike's idea of wooing a woman. God! And his stupid drinking, would he never learn and grow up? Sadly she thought probably not.

35

She arose quietly, slipping her feet into her slippers and wrapping her dressing gown around her, tying it tightly in a bow at her waist. She removed the chair from under the doorknob and unlocked the door, opening it slightly so she might be able to listen for any sound of movement from Mike's room. She was very uncomfortable at the thought that she might encounter him on the landing. Her mouth was dry, her anxiety was back; the only comfort was that he would have slept off the drink and should be his normal self, but it was still going to be awkward when they met. All was quiet. The empty silence that reached her made her wonder if he was still sleeping it off.

She was surprised as she passed his room on her way down to the kitchen to make her morning tea. The door was wide open and there was no sign of Mike. A cursory glance into the room showed his pyjamas and work clothes were piled in a heap on the floor by his bed and his bed was stripped of its sheets. She crept down the stairs, hardly daring to breathe; even the creaking of the stairs spooked her. Turning the corner into the kitchen, she was affronted by the hideous smell of vomit and his dirty sheets were dumped in front of the washing machine. Sitting on the counter was a dirty whiskey tumbler and a half-filled cup of cold coffee, they were the only signs that Mike had been up and was gone.

Mixed emotions of relief and anger swirled around in her head. He must have gone into work leaving her to clean up his mess. Damn him! She looked at the clock; no need to hurry, she had plenty of time to have breakfast and get to the office. He must have been up at the crack of dawn to avoid her. *Well!* She thought. *Thank goodness.*

Mike had got into work early, something that his editor made a mental note of because it was so unusual. He sat at his desk pouring over his notes. He was writing an article about the local rugby team, who was celebrating its bicentenary. He had to research its history, starting with the original founding father, and was quite enjoying putting it together. Things had changed a lot in two hundred years. The game then and now was a game for real men; their forward prop was about twenty and was built like a bull. Young men like him were the true heroes of the game; his speed and strength was envied, respected but envied. He was deep in thought, imagining himself to be one such hero. If only he had had the chance he would have been a regular Man of the Match.

"Hi," said a voice behind his chair. He half turned to greet the voice.

"Hi, yourself," he grinned at Debs, giving her his star smile and the little-boy-lost look that women seemed to warm so readily to.

"Fancy a cuppa?" said Debs, indicating with her head towards the corner of the large office that served as a mini kitchen.

"Why not?" Was his reply. He pushed his chair back, avoiding her toes as he did so. He stood and took her arm, leading her through the maze of desks in the open-plan layout to the cosy corner that housed the coffee, tea, powdered milk and plastic cups.

Debs pressed the red button on the half-full kettle of water and waited. Mike slipped his arm around her waist, giving her a little squeeze.

She looked up into his face and in muted tones said, "Be careful, Mike." She scanned the office. "Katie might see and make a scene."

"Oh! Don't worry I left her sound asleep. And what do I care anyway?" he retorted and duly kissed her forehead, tapping her bottom playfully at the same time.

The whistle on the kettle shrieked out and it brought the two of them back to reality, reminding them that they were standing in an open office where anyone could see them. Debs blushed and wide-eyed, asked, "Are you and Katie finished?"

"We're not married, you know."

Debs made their coffee and they went and sat on the grey plastic chairs that stood next to a small round grubby table that was used by the staff. Previous cups from that morning left a few circular stains on it, and it sported a sugar dispenser standing on guard at its centre. White plastic spoons lay on a saucer; they had been used and reused and were stained brown with coffee. Mike absent-mindedly picked one up and stirred in the powdered milk he had placed in his coffee.

"She's cross with me again," he confided. "I had a little bit too much to drink again last night. She can be quite unreasonable sometimes." Again, he flashed a winning smile.

"Anyway, how about we talk about you and me? We could do a Chinese tonight if you're free. How about it? We could meet up after work and have a bit of fun." Mike could charm the birds out of the trees when he wanted to. Katie had ruined last night; well, she wouldn't ruin tonight. What he needed was a real woman who would be interested in him and not in stupid dreams.

He had always known that Debs held a torch for him and that she had had a crush on him for a long time, but she had never revealed it. If he was honest, she wasn't really his type but she was nice enough, and damn it, Katie didn't really appreciate him. Perhaps he would be lucky tonight. Well, he certainly hoped so!

Katie ate her breakfast slowly. As she drank her tea her stomach began to churn. *It is the result of last night*, she thought. What in heaven's name was she going to do about Mike? In one short month he had forgotten his promise to her and she didn't want to go through another week of dodging him again. He would have to leave, go back to his own place as soon as possible. Sparks of light in her eyes interrupted her thoughts; a half-crescent of light obscured her vision. Her feelings of depression and anxiety were developing into a nagging headache that was soon followed by feeling sick. *Oh, damn,* thought Katie, *the signs are all there for a migraine.* She hadn't suffered one for years but she knew the only answer was to take herself off to bed and sleep. She rang work pleading sickness and assured her boss she would be back at work on Monday, no problem.

It was all so annoying. She had hoped that Mike had grown up just a little bit after the last incident. But no, last night had been a nightmare. He became a real pushy chauvinistic male when he was drunk and she wasn't prepared to spend the next few months waiting for the problem to raise its ugly head again. And it would, that much she was sure of.

But right now she needed her bed and aspirin.

Louis had been pondering on the situation that he was in. How could he make Katie believe in him? The dreams of his past hadn't worked; their shared evenings and kisses hadn't proved to convince her either. He was at a loss to know how to proceed.

She was in a deep sleep now after her disturbed night and he knew how much she needed to catch up on her sleep and renew her energy. He liked to watch her sleep, just as he had liked to watch Marina. It made him feel close and protective towards her. He glanced around her room.

Her room was neat and tidy with a photograph of her parents sitting on her dresser next to a pen and writing pad. Seeing them gave him an idea. It might not work but he must try. It had been a long time since he had held a pen or written a word but he knew if his emotions were strong enough he could move objects and do so much more; it might just be possible to write a note. He would try to leave her a message in her world, one that would prove he was not a dream.

He stood in front of the dresser thinking just how much he loved her, and in addition of his very real fear that Mike might hurt her. He could feel the power of his emotions fill him; he was ready.

He tried to pick up the pen. It took him several goes before he managed to hold it in his hand and before he was able to pull off the black lid that exposed the ballpoint. These modern people were so clever – no dip pen or ink well; instead, both were contained in one unit.

A letter had been started to Katie's mother but only part of the page was written on, so he resorted to write below the words that were there, so that when Katie came back to finish the letter she would see his message. The message would have to be brief, if it could be written at all.

Louis steadied his hand; the pen seemed to have a mind of its own when he put it to paper. An unruly line streaked across the page, out of control, but he was determined to succeed. He stood back for a moment then tried again.

I must do this for Katie and for myself, he thought.

He pressed the pen onto the page so it couldn't run away like it had on his first try. A shaky B started his message, the spider-like handwriting continuing until he finished the few words he needed her to see, then he stood back rather pleased with himself.

'Believe in me. Please believe in me, my darling girl. Louis.'

36

Katie heard the front door close. The familiar noise brought her out of her light sleep. She opened one eye and looked over to the bedside table to see the time the clock read. 6pm. Lord! She had slept most of the day but she felt much better and her head was pain free.

Mike was home from the office; he was in her house, his footsteps could be heard quite clearly downstairs. How would he react when he saw her? Her anxiety was starting to grip her again. She could feel her stomach tighten and her mouth felt dry. She needed a drink. She struggled to sit up, knowing that she wasn't ready to face him yet.

She heard his footsteps get louder as he climbed the stairs to the landing. She sat stock-still in her bed, hardly daring to breathe in case he heard her. What a relief it was to hear the footsteps stop at the door of his bedroom and the dull sound of it being closed carefully. She lay back down, wondering what she should do. She decided to wait and see if he would make contact with her.

It must have been about twenty minutes later when she heard his door open. His footsteps descended the stairs and the front door banged shut.

Well, good, she thought, *at least I won't have to see him tonight.*

There was hardly any point in getting dressed now. It was dark outside and time for her to have something to eat, so instead of dressing, she slipped her feet into her slippers, pulled on her robe and made her way down to the kitchen. Only then did she realise just how hungry she was. Her stomach made a low growl, reminding her that she hadn't eaten since last night.

She made herself a supper of pasta with green pesto and grated cheese, along with a large mug of hot tea. She grabbed a tray, placing the food on it to take back to her bedroom to eat. She reasoned that if Mike had just popped out to the shops he would be back soon and she really didn't want to see him until she felt stronger. It angered her to think of his disgraceful behaviour last night. The fear she had felt was replaced by anger and she would demand an apology from him, but not tonight. For now she would eat in the privacy of her bedroom where she felt safe.

How silly all this is. Why am I having to put up with that stupid man? Her thoughts were troubled as she climbed the stairs. When she reached her bedroom she locked the door and settled her tray on the dresser, putting it down on top of her writing pad. Distressing thoughts crowded in on her as she stared down at her food. She sat pushing the food around the plate with her fork, feeling slightly sick, and after a few mouthfuls that barely satisfied her hunger, she pushed the dish away, wondering how she was going to cope on her own? She knew there was no way she could afford the cost of running this house alone.

She felt cheated and tears were not far away. Mike had shared love with her and for a time they had seemed committed to some sort of future together, at least, that was what she had wanted to believe. It just wasn't going to happen, was it? Not with him behaving the way he did. He had changed.

Tears came slipping down her face. Whether they were tears of heartache or frustration or even fear of losing her home, she didn't know; perhaps it was a mixture of all those emotions. The floodgates were opened and the tears came.

Louis saw her place her tray over his message that wasn't a good start to his plan. His only hope was that she would see it when she took the tray back to the kitchen. He was dismayed to see her upset again. She had had a difficult twenty-four hours and all the stress was getting to her. She needed to eat something, food would make her feel stronger, but as he watched her, he saw that she was playing with the meal that sat in front of her. Her mind was elsewhere. How he wished he could communicate with her right now, but as always, he would have to wait until she fell asleep, and goodness knew how long that would be. Locking herself in her bedroom again made him realise she was still afraid of Mike and he fully understood her desire not see him until morning. It was obvious she was feeling nervous at the prospect of facing him that evening. It would mean an end to their relationship and an end to their friendship. He realised her strength was depleted and he had no power to help her with that.

Mike met Debs at China City, a restaurant off the town square.

The softly lit large room they entered was already entertaining early diners; several round tables clothed in white were laden with small dishes of delicious Chinese food.

Mr Cam came forward to meet them, making them welcome. He took their coats before steering them to a small table at the back of his restaurant. The picture on the red-painted wall behind them depicted peacocks, lotus blossoms and cranes that were embroidered in fine silk threads. The subdued lighting came from the numerous red paper lanterns that were decorated with red tassels and were responsible for the secluded intimate feel to the place.

Debs looked lovely. Mike approved of the stylish black dress she was wearing with its low-cut back; it showed off her smooth young skin and he was already imagining how good it would be to touch.

"You look wonderful tonight, Debs," he said, smiling his special smile at her. Showing her his impeccable manners, Mike pulled out a chair and helped Debs to sit down. He lingered over her, she smelt of flowers. "Nice perfume." He bent down, lightly kissing her neck. A thrill went through her. She was wearing a perfume he knew. *Miss Dior!* he thought. It was Katie's favourite perfume. *Damn! I'm not here to think about her,* he reflected crossly.

As he moved towards his own chair, he allowed his fingers to brush lightly across Debs' skin on her back. It was smooth and warm and he suddenly desired her. He was imagining his hands running over her body, touching her in the preamble before making love. He felt a thrill run through his body at his erotic thoughts.

Taking his seat next to hers, he took her hand and gave it a squeeze. His eyes looked deeply into hers, holding the moment before taking the initiative. "Let's order."

Debs was happy; her body language confirmed to him that she was attracted to him. Her eyes held his and she smiled a confident smile back. An unspoken longing passed between them. He hoped it was an unwritten promise for later that night.

The menu was scanned and food chosen and ordered.

Mike felt on top form. A pretty girl was at his side and a few glasses of wine would not go amiss along with the meal, what could be better? It would be a good start to the evening but he would be careful not to over-do it tonight. He wouldn't make the same mistake he had made last night. He wanted Debs and if he had read her right, there was a promise between them. Tonight would be his.

Forty minutes after eating a few mouthfuls of pasta, Katie was asleep. She hadn't thought she could cry any more tears over Mike but she was wrong; they flowed no matter how much she tried to stifle them. She was completely exhausted, struggling with the upset. Lots of screwed-up tissues, damp with her tears, lay all around her and despite sleeping for most of the day, she had been overcome with the need to sleep again.

Louis touched her cheeks and smoothed her hair back from her face, revealing the results of the tears, but even with red blotchy skin she looked beautiful to him.

His dislike of Mike was raised another level seeing her like this.

Louis took her hand; immediately their spirits were joined and he met her by her bed in her subconscious state of sleep. She was so pleased to see him. He held out his hand and she took it. The light shone behind her. It would light the way back to the peacefulness in that tiny kingdom that she needed so much. The tree, the meadow and the babbling water of the stream would be a magical escape from the distress and hurt that Mike had left her feeling.

"Shall we go?" said Louis enquiringly.

"Yes," she answered simply, raising her hand to clasp his; they were instantly transported to the path filled with sunlight that led to their tree.

With each step that she took with him she felt lighter, her anxiety melting away as the sun warmed her face, and she felt safe again. The sound of water making music came from the stream beyond the meadow. It filled her heart. She stopped him, holding him fast on the spot to listen to the sound. She closed her eyes, enjoying the melody that floated over the grasses, and her mood lifted. She was happy. After a few moments they walked on and stood together under the tree surveying this small beautiful world.

Her joy at seeing Louis's world made Louis reassess it; he had got so used to it that he had forgotten its beauty, she helped him to see it fresh again. This tiny world that was of Louis's making had not changed since he had died. Having lived with it for so long he was surprised to see that the grasses were moving as a breeze passed through them; he had carved no motion in the meadow. Then he saw a small speck in the sky growing in size as it came towards them. He realised that somehow Katie was having an influence on his world through her dreams. His world was being fused with Katie's imagination; new input from the dreams she was having affected his kingdom. The moment when the speck became a bird, he was overjoyed and his world had become *theirs*, it was as much hers now as it had been his.

The bird flew closer. The swallow darted this way and that, leading other specks that soon became a flock. The delicate birds were eagerly chasing each other across the clear blue sky, flying towards the blue hills in the distance.

Then he heard another new noise in his kingdom. Bees were suddenly buzzing about and visiting the buttercups and wild flowers in the meadow; butterflies and dragonflies were skimming over the top of the grasses, their colours flitting in and out as though playing hide and seek. It was summer in his world and the whole scene in front of them was coming alive, thanks to Katie. How marvellous it all was. She, his Katie, had made this happen.

It was beyond anything he could possibly have imagined and much more than he could have achieved because he had stopped seeing it and had forgotten that his imagination could influence his world behind the curtain of oak. He began to see possibilities that had never occurred to him before. His lovely Katie was sharing her dream with him and it stimulated his creative soul again. If only he could make her realise that he was really here with her, living in a secondary world attached to her reality, but invisible to her except when she was sleeping.

How could he prove he wasn't an 'erotic dream', as she had put it? He was real, he felt, he hurt, and he needed love and company just like she did.

Katie stood next to him under the tree, holding his hand. A warm and bonding pulse linked them. Words at that moment were not necessary; they shared the new living landscape hand in hand. The scene was reminiscent of the couple on the headboard he had carved all those years ago.

He was only thirty, a young man, but his dress and hairstyle belonged to a past century. How could she be made to see him as anything but this dream man? If he ever finally got her to accept him, would she only see him as a ghost from the past? That was not what he wanted her to see when she looked at him. How he wanted to be modern man, to look and dress like Mike did. Would that sort of change make a difference to how she viewed him?

How would I look with shorter hair? he questioned himself. *Perhaps something like Mike's.* In an instant his thought was passed on to Katie, who ran a critical eye over his hair. The weight he had felt on the back of his neck for years unexpectedly disappeared; the ponytail that had been so fashionable when he was alive was no longer there. He now looked like a twentieth-century male except for the clothes.

You're very handsome, thought Katie as she looked at him, wondering how just a thought had altered his appearance. But dreams were tricky like that, weren't they?

It felt strange not to have weight at his neck. He slipped his fingers through his new hairstyle, feeling it finish at his collar. His unruly hair still fell over his eyes when he moved his head but the tail that had been his fashion statement was gone. Katie had brought a kind of magic to his landscape and now she was helping him to modernise his look.

His thoughts were diverted when he heard ducks quacking in the distance and then two mallards flew over their heads. They squawked, almost in greeting, before turning away, flying low over the meadow towards the cottage and the stream in the distance.

He had thought he was bringing her into his world, whereas she was bringing her world into his and renewing it. He loved it. If she came to believe that this was not a dream, would all the things she had brought to it disappear? It was something he decided he would have to test. It might be that through his own thoughts and imagination he could keep his kingdom as Katie had imagined it.

Louis squeezed her hand, loving what he was seeing and hearing. She responded by squeezing his hand back and smiling at him with such a dazzling smile his heart sang with a new kind of joy.

The grief he had held for such a long time vanished. He never thought he would be as lucky as this, to share his world with someone who could repaint it with such wonderful creatures.

They chose a spot to sit under the tree that gave them access to the full view of the blue hills and the broad expanse of meadowland.

What a lovely place to live in. The thought flowed from her into Louis's mind.

"It's been a lonely place until now. Your gifts of life to my kingdom will be treasured as long as you are with me, Katie." He gave her a hug. "And thank you for my new hairstyle. I hope the new look suits me," he said very seriously, but he had a twinkle in his eye. He had heard her thoughts on the subject; she thought him handsome and that was enough for now.

It was strange that this figment of her imagination spoke in such a normal way. In fact, her dream was running along such realistic lines that it was very much like everyday life, except dreams weren't like that.

It was confusing; her feelings were intensifying for this Louis, her dream man, so whatever he was or wasn't, a bonding was taking place right there in her dream.

37

Up to now, Louis had always made sure he was holding her by the hand to keep her with him in his world. *How strong is her connection to my world?* he wondered. She had brought life to it and he felt that the time had come to see if she could stay without him holding her there.

He would have to let go of her hand. There was a risk that she may disappear without his touch and she would drift back to her bedroom, back to her slumber. But he must risk it.

He unclasped her hand and he moved to rest his back against the tree to watch her.

A wave of relief passed over him. The test had been worth it; she didn't disappear, confirming that she was part of his reality when she was in a dream state. He relaxed, letting the tree trunk support him while pulling his knees up so he could rest his arms on them.

His breeches pulled across his thighs and knees and his black woollen socks protruded from his leather boots.

"Why are you dressed like this?" Katie asked. Her words were spoken and when he replied to her questions in his soft deep voice it resonated so that it made her skin tingle.

She leaned over, reaching out to him, feeling the cotton cloth of his shirt under her fingers. It was surprisingly coarse even though the gathering was quite fine on it.

"Where did you come from?" she asked. "How did you get into my head?"

"I'm not in your head, Katie, I am here with you. I have loved you before you were born and I love you now."

"What are you saying? I don't understand."

"I've shown you my previous life in dreams. Remember them? I've been trapped between worlds for many years. When I was killed, murdered by my wife, I didn't understand that I was dead. When a veil of light opened up before me like a tunnel that was pulling me in, I was afraid of it, I didn't understand what it was. I resisted it, then the gate to the next life closed, leaving me stranded. I was tied to the bed that I'd made, tied by my life's blood. Wherever the bed goes, I go. I am around you daily and when you suddenly feel cold for no reason, that would be down to my nearness to you. You should never be afraid of it. Please believe me, my darling girl. Believe in me."

He caught her arm, pulling her towards him. She didn't resist and when he took her chin in his hand and gently tilted her face up so he could kiss her lips, she moved to meet him.

It started as a gentle kiss, his fingers caressing her neck, the kisses becoming harder and stronger. The straps on her nightdress were narrow and easily moved from her shoulders. His lips were working down her neck onto her shoulders; her eyes were closed, she was enjoying the sensation that was building within her. *It must be the power of love,* she thought. How she wanted to love and be loved. Here was a dream that was so emotionally charged that it felt real. Could a dream ever hurt you like in real life? Probably not; in a dream she had nothing to lose. Right now, she wanted more than kisses. She wanted to feel whole again, a woman. Perhaps this time it would happen.

His hand lingered near her breast; she wanted to feel the firmness of his hand caressing her. *It is happening,* she thought. They would make love, real love, not sex. She was ready.

She could hear the birds and the bubbling stream; everything was so real and she felt so alive.

A door banged shut somewhere out there but she only half heard it; her hands were pulling at his shirt, loosening it from where it was held at his waist. She wanted to feel his skin. She wanted to feel skin on skin. The anticipation was stupefying.

His kisses had reached the delicate V between her breasts, both his hands holding her while she worked on reaching his chest under his shirt.

She heard giggling from somewhere. She pulled back from Louis, searching his face. Did he know what it was and where the sound was coming from?

Louis was looking puzzled too; then it came again, a woman's laugh. It came from somewhere in the house, out beyond his kingdom.

Katie was starting to wake up from her dream; the connection between them was being broken.

Their moment was gone. Katie's consciousness was taking over and she was being pulled back from the sunlight against her will, leaving Louis sitting under the tree, bewildered. He was getting smaller and smaller as she moved away back into her bedroom. To awaken to what? Louis wasn't sure.

Katie was waking up from her sleep to the sound of giggling that was filtering into her bedroom from along the landing. The giggling became low laughter, a sound that seemed familiar to her but a sound that didn't belong here.

And then she knew, of course she recognised it. It was Debs. She knew that laughter; she had heard it so many times before in the office. She lay there listening to stifled laughter coming from down the hall from Mike's room.

How could he bring her here to my home? Oh God, what is Mike up to? Silly question, she knew all too well what he was doing; trying to punish her for last night. What an idiot, what a useless stupid man he was. *But how do I deal with him?*

She sat up, not amused by what she was hearing. She felt betrayed. Her thoughts were in turmoil. Yes, Mike and her had had another episode last night but instead of getting an apology from him, he was further insulting her by bringing that woman back here. The last twenty-four hours had been hell and things were not improving.

If she let this go, he would do this again, they weren't engaged. What was she thinking? Thank the Lord they weren't engaged, with a man like him it was better to have an uncomplicated arrangement.

She reflected that she hadn't always thought that way. She had actually thought they might make a go of it as a couple but now that felt as though that Mike had been someone else she had known. This Mike she hardly knew at all.

He rented a room from her and they had been lovers, but not in love. Louis was a dream, a good dream but not real. Mike was real and he had been good until he started drinking.

She didn't want to be with a drunk or a womaniser; he had gone too far this time. What she wanted was something real. Louis, that caring man in her dreams, was, after all, just her yearning to be loved and how she needed to be loved right now.

A smothered laugh sounded down the hall again. She supposed they were making love, of course they were making love. What else? *How dare he humiliate me so?*

Anger was rising within her. Throwing back her duvet she leaped out of bed and was out onto the landing and heading down the stairs at speed. Reaching the kitchen, she went straight to the radio and switched it on. She set the volume to be as loud as she could. The loud thumping beat of music coming from late-night Radio 1 screamed at her. It almost hurt her ears. She deliberately left the kitchen door wide open so the sound could be heard upstairs. If they could disturb her, then tit for tat, she could disturb them. She was defiant. They had abused her trust and ruined her dream.

As far as she could judge as she strained her ears above the music, the laughter from Mike's room had ceased and all was quiet.

Well, good, she thought.

Her stomach reminded her that she was hungry. It rumbled and grumbled at her, she had barely eaten that day.

Well, she was in the kitchen and she had nothing else to do but wait to see what the consequences of her action would be, so she put the kettle on and raiding the breadbox, put two multi-grain brown bread slices into the toaster, then sat at the table and waited.

Debs and Mike laughed a lot during the meal they shared at China City.

Mike was surprised; he was actually really enjoying being with her and he was changing his opinion of her – she might be his type after all.

The food had been exceptionally good from the starter of Peking duck, plum sauce and pancakes to the Chinese gooseberries dessert to finish. They had drunk a couple of gin and tonics plus a bottle of French white wine with the meal. They had spent three hours eating the many courses that came with the set menu for two, enjoying every morsel. Both were feeling very relaxed and satisfied and they were more than ready to make a night of it. Both had expectations of completing it by sharing love together.

Mr Cam called a taxi for them and when Mike gave the address to the driver, it was to take them back to his lodgings, the home that he shared with Katie.

They could have gone back to Debs' but Mike was still indignant with Katie for the rejection he felt from the previous evening and was out to prove to Katie that he could have any girl he wanted. She was bound to be jealous.

The two of them were like teenagers on a first date on the ride back in the cab and spent their time cuddling up, sharing kisses and giggling. Mike was unrepentant at his motive and he was pleased at the thought of making love to Debs right under Katie's nose.

They had made a pact to be as quiet as possible when they got to the front door, slipping inside and making their way through the house and to the stairs, smothering their laugher and tiptoeing while holding their shoes to mount the stairs. Holding a finger to their mouths in joint agreement of silence, they half staggered forward but in doing so let the front door close itself rather loudly behind them.

The effect of the wine was apparent as they climbed the stairs; they were stumbling and hanging on to one another as they went. After closing the door to Mike's room they both burst out in laughter and collapsed in unison on his double bed, their legs raised in the air, before rolling together to the middle of the bed. The promise was in both their eyes as they started to undress.

They were too intoxicated for any meaningful foreplay and got right down to it, fumbling over buttons and zips, which only increased their hilarity.

Trying to make love can be difficult when certain bits of you don't work quite as well as they do when you are sober. Mike was having a trying time but Debs egged him on in between laughter and giggles until at last they came together as one.

Still joined, they were jolted out of their skins by a sudden blast of music that came from downstairs.

"God, she's up," cried Mike. "That stupid bitch is trying to deafen us." They both hugged each other and Mike finished what he had started, leaving both of them only half-satisfied.

Debs whispered in Mike's ear, "Lets go to my place out of her way, the night is still young." Nodding in agreement, Mike kissed her quickly on her lips. They sat up in the crumpled sheets, grabbed their clothes and dressed quickly.

"We'll have to get a taxi," said Debs.

"No problem," answered Mike, "there's a call box just down the road, we'll wait there."

Five minutes later they crept down the stairs and out into the night, shutting the door with care behind them, leaving Katie sitting in the kitchen eating toast and being deafened by the sound of hard rock music blaring out from the radio, not realising they were gone.

How she wished she had earplugs; hard rock music wasn't to her taste but she'd put up with it to make her point.

She wouldn't be able to hear the toast pop up with the noise but the steam from the kettle told her when it was boiled. She got up to make her tea just as the toaster threw up hot brown toast that smelt so good to her famished self. She went to the fridge, grabbing butter and marmalade. She was going to enjoy this.

She returned to the table with her bounty on a plate along with a mug of steaming hot tea. She had almost finished her toast when a draught from the front door came travelling around her ankles. She stood up and went into the hall. The door was closed but though the frosted glass panel, a figure was caught by the street lamp walking away.

"Good." She turned back to the kitchen and turned off the radio. The silence was bliss. She finished the last bit of toast and there was no noise upstairs so she supposed Mike had gone with Debs. She wasn't totally sure but she couldn't stay in the kitchen all night. Taking the mug of tea in her hand, she made her way to the stairs.

She didn't know whether to laugh or cry but whatever, she wouldn't sleep well tonight, and tomorrow she would have to face Mike.

"Oh, deep joy," she said out loud and with feeling.

The climb back up the stairs was difficult; her feet felt like lumps of lead and the last thing she wanted was to bump into her lodger on her way back to her room if he was still there.

She survived the short trip to the top of the stairs and on passing Mike's room she saw the door was wide open. She didn't need to be afraid after all, he was gone. She sighed a deep sigh of relief.

Katie closed the door to her bedroom, leaning her back against it, resting there for a moment before taking a deep breath and pushing herself forward, heading to her dresser with her tea.

Damn! Her tray with the plate of leftover pasta from earlier that evening was sat there looking at her. The pasta was an unappetising heap, dried solid and stuck together, and the green pesto was caked to the side of her plate.

I can't leave it there till morning, she thought. *It might smell and anyway, it will need a soak in the sink for a few hours to clean it properly.*

The thought of venturing out of her safe room and going down the stairs was quite intimidating. What if Mike came back before she had managed to get to the kitchen and back? It was difficult but she knew she couldn't allow herself to be scared of Mike and that he would have to be faced some time.

She put down her cooling tea and, full of determination, reached out, taking the tray in her hands. She lifted it up. Something was sticking to its underside. What on earth was it? Then she remembered. "My letter to Mum," she said out loud. "Oh flip, the tray must have been damp when I put it on the dresser."

She parked the dirty plate to one side and lifted the tray high to see where the pad was joined to it. Gently, she eased it away from the wooden tray, leaving only a little paper stuck on it. *Well, that will come away easily enough with a damp cloth and some elbow grease.*

It was the letter that she wanted to save; she scanned the leaf of paper and realised that it was too damaged. She would have to rewrite it but there seemed to be a postscript at the bottom of the page that she couldn't remember writing. What was it?

The hand that wrote those spidery letters was not hers. No one had been in her room but herself. She re-looked at the bottom of her letter. The words were written in script, an old-fashioned type of handwriting, but the words were very clear.

'Believe in me. Please believe in me, my darling girl. Louis.'

It was a replay of what Louis had said to her that evening in her dream. She caught her breath. She felt the hairs rise on her neck and arms; a chill came into the room.

Louis was beside her. Thank God she had seen his note. Would she understand at long last, would she believe now? Thought Louis.

The tray and dirty plate were forgotten. Katie sat down quite heavily on the padded stool by the dresser. What was she supposed to think? Her dad always said she over-thought things, but really... She paused her thoughts that were pushing through in her mind and she went back to when the dreams had started. He had explained about himself, but that didn't explain how he got into her dreams?

It had all started when she had bought the bed, hadn't it? No, hang on a minute – she had an overwhelming desire to buy it even though she hadn't the money for it. She caught her breath, remembering that dark warehouse and her desperation as she walked away from it, needing it, wanting it. Was that Louis's doing?

She remembered the first night she had slept in it, the comfort and calm that wrapped around her, what she felt was wonderful. Then came the dreams; a history, then Louis introducing himself. She should have known then that something was different; dreams were usually muddled but they had been so real.

Oh! And then he had died, that awful scene with that woman with a knife. Again it had been all wrong for a dream. She remembered seeing it almost as a news flash on the television.

Was he a ghost, an apparition, or was it more than that? Could he be living in a different reality to hers? A reality that ran side by side? Was the fabric between their worlds so thin that he was able to visit her in her sleep and take her into his world, a world she could happily share in?

So much had happened in the last twenty-four hours: promotion, betrayal, and maybe she had fallen in love with a ghost. If he was real enough to write her a message, he was real enough for her to believe in.

When Louis came to her later in her dreams, she was ready to believe in him no matter what he was. She knew him to be kind, warm and considerate, but most of all, a gentleman.

He knew when he looked in her eyes that a change had taken place; he was no longer that man in her erotic dream and the look she gave him was a powerful look of love. That love which had been denied for so long could not be smothered any longer.

They spent the night lying in the shade of their tree shielded from the sunlight. In the background they could hear the songs of the birds and the soothing sound of the music from the stream. They came together whole-heartedly, all vulnerability gone; doubt no longer plagued Katie's mind. Whatever he was, he was hers and she was his. And for a while both their worlds came together and the world stopped spinning for them.

38

The morning light crept from under her curtains and changed the colour of the carpet from a dull grey to a soft blue. The fingers of light spread over the room, heralding the start of a new day.

Under the covers her form was curled in the foetal position, the light eventually reaching her eyes and calling her to wake up. Uncurling herself, she stretched her whole body, starting with her back and legs, and then she stretched her arms up towards the ceiling to relax her stiff muscles. As the back of her hands touched the headboard, she smiled, feeling happy for the first time in as long as she could remember.

It had been perfect. Making love with Louis made her realise nothing could match the intensity of the intimacy that they had shared last night, that sex was a poor relation to real love being shared by two people in the act of lovemaking.

It had been so precious. Her thoughts of what they had shared made her body tingle. She remembered the feel of his skin under her hands and rejoiced in the fact that Louis had made love to her slowly, with care, making sure that they both hit every stage of lovemaking together until the climax came, leaving them exhilarated and clinging to each other.

She could hardly wait for the evening to come.

She turned over and looked at her alarm clock. 7am. Another fifteen minutes to linger in her warm bed and think of Louis.

She drifted; her eyes closed.

He had come to take her back to his world last night. He was so handsome and love shone out of his dark brown eyes when he looked at her. His newly cropped hair was rather unruly and it fell over his eyes when he knelt to offer his hand to take her back to his kingdom. She had no regrets but felt it rather strange to love a ghost. He was so aware of where he had come from and the pain of his journeys through the centuries. And he was here in a world he had created first in wood, but one that had gone deeper and become alive on another plane. A ghost, then; how else could she describe him? How could she not have seen that he wasn't a dream? Well, now she knew.

The alarm went off, making her jump. She rubbed the sleep from her eyes and reached over to turn off the offending racket. That done, she sat poised on the edge of her bed, ready to get up and meet the day. When she glanced over to the dresser she saw the plate of pasta lying where she had left it the night before alongside the half-full mug of cold tea that would have developed a skin on top by now. She sighed. She had forgotten all about them. Still, what the hell? Nobody had died.

Walking around the bed, she grabbed the tray and placed the dirty articles on it. She slipped her feet into her mule slippers and made her way onto the landing to go down to the kitchen for breakfast.

His door was closed!

She was sure it had been open when she came up last night. Had she closed the door without remembering? She thought not. That only meant one thing: Mike was back. She wondered what had happened between Debs and him last night.

She crept past his door; if he wasn't awake yet that was okay. She'd rather have a cuppa with some toast before seeing him, food to fortify her before what would be a difficult meeting.

Mike learned after they had left Katie's that Debs only lived a few streets away. Not worth hiring a cab for that little distance and besides, he knew an off-licence that was quite near that stayed open late. He was quite keen to buy a bottle of whiskey.

"Let's oil the wheels a bit, eh, Debs!" he said, laughing and giving her a slap on her bottom that was harder than it should have been.

She had begun to think that inviting him back to her place was not such a good idea. *Mixing his drinks has made him loud and aggressive,* Debs thought, her bottom feeling tender after Mike's heavy-handed love tap. The wine and the shot of whiskey he had drank back in his bedroom just before they had left had made him bullish, so unlike the Mike she had shared love with and the one she knew from the office.

By the time they left the off-licence, the damp evening had turned into a wet one. The rain was slight and even though it was dark, Debs could see heavy clouds hanging there, hiding the moon and stars, and the spitting rain promised to become heavy. They were still a few streets away from her lodgings. *Too near for a taxi but far enough to get a soaking from the heavens. Why didn't I insist on taking a taxi in the first place?* thought Debs. The poor lighting on the dark street with the uneven paving was proving to be a bit of a challenge for her. The pair of new high heels she was wearing were great to look at and sit in but were not designed for walking.

The fun evening they had shared was dampened by the weather and the spit of rain became a heavy shower that was seeping through their clothes. If they were out much longer they would be soaked to their skin.

Mike was getting irritated because she was walking so slowly.

"Come on, will you?" he said again and again, pushing her slightly, encouraging her on. As they neared the terraced street where Debs lived she developed a limp. There was only a few yards to go but each step she took was agony and she could feel liquid sticking to her heel where a blister had burst.

She felt like a drowned rat; her coat was wet through to the lining and although she had tried to protect her hair by holding her handbag over it, it had proved a waste of time.

"We should have got a taxi, Mike, now we're wet through," moaned Debs. "And for goodness' sake, be quiet when we get inside, I don't want my landlady waking up," she added.

"Mum's the word, my little precious," replied Mike. His irritability had gone in anticipation of the next hour or so. "I can't wait to get our clothes off," he said knowingly, giving her a wink and elbowing her in her ribs as she was trying to find the vale lock with her key. "To dry, of course." He laughed at his own sense of humour.

"For God's sake, Mike, let me get the door open."

Standing in the tiny narrow hall, Mike could see a shabby patterned carpet running up the stairs, leading to a dimly lit landing. A 60-watt bulb hung there without a shade.

No matter, I'm not here for the décor, he thought.

"Go on, Mike," Debs encouraged him in whispered tones. Putting her finger to her lips and indicating with her head to a door that belonged to Mrs Green her landlady.

They managed to get up the stairs and into her room without making a sound.

Debs' pad was okay; a shabby room in need of a good coat of paint. The furniture was old-fashioned, apart from the three-quarter bed in the corner that sported a white studded headboard and a cherry-coloured double-sized quilt. A new white bedside table sat beside it. It was a bed-sit, a lot like his was before he moved in with Katie.

Debs kicked off her shoes and walked over to the three-bar electric fire, putting on just two rungs.

"Give us a shilling for the meter, Mike. That fire eats electricity and we should try to dry your clothes a bit before you leave." She erected an old wooden clothes horse in front of the fire before discarding her coat and slipping out of her little black dress, which she carefully placed over a wooden rail. It was damp but not wet, and she was sure it would dry without any damage. Mike passed her his coat and jacket and she placed them next to her clothes to dry off.

She limped across to her bedside table and pulling out a drawer found some Band-Aids, antiseptic and cotton balls, and set to cleaning up her heels and big toe that were weeping and throbbing from the blistered skin.

Sitting in her underwear on the bed seemed to indicate to Mike that he was on a promise. He was totally oblivious to her sores or how wretched she was feeling.

The night had started so well, full of fun, and two consenting adults had in the main enjoyed being together. Now she was tired and in pain and just wanted to get rid of Mike as soon as she could without offending him.

Mike, however, had other ideas. He found two glasses in what passed as a kitchenette and poured two very large glasses of whiskey, placing one next to Debs on her bedside table before sitting down next to her, waiting for her to finish tending her injuries.

Both her heels and one toe were now covered with plasters, much to her relief; she couldn't possibly have got into bed with them weeping the way they were. Mike patted her knee when she was finished and leant over to plant a kiss on her neck. She moved back out of his way.

"Not now, Mike, there's a love."

He took a long swig of the amber before putting it down beside Debs.

"Oh! Come on, give us a kiss," implored Mike. "Don't be shy," he said, encircling her with his arms and pushing her down on the bed. "What you need is just a bit of encouragement," said Mike, before trying to nibble her ear.

But Debs would have none of it. "Are you deaf or something?" she retorted. "I'm tired, my feet hurt; why don't you just drink up and go?" And she pushed him away before sitting up and turning her back on him, ignoring the drink he had poured for her.

He felt cheated and, damn it, he was being rejected again. Well, that wasn't going to happen again tonight.

She had said 'the night is young'; that was a promise, wasn't it? He had wined and dined her and walked all the way to her pad in the rain. She owed him. *She owed him.*

His temper was rising. He could feel his self-control seeping away from him. He reached out and grabbed his tumbler, drinking it down in one gulp.

She wasn't playing fair. Well, sometimes women say no when they mean yes, she was just playing hard to get. He put down his empty glass very deliberately and turned his full attention to Debs.

He trailed his hand across her back before pinging her bra open and trying to remove it. It caused her to round on him, holding the bra in place while she shouted in his face.

"What's wrong with you? We've had a good evening but now it's over. Time to go, Mike." She stood up and pointed to the door.

"It's over when I say it is," retorted Mike, grabbing the wrist of the hand that indicated the door and twisting it in temper. She let out a stifled cry; her wrist felt crushed and her skin was burning from the twist. This was not the Mike she knew.

Trying to hold her bra in place to save her modesty she shouted at him.

"You're drunk!" she shouted in his face. "Some men become happy when they drink but some men change personality and not for the better. You're an arrogant bastard. Do you really think I could have sex with you now?" she said, holding her wrist. "Never! Never, not against my will."

That was the moment that Mike lost it. Instead of backing off, he pushed her with some force back down on the bed, her bra dropping onto the quilt as she used her arms to soften the landing.

Mike was on top of her before she could move out of his way, his hands passing over her body, his lips groping for hers. He was so heavy, she couldn't move under his weight. With all the strength she could muster, she hit him with clenched fists around his head, boxing his ears and kicking her legs, trying to move the man off her.

Now she was scared. It was as though Mike was someone else; he had not heard a word she had said and he was totally oblivious to her fear. She felt he had forgotten she was a person and was nothing more than a toy for him to play with. But she would fight. He wouldn't take her easily.

She screamed out in a loud voice, "Don't touch me! Someone help me." Tears welled up in her eyes, her mascara turning them black as the tears ran down her face.

It was then that Mike saw her distress. His sanity returned and he realised what he was doing. He had shocked himself and moved off her. He sat kneeling beside the sobbing woman.

"Debs, Debs, I'm so sorry. I got carried away. Forgive me, please," he begged.

"I hope God strikes you down, you pervert," she shouted back, wiping her tears away with the back of her hands. "I'll never forgive you."

They were stunned to silence by the forceful hammering on the bedroom door and an anxious voice asking if everything was all right, and should she ring the police?

Their shouting had woken up Mrs Green, a light sleeper and Debs' landlady.

Again the voice asked, "Are you alright, dear, should I get help?"

Debs was over to the door in two strides, grabbing her discarded coat on the way. She covered herself up and opened the door, smiling with relief at the fifty-something-year-old woman standing there in an electric blue dressing gown with pink curlers in her hair. Debs' eyes were red and the black marks on her face were evidence of her tears.

"Sorry, we didn't mean to wake you, Mrs Green. We were just having a difference of opinion. Mike's going now, anyway, aren't you?" she said with force, looking back at him.

It was past midnight and the night was over.

A shame-faced Mike collected his jacket and coat from by the fire. They were still wet. He passed Mrs Green, not daring to look at her. The heat had gone out of him; he was like a dog with its tail between its legs. He slunk out of the bedsit and ran down the stairs, slamming the front door as he passed through it into the dark night.

Debs, on her part, would be forever in Mrs Green's debt. She had had a narrow escape, one she would never forget.

Mike's clothes were still wet but at least the rain had stopped and the walk back to Katie's house would help him to sober up. There was just him, the moonlight and the puddles that the rain had left. The streets were empty of people.

The shock of what he had nearly done wasn't lost on him. Only the fear he had seen on Debs' face had stopped him from pursuing a path he could never have thought of committing when he was sober. He had fallen foul of the drink again.

His frustration and temper had taken him over again.

'A different person.' Katie had said that and now Debs.

She hadn't deserved his forceful advances, he had assaulted her but would he have gone on to rape her? God! What the hell had he been thinking?

A bitter taste of self-loathing was eating at him.

He should have moved on years ago when he saw that this job had no prospects. He should have found a new career in a different town, but he was a coward with no hope and no aims, and now he had descended into a miserable violent drunk. Could he lower his standards any more?

He walked the streets in an attempt to clear his head. He had nowhere else to go except back to Katie's home.

It was 1am when he found himself in front of the door he had left so merrily a few hours earlier. He would have to be as silent as the grave when he let himself in; the last thing he needed was to face Katie, and it was best he slept off whatever was left of the drink inside him.

God! He had done it again, drunk too much and become aggressive and selfish, only seeing what he wanted. He was coming to the conclusion that Debs was right he did have a problem.

Tomorrow! No, today. I will have to face up to it, he thought.

Tired and still damp, he was only too happy to strip off and drop into his bed and sleep, sleep like the dead, that way he could forget tonight. Come the morning – well, that was a different matter.

Katie closed the kitchen door as quietly as she could to keep any noise to a minimum. A thought passed through her mind as she moved towards the sink: 'let sleeping dogs lie'.

Setting her tray down on the counter, she threw the cold tea down the sink and cleaned the pasta off the plate before running warm water into the bowl. Adding washing-up liquid, she placed the pots in the water to soak. They could see to themselves while she made herself some breakfast.

She was hungry; she had hardly eaten anything the day before what with her migraine and all. A simple meal of eggs on toast represented a feast to her that morning.

The kettle boiled quickly, she put some of the boiling water into a small pan and added a splash of vinegar. She would spoil herself and have two poached eggs. She turned the knob, pressing the igniters at the same time. The gas hob sprung into life. The flames leaped up before settling down to hug the bottom of the pan. The bread from the bread bin that she held in her hand was a little stale but she was going to toast it anyway, so it hardly mattered.

She pushed the 'on' switch on the kettle, bringing it back to life before pouring the hot liquid over the black flakes of Assam tea in the bottom of her bright yellow teapot.

By the time the toast popped up, she had cooked her eggs. The table was set for one and she was ready to eat. It was only 7.20am.

There was a brief chill in the air. It came quickly and was gone. She knew Louis had come to join her for breakfast. Though she couldn't see him, she felt his closeness and that made her happy.

Mike had woken to the gurgling in the pipes that ran under the floorboards of his bedroom; somebody was running water in the kitchen. The muted sound of the kettle singing came upstairs and he was awake. She was downstairs making breakfast. Creeping about like a mouse, he dressed in silence before pulling on his trainers. How was she going to greet him after last night? He feared the worst.

He went down the stairs two at a time, trying to avoid the creaks and groans of the wooden stairs; even with carpet their voice could be heard. Today was not a day to invite a sound from them.

He opened the kitchen door quietly; she had her back to him. How was he going to play this? She would want him to leave, that was sure, but that was the last thing he wanted.

She stood in her nightclothes; she was so petite and really very pretty. She looked so good on his arm. He loved it when other members of his sex looked on with approval when they were out together.

He had gone out of his way to prove to her that she wasn't the only fish in the sea and he had tried to make her jealous. It had been a stupid thing to do. Had he burnt his boats completely? They said that the best form of defence was attack. Was that the line he needed to take? It was worth a try.

When she turned to acknowledge him he had not quite made up his mind on the approach he would use, but he knew that he definitely didn't want to leave.

She offered coffee. He certainly needed one right now, and to talk. If she had the whole day to think about the situation, she would realise she needed his money to keep the old homestead together.

She jumped when she turned the radio on and hard rock blasted out at her. He had to smile. Well, at least that broke the ice.

She was washing up her dirty plate when she heard the door open. Her back was to it but she could already feel the tension that entered the small kitchen with his arrival.

"Good morning, Mike," she said, without turning or stopping the chore she was undertaking. She felt an icy draught of cold air circulate the room. Louis was alarmed. She knew he was worried for her. He didn't need to be, she felt fully in charge that morning.

She turned her head, glancing at the six-foot hulk of a man framed in her doorway. The face she read was not consolatory, if anything it was defiant. Standing before her was the schoolboy who must win whatever the game is. She wondered what game he was playing now.

Uncertainty filled her mind. She mustn't doubt her own strength now, she must face him and tell him to go and she must find a new lodger to help with the cost of running her home.

He had kept his own place on, thank goodness, which he sublet. She didn't know the terms on which he rented his place out but it was possibly on a quarterly contract. When, she wondered, did that run out? If she had to put up with him until he could move back to his old home, well, so be it. But she would have strict rules about his behaviour in her home and he would only be her lodger from now on. *Louis is my lover now,* she thought defiantly.

Disguising the way she really felt, she said in a light-hearted voice, "Come on in, Mike, I'll make you some coffee, then I must get ready for work. We can talk later." They worked every alternative Saturday and today they were both due in the office.

Katie felt vulnerable dressed as she was in her nightdress; how stupid to come down not dressed, but she would be able to slip back upstairs once he had his coffee. She put on the radio to break the tense silence, forgetting she had left it on a rock station from the night before, and the music blasted out on the top setting. Somehow it broke the tension, bringing a smile to Mike's face as he lumbered into the kitchen and sat at the table. She quickly made a large mug of strong black coffee, placing it front of him and pushing the sugar bowl and a spoon towards him.

She needed to shower and dress and time was ticking on. Both of them were due in at work for 9am. He was already dressed so she was on catch-up. She left the kitchen, quickly aware that he was already stood and was at that moment putting bread into the toaster. It was a relief to feel that the morning had become normalised but it would be stressful sharing the journey together into work.

The talk would have to wait until that evening. It was probably best that way. Both of them should have time to think through where they stood, and it would give her time to choose her words and practise her speech before tonight.

Mike sat eating his buttery toast. He shivered, suddenly feeling very cold sitting at the table. The short-sleeved polo shirt just wasn't warm enough that morning; he must take a light jumper with him to work. The hairs on his arms were standing on the end of his goosebumps. Perhaps he was getting a cold; the rain and the damp had left him in a shivering state last night, it had taken hours to get warm before he could sleep when he got into his bed.

He would make himself some more hot coffee and take a couple of aspirin, and try to ward off any illness that was lurking around ready to take him down.

Louis sat opposite to him, trying to understand what made this man tick. He wished that he could do more than just look on. It was frustrating and worrying that Mike seemed to oscillate between being a good guy and a downright wrong'un. His fear for Katie was perhaps unfounded; he had seen Mike in both moods and, providing he stayed off the booze, Katie would be all right, he was sure of it. But should Mike drink… well, he would be around tonight to watch the proceedings. His strength was through his emotions and with emotion he had fought men before.

By the time Katie had dressed and returned to the kitchen, Mike had already left for work.

She was filled with a kind of dread as she travelled to work. It was the not knowing what she was to face that Saturday morning that made her nervous. The last thing she wanted was to have a show down with him in the office. But as so often when you have rehearsed a scenario, it wasn't needed; she had nothing to fear. Mike was out all day with the paper's photographer on assignment, interviewing an all-woman water polo team. The women were at the top of their league having taken part in tournaments all over the country. It was a human-interest story that Mike didn't particularly like to report on but it was part of his job. On the plus side, these ladies were young and fit and he would able to look over the cheesecake and maybe chat one of them up.

He would not be back into the office that day which suited him; if he could put off that talk with Katie for a few hours, he would, and he would make his own way home when he finished.

Katie was relieved he wasn't in the office. As the day unravelled it was obvious that Debs had a tale to tell, and she seemed to spend most of the morning surrounded by women in the office telling it. Katie was sure that the gossip whispered to one another included Mike and last night. Debs' wrist was wrapped in a thick crêpe bandage. Had she fallen or was it a sprain? *What on earth has happened to her?* Katie thought as she started feeling stress build up in her.

Whatever it was, Debs was sharing it with all the women staff. Their faces showed some shock but there was also an element of enjoyment on their faces as they gossiped, sharing it in whispers behind their hands to one another.

They kept looking across at Katie with knowing looks and nodding heads. By lunchtime, Katie could stand it no longer and marched over to Debs' station and asked her outright what was going on and what had happened last night.

"Only tried to rape me, didn't he," confided Debs in a whispered voice. Katie could see that tears were not far away. "He hurt my wrist when I told him to get out of my flat." She indicated towards the bandage. "If it hadn't been for my landlady... well, you know." There was just a hint of a tremor in her voice when she said it.

Katie knew her fear; she too had known Mike's aggression. Nevertheless, she was shocked.

"Will you go to the police?" Katie asked, putting her arm around Debs' shoulder, wanting to comfort her. Debs' eyes filled with tears.

"I can't, it would be difficult seeing that we made love at yours before he came back to mine," she confessed. "I don't want the humiliation of it all. It started out so well," she went on. "He was a real gentleman. We had a lovely meal and a bottle of wine. We had a good time and I really liked him; he said you and he were finished so I was pleased when he asked me out. Then he started drinking whiskey at yours. After that, he got above himself. Pushy and aggressive. It was the drink, I'll swear it. I'll never go out with him again, that's for sure, and neither will any of the girls from the office, I've seen to that." She said it with a certain amount of triumph in her voice, and then she added, "You're welcome to him."

How Katie got through the day at work, she wasn't sure. By 5pm she was ready to go home, tired and dreading the evening that was to come knowing that it was going to be very difficult.

It was with a heavy heart that she returned home. Mike really needed help, that much was sure. But how was she going to help him when she wanted him out of her life and out of her home? She couldn't let it go. That talk had to take place; pretending that nothing had happened was something she couldn't live with.

In the moments between the interviews he had to take, Mike thought about nothing else but his position with Katie. He knew that as a couple they were finished. He dreaded the talk that was coming that evening; he was sure she would ask him to leave and after last night, he could hardly blame her. He realised that he had acted like a bloody fool inviting Debs back to his room. It was not his finest hour.

He enjoyed a drink but he could control it, he knew he could. He still had half a bottle of whiskey in his bedroom. He promised himself he would get rid of it as soon as he got home. He didn't need the temptation of it sitting there looking at him; better to pour it down the sink than risk another disaster like the one last night with Debs.

Debs! A prang of conscience hit him. He hadn't meant to hurt her but he had felt so cheated. She had invited him back to hers, told him that the night was young and he believed he was on a promise. Then she went back on her word. God! His reputation would be ruined if she gossiped about him at work. Had he set in motion a train of events that he would not be able to stop? Would he lose his job? Would he have to move back to his old bedsit? He must try to salvage something or his life could be in ruins. Depression was not far away.

By the time he arrived back in his bedroom, the brooding had developed into a bad mood. He needed a pick-me-up and instead of pouring the whiskey away, he found an old plastic beaker and poured himself a large drink.

Mike sat on the edge of his bed, downing the amber liquid, and remembered when he had shared the bed with Katie and Debs. They were good memories. A wry smile hovered on his lips.

"I'm a bit of a stud, aren't I?" He nodded, agreeing with himself, and promptly poured another drink.

There was a change of mood by the time he had finished the bottle. He was remembering Katie. It was always his bed, they had never shared hers; that bloody bed that she loved so much, all carved and fancy. Perhaps it needed a new look. Perhaps he could carve his and Katie's initials on the tree on that bloody headboard in an ironic gesture.

He had a penknife from when he was a boy tucked away in his odds and ends drawer in his tall boy. He relieved it from the drawer, turning it over in his hand before taking it out of its sheath.

It should be sharp enough, he thought, trailing his thumb over the blade. "What a joke," he said loudly, agreeing again with himself.

He realised he would have to be quick if he was going to do it. Katie would be home soon. He moved across the landing to her room. Knife in hand, he opened the door. He would carve a heart with their entwined initials on it. The tree was now in his sight; whatever else, she would remember him.

Louis heard the door open and watched Mike walk in with the knife in his hand. What was this man up to?

Mike crawled onto the bed, kneeling at its centre facing the headboard and the tree. He threw the pillows to the right and left of him to give him more space and they landed softly on the floor. The mattress was soft under his knees and he was unsteady because of his drinking. Nevertheless, he unsheathed his knife and prepared to cut the wood.

A cold blast of air covered him just as he was about to cut the tree with the point of the blade. Louis was furious. This stupid man was about to vandalise his work of art. Anger flooded into Louis, giving him the strength and the ability to act, and act he did, by shoving Mike off the bed with some force.

Mike landed heavily on the floor, hitting his head on the bedpost as he fell. His knife shot out of his hand, landing under the bed out of his reach. He would have to crawl under the bed to retrieve it. But even lying on his belly he couldn't reach it; he needed to move the bed to one side. Standing up, he felt dizzy and a little sick. He couldn't understand how he had fallen off the bed and he could feel a lump under his finger when he touched his head. The dammed knife would have to wait.

Now his head hurt and he touched it gingerly. The whiskey had gone to his head and he felt the need to lie down. He turned and left the bedroom, getting back to his room just as the front door opened. Katie was back.

She kicked her shoes off in the hall and went into the kitchen. Mike's coat was hung in the hall. *So he is in.*

Normally they had supper together after work and it might be easier to talk over a meal. It would have to be tomato sauce and pasta tonight as she hadn't shopped for a couple of days. She would ask him to join her but in the meantime she put out salted peanuts in a dish as well as a bowl of crisps; they could nibble on them until the food was ready.

She made a pot of tea and carried a mug of the hot beverage up to her room.

What on earth had happened here? Both her pillows were on the floor and she certainly hadn't left her bedroom like that. Had Mike been in her room? Why would he have been? Everything else looked normal; nothing else was moved.

She picked up the pillows, putting them back where they belonged, and changed her clothes. What should she do?

It was with some trepidation that she knocked at his bedroom door. She heard a muffled voice call out to come in. He was laid on his bed with his eyes closed. She could smell the whiskey from the doorway and saw the discarded mug on his side table. *Oh, Mike! Not again,* she said to herself.

"Have you been in my room?" she said in a curt voice. Mike turned to look at her.

"Just wanted to see that carving," he said sulkily.

She decided not to question him further. He had been drinking; who knew what went on in that mind? He probably didn't know either.

"Look, Mike, I'm making supper – why don't you come down when its ready and we can talk?"

Reading the signals the way he wanted them to be, Mike cheered up. *She can't be all that angry with me if she wants me to join her for supper. She may not want me to move out after all.*

He started to feel more confident, even ready to argue in his defence. After all, it wasn't all his fault; women egged men on, didn't they?

Katie had turned around and was on her way downstairs when he sat up in preparation to stand. His head was sore. He touched the tender spot under his fingers. The bump had grown larger since he lay down. How he got it would be his secret.

"That damn bed," he uttered, "and those damn dreams. We were okay until those dreams started." His mood became darker. He remembered that she talked about a Louis, not flesh and blood like him, a bloody dream.

He stood up. His anger was building as he headed for the door. He remembered his knife that he had left under her bed; the sheath was still in his pocket. He'd collect it before going downstairs. He couldn't risk her finding it under her bed; she would know he wanted to vandalise her precious bed.

Louis saw Mike move quickly into Katie's bedroom and move the bed over just enough to reach the knife. Going down on all fours, he crawled under the bed and retrieved his property and, restoring the bed to its original position, he carefully put the knife into its sheath and left the room.

Mike made his way down the stairs, closely followed by Louis, who was concerned by Mike's odd behaviour. It seemed obvious that Mike had been drinking and Louis knew that meant he couldn't be trusted.

Katie was busy cooking when she felt that coldness enter the kitchen. She turned towards the door with a smile. She couldn't see him but no matter, she knew Louis was there. But instead she saw Mike with a look of thunder on his face. There definitely was a feeling of rage flowing from him; how was she to deal with him?

She kept calm. If she didn't antagonise him and got some coffee into him with some food, she may avoid his temper tantrum.

"It's not quite ready, Mike, why not sit down and help yourself to the nibbles while I make you some coffee?"

"Thought we were going to have a talk?" Mike muttered.

"I'll get you coffee then talk, if that's okay."

She busied herself. Pushing down the switch on the kettle, she found a mug and put a spoonful of coffee granules in it, ready for the boiling water.

"Mike, we can't go on like this. I think it would be better if you went back to your own place. You can stay here until your tenant's term is up but we that is our relationship, is over. But you know that, don't you?"

Mike was suddenly deflated. His body felt as though he had had a body blow and was winded. For a moment he was dumbstruck and then his temper erupted.

"You can't do that to me, I won't go," he snapped. "I helped you when you needed someone to share, we had something special."

His hand went to his pocket and he fingered his knife, still in its sheath. He had tested it, it was sharp. He could hurt her, yes he could. Who did she think she was, treating him like this?

The thought passed through his head and it shocked him. Was he seriously thinking of harming her? What was he becoming? God, he had done it again, that damn whiskey. He shook his head. It was true, he had changed, just as Katie and Debs had said. He couldn't control it. The whiskey that he had thought relaxed him made him mean.

Reaching for the chair, he sat down. He had to do something about it and quickly, or he would lose everything he valued.

Katie's voice was soft but the words he had dreaded hearing rang in his ears like a death knell.

"Mike, it's over. Let's be grown up about this; I can't live with your drinking and you can't live without it. We can still be friends."

"Friends, I don't want to be friends," he whispered back. 'You can't do this to me."

The kettle sang, steam rising from its spout as it turned itself off abruptly.

Katie poured the boiling water into the mug and placed it in front of Mike.

She kept her voice calm, not wanting to aggravate him more than he was already. "Let's stay calm, Mike, I'm sure it will all work out for both of us."

He needed coffee; he needed to be completely sober if he was going to persuade Katie to change her mind. The table held the nibbles that Katie had put out. He must put something in his stomach. He grabbed a handful of peanuts and stuffed all of them into his mouth. He could hardly turn his mouth over to chew them but he wanted the nuts to soak up the booze and he needed lots of coffee. He must get sober.

How it happened, Katie wasn't sure. Mike reached for the coffee but he fumbled with the handle and dropped the mug; the hot black liquid spilled from the mug, spreading quickly down into his groin. His mouth was still full of half-chewed peanuts. At the shock of being burnt with scalding hot coffee he jumped up, taking in a quick intake of breath. The half-chewed peanuts hit the back of his throat and lodged in his windpipe, blocking his ability to breathe.

Katie watched in horror as Mike tried to clear his throat. Coughing only seemed to make it worse; his hand was clutching at his neck, his complexion changing very quickly from normal flesh to a bright pink.

She must help him and get him water to wash down the nuts and clear his throat. She rushed to find a glass and filled it with tap water but when she turned back to him he was dropping to his knees, his red face tinged with purple.

"Oh my God, Mike!" She was on her knees beside him, still holding the water; she tried to get him to drink. With the glass forced to his lips, she held his head, trying to get the water into his mouth, but the clear fluid spilled out of his mouth as fast as she tried to get him to drink.

Katie was unsure what to do next to help him.

Louis was at her side watching the scene as it unfolded, wondering how those small nuts could cause such a problem.

It was obvious that time was running out for Mike, the purple-blue colour on his face and lips was telling a tale; he was no longer clawing at his neck with his hands, his neck was bulging and his choking sound was reduced to a gurgle.

He was laid on his back, his eyes rolling up into his skull. Katie was trying to put Mike on his side but his body was just too heavy for her to move him. If she could move him and get to his back she might be able to remove the blockage by hitting him between his shoulder blades.

She was struggling to help this choking man but was failing miserably.

Louis came to a decision. He could blend into Mike's body just as he had years before to help Lucy.

It was easy; all he had to do was merge into the body that Mike occupied. When he was installed in Mike's body, he hoped his strength would save him.

His throat became Mike's, his lungs became Mike's and with his strength and Katie, they turned the dead weight of Mike's body over and Katie was able to attack the centre of Mike's back with heavy strokes, as she tried to expel the blockage from Mike's throat.

Katie was beside herself; she had to help him no matter what, and there on her knees she pleaded. "Please don't die. Please don't die." She repeated it over and over each time she hit the centre of Mike's back between his shoulder blades. She was so frightened for him, her tears were unstoppable, she had to save him.

Louis could feel that the spark of life in Mike was very weak. The blockage in the throat was solid. Louis could feel the swollen tissue, scratched from the nuts that lay there. He could feel Mike losing his battle for life. His spirit was slowly leaving his body and being drawn into the next realm and Louis couldn't stop his passing.

Louis could feel Katie's fist as it made contact with Mike's back; he felt every thump and he heard every plea she was making, willing Mike to recover, but the light of Mike's spirit had gone.

Finally Katie resorted to clasping her fists together, and with her hands raised she gave a mighty downward swing, hitting Mike's back, not knowing that he had already passed on.

Louis was in the process of leaving Mike's empty shell when her double fist landed on his back, shaking Louis and making him shudder. Louis was still in Mike's body; the blow had landed with such force that it threw his head backwards and forwards quite violently, dislodging and unblocking the windpipe just enough for air to pass to the lungs. *God, that was a strange sensation*, he thought, but when he tried to move out of Mike's body he wasn't able to.

Louis gulped hungrily for air; it was the first time for many years that he needed to breathe and it felt so strange. He coughed and coughed, spitting out the offending objects that were choking him, before gulping in more air to his aching lungs. His eyes watered with the effort of coughing and he spat out still more nuts to clear his throat of the blockage.

He moved now, feeling the weight of the body as he rolled onto his back. It was so heavy. He had forgotten how it felt to be mortal; his spirit body had no weight at all. He could feel a heart beating in his chest. What had just happened?

He opened his eyes as he heaved himself into a half-sitting position. He looked into the red-eyed, tear-stained face of Katie. Her fists were ready to strike again. He raised his arm, stopping her in mid-flight.

A feeling of relief flooded her body and she responded by taking him into her arms, rocking him to and fro like a child who needed comfort. He was alive.

Louis smiled. His chest was heaving, drinking in the air, and he wondered how this miracle had happened. He had lived in his netherworld hoping for such a moment but never at the expense of another man dying. Yet here he was, alive and looking at the woman he loved.

She smiled down at him.

"Mike, you're back," said a much-relieved Katie.

"Not exactly."

The voice she heard wasn't Mike's, but it was a voice she knew. The eyes she was looking into were not Mike's either but she would know those kind eyes anywhere and when the voice said, "Believe in me, my darling girl."

Then she knew.

ABOUT THE AUTHOR

Brenda trained as a dress designer at the Bradford College of Art before going on to start her own manufacturing company in West Yorkshire. Fifteen years later she moved to Hertfordshire and started to paint. She has always loved drawing, painting and words, tools to make narratives and stories.

She developed stories for young children before moving on to poetry and short stories. Married with four children, she teaches art and exhibits her paintings in local galleries.